CW01123464

Page Two

SCEPTRE

Also by Sarah Grazebrook

A Cameo Role

Page Two

SARAH GRAZEBROOK

SCEPTRE

Copyright © 1997 Sarah Grazebrook

First published in 1997 by Hodder and Stoughton
A division of Hodder Headline PLC
A Sceptre Book

The right of Sarah Grazebrook to be identified as the Author of the Work has been asserted by her in accordance with the Copyright, Designs and Patents Act 1988.

10 9 8 7 6 5 4 3 2 1

All rights reserved. No part of this publication may be reproduced, stored in a retrieval system or transmitted in any form or by any means, without the prior written permission of the publisher, nor be otherwise circulated in any form of binding or cover other than that in which it is published and without a similar condition being imposed on the subsequent purchaser.

All characters in this publication are fictitious and any resemblance to real persons, living or dead, is purely coincidental.

British Library Cataloguing in Publication Data

Grazebrook, Sarah
  Page two
  1. English fiction – 20th century
  I. Title
  823.9'14 [F]

ISBN 0 340 67515 2

Typeset by Palimpsest Book Production Limited,
Polmont, Stirlingshire
Printed and bound in Great Britain by
Mackays of Chatham PLC, Chatham, Kent

Hodder and Stoughton
A division of Hodder Headline PLC
338 Euston Road
London NW1 3BH

1

'Ommmm', 'ommmm', 'shanteeee'. Peace and calm. Ruth Page sat cross-legged in her corner as, swathed in leotards and leggings, the dozen or so yoga students exhaled their generalised anguish and sniffed in the elixir of life. Up one nostril and down the other. Left, right. Left, right.

The woman next to her had a cold. 'Obbbb, obbbb, shanteeee', cough, cough, cough. Ruth ordered herself to concentrate. In with hope, out with despair. Breathe it away. 'Listen to your own breath,' exhorted the teacher. 'Search for your inner light.' Ruth searched furtively for her handkerchief. She loathed this bit. Bad enough her own nasal fallout cascading around her, but the sound of other people's made her bilious.

She was glad the lights were dimmed. Soon they would be into relaxation. She liked that. Lying under a blanket on a cold February afternoon, eyes shut, drifting away into their own cosmic whatsits.

Not that Ruth ever drifted away. No sooner did the Buddhist chimes come tinkling from the cassette than her normally stoic thought processes would screech into overdrive. Plans were laid for redecorating the bathroom, recipes rehearsed, letters composed, and over them all hovered the silent banner headlines: 'Choked to Death on Dental Floss'; 'Killed by Her Own Drill'; 'Suttee of Deserted Dental Technician'.

It amazed Ruth that, though in the ordinary course of events she felt very little animosity towards the woman who had stolen her husband, her entire being cried out for vendetta every time the teacher mentioned tranquillity.

A hand reached down and wobbled her chin. 'Still very tense, Ruth. Try and relax. Let your body melt away.'

• Sarah Grazebrook

Would that she could. Laureen Denkell would melt. She was exactly like one of those Barbie dolls: plastic skin, candy floss hair, and FAT? By the time she was forty she'd be elephantine. Didn't Duncan know that? Another year and he'd have to have the doors widened. Perhaps they wouldn't have doors at all. Just open-plan, so that Laureen could roll from space to space without damaging the basic structure.

'That's better. Now you're smiling. Now I'm just going to read you a few lines from a favourite Urdu poet of mine. Take from it what you need. We're not all alike. We need different things. Some of us need one thing and some another.'

The poem had not gained in translation and while the teacher spoke of flowers opening and boughs unbending Ruth thought about being a single woman again. Officially single.

She wondered how she would describe herself to people now. 'Hullo. I'm Ruth Page. A divorcee.'

'And what do you do?'

'I'm divorced.'

'Newly divorced', perhaps? That smacked of desperation. 'Highly desirable detached property. Fresh on the market. One male owner. Room for improvement but basically sound.'

Lies, all lies. Not at all sound. Single. A cast-off. Lonely. Certainly not highly desirable. If she'd been that, Duncan would have desired her, and not that Milwaukee dirigible.

A whole year without him. Christmas, the birthdays, their anniversary. A year was a long time – much longer than the twenty-three they'd spent together. Perhaps that was because Martin had gone too.

Just six weeks after Duncan Page had announced he was leaving his wife for his orthodontist, their son had gone up to university and Ruth, who for her entire adult life had been a wife, a hostess, a mother, had become redundant overnight. A wanderer in her own home, unwanted, uncentred, unnecessary.

Not that she had been entirely surprised by Duncan's defection. She had known about Laureen for some time. Had she minded? She wasn't sure. Somehow it had never occurred to her that her husband would actually leave her. Why should he have done? She kept house; she cooked, not adventurously, but well; she looked after him, visited his mother, entertained his business acquaintances, even emitted small half-genuine moans when he occasionally felt the urge to climb on top of her and thrust away ritually for five or ten minutes.

She had not complained when he had spent weekends away, evenings out. She had been sympathetic when he had rung ten minutes before guests were due, to say that he was running late and might not get away at all. Yes, she had been very understanding, going about her voluntary work, her PTA duties, her sponsored coffee mornings with a dedication and reliability few could deny.

And for this she had been left.

Duncan had been quite ruthless in his justification. They had been growing apart for years. She herself, it seemed, was mainly responsible for this. She hadn't 'grown' with the marriage. He had done his best, but now he could see no way forward for them and besides, there was Laureen. He couldn't hide it from her – he knew it would come as a shock – he had no wish to hurt her, but he and Laureen were very much in love, had been for years. And now that Martin no longer needed them . . . That HAD hurt. More, a million times more than Duncan's carnal roisterings with the American marshmallow.

But he was wrong. Martin did need them – her, anyway. He wasn't just her son, he was her friend. Something Duncan, for all his brusque 'men's talk' and Sunday expeditions to the pub, could never fathom.

She had seen the look in his eye, half curiosity, half irritation, when he entered a room and found them capsized with laughter over some unrepeatable piece of trivia. Their trips to the cinema, Martin's critical interest in her clothes and her hair. 'Positively unhealthy', Duncan had called it – when he could be bothered to notice.

No, it was not Duncan that Ruth missed, but Martin. But he was growing up and he was happy, and so she had filled her life with more voluntary work, taken up yoga and even retrieved some of her Italian books from the loft, where they had stayed almost since the day she left university, married Duncan and started on the road to non-existence.

'I want you to start to come out of your relaxation now. Very slowly. Feel the tips of your toes, your fingers, glowing with warmth and energy . . . be aware of each part of your body.'

Ruth rolled on her side, aware only of a dozen middle-aged women creaking like an unoiled boat. She opened her eyes. The woman beside her, whose nose was certainly glowing, blew steadily into a wodge of paper hankies. She looked serene enough.

Ruth rolled up her mat, folded her blanket and put on her coat. Just as she always did. She wondered if they could see the difference. The Divorcee's Fold, she thought idly and wondered if she should button her coat on the other side. Perhaps she should wear a key-ring suspended from the middle button? This was ridiculous. How could anyone tell that today was the day she became a single woman again? Like losing one's virginity. If they weren't there, they couldn't know.

Remembering her own deflowering she reflected that they probably wouldn't have known anyway, such a non-event had it been. She should have guessed then. Heeded the signs. 'This woman is on her way to a non-life.' And today was the non-day of them all.

'Mum? . . . It's Martin. Are you all right?'

Ruth, second gin in hand, stood hunched over the phone. 'Hullo, darling. Of course I'm all right. Why shouldn't I be?' She could sense him doodling at the other end of the line. She wondered what he was drawing. Probably a melon head with golf ball ears, that was what he usually did. It always reminded her of Duncan's sister, Joy. She must ring Joy. She knew she must. She had been putting it off for days – weeks. It was ungracious of her after all Joy had done, sorting out a place for her to stay so that they could let the London house till it was sold, sending her helpful leaflets about her rights as a divorced woman – none, it appeared – and peppering her with advice about how not to sink into depression, all of which might have sent any sane woman to the brink of Beachy Head had she lacked the foresight to ignore it. Fortunately Ruth had known her sister-in-law long enough to let her good intentions wash over her, much as she had let her husband's bad ones.

Now there was less than a week left. She must make the effort.

Martin's voice. 'It's just that . . . You know . . . Dad told me it was today.'

'Yes.' What else was there to say? But he wanted more, she knew that. 'Honestly, darling . . . Martin . . . it doesn't matter. It's just . . . the formal end . . . You know . . . It's all been over for ages now. This is just a formality . . .'

She heard Martin swallow. She hoped it was only beer. 'Yes. Well, anyway, I just thought I'd ring. I'll be up at the weekend to collect my stuff.'

'I've got most of it packed up.'

'Thanks, Mum.'

'Friday or Saturday?'

'Saturday, probably. Maybe Friday. I could bunk off my tutorial.'

'No don't do that. Saturday will be fine. I'll get some pork.'

'Smashing. Er, Mum . . .'

'Yes?'

'Did Dad say anything to you?'

'I haven't heard from your father for weeks.'

'Oh. Oh, well never mind then.'

'What is it, Martin?'

'Nothing, honestly. You know Dad. Got to go now. I'm meant to be playing darts. See you soon, Mum.'

'Bye, darling. Don't overdo it.'

'What?'

'Any of it. The darts.' She heard the phone click. The loyalty, she thought. Don't overdo that.

The phone rang again. Ruth stiffened as she recognised Joy Blakeney's voice. 'Ruth . . . How ARE you? We've all been so worried. I wanted to ring but Christopher said not to. He positively refused to let me. Goodness knows what he was hoping to achieve. Anyway, tonight I said I must ring. "Goodness, she's only got a week," I said. "The poor thing must be at her wit's end, what with those awful people panting to move in . . ."'

'They're very nice, actually. They couldn't have been more accommodating.'

'Yes, well if you say so, Ruth. But honestly . . . fancy Duncan letting them come round the house while you're still in it! What can he have been thinking of? I think this whole idea of renting is quite appalling. I'm sure it's against the law.'

'It's only for three months. It was that or sell at a loss.'

Joy clicked her tongue dismissively. 'That's Duncan all over. Money, money, money. It's all he thinks about.'

'Well, he is an economist,' said Ruth without enthusiasm.

'He's a skinflint. Always has been. Do you know, on my twelfth birthday he gave me a bar of fruit and nut chocolate? He knew I hated raisins, so he'd unwrapped the blooming thing and picked them all out. Every single one. I never told you that, did I? That's the sort of man you got yourself married to. You're well out of it, Ruth, believe me. Mind you, I bet this house business was all HER doing. Of course it was. But never mind. You're not to think about it. Put her right out of your mind. We all have.'

'Yes, I have too. More or less.'

'Of course you have. And I'm a fool for reminding you. Dragging up old skeletons. Christopher says I do it all the time. But not this time. That woman is absolutely persona non gratis in this household, and always will be. And I've told Duncan to stay away too. He may be my brother but I think he's behaved disgracefully by you. Disgracefully. And it's not even as though she's pretty. All that fluffy hair. She reminds me of . . . Who is it she reminds me of . . . Christopher . . . Chrissie, darling, who did I say Duncan's floozie reminds me of?'

A distant rumble from Christopher Blakeney then, 'That's it. That woman who writes all those awful books. You know who I mean.'

'Joy, are there any problems with the cottage? I know I should have rung earlier . . .'

'No. None at all. Everything's gone like clockwork. That's why I rang. I thought you'd want to know. I had lunch with Duncan the other day. Well, not lunch exactly. More like coffee with food. I absolutely refuse to sit down at the table with him after the way he's behaved to you, but I was up for the Cezanne exhibition and it seemed like a good time to get things tied up. Anyway, darling, you've nothing to worry about. The Taylors think you're marvellous to be looking after things for them while they're away.'

Ruth felt a twinge of nervousness. 'It is only the cottage, isn't it, Joy?'

'Of course it is. And the garden, but that's the size of a window box.'

'I'm not all that good at gardening.'

'Don't worry. Chrissie and I will be on hand to assist. Anyway things look after themselves at the seaside. Not like your prissy town plants. Now, who's moving you? Is Martin taking time off?'

'I'm not sure yet. I don't really want him to miss any more lectures. Besides, I shan't be bringing all that much. I'm sure I shall manage fine.'

'Nonsense. You can't possibly do it by yourself. You need a man. I'll tell Christopher to take the day off. He can come up the night before. Yes, that's what we'll do. I'd come myself but I've got a WI craft morning. You must join the WI, by the way. You're just the sort of person we're looking to recruit. Plenty of spare time. No ties. Might rope you in for Meals on Wheels, too. You'll enjoy that. Lots of "characters" – some of them are quite interesting in their way. What's that, darling? . . . Oh, Ruth, I must go. There's a gardening programme I've simply got to watch. Give me a ring if there are any problems. Chrissie'll be up on Monday evening. Don't bother to feed him. He can get something on the way . . . Yes, yes, I'm coming . . . Honestly, what a fusspot. As if I didn't know how to divide an aster! Men! Bye bye, Ruth love. We're longing to have you down here. Just what you need. A complete break. New leaf and all that. No moping now. Bye.'

'Bye, Joy. Thanks for ringing.'

Ruth went back to her depleted sitting room. Duncan hadn't taken much. It had been mutually agreed that most of the furniture must remain, at least for the three months' tenure of the Webster family, but the picture over the fireplace had gone and a couple of table lamps. The room looked larger, shabbier in the overhead light. Walls that were once a warm apricot were now Social Security cream. She could see where the carpet had frayed at the edges, and the dark treacly stain of the linseed oil Martin had kicked over while embalming his pencil case to bury the last of the hamsters in.

• Sarah Grazebrook

This was no good. One thing she had promised herself when Martin left: no brooding. And she had stuck to it. An hour after seeing him off at the station she was up to her knees in the debris of his room.

Yes, she'd managed Duncan's departure, then Martin's, and she was damned if she was going to let her own defeat her. Not for her, wandering from room to room remembering the good times. What good times, for God's sake? There hadn't been any. Just mediocre times, interspersed increasingly with lonely times and culminating finally in bloody awful times.

She would miss the house. She supposed she would. But why? She'd never liked it particularly. Or the garden, which managed to attract whatever rain, wind or shade was on offer to Ealing throughout the year. The neighbours she scarcely knew. They were Polish and, though resident in the United Kingdom for thirty years, still conversed mainly in broken sentences, centred conscientiously round the weather and the royal family.

She had friends. Or did she? Mostly they were the wives of Duncan's business associates. She had lost most of her own when she'd left university. They'd kept in touch at first but domesticity had proved anathema to ambitious graduate women, and now she was down to occasional Christmas cards enclosing scribbled details of recent promotions. There was no one she would really miss. Certainly no one who would seriously regret her going. She was a useful amiable woman, unexceptional in every way. The wallpaper of other people's lives – her own husband's, even.

Glad that she had avoided the sin of self-pity, Ruth poured herself another gin and got out the photo albums to prove her point.

When she had finished crying she made herself a bowl of soup and watched an episode of *Casualty*, in which a man put his head very forcefully through a plate glass window. She noted a certain likeness to Duncan in the man's demeanour and went to bed on a note of increasing optimism.

2

Ruth stood among her cases in the hall of Bell Cottage and wondered why she'd ever agreed to the arrangement.

The place was freezing, despite Christopher's valiant and ultimately successful efforts to get the central heating going. She could feel the draught under the doors and through the ill-fitting window frames as she moved from room to room, clutching wretchedly at the clanking radiators in the hope that some warmth had managed to seep through to them.

The sitting-room was quite pretty. It was at the back of the house, facing on to the 'window box' garden which Ruth now perceived was the size of a paddock. It had french windows that in anything but this north easterly gale might be considered an attraction.

The dining-room was coffin-shaped and accordingly gloomy, with a hideous mahogany dresser taking up all of one wall and the rest of the furniture crammed against the other.

The kitchen was pokey, with bottle green units and lino revealing a stone floor through the cracks. The cooker was gas, which Ruth had never used, and the fridge let out a hum worthy of a Geiger counter at Chernobyl.

Upstairs was scarcely more encouraging, both bedrooms being yellow – a colour Ruth had never got on with – and the bathroom bright pink, which she concluded had been done to create an impression of warmth since there was certainly no other means of achieving it as far as she could see.

It was getting dark. She supposed she had better find the shops. Christopher had given her directions, murmuring something about 'not expecting too much'.

• Sarah Grazebrook

She set off and found a dilapidated newsagents selling milk and what could best be described as Survival Rations, most of which were past their sell-by date. She bought some basics and hurried back up the lane to Bell Cottage.

Something moved in the hedgerow and Ruth squeaked in terror. A rabbit ran across her path. She breathed again and told herself what fun it was to be in the country. Nonetheless, it was with some relief that she let herself back into the cottage and bolted the door behind her.

She drew the curtains, pausing for a moment to take in the clear light of the skyline, uninhibited by buildings and sodium glare. Branches jabbed the air like ink scratchings on turquoise blotting paper. The stars were out – far more than she had ever seen in town. From further down the lane she could hear the sound of the sea thrashing against the shingle beach. The sort of sound her yoga teacher charged seven pounds ninety for on a relaxation tape, albeit you got a birdcall or two thrown in. As if to oblige, a solitary owl hooted, and somewhere down below a phone began to ring.

It took Ruth several moments to connect the ringing with herself. As she sat on the unmade bed wondering whether two duvets would be enough to stop her freezing to death, if Laureen would get her jewellery should they fail, and why some idiot didn't answer the phone, it occurred to her that hers was the only house for two hundred yards, and consequently the idiot must be she.

She had some difficulty locating it under the pile of towels which Christopher had dumped on top of it.

'Ruth, darling. It's me, Joy. I am so sorry I wasn't there to let you in. We had a meeting about this blasted pageant and I couldn't get away. Are you all right? Did Christopher see you in okay? He went shooting off to the office as soon as he got back, as though they couldn't get through one dreary day without him. I ask you. Did he say, by the way? About tonight?'

'No,' said Ruth, her heart sinking.

'Oh well, it's nothing. Absolutely nothing. Just a chance to meet a few of the locals. We thought you'd like it. No need to dress up. We're all pretty informal at the seaside, you know. Country Cousins, and all that. Chrissie'll pick you up about six. Does that give you enough time? He could make it a quarter past.'

Ruth leant her head against the wall. 'What exactly have you got planned, Joy?' she asked, trying to sound enthusiastic.

'Oh, didn't he say? He is a pest. No, it's just a few friends. I'm doing a chili. Well, you'll need something warm after all that unpacking, won't you? Besides that cottage is so perishing, I always find. Not that that'll bother you, I don't suppose, but I'm hot-blooded so I simply die every time I go near the place.' This was the best news Ruth had had all day.

She rallied herself. 'It's awfully kind of you, Joy. But you really shouldn't have gone to so much trouble.'

'Nonsense. It's not trouble at all. We're looking forward to it. I've told everyone about, you know, everything, so you've nothing to worry about. They're all frightfully sympathetic.'

Ruth put the phone down wondering if she could possibly repack her car and get away from the cottage before Christopher Blakeney returned to escort her to this ultimate humiliation. How could Joy? How could Christopher have let her? What on earth had she done to deserve not only a husband who deserted her, but in-laws to trumpet it to the world at large? Hadn't the purpose of her coming here been to escape all that? Some escape, her very first evening spent receiving the condolences of the entire town. She could just imagine the conversation. 'You must be Joy's sister-in-law. The one her brother's just dumped.' 'Of course a lot of men leave their wives for younger women. You're in no way exceptional. I expect you know that?'

I certainly do, thought Ruth, hating the seaside with a savagery she had not known herself capable of, except during relaxation.

Christopher Blakeney looked even more fed up than Ruth when he arrived to pick her up at ten past six. The last thing he had needed after missing a full day's work was to be asked to spend an evening making small talk to their neighbours. And Joy's chili, which she reserved specifically for occasions of this sort, always gave him heartburn. Or perhaps it was the company. Either way he was less than gracious as he bundled Ruth, hair still damp since she couldn't find her hairdryer, into the car and rattled off down the lane towards Harbinger House.

• Sarah Grazebrook

They drove in silence, Ruth painfully aware of the resentment oozing from her host. 'I'm awfully sorry about this,' she ventured at last. Christopher relaxed somewhat. 'It's not your fault, Ruth,' he admitted. 'Why Joy has to do this on your very first evening. I mean it's not as though you're down for a weekend, is it? You're going to be here for months and months.' He sounded so depressed at the prospect that Ruth smothered a laugh. Christopher glanced at her curiously. 'What's so funny?'

'Nothing. You just make it sound like a prison sentence.'

Christopher sighed. 'Wait till you meet this lot,' he said. 'I know which I'd prefer.'

Contrary to Joy's promise that people did not dress up at the seaside, the assorted guests looked as though they were waiting to collect their OBEs. The men were in suits and the women sported a variety of rich wool sheaths, several glittering with lurex thread, clearly a feature of coastal fashion. Ruth fiddled nervously with her damp fringe and tried to look as though a guernsey sweater and slacks were *de rigueur* for cocktail parties in London.

Joy was talking to a lugubrious-looking man who hung over her like a lamp-post as she chattered non-stop into his wine glass. Occasionally he would lift it to his lips and suck a small quantity into his mouth where it washed from side to side until he was ready to swallow. He accompanied this movement with a swaying of his feet. The effect was of a man on board ship.

Catching sight of Ruth, Joy immediately seized his arm and hoicked him across the room. 'Ruth, how marvellous. You're here at last.' She flung a murderous look at Christopher who was doing extravagant things with a coat hook. 'This is Adrian Mills. He's in television so you'll have a lot of things in common.' The two of them gazed at each other in mutual bewilderment. Eventually Ruth's training came to her aid. 'I'm afraid I don't know much about television,' she muttered apologetically, 'apart from what one reads, of course.'

Adrian peered down at her with acute suspicion. 'What have you read?' he snapped.

Ruth baulked. 'Well, nothing, really.'

Adrian relaxed. 'Do you watch Delia Smith?' he asked.

'Sometimes,' said Ruth cautiously. It seemed a fair response.

Adrian smiled a feline smile. 'So do I,' he confided. 'I think she's pretty smart.' Ruth nodded energetically and accepted a deep-fried pebble from a silent woman with a tray.

'Some people say she's overrated,' continued Adrian, his eyes narrowing slightly.

Ruth chewed hard on her pebble. 'Oh no. I think she's lovely. She makes everything sound so easy. And her recipes work. Even I can do them.' She laughed demurely, as she always did at this point.

'Can't you cook either?' demanded Adrian with more antagonism than their acquaintance seemed to warrant.

'I do my best,' said Ruth, somewhat at a loss. Adrian softened slightly. 'I'm a plain enough man,' he confided. Ruth thought this true but was too well-bred to respond. 'Meat and two veg with a decent pudding, and perhaps a bit of cheese, that's all I ask.' He accepted another stone from the tray and strode away to talk to an equally plain man who was shouting into a mobile phone.

Joy seized her again and propelled her towards two women, one large and Junoesque and the other thin with darting eyes.

'Grace, Violet, this is my sister-in-law, Ruth Page. She's looking after Bell Cottage while the Taylors are away,' Joy recited unconvincingly. The women smiled knowingly and said they hoped she would enjoy her stay. The larger woman, who was Grace, put a reassuring hand on Ruth's shoulder and said if she ever wanted to talk she would give her her phone number. Ruth thanked her, but did not take up the option.

Violet asked her if she swam at all, adding that they were looking for someone like her. Ruth wondered whether this meant she resembled a missing swimmer, or that Violet had some as yet undisclosed purpose for her that had to do with cold water. Neither thought appealed.

While Violet was refilling her glass Grace confided, sotto voce, that her friend was a very nice woman, but that Ruth should be a bit careful. Before she could elaborate they were joined by a man whom Grace introduced as her husband, Garth Forland.

'I was just telling Ruth about Violet,' Grace murmured in her conspiratorial way. 'What?' asked Forland loudly. Grace shook her head helplessly. 'You know.' She turned to Ruth. 'Mind you, she'd have been nowhere if it weren't for Joy. She owes it all to her.'

Violet returned, plainly unaware how much was due to her hostess, because she was complaining about the lack of bottled water in the Blakeneys' fridge.

'You'd think she'd have got some in,' she grumbled. 'All I could find was this economy orange stuff. I'm sure it's got additives. Joy wouldn't let me look at the label but I know I'm right.'

'Don't fuss, Violet,' ordered Garth Forland firmly. 'Water's water. Orange is orange. That's all there is to it.' His wife moved away to talk to Adrian who had been deserted by the man with the mobile phone and was now sitting on a radiator consuming a bowl of peanuts.

'So. What's your handicap, Ruth?' Forland demanded, helping himself to a whisky. 'Don't be shy. We're used to all sorts down here.'

Ruth was struck with the ghastly thought that Joy had finally exceeded herself on the subject of her own present difficulties. 'Cannot please husband in bed,' flashed accusingly across her mind. 'Refuses to wear wires on her teeth'.

Forland was watching her impatiently. 'You do play?' He prompted at last. 'Golf?'

'Golf? Oh . . . no, I'm afraid I don't,' answered Ruth. 'Only the crazy kind, anyway.' Garth smiled thinly, plainly thinking she was a little crazy herself, and moved away to talk to other guests.

'By the way,' whispered Violet, who had got over her distaste for the orange juice by adding a substantial measure of gin to it, 'watch out for Grace. Oh, she's my best friend and I wouldn't hear a word against her, but she can be a bit . . . sometimes, if you know what I mean.'

Ruth closed her eyes and nodded meekly. When she opened them again Violet had gone, to be replaced by a plump, pretty young woman with anxious eyes and wild brown curls.

'Hello,' she said. 'You're Ruth, aren't you?'

The newcomer, too, wore wool and lurex, but of them all she looked the least comfortable and the most attractive. She held out a hand sticky with cocktail sausages. 'My name's Gwen Pritchard. I'm in the basement.'

'Here?' asked Ruth, then felt she had sounded unfriendly. 'I'm sorry. It's just I didn't know Joy and Christopher had a . . .'

'Lodger? Yes, me. They're doing me a huge favour. It's only temporary, of course, but I'm sort of between posts at the moment, if you see what I mean.' Observing that Ruth did not, she went on, 'I broke up with my husband – not husband, really. "Partner", I believe they're called nowadays, and he holds the mortgage on our flat so I didn't really have a lot of choice in the matter. Joy and Christopher have been wonderful. Without them I don't know where I'd've been. And of course they've been so good to Adrian, what with all that business . . . and Violet, of course. I don't know how they manage to find the time.'

Ruth felt a blanket of gloom descending on her. Any minute now the blind mute child would doubtless be wheeled in, to attest by a series of wonderful, vase-breaking gestures the difference her brother and sister-in-law's charitable input had made to its hitherto useless life.

Violet reclaimed her and explained that it was her hope to recruit a triathlon team from amongst the women of Westbridge. They would be required to run three miles, swim one, and bicycle sixteen, with the option of running up a one-in-three gradient, their bicycles held high above their heads. This, apparently, procured no penalty points.

When Ruth expressed a genuine fear that it might procure a heart attack, Violet dismissed her qualms by informing her that an EEC grant was available. She didn't specify whether it was for achievement or medical care.

Joy rescued her at this point, if 'rescue' was the right word for dragging her round the remaining guests explaining that she was 'down here for a bit of rest, if they knew what she meant'. Since it was perfectly clear that every single one of them was sufficiently versed in the details of her marital break-up to equip them for the finals of *Mastermind*, Ruth found the exercise rather demoralising.

The chili was served, everyone squeezing uncomfortably round a long pine table as Joy dolloped lumps of it into bowls which were passed solemnly down the line as she exhorted them to help themselves 'to the rest'. From where Ruth was sitting this appeared to consist of the salt and pepper, though she had a suspicion that further up the table salad and rice were being swopped by the privileged few.

She found herself once more next to Adrian Mills who had managed to secure himself a large piece of French bread, but showed no signs of wanting to share it.

On her right sat Gwen, meekly grateful for her portion of sludge and accordingly useless in any potential uprising.

'Aren't you going to finish that?' asked Adrian fiercely as Ruth pushed the stodgy beans around her bowl.

'I'm a bit full,' she lied, thinking how much she would give for her own kitchen and a poached egg on toast.

'I hate waste,' said Adrian darkly and poured himself the last of the wine.

Plates were gathered in and trifle appeared. This too was dished out with religious intensity, producing cries of 'Oh Joy, you shouldn't have,' as the guests dug deep into the gooey mass. Ruth was of entirely the same opinion but for possibly different reasons. She struggled on, goaded by an increasingly ratty Adrian and was on the point of asking him whether he would like to finish hers himself, when a bleeping from inside his jacket drew him muttering into the hall where he could soon be heard remonstrating crossly with whoever was on the other end.

Joy took this opportunity to squeeze herself into his seat. 'Everything all right, Ruth, is it? I'm sorry. I've neglected you terribly, but every time I looked across you seemed to be chatting to someone or other, so I thought you must be managing.' She placed a sisterly hand on Ruth's arm. 'I know how hard it must be for you, believe me, I do. But we Westbridge folk are a friendly lot. You'll soon feel at home, really you will.'

Ruth smiled wanly. 'I'm sure I shall. Honestly, Joy, I can't thank you enough for all you've done, but you mustn't worry about me. I shall be fine. I just need a bit of time to adjust.'

'Of course you do. And we're all here to help you do just that.'

Adrian returned looking seriously irritated. Joy relinquished his seat and hurried away to stop Christopher opening any more wine. Ruth, sensing that this was not the moment to offer him her trifle, turned to Gwen who was sitting with her hands folded in her lap, gazing adoringly at the back of Garth Forland's head.

'Have you lived here long?' she asked. Gwen dropped her eyes and sighed distractedly. 'How long is long?' she asked. Ruth was slightly flummoxed. 'I don't know. It's just I was wondering if you could tell me where the library was, and if there's anywhere I could get my hair cut – that sort of thing.'

Gwen gave a deprecating smile. 'I'm sorry. There I go again. Only thinking of myself. There's a frightfully good optician on the corner by the butcher's, and a super health shop. They do a special offer every month. It's zinc at the moment. You get sixty tablets for five pounds forty-nine. That's two months' supply. Pretty good, eh? And of course there's . . .' she paused delicately. 'No, you wouldn't want to hear about that.'

'Wouldn't I?' asked Ruth politely, thinking Gwen was probably right.

Gwen sighed and gave a little shudder. 'No, I'm sure you wouldn't. It's just the second-hand bookshop I work in. Only part-time. Afternoons, mainly.' Her hands fiddled distractedly with her paper napkin.

'I like second-hand bookshops,' Ruth prompted. 'They're much more interesting than new ones.'

'Oh, do you think so?' Gwen's eyes grew round with pleasure. 'I'm so glad to hear you say that. You can't imagine what it's like sometimes when I tell people about it. It's as though . . . as though . . . I expect you think I'm terribly silly?'

'Why should I?' asked Ruth cautiously.

'Oh, because . . . because . . . Well, never mind about that. It's in a little side street behind the market. "Penny Dreadful", it's called. It would be so marvellous if you could pop in one afternoon and we could have a chat. Thursdays are best. I don't know why but no one ever seems to go shopping on a Thursday in Westbridge. Not for books, anyway.' She gave a quick laugh. 'Anyway, THEY aren't there on a Thursday.'

'They?' Ruth repeated.

'The owners. Paul and Jenny Redwood. The slave drivers, I call them. I told Garth Forland and he thought it was fearfully funny.' She giggled shyly. Ruth smiled politely.

• Sarah Grazebrook

'Have you known Adrian long?' Gwen asked quite suddenly. Ruth shook her head in surprise. 'Joy introduced us tonight. I didn't know anyone before this evening. Why?'

Gwen blushed. 'Oh, no reason. It's just I saw the two of you talking and I just sort of got the feeling, you know, that you KNEW each other, if you see what I mean.'

'No,' said Ruth firmly. 'We don't at all.'

'I haven't offended you, have I?' asked Gwen in mortification. 'I didn't mean, you know, to suggest anything.'

Ruth smiled, suddenly very weary. 'Of course you haven't. Why should I be offended? I've thoroughly enjoyed my evening. It was extremely kind of Joy to go to all this trouble.'

Gwen beamed. 'Yes. And just think, if she hadn't, we might never have met.'

'No,' Ruth agreed. 'We might not have.'

The guests began to go. An elderly couple who had hardly spoken to her all night, suddenly descended and said she would be welcome at their pottery class any time she liked. There was a small deposit for clay and she would have to pay for her own glaze but apart from that it was a very economical hobby and one they felt sure she would enjoy.

When everyone had gone, including Adrian with a canister of left-over chili, Joy made coffee and asked Ruth what she had thought.

'Everyone seemed very nice,' Ruth answered, trying to remember any of their faces.

'Even the Forlands?'

Ruth smiled. 'I'm not a golfer.'

Joy sniffed. 'Neither is he. Though you wouldn't know it, to hear him rabbiting on. Did Violet Sampson get at you, by the way?'

'Get at me?'

'She means, has she got you crossing the Sahara on a moped?' intercepted Christopher, who was trying to sort out his witness statements for the morning.

Ruth laughed. 'Well, she did say something about swimming, and running up a hill with a bike on my shoulders.'

'The woman's completely mad,' Joy declared, moving the sugar further away from Christopher. 'Take my advice and steer well clear of her. Rowena M. tore her cartilage to shreds on that stupid marathon.'

'Rowena M. should have known better,' observed her husband.

'Which one was she?' Ruth asked, trying to think who among the people she had met that night, could possibly have entered for a marathon.

'Oh, she wasn't here tonight,' said Joy briskly. 'In fact I won't have her in the house since last time.'

'Which is perfectly absurd, as you very well know,' observed Christopher, folding up his papers and replacing them in his briefcase. 'Come on, Ruth. I'll drive you home. You must be whacked.'

'I am rather,' Ruth admitted, wondering vaguely what heinous crime the woman must have committed to merit exclusion from Joy's chili parties. Christopher went to fetch her coat. 'By the way, what did you think of Adrian?' Joy asked casually.

Ruth paused. It was difficult to tell from her sister-in-law's tone what response she was looking for. Presumably not her natural one that he was dull, petulant and greedy. 'I didn't really get to talk to him much,' she demurred.

Joy looked disappointed. 'Oh didn't you? And I specially made sure you were next to each other. Mind you that dratted wife of his rang up halfway through, didn't she? You'd think she'd give him one evening off. Ah well.' She yawned and ate a peanut which had fallen on to a cushion. 'That's Rowena for you.'

3

Ruth woke the next morning to the sound of pouring rain. She opened her eyes, shuddered at the glaring yellow walls, readjusted the duvets and tried to get back to sleep.

After ten minutes of shifting from side to side she acknowledged defeat and forced her feet out on to the austere beige cord.

She had trouble with the gas hob, firstly because she didn't know which knob to turn and secondly because she was terrified. When it finally lit with a mighty pop, she leapt backwards and jarred her heel against the fridge.

I hate this place, she thought, rubbing her heel and trying to think of some soothing yogic affirmation which might ease her desire to take her sister-in-law by the throat and very slowly throttle her.

There was a ring at the front door. Ruth clutched the kettle defensively. Surely not Joy at this hour? She wasn't even dressed. Perhaps it was the postman. She'd rather he didn't see her in her dressing-gown. If she kept quiet he would doubtless go away.

The bell pealed out again. Then again. Whoever it was obviously had no plans to move on. Reluctantly Ruth huddled her dressing-gown round her and plodded through to the hall.

'Mrs Page?' A ruddy young giant in dungarees was beaming down at her.

'Yes?'

'I've got her for you.'

Ruth, whose thoughts had so lately been fixed on Joy's murder, had a sudden fear that her wishes had fathered the opportunity. 'Who?' she asked rather sickly. For reply the youth turned and trotted back to a battered van parked by the gate. Here he was set upon by two Rottweilers and an angry hyena, or so it sounded to Ruth as he opened the back of the vehicle.

He leant inside, further infuriating the inmates, and emerged seconds later with either the back legs of the Rottweilers or the front ones of the hyena. In fact they turned out to be all four of a small fat dachshund, which he tucked stoically under one arm before reaching inside for a large leather holdall. Kicking the doors shut, he carried both dog and bag up the path. At the porch he released the animal, which immediately flew past Ruth into the hall and began making a nest with the new woollen jacket she had been foolish enough to leave on a chair.

'There,' said the youth pleasantly. 'She's glad to be home, that's for sure.' He deposited the holdall on the step and drew a pad of invoices from his shirt pocket. 'If you could just sign for her.'

Ruth felt her mouth opening and shutting like a fish. She pulled herself together. 'I'm terribly sorry,' she finally managed, 'but there's clearly been a mistake.'

The youth frowned. 'Bell Cottage?'

'Yes.'

He consulted his invoice. The beam returned. 'No mistake. It says here "Lollo", that's her.' He jerked his head in the direction of the dachshund, who had now pulled Ruth's towels off the telephone and was performing some kind of ritual fertility dance on them. 'To be delivered Wednesday the fourteenth. Bell Cottage. Mrs Page to take charge.'

Ruth traced small circles on her forehead. She must not panic. That there had been a mistake could not be in doubt. How such a mistake could have occurred was a mystery, unless it was Joy's idea of a joke. Common sense reminded her that Joy would not know a joke if it walked up and bit her, which this particular one looked more than capable of doing.

She tried reasoning. 'Look, I'm sorry. I'm sure it's not your fault and I'm sorry you've had a wasted journey, but really I know nothing about this dog . . . Lollo, or whatever you said it was called.'

'She's a she,' corrected the youth.

'She, then. There you are. I know nothing about dogs. I've never owned one in my life. I'm more of a . . . rabbit person myself, if you see what I mean,' she added, hoping to placate him.

The youth furled his upper lip. 'It's nothing to do with me,' he maintained. 'You'd best phone Mrs Francis if you're not happy. I can't hang around. There's four gerbils and a guinea pig to do before nine o'clock. You get in touch with Mrs Francis.' He thrust the unsigned invoice into her hands and set off down the path before she could object.

'This is ridiculous,' said Ruth out loud, gazing distractedly at the piece of paper in her hand. She became aware of a screaming sound. Good, she thought maliciously, it's hurt itself, but the noise was coming from the Taylors' kettle which had all but boiled dry in the fracas.

She poured what remained of the water into the teapot and looked around for some means to toast bread. Lollo had followed her into the kitchen and was watching her avidly, a steady stream of saliva dripping from her hospital corner jowls. 'And I don't know what you're looking at,' grumbled Ruth as she once more leapt back from the grill. Lollo sat down and began to pant. Ruth put some bread under the grill and went to phone the odious Mrs Francis who had landed her with this overweight sausage.

Pets Paradise was closed till nine o'clock, the answerphone informed her, in between playing 'Old Shep', which struck her as sinister, and 'How Much Is That Doggie In The Window?' which was downright revolting, but if she would like to leave a message after the bleep someone would get back to her as soon as possible.

Ruth left a message saying she must speak to Mrs Francis most urgently and giving the Taylors' number. She went back to the kitchen where plumes of black smoke apprised her that gas grills were not the same as toasters. 'Thanks a lot,' she snarled at Lollo, who was still dribbling in a manner inconsistent with what was on offer.

She opened the back door and wafted the smoke out of it with a teatowel. 'I hate this place,' she informed the neighbourhood. 'I haven't even been here twenty-four hours and I hate it. I lived in London for twenty years and I didn't hate it once.' As if to

• Sarah Grazebrook

agree, Lollo let out an enormous belch and sicked up a button from Ruth's new coat.

The receptionist from Pets' Paradise was less than helpful. 'Mrs Francis is on holiday,' she intoned at intervals, as though the repetition would eventually persuade Ruth to accept her fate. 'Well who sent this bloody dog to me?' Ruth finally screeched. There was a silence, followed by the click of a receiver being replaced. That's it, she thought. I've done it. The police will be round here next. I've made an obscene phone call. Imagine the headlines. 'Deserted wife abuses teenage receptionist'. 'Dog Hater rejects lovely Lollo'. She became aware of a retching sound and was just in time to prevent Lollo from depositing the burnt toast, which she had thrown into the garden for the birds, all over her towels which were still lying in the hall where the beast had dragged them.

If Ruth had not known Joy better she would have thought she sounded a little embarrassed when she finally came to the phone, having sent her cleaning lady to answer it and then, by a series of shouted instructions, implied that nothing short of a 'life and death' emergency could drag her away from potting her geraniums.

'Tell her it is "life and death", please,' said Ruth in a strangulated voice.

'Ruth? How are you, dear? Not suffering too much from last night, are you? I told Chrissie to go easy on the wine but he's such a generous sod when it comes to entertaining. Loves to push the boat out.'

'Joy, you didn't tell me the Taylors had a dog.'

There was a pause. 'Didn't I, dear? I thought I had. She's such a sweet little thing. No trouble. Terribly affectionate. Wonderful company.'

'Why did you tell them that I would look after it while they were away?'

Ruth had finally got hold of Mrs Francis' assistant who had been most adamant that her instructions were to deliver Lollo at the earliest opportunity to the 'nice lady who was going to look after her for the next few months'.

'It's better she should be in her own home,' the woman had reiterated with sickening rationality. 'That way she won't miss

Mummy and Daddy so much. She's got all her medis in her little bag. The instructions are with them so you've nothing to worry about.' Ruth had enquired what 'medis' might be.

'Medication. I'm afraid she's got quite a lot. Well, they do, don't they, dachshunds? Blood pressure. But so long as you keep her regular there shouldn't be a problem.'

Ruth had debated asking whether buttons and burnt toast constituted a regular diet, but had decided instead to attack the problem at its root.

'It can't stay here, Joy. Surely you realise that? I did ask you if there were any conditions attached to my using the cottage.'

'It's not a condition. It's company for you. Goodness, you don't want to be stuck out there miles from anywhere with no form of protection.'

'Protection? Joy, I've come from West London. There are more muggings there in one afternoon than there probably are round here in a quarter.'

'Muggings aren't the only form of crime,' responded Joy energetically. 'You're only three miles away from Barlan.'

'What's that?'

'An open prison. I should think you'd be grateful to have a dog around the place.'

'Well I'm not,' said Ruth stubbornly. Duncan had often complained to Joy of Ruth's obstinacy. She began to perceive what he meant. 'Anyway, it's a horrible dog. It's been sick twice already, and it's put its filthy paw marks all over my new coat.'

'That's affection. She probably wants a cuddle, poor lamb,' said Joy maternally.

'Perhaps in that case you'd like to come and cuddle her,' said Ruth coldly, 'because she can't stay here.'

There was a deep sigh. 'I suppose I shall have to see what I can do.'

'If you would. I'm sorry to be a pest, Joy. I do appreciate what you've done for me, but dogs are out, I'm afraid. Completely out.'

Joy sighed deeply. 'That's all right, Ruth dear. We all understand.'

Ruth, a mild woman by nature, felt the hairs rising on the back of her neck. 'What do you understand?'

'Well, it's revenge, isn't it? Oh, don't worry. I don't blame you. None of us do – will. It's just it seems a bit hard to take Duncan's transgressions out on poor pretty Lollo.'

'Lollo isn't pretty,' said Ruth automatically. 'She's fat and ill-mannered and destructive.'

There was the tiniest hint of satisfaction in Joy's voice as she murmured 'Exactly' into the receiver.

Ruth spent the morning unpacking, coming to terms with her gas cooker, and fighting Lollo off her bed linen. For some reason the creature seemed obsessed with dragging everything, including the newspapers in which most of Ruth's breakables were wrapped, into the hall and making a nest with them.

It was quite a neat nest, based mainly under the telephone table, but protruding sufficiently to cause savage snarling if Ruth happened to step on a border as she trailed up and down the stairs.

After lunch, which consisted of tinned soup so bland that even Lollo resisted it, Ruth decided that she must explore the town or starve.

She had never considered herself a gourmet, nor even a fussy eater, but if she were to be confined to the offerings of the local newsagent she could see that she would be dead within the month. Besides which, the price of dog food seemed to be on a par with caviar at Fortnum and Masons and, much as she disliked the portly Lollo, Ruth had no intention of watching her systematically starve or, worse still, exist on a diet of coat buttons.

Over her coffee she considered her position. Joy wouldn't dare leave the dog with her indefinitely. Her local cred demanded that the brute be returned alive. Besides, there were so many people in Westbridge who appeared to owe their very existence to Ruth's saintly sister-in-law that the thought of supporting Lollo for three months would probably instil in them a sense of purpose not equalled since Sidney Carton mounted the scaffold.

The rain had abated as Ruth rooted through Lollo's holdall for something approximating to dog food. Little though she knew about pets, there seemed nothing amongst the vitamin pills, antihysteria lozenges and hyper-activity capsules that equated to a slap up doggie meal. Lollo sat beside her dripping patiently.

At the bottom of the bag was a sheet of paper. Ruth glanced at it, then stared. What she had assumed was a left-over copy of the Taylors' Australian itinerary was actually a list of Lollo's prescribed medication and the times at which she should take it.

It made fascinating reading. She looked at her watch. Apparently by ten past two, which it now was, Lollo should have been the recipient of two doses of cod liver oil, a pep-up Doggie Bounce Bar, three spoonfuls of brewer's yeast and a Camomile Canine Pacifier. It said nothing about food.

A low pitched whine reminded her that Lollo had not been out since she arrived. She opened the back door. Lollo leapt through it and made for the nearest flower bed where she crouched vindictively over the beginnings of a geranium. Ruth watched in distaste. Better far to do these sort of things in the open country, she decided. She searched around again and found Lollo's lead, a strange apparatus more like an electrical extension cable than a means of controlling a dachshund.

Spotting this, Lollo came shooting back into the kitchen, and began to perform a series of pirouettes, each requiring a savage stab at Ruth's legs on the final twirl. 'Stop that,' Ruth implored. 'Keep still a minute, can't you?' But the sound of her voice only excited the dog more and it was some time before she succeeded in attaching the strap to Lollo's puny tartan collar.

Lollo seemed to regard the attachment of her lead as a licence to bungee jump at every passing vehicle, pushchair or pedestrian. Ruth quickly came to realise that the extension lead was not for her convenience as she watched helplessly while Lollo shot out of reach, snapping and yapping at everything in sight. It seemed grossly unfair to her that, though the monster experienced no problems in getting it to unwind, she herself had not the slightest idea of how to retract it. She squeezed the handle feverishly, but it continued relentlessly paying out so that she was reduced to winding it round her elbow like a seaman tying up a boat.

She found the town centre which had a pedestrian precinct, the usual shops and an injunction that dogs should not be allowed to foul the pavement. This Lollo duly did with much panting and grunting to the dual delight and indignation of the mothers and children observing the process.

Ruth's heart sank as she overheard mutterings about a Dog

• Sarah Grazebrook

Warden. Help was at hand, however, in the form of Gwen Pritchard, clearly free of the slave drivers' demands, who came rushing out of the health shop crying, 'Oh poor you. Isn't she a treasure? A naughty treasure, though,' with which she crouched down, scooped Lollo's offerings into a carrier bag and deposited it deftly in a Poop Bin, sight hitherto unknown to Ruth. Both mothers and children turned away disappointed.

'Thank you,' said Ruth with heartfelt relief. 'I don't know what I'd've done otherwise.'

Gwen gave a deprecating laugh. 'Oh, rubbish. How could you be expected to know it was "défense d'uriner"?' She laughed again and gave Lollo a life-threatening hug. 'And YOU are a naughty girl. YES you are. YES you are.' Lollo responded well to this by covering Gwen's skirt with mud and licking her face ferociously. Ruth sought to pull her off but Gwen showed no distaste and continued to play with the dog's ears and assure her that she was beautiful beyond her dreams.

A thought struck Ruth. 'I don't suppose you could do me another favour?' she began. Gwen looked up surprised. Two favours in one day might yet establish her as a useful person.

'Of course. Anything. If I can.'

'It's just I really need to do some shopping. I need some food for Lollo,' Ruth added hypocritically. 'I was wondering if you could possibly hang on to her while I nip into the supermarket? I'll only be a minute, but they certainly won't let me take her in there and,' she summoned dramatic resources she did not know she possessed, 'I wouldn't want to leave her tied up all by herself outside.'

Gwen was delighted. She would take Lollo for a teeny walk round the park and meet Ruth in fifteen minutes by the exit.

Ruth dashed into the store, bought two bottles of wine, one tin of dogmeat, some fruit and a frozen chicken dinner. That would get her through the night. Tomorrow she would be able to do some proper shopping and take it home in a taxi. Tomorrow, when Lollo had gone.

True to her word, Gwen was waiting for her when she came out. 'Oh poor you. You're so loaded. Let me help you.' Ruth protested that she was more than capable of carrying a couple of bags of shopping, but Gwen was now into true Samaritan mode and insisted on accompanying her back to the house, carrying the heavier of the bags and keeping hold of Lollo, who trotted meekly beside her new friend with only the tiniest hint of smugness.

Back at the cottage Ruth made tea. Gwen had some herbal biscuits she had bought at the health shop and insisted on sharing. Lollo had one too, but clearly felt much the same way that Ruth did, that they tasted of toothpaste, and left hers half-digested on the sitting room floor.

Tea finished, Gwen gazed longingly out of the french windows and said how much she missed her garden. 'Do you like gardening?' asked Ruth, hoping to exploit Gwen's willingness still further.

'Oh yes. I love anything to do with Nature. Don't you?'

'I hadn't really thought about it,' Ruth confessed.

'We're so alike, we two, aren't we?' Gwen enthused. Unsettled, Ruth poured more tea. 'We both love animals, and flowers and things,' Gwen continued. 'And of course we've both had such rotten luck – with men, I mean.' She cast a quick glance at Ruth and added more cheerfully, 'And we've both been saved by Joy and Chrissie. We're both very lucky people in a way. And now we've met each other. It's almost like Fate, wouldn't you say?'

Fortunately Ruth was saved by the telephone from having to say anything. She excused herself and hurried to answer it. It was Martin. 'Hi, Mum. I just wondered how you were settling in.'

'Fine, darling. Shouldn't you be in a lecture or something?'

'It's Wednesday,' said Martin in a righteous voice.

'And?'

'And I don't have any lectures on a Wednesday. How is it? Has Auntie Joy driven you mad yet?'

'Of course she hasn't,' said Ruth rather too quickly.

'What's she done?'

'Nothing. Nothing at all. In fact she's been very helpful. She laid on a special supper last night, so I could meet all the locals ...' She heard Martin chuckling. 'Don't you start laughing. Some of them were very nice. I'm having tea with one of them at the moment, as a matter of fact. She's extremely pleasant.'

'So you're all right?'

'I'm all right. How about you?'

'Wonderful. Fine. Can I come and see you soon?'

'Come whenever you like. You'll love it here. Lots of cold air and rain and things.'

Martin laughed. 'Missing London already, are you?'

Ruth smiled. 'A bit. I must go. I've got a guest.' There was a high-pitched squeal and Lollo came rushing into the hall carrying Gwen's scarf.

'What the hell's that noise?' asked Martin as Ruth struggled unsuccessfully to retrieve the object.

'Oh nothing. Just a dog.'

'Have you bought a dog, Mum?' asked Martin in genuine surprise.

'I certainly have not. It's just . . . visiting. I'll tell you about it when I see you. Oh Lollo, you swine. Look, I'll have to go, darling. The little sod's tearing this scarf to shreds. Talk to you soon.'

'Bye, Mum. Don't go overdoing this "Country Life" business, will you?' Ruth laughed and put the phone down. Gwen came tiptoeing out to see the remains of her scarf disappearing into Lollo's nest.

'I'm terribly sorry,' Ruth apologised. 'I tried to get it back from her but she's got teeth like a vice.'

Gwen shook her head vigorously. 'It doesn't matter, honestly. Not in the least. It was only an old one. One that Henry gave me.' Her voice dropped and a look of poetic grief came over her face. Ruth felt dreadful.

'Was Henry . . . ? Is he your . . . ?'

Gwen nodded then shook herself and gave a brave little smile. 'So, that's the end of that. I shall take it as an omen. Off with the old, on with the new.'

'You must let me pay you for it,' said Ruth firmly. Gwen looked shocked. 'Certainly not. I wouldn't dream of it. No, it was meant to be. In a way,' she glanced at Ruth shyly, 'it sort of seals our friendship, if you see what I mean.' She picked up her coat. 'I must be off. I promised to help Joy finish lining her curtains this evening.'

'Well, thank you so much for carrying my shopping and everything,' Ruth murmured, trying to ignore the proffered bond. 'I expect I'll see you over at the house some time.'

Gwen smiled excitedly. 'Oh, yes. Lots of times. You must come and have tea with me.'

'That would be very nice,' said Ruth, her heart sinking.

'Tomorrow?'

Ruth swallowed. 'Tomorrow's a bit difficult for me. I've got to see the bank manager and sort out a few things.'

Gwen nodded sympathetically. 'It's horrid, isn't it? All that. Well, if you need a shoulder to cry on, you know where I am.' She gave Ruth a smile so full of compassion that Ruth felt she had been squeezed like a lemon. She waved her, smiling, down the path and watched to make sure she was off the premises before going inside and shutting the door firmly behind her. Lollo was in the sitting room lapping the dregs from Gwen's teacup. The animal turned as she came into the room and Ruth could have sworn it smiled.

4

Ruth's interview with the local bank manager proved a rather bruising affair.

In the past her only contact with the species had been at cocktail parties and via statements informing her that she was neither rich nor bankrupt. This had seemed appropriate to Duncan Page who, as an economist, had felt honour-bound to see that his wife did not live in penury, nor yet in a style that was preferable to her previous one. He didn't want her to be wretched in her abandoned state, but nor did he see why she should find it an improvement. Thus Ruth's life in London had chugged along on a reasonably even keel, the bills being settled, with a small contribution available for her personal needs. Now, it seemed, things were to change.

The bank manager, whose name was Mervyn Parsons, ushered her into a small blue office and sat her down while he opened a file and extracted a solicitor's letter. Ruth immediately recognised the logo of Millet and Bailey, her husband's representatives in the recent divorce.

'Mrs Page,' Parsons began. He had a surprisingly deep voice and Ruth automatically found herself listening to the timbre rather than the content of what he had to say.

After a few moments, however, she came to realise that what he was telling her was not to her advantage.

Duncan, despite their so-called 'friendly' divorce, was maintaining via his solicitor that, now she no longer had the mortgage to contend with, and was no longer subject to London prices, he could not be expected to continue her maintenance on the previously agreed level.

• Sarah Grazebrook

'But I thought that had all been settled,' she stammered distractedly as Parsons laid down his pen. 'And anyway, why have they written to you? Surely they should have contacted my solicitor? Or me, even. I know nothing about any change of arrangement.'

Mr Parsons folded his hands and affected innocence. 'I really can't say, Mrs Page. Except, of course, that before we can permit anyone to make regular withdrawals from our branch we naturally have to be satisfied that they have the funds to sustain them.'

Ruth's mouth went dry. 'But I do. I'm sure I do,' she pleaded. 'Obviously there's been some kind of mix-up. I shall get on to my solicitor the moment I get home and see that it's sorted out.' She hesitated, feeling much as Oliver must have done when faced with Mr Bumble. 'Does that mean I can't have any money?'

Mr Parsons sucked his teeth. It was his concession to a humane approach. 'You may use your cheque card up to its cash limit, Mrs Page, but with regard to regular withdrawals,' he sucked again, 'I think perhaps that should be left until the situation has been clarified.'

He showed her out. Ruth slunk past the tellers, convinced that they were telling each other about her disgrace.

How could Duncan? What a miserable mean slug of a man he was. To do this behind her back, without ever hinting what he had in mind. To think that she had given up their house in London at his suggestion, to help him out. How many wronged wives would agree to be put out of their homes and transported – there was no other word for it – to this offshoot of the Arctic Circle, just so that their philandering louse of an ex-spouse could have more to spend on his American butter mountain?

'Hullo there.' Grace Forland was bearing down on her, not unlike a mountain herself in a navy duster coat with wrap-around shawl.

'Oh . . . hullo. I'm sorry, I didn't see you,' Ruth floundered. Grace seemed undismayed and gazed compassionately down at her, like someone observing a squashed hedgehog.

'That's all right. I could see you had things on your mind.' Her voice reverted to Agony Aunt. 'Everything all right, is it?'

'Yes,' said Ruth sharply then, embarrassed, 'thank you.'

'You must come and have coffee.'

'Thank you. That would be very nice.'

'How about the twenty-seventh of March?'

Ruth stared at her. It was six weeks away.

'Are you free then?'

She collected herself. 'I think so. I haven't actually got my diary . . .'

'No, no, of course not. Why don't you give me a tinkle? You've got our number, haven't you?'

'Yes, thank you. I will.'

The counselling part over, Grace confided that she was going to have her feet done.

'Oh.' Ruth cast a surreptitious glance at Grace's feet. They were large, but not disproportionately so.

'Reflexology,' Grace continued. 'You should try it. Wonderful. You'd be amazed what they can spot. Garth's got a dicky liver. I bet you wouldn't have guessed.'

Ruth admitted that she was not in the habit of guessing people's ailments.

'No. Exactly. I blame the golf. All that air. And he bicycles. It's bound to take its toll.'

Ruth agreed, it being the easiest option. Somewhere a clock struck twelve. Grace started in horror. 'Heavens, is that the time? I shall be late.' She turned to go just as Mr Parsons emerged from the bank in search of his lunch. Grace waved her shawl in semaphore. 'Merv, yoo hoo. Come and meet Mrs Page. She's just moved down from London.' The two of them smiled stonily at each other while Grace informed them in turn of the other's claim to her affection. Parsons was 'an absolute sweetie, considering what he does!' And Ruth was 'a very dear friend and Joy Blakeney's sister-in-law.'

Parsons gave her a glance that said either meant the end of her hopes of an overdraft, before making off down an alley on the pretext of needing to buy some mineral water.

Grace departed in search of her reflexologist and Ruth, irritated, humiliated, and hungry, went into the local supermarket and spent fifty-two pounds on her credit card.

Wheeling her trolley round the aisles, she nursed a perverted hope that she would encounter Mervyn Parsons at the checkout, to which end she purchased a scratch card, which she ostentatiously scraped at while the assistant calculated her bill.

Lollo was indecently pleased to see her, bouncing up and down like a yo-yo, claws tearing indiscriminately at Ruth's tights. 'Get off me, you monster,' Ruth admonished, fighting to keep her groceries above the creature's jawline. 'I don't know what you're so pleased about. None of it's for you.'

She made them both lunch. Pills and mush for Lollo and smoked salmon sandwiches for herself. She opened a bottle of wine and toasted Mr Parsons whom she fervently hoped was now choking on his mineral water.

Lollo, having finished her mush and deposited most of her pills in a neat pile behind the cooker, bounced even higher to see if she could bully Ruth into dropping her sandwich. 'Do stop that,' Ruth ordered, pouring herself some more wine. 'I'll take you out when I've finished.' The dog, who was plainly versed in the language of broken promises, set up a determined yowling till Ruth opened the back door and half threw her into the garden. 'When I'm ready,' she snarled, emboldened by the wine. 'And that won't be till I've rung your rotten Auntie Joy.' Shocked by her own vehemence she made herself some coffee and ate three or four chocolate biscuits.

Joy was not at home. Ruth left a message saying she was about to take Lollo for a walk, but that Joy could collect her any time after four o'clock, adding rather ominously that she had no more dog food in the house.

When she returned Lollo was busy uprooting an exotic-looking plant from the patch marked 'herba urceolaris rara'. Whilst having no idea what the label meant, Ruth sensed that it would upset the Taylors, so left her to it while she had another glass of wine.

The two of them set forth just as the wind performed its customary coastal somersault. Ruth pressed on defiantly in the direction of the beach, Lollo trotting beside her, fur flattened like a weasel, stopping to sniff at every twig and pebble till Ruth lost patience and yanked her ferociously with the never-ending lead. Lollo immediately gave a very decent impression of turning blue and performed several cartwheels before coming to rest in a pile of picnic detritus, which she crammed down her restricted gullet with the skill of a conjuror disappearing a tablecloth.

They walked for a while in relative calm. Ruth was getting used to the wind and was even beginning to enjoy it in a perverse way. She found the need to fight the elements gave impetus to her rehearsed conversations with her solicitor, not to mention Duncan, should the need arise.

It was while she was embroiled in one of these that disaster struck. One minute she was struggling along, decimating Duncan's miserable defence with the stunning conciseness of her argument, the next she was being dragged helplessly as Lollo streaked in the direction of a large black mongrel who was belting towards her, tail erect, with the dedication of a suicide bomber.

Before she could prevent it the two were entwined.

From the noise they were making she had no doubt this was the prelude to a bloodbath and, though she felt no affection for Lollo, neither did she wish to see her torn apart before her eyes. Added to which, if she did not extract herself from the cat's cradle round her ankles it seemed perfectly possible she might be the next victim. Grim tales of 'tasting blood' came to mind. She struggled to gain control of the lead.

'Let go this minute, you dozy bugger.'

Ruth dropped the lead like lightning and turned to see who had seen fit to so label her. A stocky man with thick black hair and weather-beaten face was striding towards her, a large stick swishing menacingly in his hand. Ruth swallowed and tried to remember which pocket she had put her keys in.

'Is that your dog?' he demanded as he approached.

'No,' said Ruth. The man snorted and looked pointedly at the hand so lately holding Lollo's lead. 'That is, I'm looking after it – her – for a while.'

'You call that "looking after her", do you?'

Scottish, thought Ruth. They're always violent. She turned to where frightful noises were coming from the clump of bushes behind which Lollo and the black dog had disappeared. 'Couldn't you call your dog off, or something?' she pleaded weakly.

The man whistled. There was a pause in the squealing, then it resumed. The man snorted again and thudded across to the bushes. Ruth followed at a distance, rehearsing what she would say to Joy and eventually the owners about the untimely decease of their pet. Her reverie was broken by the sound of the man's laughter. Sadist, she thought, quickening her pace.

The sight that greeted her was not a pleasant one. Lollo had disappeared completely, save for the odd bit of silky fur protruding from under the mongrel's body as he rocked rhythmically back and forth, a look of satanic relish in his eyes.

'Oh my god,' said Ruth. 'Get him off her. Do something.'

The man laughed again. 'I'm not daft enough to put myself between Tyson and his oats, hen. You can if you want.'

'But he's smothering her. She's not even my dog. I really think you're behaving irresponsibly.'

'I am?'

'Yes. I mean he is your dog. And he's the one that's . . . I don't know what I'm going to tell the owners.'

With a mighty sneeze Tyson detached himself from Lollo and ran panting off towards the beach. Lollo lay for several seconds squeaking like a canine Lucrece, then gradually hauled herself up, shook herself violently and came pattering coyly over to Ruth.

Ruth snatched up her lead angrily and wound the surplus round her wrist. The man watched with some amusement. 'Bet that's cured her headache,' he said more amiably. Ruth pursed her lips and swept the now-acquiescent Lollo back the way they had come.

'By the way,' came the man's voice. 'There's a button underneath the handle to shorten the lead.' Ruth took no notice but once out of sight she investigated and found he had been telling the truth. She unwound the lead from her wrist and adjusted it to a manageable length. At least she'd learnt something that day. She only wished it had been before, rather than after the fiasco. And from someone slightly less objectionable than the man on the beach.

Lollo's 'headache' might be cured, but she had a splitting one. She really shouldn't drink at lunch-time. Especially as she still had to phone her solicitor. And Joy.

She made herself some black coffee and rang her solicitor first. Mr Draper was not in that afternoon, she was informed, and he was in court all tomorrow morning. Could anyone else be of assistance? 'No, thank you,' she replied wearily. She didn't feel up to discussing Duncan's latest apostasy with a teenage clerk. 'I'll ring back.'

Joy was scarcely more helpful. 'Ruth, how are you? Everything all right? I saw Grace Forland this afternoon. She said she'd bumped into you in the town. She thought you were looking a bit peaky. I said it would be the sea air. It always plays havoc with the system for the first few days. You'll soon get used to it. You must come and have lunch at the weekend. I'll try and get hold of Adrian. He likes a good roast.' She paused as though to allow Ruth to assimilate her good fortune.

'Joy, what have you done about Lollo?'

There was a pause. 'Actually, Ruth, I'm drawing a bit of a blank on that at the moment. I phoned Violet. I was absolutely sure she'd be game, but she's off on a charity hike for Lithuanian music students at the moment. Not sure how long. Then I tried a couple of other buddies but they weren't all that keen. Lollo's a bit of a "love her or hate her" type dog, if you see what I mean.'

'Well, I hate her,' Ruth snapped before she could help herself. There was silence on the end of the phone. Lollo pattered over and sat by Ruth's feet, fixing her with an adoring gaze. Ruth was overwhelmed with guilt. 'I don't really hate her,' she murmured.

'I'm sure you don't,' Joy broke in, forgivingly.

'But I can't keep her here. For a start I've got no more dog food.'

'Can't you give her some mince or something?'

'I haven't got any mince.'

'Well, anything. What you're having.'

Ruth blushed, remembering how in rebellion she had bought a piece of fillet steak for her dinner. 'What about the dog's home? Pets' Paradise or whatever it was called. Why can't they take her till Violet gets back?' The silence this time was tangible. 'Joy, are you still there?' Ruth asked at last.

'Yes. Actually I did try them. Once I was sure no one else wanted to take her on.'

Ruth swallowed. Bugger Duncan. 'If it's the cost you're worried about,' she said hesitantly.

'That is a major consideration, certainly.'

'I would be willing to pay for her to go there. I really think it's important she should be somewhere where she can be looked after properly.'

'It's not cheap, you know.'

'I realise that.' Ruth suddenly understood why the Taylors had agreed to let her live in their igloo rent free. It was infinitely cheaper than having to board their yard of lard for three months. 'Nevertheless . . .'

There was a sigh of relief from the end of the line. 'Well, if you're absolutely sure . . .'

'I am.'

'I'll get on to them in the morning and explain that you'd like them to take Lollo back, full board, from . . . let's see, the eighth of March.'

Ruth stared at the phone. 'The eighth? But that's next month, Joy. I was thinking of tomorrow.'

Down the line Joy was thinking how difficult relatives could be. 'Yes, well, of course, normally that would be the case.'

'Normally?'

'Normally, yes. But they have promised there will be a place for her the minute . . .'

'The minute what?'

'The minute she's out of season.'

5

'Five nine one five seven five two.'

Laureen Denkell's twang made it sound like a song.

Ruth felt the same cold pang she always felt when she heard her voice. 'Could I speak to Duncan, please?'

'Who is it calling, please?'

'Ruth.' As you bloody well know, she thought. She was surprised at how aggressive she was becoming, if only in her head, but the last few days had stretched her to breaking point and she didn't think it would take much to finish the job.

'I'll just get him for you.'

After a few moments Duncan came on the line. 'Ruth?'

'Yes.'

'What's the problem?'

Ruth felt the white light of fury shooting through her. She took a deep breath. 'I think you know what the problem is, Duncan.'

'Not sure that I do.'

'Well, perhaps I should refresh your memory. Do you remember signing an agreement in the presence of both our solicitors saying that you would be responsible for the mortgage, all service bills and that on top of that you would make me an allowance of three hundred pounds a month to live on?'

'Ah.'

'Yes, you may well say "ah", Duncan, but you're not going to wriggle out of it. How dare you tell the bank that you weren't going to pay my maintenance? How dare you spring this on me? After I've moved out of our house – my home – just to help you.'

'Oh, come on, Ruth. You know it wasn't like that. The house was far too big for you. You were just rattling around in it. Especially now Martin's gone.'

'And don't drag Martin into this. He isn't "gone", if you want to know. He and I see a lot of each other. We enjoy each other's company.'

'Yes, well, don't let this empty nest thing get out of hand, will you? Martin's got his own life to lead.'

'A fat lot you'd know about that.'

'Don't start, Ruth.'

'He'd've been leading his own life from the day he was born if you'd had your way. The same as I was.'

'Ruth, we've had all this out before. Don't let's start it again.'

Ruth felt ashamed of her outburst. She sounded like some twisted harridan, not a sensible independent woman who had rung up to sort out a small hiccup in her financial arrangements.

'I want my allowance in full, Duncan. Otherwise you'll be hearing from my solicitors.'

'Ruth, be reasonable. How can I possibly fork out seventy-five quid a week on top of the mortgage . . . ?'

'You're not paying the mortgage. The Websters are.'

'Yes, I know, but I'm responsible for it.'

'That's not quite the same. And anyway that doesn't affect what you agreed to give me.'

'Yes, but be reasonable, Ruth. It can't possibly cost the same to live in some hick seaside town as it does in London.'

'As a matter of fact I think it may cost a good deal more.'

'What do you mean?'

'For a start the place is freezing.'

'That's sea air. You'll get used to it.'

'It's not sea air. It's living in a damp cottage, Duncan. And if you think I'm going to catch pneumonia just so you can take your dentist out to dinner twice a night, you're very much mistaken.'

Duncan's voice was full of reproach. 'Please don't refer to Laureen as my "dentist". You know it only cheapens you.'

Ruth saw tiny pinpricks of light before her eyes. 'I daresay it does, Duncan. But not sufficiently to cut my allowance by thirty-three percent. How can you expect me to live on fifty pounds a week?'

'Things are cheaper in the country.' A whine had entered her ex-husband's voice. She remembered how it had been the first thing to make her dislike him.

'I've seen no evidence of that. And anyway, there's the dog.'

'The DOG?'

'Yes.' Ruth tried to give the impression by her tone that they were talking a stone of steak a day.

'Are you telling me you've bought a dog, Ruth?'

'Not bought, no. I'm looking after it.'

There was relief in Duncan's voice when he spoke. 'Well, naturally, that's your business, Ruth. But I have to tell you that there's nothing in our settlement about supporting a dog. I hardly think you can cite that as a legitimate expense.'

Lollo came and sat supportively on Ruth's left foot. She had been quite nice since they had got home, leaving her tablets by the wastebin, rather than shoving them into spots the hoover could not reach, and eating the makedo supper of chicken and brown bread with a relish that made Ruth feel like a canine Cordon Bleu.

She reached down and gave Lollo's ear an affectionate twitch. Lollo licked her hand.

'Actually, Duncan, I'm walking a guide dog for the blind. And if you're going to make difficulties I'm quite prepared to go to the Press.'

There was a silence. Ruth pictured Duncan's lower lip which would hopefully be giving Laureen apoplexy by now. 'Would sixty be all right?'

Ruth sighed. 'Sixty would be an improvement.'

'I'll speak to Millet in the morning.'

'Duncan.'

'Yes?'

'Sixty and I want Martin's car serviced.'

'For God's sake, Ruth, your father left Martin a fortune.'

'He left him everything he had, Duncan. It's not quite the same thing. Anyway, as his own father I'd've thought you'd've wanted to give him all the help you could.'

- Sarah Grazebrook

'I do. Of course I do.' There was a sickly pause. 'But I've got other responsibilities now.'

You are a horrible person, Ruth thought. You don't even know the harm you do.

They watched television till two o'clock, Lollo curled up beside Ruth on the couch, a plate of chocolate biscuits between them. 'We shall get fat,' Ruth informed the dog as she broke the last biscuit in two. Lollo grunted contentedly and chomped on her portion. Ruth gazed at Harrison Ford's anguished features and promised herself that in the morning she would get a life.

She slept late and was only awoken by the sound of Lollo squeaking to go out. Shivering, she made her way down to the kitchen to be leapt upon and licked. Whilst not actually enjoying the experience, she had to acknowledge a certain pleasure in being so necessary a part of Lollo's existence, at least for the time being.

She had never owned a pet, Martin's hamsters apart. Cats had never appealed to her and Duncan was allergic to dogs, or so he had maintained, though Ruth had long suspected it was the idea of walking them that brought him out in spots.

It had not bothered her, since all the people she knew who did own them seemed to spend their lives ferrying them between vets and willing relations, or cancelling holidays and invitations because the relations were no longer willing and the vets too expensive.

She was glad that she had been firm with Duncan. Somehow it had seemed easier from this alien territory. He had always managed to make her feel as though he were doing a favour when she asked for anything connected with the London house. As though it were by his benevolence alone that she were living there. True, he was responsible for the mortgage, but her parents had put down the deposit as a belated wedding gift, and without that they would certainly not have been able to afford anything like it.

Ringing from Bell Cottage she had felt a sense of control over her affairs which she had never known before. Independence. She now realised that what had passed for that in London during her year on her own, was in fact isolation. Here she was mistress of her own fate. It was for her to decide whether she got up or stayed in bed, ate or starved, entertained or became a recluse. She was free. A New Woman.

'Duncan of the DTI', she thought with a sudden flash of amusement. Grown in the dark of a scruffy windowless office, in the basement of a vast characterless building. Dazzled by the glow of the American puff-ball's dentures. Good luck to him. Good luck to them both. Duncan had been Page One of her life. Westbridge would be Page Two.

As if to underline the benefits of choice, Joy rang at nine-thirty to tell her that she was to come to lunch with them on Sunday, that she had promised Grace Forland that Ruth would help two mornings a week in the Animal Welfare charity shop, that the Trents were very upset that she hadn't shown up at their pottery class the evening before, and that Gwen Pritchard had bored both her and Chrissie rigid by cataloguing Ruth's virtues to them instead of getting on with lining the curtains. Joy didn't know when they were going to be finished at this rate and she had so wanted to be able to show them off before the evenings got too light to be worth drawing them.

She rang off with a sombre warning about the dangers of letting Grace down. 'She can be a bit funny, if you know what I mean.'

Ruth replaced the receiver wondering if it would be possible to enrol for a class in Local Innuendo, as it was difficult to see how she would ever sustain a single conversation without some background to the mental state of her new acquaintances.

After breakfast she rang her solicitors and left a message to say that she had agreed to let Duncan drop her maintenance to sixty pounds a week, on the understanding that he paid for their son to have his car serviced plus a year's subscription to the AA. She was rather pleased with this addendum as it would annoy her ex-husband mightily and stop her worrying about Martin breaking down.

The sun was putting in fitful appearances and, though there was no heat in it yet, Ruth felt unaccountably cheered. She decided to take Lollo out before lunch in the hope of avoiding the unpleasant Scot and his creature.

• Sarah Grazebrook

Lollo, though pleased to go out, seemed undeniably disappointed to have missed the rendezvous and consoled herself by rolling in a pile of discarded fish-bones. Ruth refused to let her back in the house till she had doused her with a bucket of soapy water, which Lollo took as an invitation to run round and round the garden yelping, before plunging into the compost heap at the far end and returning to Ruth in a worse state than ever.

Despite herself Ruth found she was laughing. She filled the sink with more soapy water, lined up several towels and, wrapping one of them round the dog and another round her waist, lifted Lollo cautiously into the air and winched her into the water.

Lollo struggled savagely, little pointed fangs snapping at Ruth's hands as she tried to bath her. 'Calm down,' Ruth muttered. 'CALM DOWN, do you hear.' Lollo showered her with muddy water. 'You little sod.' Lollo now had two paws on the edge of the sink and was preparing to leap. Ruth pushed her back in, soaking them both. 'Now STAY in there, before I drown you,' she ordered. Lollo rose to the surface again and let out a heart-rending wail which turned halfway through to a bark of furious intensity. 'What's the matter with you now?' Ruth, half-blinded by soap, turned to find a fresh towel and was confronted by Grace Forland's horrified face pressed against the kitchen window, her features flattened like a gargoyle as she strove to see what Ruth was up to.

Ruth stared back mesmerised. Lollo took the opportunity to hurl herself over the side and shot away through the house, muddy water spreading like a river behind her.

Meanwhile Grace, features now remodelled to a more standard shape, was miming that she be allowed to come in. Ruth dried her hands and opened the back door. 'I'm sorry about that,' she said limply. 'I was just giving Lollo a bath.'

Grace nodded nervously. 'Everything all right, is it?'

'Yes,' said Ruth, tired of being asked.

'Only I don't think the Taylors used to bath her all that often.'

'Didn't they?' asked Ruth, suddenly protective of her animal skills. 'Well, that explains a lot, of course. Can I offer you a cup of coffee?'

'Thank you,' said Grace, plainly able to accept, if not offer refreshment without a six-week waiting period. There was a loud thud from upstairs. 'If you'll excuse me,' said Ruth and rushed to see what had happened.

Lollo was sitting in the middle of Ruth's bedroom, swaddled in the duvets, now also mud-streaked and damp. The standard lamp was lying at a drunken angle across the floor where Lollo had caught her paw in the flex, and a glass of water that Ruth had forgotten to bring down with her in the morning was upended over the dressing table. 'You know what you are?' Ruth told her in a rising crescendo. 'You are a bloody nuisance and I wish I had drowned you.' She went out, slamming the door behind her to be faced with Grace, peering anxiously up the stairs. 'Do you need any help?' she enquired tentatively. Ruth contemplated asking her to help her bury Lollo alive in the back garden, but instead said everything was under control and left Grace in the sitting room while she went to tackle the gas.

Grace drank her coffee sugarless, since Ruth had none, and talked at some length about the value of the work done by the Animal Welfare shop.

Ruth got the distinct feeling that Grace was now regretting having put her up for the Tuesday\Friday mornings' slot, particularly since it seemed that these were the hours when 'Only Madge Jordan is available'. Ruth asked how many people normally worked in the shop and was told two. This led her to suspect that Madge Jordan was the problem, not the ratio.

'What would I have to do, exactly?' she asked as Grace struggled with her coffee.

'Oh not much, really. Just help out. Whatever needs doing. Joy did say that you had done this sort of thing before.' A note of accusation had entered her voice, but Ruth put it down to the lack of sugar.

'I did a bit for the Red Cross and Save The Children from time to time. I haven't worked for an animal charity before.' Grace's face registered no surprise at this.

'I just wondered if it was different in any way?' Ruth continued blandly.

Grace shook her head. 'No, no, I'm sure it isn't. All these shops are much of a muchness, aren't they? And it will give you

• Sarah Grazebrook

something to do, which is so important in your circumstances, isn't it? Keep busy. That's what they say.'

There was another furious scrabbling from above. Grace rose. 'Well this has been nice. Thank you for the coffee. You know where the shop is, do you?'

'No,' said Ruth who had foolishly assumed Grace might have been going to pick her up.

'It's just down the High Street, opposite the library. If you could get there about nine. I've told Madge Jordan you'll be coming. By the way, don't worry if she's a bit offhand to begin with. It's just her way.'

Grace departed, mentioning as she went that she would see Ruth at the Blakeneys' for lunch on Sunday when they were all going to discuss the pageant, so she wouldn't spoil it for her now.

Ruth cleared away the coffee and mopped up the worst of Lollo's ravages. The prospect of Sunday lunch with Joy, Christopher, the Forlands and the peevish Adrian Mills left her with the distinct impression that there was not much left to spoil. Gloomily she opened the fridge, spied the half bottle of wine left over from yesterday's lunch, poured herself a large glass and went to wrest her bedding back from the Beast of Bell Cottage.

6

Ruth arrived outside the Animal Welfare charity shop at ten to nine.

She had got up early to walk Lollo, then scattered a handful of pills in the dog's path, swallowed some toast and driven into town. She parked her car opposite the library and was annoyed to find it would cost her two pounds fifty for the privilege of donating her morning to Good Deeds.

There were two large rubbish sacks on the shop step. Ruth stood by them for a while then went and scrutinised the window which had 'Household Sale. Starts Friday' taped in large red letters across it.

As evidence there were several coloured blankets and a couple of faded lampshades underneath the sign. Further back Ruth could see a set of saucepans and some bathroom scales.

'Can I help you?'

She turned to see a broad-shouldered woman with a pronounced moustache and unruly grey hair frowning at her from the doorway.

'Are you Mrs Jordan?' asked Ruth.

'I am. We don't open till half past, you know. You'd be better off coming back then. I don't make exceptions.'

'I'm Ruth Page,' Ruth explained. 'Grace Forland said you were expecting me.'

Mrs Jordan's frown intensified. 'Oh yes. She did mention something about finding someone. I never believe a word she says.' She thrust her key into the lock, gave it a savage twist and kicked open the door, dragging one of the rubbish sacks behind her. 'Bring that other one, will you? Might as well make yourself useful.'

• Sarah Grazebrook

Ruth picked up the bag which seemed abnormally heavy and heaved it into the shop. 'Shut the door, can you?' commanded Mrs Jordan, 'otherwise we'll have a hoard of marauding peasants on our tail.'

Ruth did as she was bid. Madge Jordan had disappeared into a recess at the back of the shop. 'All the new stuff goes out here for sorting,' she bellowed through a curtain.

Ruth followed with her sack. 'Would you like me to make a start?' she asked, hoping to sound both willing and efficient. Mrs Jordan looked up in surprise. 'You can if you want. I usually leave it for the Monday bunch. Lazy cows. No customers on a Monday, you see. I said it should be on a rota. Would they have it? Would they hell! Know which side their bread's buttered, that lot. All the sales start on a Friday, you see. I bet Lady Muck didn't mention that to you, did she?'

'I don't mind. Really,' said Ruth. 'I'd rather be busy, actually.'

'Would you? Actually?' mimicked Mrs Jordan. 'Well that's good because I've got to get my front tyre changed at ten o'clock. I daresay you'll be able to hold the fort on your own for an hour, won't you?'

'I'll do my best,' said Ruth. 'Is there anywhere I can hang my coat?'

'Out the back if you don't want someone offering you a quid for it.'

Ruth hung her coat up. The recess opened on to a larger room, crammed full of rubbish sacks from which boots, clothes, curtains and other items oozed. Some of them had been partially unpacked and a quantity of tee-shirts and anoraks lay in untidy piles around the floor. In one corner was a sink and drainer on which rested a kettle, some sugar and several mugs.

'Put the kettle on while you're in there, will you?' came the command. 'Coffee's in the box by the window. And the milk and that.'

Ruth hunted around, found some teabags, the coffee and a tin of powdered milk. 'Do you want coffee or tea?' she called.

'Coffee. Black. Three sugars.'

'No biscuits?' queried Madge Jordan when she took it through.

'I didn't see any.'

'Don't tell me those toads have finished them off again.' She strode into the back room and rummaged cursing in the supply box.

'Would you credit it?' she demanded when she came back. 'I put a full packet of shortbread in there on Tuesday. I'd only had two. Never think to replace them, you see. Animals, you see. Animals at heart.'

Ruth wondered briefly if Madge Jordan was all that suited to her chosen charity.

It was twenty past nine. Several women with large empty shopping bags were beginning to gather outside the shop. They looked very cold.

'Is there anything that needs doing before we open up?' Ruth prompted.

'No. Only the till. And you can't do that.'

'Why not?'

'You're not accredited. Besides, I've got the key.' Mrs Jordan sat down opposite the shivering bargain hunters and lit a cigarette.

Ruth looked at her watch. 'I don't suppose it would do any harm to let them in a few minutes early, would it? Especially if you've got to get your car done?'

Madge Jordan gave a throaty laugh. 'Let 'em freeze, say I. They know the form. It's the same lot every week. They sell it on, you know. See that one with the scarf?' She pointed ostentatiously at an emaciated woman in a headscarf. 'Watch her. She always comes the "it's for Bosnia" rubbish. Sells it down the market. I've seen her. Whatever the price is, double it for her. That's my advice.'

Ruth glanced away in embarrassment. She felt sure the woman must have heard every word. It was like being in a goldfish bowl with all these people staring in. She picked up her cup and took it through to the back.

When she came back Mrs Jordan had opened the till and emptied the float into it. She was now standing by the door staring at her watch like the starter of the Grand National. The customers vied for position accordingly. The Town Hall clock chimed the half just as she released the catch. The crowd, for so they seemed to Ruth, despite being few in number, surged

• Sarah Grazebrook

forward, whipping expertly through the net curtains, bedspreads and clothes rails before sweeping on to the till, behind which she had retreated.

'How much for this, love?' asked the headscarf, waving a jumper clearly marked two pounds fifty under Ruth's nose.

'Two pounds fifty,' she stammered, avoiding Mrs Jordan's eye.

'Only it's for Bosnia. The little kiddies have nothing to keep them warm.'

'Yes. Still, it's a very nice jumper. And all our proceeds go to charity, too, you see.' Ruth smiled deprecatingly to show the matter was out of her hands. The woman sniffed and dropped the jumper into a bin marked 'Everything Fifty P'. Another woman snatched it up and waved a fifty pence piece at her. 'Here you are, duck. I don't need a bag.' She was gone before Ruth could protest. She daren't look at Madge Jordan whom she felt sure was registering her every move with a view to having her prosecuted for defrauding the Animal Welfare Trust.

A middle-aged man thrust his way forward. He was carrying a pair of velvet curtains. 'How much for these?' he demanded. Ruth hunted for the label. 'I'll give you a fiver,' said the man, rolling them up and thrusting them under his arm.

'If I could just look at the price tag,' Ruth pleaded, but it was hopeless.

By a quarter to ten they had gone. The till was fifteen pounds richer and the shop, by the look of it, half empty.

She awaited Mrs Jordan's wrath. She seemed to have disappeared. Probably phoning head office, Ruth thought despairingly. It wasn't her fault. She'd done her best. Some best. Animals were doubtless being exterminated left, right and centre as a direct result of her failure to secure their funding.

'Here we are.' Madge Jordan, cigarette dangling from her lips, emerged from the back carrying two fresh cups of coffee.

'Oh. Thank you,' said Ruth in relief. 'I'm awfully sorry – you know – about that.'

The woman gave her hoarse laugh and flicked ash into a vase. 'You did fine. Takes a bit of getting used to, that's all. I'll have this then I'm off to Quikfit. You'll be okay now. It's always the first half hour that's the worst.'

She showed Ruth how to lock the till. 'Have a look through that lot out there, if you like. See if there's anything you fancy.' At the door she stopped. 'Are you a friend of Grace Forland?' she asked doubtfully.

Ruth swallowed. 'I haven't really known her very long. I've only just moved down here. My sister-in-law introduced us. Joy Blakeney. I don't know if you know her?'

Madge Jordan's face showed very clearly that she did. 'Now I know who you are.' She nodded sagely. 'You're not what I'd imagined.'

Ruth smiled uncertainly. 'What did you imagine?'

Madge Jordan shrugged. 'A raving nutter, I suppose.'

At half past ten Grace Forland crept in. It was not a movement Ruth would have associated her with, but there was really no other way to describe the manner in which she entered the shop. Her eyes darted furtively around the room as she padded towards Ruth. 'Is everything all right?' she whispered. Ruth nodded. 'Is . . . is Mrs Jordan here?' Grace croaked quietly, her eyes still flickering like a pickpocket's.

'She's popped out for a few minutes,' Ruth hissed, infected by Grace's tone. 'She should be back any sec.' Grace Forland looked first relieved then unnerved. 'Well I . . .' she began, glancing behind her. 'I won't keep you from . . . I can see you're busy. I just wanted to make sure . . . So, everything's fine, is it?'

'Yes, thank you, Grace. Perfectly fine. Mrs Jordan's been extremely helpful.'

'Has she?' said Grace, unable to disguise her amazement.

'Yes. I'm sure we shall get along fine.'

Grace retreated, muttering that she would see her at Joy's on Sunday. Not if I see you first, thought Ruth, and found herself laughing.

The laugh was very quickly wiped off her face, however, by the arrival of the next customer. Since Madge's departure she had had a very easy time of it, sorting through the school uniform bag and the swimwear. A couple of people had come in to browse and one of them had bought a cardigan, but the woman had not queried the price nor tried to stuff it in the bargain bin and Ruth had begun to think she might even get to enjoy herself at the shop.

• Sarah Grazebrook

All this was destroyed, however, by the entrance of the surly Scot. He did not register her at first, making straight for the rack of men's jackets and whittling through them with every bit as much professionalism as the earlier intake.

Selecting one, he divested himself of the ancient Barbour he was wearing, and plunged his arms into the sleeves. Then, still wearing the jacket, he picked out a pair of trousers and measured them against his legs.

'Can I use the changing room, hen?' he enquired, still more intent on his own appearance than hers. Ruth was stirred from her discomfort by the need for action. She looked around. There was no sign of one. She hesitated. 'I suppose you could use the back room,' she said, 'if you want to try things on.'

'I wouldn't ask if I didn't,' said the man logically. Ruth held aside the curtain. She felt she should follow him in to make sure he didn't stuff his pockets with anoraks and teabags, but equally she was not keen to witness him removing his trousers. It smacked of voyeurism.

She was saved by the return of Madge Jordan, a large bag of shopping in either hand. 'Got some more biscuits. I'm going to hide the bloody things this time. I'll put them in the undies sack. No one ever goes near that.'

Before Ruth could stop her she had barged through to the back of the shop where there was the sound of Scottish expletives drowned by a guffaw from Mrs Jordan. 'Gawd, Bill, you'll never get into those. What are you playing at, you vain bugger?'

'They're for a wedding,' came the man's disgruntled voice.

'Not yours, I hope,' cackled the woman, marching back into the shop where she began to flip expertly through the men's clothes.

'That'll be the day,' came the response.

Madge raised her eyes to Ruth. 'Have a look at those jackets, over there, will you? See if there's anything in a forty-two.'

Ruth did as she was bid. Madge had disappeared into the back again, armed with several pairs of trousers. Ruth could hear them arguing.

'They're too tight.'

'Rubbish. Try these blue ones, then.'

'I don't like blue.'

'Yes you do.'

'I do not. Get your hands off me, woman. What are you trying to do?'

'Not what you're hoping, that's for sure.'

'You must be joking, woman. Don't you know I've got half the women in Westbridge lusting for my body? Not those.'

'Why not?'

'They make my bum look big.'

'Your bum is big. It's these or the blue ones. That's all we've got.'

'I don't like blue.'

Ruth meanwhile had found a navy blazer and two rather shabby suit jackets that seemed to have got separated from their bottoms. 'Any luck?' Madge called to her. She swallowed and took them through. The Scot was still struggling with his zip. Ruth held them out. Madge grabbed the blazer. 'Here we are. This is nice. It'll go with the blue ones. Make you look nautical.'

'I don't want to look nautical,' grumbled the man. He looked up and caught sight of Ruth for the first time. 'Oh,' he said, seemingly unperturbed. 'What are you doing here?'

'I . . .' said Ruth.

'She's come for a sight of your equipment, of course,' said Madge, barking with laughter. 'Why? Do you two know each other?'

'No,' said Ruth.

'Yes,' said the man.

The bell rang in the front of the shop. Ruth hurried through. It was the woman with the headscarf again. 'Are you on your own?' she muttered, coming very close.

Ruth took a step back. 'Is there anything I can do for you?' she asked.

The woman took a pace forward. 'I just wondered if you've got a few things you'd be thinking of throwing out? Things you wouldn't be charging for?' she hissed.

Ruth shook her head vehemently. 'I don't think so. You'd be better off talking to Mrs Jordan about that.'

The woman sniffed. 'She never throws nothing out,' she said sulkily.

• Sarah Grazebrook

Ruth smiled nervously. 'Well, even so. It's not really in my hands.'

'It's for the kids in Africa,' the woman wheedled, her hands raffling through the jumpers. 'Just a few woolies and that. This is a nice blouse.' She pulled a cotton blouse off its hanger and studied it critically. 'How much you asking for this?'

'Whatever it says on the label.'

'Only it's for the kiddies . . .'

'I know,' said Ruth. 'In Africa.'

'Bosnia,' the woman corrected.

'It's three pounds.'

'Three quid!' the woman expostulated. 'That can't be right.'

Ruth removed it rather firmly from her hands. 'No,' she said. 'It isn't. It should have said six.'

When the woman had gone, Madge summoned her to look at the Scot who was now dressed in the blue trousers, the blazer and a cream shirt which she had found for him. He looked almost presentable.

'What do you think?' asked Madge.

'Fine,' said Ruth politely.

'Just fine?' squawked the Scot. 'Is that all you can find to say?'

'What do you expect me to say?' Ruth retaliated.

The man considered. 'How about, "You look like the very flower of Scottish manhood. When I gaze on you my heart leaps with a passion no other man has ever stirred in my fragrant woman's bosom". Something on those lines?'

Ruth stared at him.

'Take no notice of Bill,' Madge Jordan chuckled. 'He thinks he's a poet as well as everything else.'

'I am a poet,' insisted the man. 'As well as everything else.'

The town clock chimed one. Madge looked at her watch. 'Thank God for that,' she said. 'Come on, Cinderella. Get your togs back on.'

'How much are you going to rush me for this lot?' the man demanded as he struggled out of the blazer. Madge sucked her cheeks. 'Fifteen quid, the lot.' Ruth waited for the outburst, but to her surprise the man did not quibble. Instead he gave Madge a twenty-pound note and refused to take any change.

When he had gone Ruth washed up the coffee cups and waited while Madge emptied the till. 'So, what do you think?' Madge asked her as they were leaving the shop. Ruth smiled.

'I've quite enjoyed it. The Bosnia woman apart.'

Madge nodded. 'You always get those. You get used to it. You'll get used to Bill, too.'

Ruth stiffened slightly. 'Does he come in a lot?'

Madge shrugged. 'Only when I'm there. He can't stand the rest of them. He's a nice bloke. I like him.'

'What does he actually do?' asked Ruth. 'Apart from being a poet, I mean.'

Madge laughed. 'Some poet, Bill Bartholomew. He writes. Not sure what. Bread and butter stuff, mostly, I think. Ghosts articles for scientists and statisticians. Tries to make them sound like human beings. He does all right. He used to be in Fleet Street, as I gather. Dropped out when Murdoch moved in. Does quite a bit for the local rags. Sometimes he gets a commission from one of the nationals. Lives like a king for a few months, then it's back to the grind. And the charity shops. Funny bloke. I like him. Bit of a ladies' man, or so he reckons. He's got the gift of the gab, that's for sure. Don't you go falling for it, though, will you? I know it can get a bit boring down here if you've been used to London life. Got to watch yourself. People do odd things at the seaside.'

Ruth drove home, reflecting that however dreary things got, she would not be bored enough to fall for Bill Bartholomew.

7

Lollo had made another nest, this time of an old towel which Ruth had left near the front door to wipe the dog's paws, and a collection of free newspapers which had evidently been delivered in her absence. Although the mess was huge, the damage was not, so Ruth accepted the animal's declarations of affection and went to prepare their lunch.

She had stopped off at the butcher and bought some sausages and a pound of undefinable meat labelled 'Dog'. From the look of it, that might very well have been what it was, but the man assured her it was the finest offcuts of his entire stock and that two local mutts had won Crufts as a direct result of eating it. Ruth did not believe a word of it, but she was parked on a double yellow line and therefore not in a position to argue. She was also persuaded to purchase a large yellowing knuckle bone which, the butcher had assured her, 'they all love'.

Lollo showed appropriate suspicion, given the bone was big enough to be a relation, and refused to come near it till Ruth had powdered it with brewer's yeast, to which the animal was plainly addicted.

Ruth felt undeniably hurt by the rejection of her gift, but not enough so to prevent herself opening a fresh bottle of wine and having scampi and garlic bread for her own lunch.

I never ate like this when I was in London, she thought wonderingly as she poured her second glass. I didn't even have this with Duncan, when we were married. FIRST married, even. Still, it's very nice.

Saturday brought a letter from Duncan's solicitor endorsing the

• Sarah Grazebrook

new financial arrangement, one from her own telling her on no account to consent to it, and a brochure from Pets' Paradise outlining the cost of full board on a weekly basis for Lollo.

Ruth stared at it incredulously. She could have had a month in the Canaries for the same price. Lollo obviously sensed she was in trouble because she kept well out of the way while the new nanny burnt her toast and shouted at the antiquated coffee pot.

Later Ruth sat down and tried to work out how she was going to manage, but whichever way she calculated it all came back to one thing. She was not. There was not enough money for her to pay for Lollo's board and survive, let alone live.

Dark thoughts began to enter her mind. A walk on the cliff, Lollo chasing a rabbit, an unseen mineshaft; the sudden screech of brakes, Lollo's podgy little body lying prone in the road. Tears poured down her face. This is ridiculous, she thought. I don't even like the animal.

She must be practical. She couldn't afford to send her back to the kennels, and she certainly wasn't going to keep her at Bell Cottage.

Lollo trotted past dragging the clean duvet cover Ruth had left on the ironing board. 'You rat,' she squawked, wrenching it away from her. 'You are living on borrowed time. I hope you know that.' Lollo gave a frightened yelp and went and hid under the dining-room table.

Ruth cleared away her breakfast things then went for a long walk on her own. When she came back the dog had moved back into the sitting-room and was asleep on the couch. In the kitchen Ruth found a small heap of sick containing both the solicitors' letters and the price list from Pets' Paradise Boarding Kennels.

Sunday dawned fine with a strong breeze that carried the first hint of an end to winter. At half past ten the phone rang. It was Joy. 'Just checking you're all right for lunch?'

'Yes, thank you, Joy. I'm looking forward to it.'

'Twelve. We'll eat about one. I know it's early but Adrian has to get away.'

Ruth assured her that she would be with them by twelve,

thinking that to organise a lunch party round Adrian Mills was a sign of serious desperation.

She had a long bath then went to get dressed. She did not intend to be fooled again into 'casual' wear, so spent an uncomfortable five minutes fighting the zip of her Jaeger skirt. She really would have to lose some weight. But why? Who was there to care whether she was fat or thin, apart from herself? And she wasn't all that bothered. So long as she didn't get like Laureen Denkell. She shuddered, not merely at the thought of it but at the gruesome prospect that if she did, Duncan might sicken of his American soulmate and make a beeline back to her. She laughed out loud in the sudden realisation that she didn't want him back. This is progress, she told herself.

Her pleasure was brought to an abrupt halt by the sound of a mighty splash, followed by a frantic scrabbling and hysterical squeaks from the bathroom. She rushed in to find Lollo, clearly alarmed by the depth of the water, plunging around in the bath like a diminutive dolphin.

'Oh, you idiot,' said Ruth, trying to get hold of her. The dog wriggled like an eel, but eventually Ruth grabbed her slippery fur and hauled her out. She flung a towel over her, rubbing viciously. Lollo shrieked and snarled, before ripping herself free and escaping down the stairs into the back garden. Ruth chased her, cursing, since if Lollo took another plunge into the compost she could not see herself getting to Joy and Christopher's before supper time.

'Come back here this minute,' she screeched. 'If I get my hands on you I'm going to kill you. Do you hear? KILL you, I said.' At which moment Grace Forland's panic-stricken face appeared round the corner of the house.

'Hullo, Ruth,' she quavered, clearly expecting to have to talk down a machete. 'We wondered if you'd like a lift? Is everything all right?'

Lollo and Ruth sat in the back of the Forlands' car. Garth had said very little, but the occasional glance he gave Ruth in the car mirror spoke eloquently of his feelings about dog murderers.

A huntsman himself, he saw Ruth's perpetual efforts to drown the Taylors' dachshund (for Grace had told him about the other occasion), as nothing short of certifiable. Hanging was too good

• Sarah Grazebrook

for her. He would say as much to the Blakeneys when he got them alone. Care in the Community was all very well, but this Page woman was a menace. No other word for it. What next? The hounds? He gripped the steering wheel angrily. She'd better not try it.

Ruth sat frostily beside her presumed victim, ignoring Lollo's proffered nuzzles and whipping her hand away from the sycophantic licks the animal kept aiming at her. She had had to change her skirt and, though infinitely more comfortable in her trusty plaid, she knew full well it made her look like a potato.

Grace twittered on about spring, and the price of carrots at the farm shop, ignored by everyone including Lollo, who had come to associate her arrival with rough towels and hairdryers and therefore disliked her accordingly.

Adrian Mills was already there when they arrived. He was perched on a stool, hoovering his way through the peanuts, while Christopher Blakeney polished sherry glasses and gazed forlornly out at the garden he would have loved to be tending.

'Hullo, Ruth. Settling in okay?' He kissed her on the cheek. 'Good God, what's that?' as Lollo, shinier than ever, shot between his legs and made off down the hall. There was a scream from the kitchen, followed by a clang.

'It's Lollo,' said Ruth without emotion.

'You've brought the dog?'

'Wasn't I supposed to?'

'Yes. No, it's just that Joy's a bit funny about them.' Another scream testified to this. 'Chrissie .. ee .. eee. Come and help me. There's this dog in here, eating everything. Quick!'

Christopher pattered off. Adrian had now finished the peanuts and was prowling in search of further titbits. Garth was pouring sherry. He handed a glass to his wife and one to Ruth.

'Cheers,' he said ominously.

'Cheers,' said Ruth, wondering what she had done to offend him.

Forland prepared to give her one last chance. 'Ever ridden to hounds?'

'No,' said Ruth.

The chance gone, Forland snorted and went over to the

sideboard where he dumped his sherry and helped himself to a whisky.

Grace turned to Adrian. 'How are things going, Adrian? Still juggling all those balls?'

Adrian scowled. 'Naturally.'

'What do you actually do?' asked Ruth, trying to look interested.

'Producer,' said Adrian.

'What do you produce?'

Adrian regarded her as though she had crawled out from under a stone. 'I'm freelance. Whatever's on the agenda, naturally. We're heading for the millennium, in case you hadn't noticed.'

Somewhat needled, Ruth resisted the urge to say she was surprised anyone in Westbridge had even remembered to change their clocks. Instead she gave him what Duncan decreed her 'difficult' smile and excused herself on the grounds that she needed to ask Christopher about the groundsel round her drain-pipe.

Just as she was regaining her equilibrium there was a further rumpus from the kitchen, followed by the sound of Gwen Pritchard pleading to be blamed.

'Oh, do go away, Gwen,' came Joy's none too friendly stricture. 'And take that blasted animal with you.'

Gwen appeared shortly after, carrying Lollo. There was evidence of flour on both their fronts. 'Hello, everyone,' she smiled demurely, her eyes immediately fastening on Garth Forland who was beaming at her in a way which could best be described as 'rogueish'.

She set Lollo down. The dog immediately shot off back to the kitchen, this time to be returned by Christopher, looking exceedingly grim, and saying he hoped no one minded if lunch was a bit late.

Adrian Mills looked as though he minded very much indeed, but even he could not reasonably complain, given that Joy too, looking very tight-lipped, had now joined the company.

Gwen had ceased to look dewy-eyed and was once more apologising for what Ruth gathered to be the upsetting of the Yorkshire pudding mix.

'Yes, all right, Gwen. It's done now,' snapped her hostess, whereupon Gwen retreated to a corner and busied herself with

• Sarah Grazebrook

studying the flower arrangement, though Ruth suspected she was fighting back tears. It all seemed a bit excessive for half a pint of batter which, unless Joy had changed a lot in the last six months, would almost certainly have come out of a packet.

She wondered if anyone else had been invited, but it appeared not, for after another sherry and the eviction of Lollo into the back garden with half a salami, Joy disappeared once more into the kitchen and Christopher led them into the dining room.

Lunch consisted of beef, insufficient for seven adults, an assortment of overcooked vegetables, and the Yorkshire puddings which were loudly and excessively praised by all present, although only Adrian managed to eat his in their entirety. To Ruth they tasted like rubber, and she harboured an ignoble wish that Lollo had been more thorough in her attack on the raw ingredients.

Pudding was another sticky affair, doused in a blanket of custard. Adrian had Ruth's. She expected Joy to object when she murmured weedily about watching her waistline, but to her surprise her sister-in-law said nothing, although she saw her nudge Christopher heftily when Adrian scooped the plate from in front of her.

Coffee took them back to the lounge and it was here that serious discussion of the forthcoming pageant took over. Ruth listened half-heartedly. As far as she could gather it was destined for the beginning of June and centred round the forced bussing of several hundred schoolchildren from the Isle of Sheppey, before the bridge linking it to mainland Britain was closed for its annual refurbishment.

Why it should be necessary to cause this much havoc amongst the peaceful inhabitants of Swale was quite beyond Ruth's comprehension or interest. She was too busy trying to calculate how long she would decently have to stay before making her excuses and getting back to the Sunday papers.

'What we need is a script.' Joy's voice cut across her thoughts.

'Why on earth do you need a script?' demanded her husband. 'I thought the thing was silent. I thought that was the point of pageants.'

'Well, it is. Of course it is. We all know that.'

'Why do you need a script, then?'

'Oh Chrissie, don't be so obtuse. How is anyone going to know what they're supposed to be doing if they haven't got a script?'

'I thought the director would see to all that. I thought that was what directors were for.'

There was a sound like a donkey being circumcised, but this turned out to be Adrian laughing. Something which, fortunately, he did very little of. 'Very good,' he said bitterly. 'Very good indeed.'

Christopher looked suitably cowed.

'The director needs a script so he can handle the actors, darling. Remember, this isn't just a matter of half a dozen stalwarts from the Westbridge Players. There are thousands going to be involved in this. THOUSANDS.'

'Are there?' asked Grace shakily. She had been asked to take charge of the costumes.

'Well, not thousands. But you know what I mean. It's a community thing. I want EVERYONE to get involved. And not just people. Horses, cattle, children, even. All I'm saying,' Joy threw back her head to demonstrate the enormity of her vision, 'is that there should be a written outline. I mean, look at it this way, we're covering a huge vista in local history. We're going from the first Romans – Julius C., Saint Augustine – right through to the present day.'

'Michael Heseltine,' suggested Christopher drily.

'Well, why not?' his wife turned to him in all seriousness. 'He's a national figure. And he's been down here.'

'So's Glenda Jackson,' said Christopher. 'Perhaps we could get her to play herself.'

Joy sniffed. 'I don't think that would be a very good idea. She's never had any clothes on in any of the films I've seen.'

'I say,' interrupted Garth Forland who had drunk a good deal over lunch, 'that would be a good idea.'

'What would, dear?' asked Grace, her eyebrows twitching very slightly.

'No clothes,' continued Garth as though it was the most sensible thing in the world. 'Lady Godiva and all that. And you'd get your horse in. Sounds fair to me. Gwenny here would make a lovely Lady Godiva.'

Joy gave a tinny laugh to show he was wasting time. 'I shall

• Sarah Grazebrook

have to put my mind to this, I can see. There must be someone in Westbridge who can write. What about that class you go to, Gwen? Is there anyone there who could knock out something for us?'

Gwen thought. Out of the corner of her eye Ruth could see Lollo digging up a clump of fine stemmed flowers by the greenhouse. 'I suppose . . .' Gwen demurred, 'Oh no, he wouldn't do. There is . . . but she's more of a poet, really . . . It's a bit difficult . . .'

'I should have thought out of a dozen aspiring authors there would be one person capable of penning a draft pageant,' said Joy briskly. She sighed. 'Still if there isn't . . .'

'There is one person I could ask,' said Gwen, emboldened by the fear of losing her assignment. 'I don't know if he'll do it. I can't promise anything.'

'No, no, of course not,' Joy responded. 'You just see what you can do, Gwen. In the meantime I'll get on with sorting out old Mr Clifford for the music.'

'Harry Clifford?' exclaimed her husband. 'He must be ninety. You can't ask him to be in charge of the music. It'll finish him off.'

'Nonsense. Old people like things to do. Otherwise they vegetate. Everyone knows that.'

'There's a difference between having things to do and leading a brass band through the high street at the age of ninety, Joy, for heaven's sake.'

'Oh don't be so dramatic, Chrissie. He won't have to do anything like that. And anyway he isn't ninety. Not till next year. I've talked to him about it. He thinks it's a marvellous idea. I wish everyone else had been so co-operative.' Joy's nose began to twitch rather alarmingly.

Ruth stood up. 'Joy, Christopher, thank you for a lovely lunch. I've really enjoyed it, but I'm afraid I must make a move.'

'I'll come with you.' Adrian shot out of his chair as though it were an ejector seat. Joy studied them knowingly.

'Oh, Ruth, must you? I've got all sorts of plans for ways you can make yourself useful. Still, we can talk about that another day.' She escorted them to get their coats. 'I hope we haven't made you late, Adrian,' she murmured simperingly as Adrian was popping a last chocolate into his mouth.

'You have a bit,' he said ungraciously. 'Still, it's not that vital. I wouldn't have to shift at all if it wasn't our damned anniversary.'

Christopher came to the door. 'Is Adrian giving you a lift?' Ruth shook her head vehemently. 'I'm walking. Lollo needs the exercise. So do I, probably.'

Christopher grinned. 'Wish I could come with you. They'll be at it for hours in there. And the worst of it is, nothing will have been decided by the end of it. They haven't even got a director sorted out. It'll end up being the vicar again, you mark my words.'

Ruth smiled sympathetically. She called Lollo who came scampering round the corner, nose and paws covered in mud. Ruth hustled her away before Christopher had time to connect it with his flower-beds.

8

Ruth was surprised to get a phone call from Violet Sampson on Monday evening. Briefly she nursed the hope that she was going to take Lollo off her hands. Joy had seemed to think it would appeal to her, but the purpose of her call was to see if Ruth would be interested in an orienteering expedition she was organising in aid of a Tibetan monastery she had heard about on the radio.

'You'll need to get sponsors, but that shouldn't be too hard, should it?'

'No,' said Ruth, who knew six people in the county. 'I could ask my bank manager.'

'It's quite a simple route. Along the Saxon coastline for the first ten miles then inland through a couple of woods and back via the Alkham Valley. You'll need plenty of water and some decent shoes. I expect you've got those?'

'I'm awfully sorry, Violet. I'm afraid I'm not up to that sort of activity. I'm really not fit enough.'

'You can get fit,' said Violet with a note of surprise. 'I thought that was why you'd come down here.'

It was Ruth's turn to express surprise. Exactly what tales had Joy been spreading about her? Not only that she was a rejected dog-mad divorcee, but also that she was vying with Ranulph Fiennes for a Millennium grant?

'I'm sorry.'

She could hear Violet tapping on the end of the phone. 'In that case, would you be willing to sponsor me?'

'Certainly,' Ruth responded, relieved. 'I'd be happy to.'

'Good,' came Violet's clipped voice. 'It's not till Easter. I'll put you down for a pound a mile, shall I?'

• Sarah Grazebrook

Ruth replaced the receiver with a heavy heart. She had just kissed goodbye to the best part of twenty pounds. There was no doubt in her mind that Violet would complete the course, probably with a bicycle held high above her head – for which, no doubt, there would be a bonus donation of fifty per cent.

She went back to her supper. The wind had begun to blow again. So much for the end of winter, she thought as she pinned the curtains together in an effort to keep out the draught. It was nearly the end of February. Three months of this place. Three months of Joy. Three months of Lollo, too, if she didn't think of something soon. How was she going to get through it? Visions of herself as a gibbering wreck flashed before her eyes. Correction. A gibbering penniless wreck. There were no two ways about it. She would have to get a job.

'How was your weekend?' asked Madge Jordan when she arrived next morning.

'Fine,' Ruth lied.

'You don't look as though it was fine. Put the kettle on, will you? I'm bursting for a fag.'

Ruth made some coffee then set about sorting the new bags of clothes that had come in over the weekend. She found some nice slacks which Madge let her have for a pound. 'There you are. Told you it was a good place to work. You always get first pick. Never need to buy a coat again. New, that is. Where did I put those biscuits? If those gannets . . .'

'You put them in the bra sack,' Ruth reminded her.

'So I did.' Madge rummaged and came out with the chocolate digestives plus a boned corselet in a striking shade of pink. 'How about this?' She held it against herself and did a couple of twirls.

Ruth laughed. 'It's a bit daring for round here, wouldn't you say?'

Madge Jordan shook her head. 'Don't you believe it. This place is a hive of intrigue. Look at me. You wouldn't think I'd done six years for GBH, would you?'

'No,' said Ruth, shaken.

'I haven't,' said Madge, 'but some of them have. Or very near. The last owner of the antiques shop was done for armed robbery, and his son was charged with receiving. Then there was a hairdresser who set fire to his shop ten days after the decorators had finished. Couldn't pay them, you see. And a butcher who did a moonlight flit. Lost all his money in the Mad Cow scare. Not to mention the bootleggers. Oh, it all happens round here. Highest crime rate in the south east, Kent. Have one of these.' She unwrapped the biscuits. 'And tell me what the problem is.'

Ruth was a bit unsettled that her worries should be so obvious to a virtual stranger. She smiled evasively. 'It's nothing really. My sister-in-law told the owners of the cottage where I'm staying that I would look after their dog while they're away. I've said I can't, but the only alternative seems to be sending her back to the boarding kennels and it really is rather a price. Added to which I seem to have let myself into sponsoring one of Joy's friends in some charity run for a Tibetan monastery.' She sighed. 'To be honest, I could do without it at the moment.'

Madge ate another biscuit. 'That'll be Violet Sampson,' she said, showering Ruth with crumbs. 'Mad as a hatter. What's she doing this time?'

'I think it's orienteering. She wanted me to do it at first . . .'

'Then when you said you wouldn't she asked you to sponsor her. Yes?'

'Yes,' said Ruth, amazed.

Madge nodded. 'Does it every time. Don't worry. We've all been through it. You've just got to hope she breaks her leg in the first half-mile. It's got to happen one day. Why don't you set this dog of yours on her? What's wrong with it, by the way?'

Ruth grimaced. 'Nothing, really. It's just I don't like dogs much. Not this one anyway. She's such a pest and she keeps being sick and things. She dug up all Christopher's dahlias when I went to lunch on Sunday. I can only assume he hasn't found out yet or he'd've been round to do GBH to me.'

'Fancy not liking dogs,' said Madge. 'Beat humans any day, in my book. What sort of dog is it?'

'A dachshund. She's called Lollo.'

'Oh well, they are a pest, it's true. Still, nothing a bit of love and affection won't cure. You'll see.'

'To be honest I haven't got much love and affection to spare at the moment,' Ruth admitted. 'I thought when I came here

• Sarah Grazebrook

I'd have a chance to sort myself out. Clear my head. Start again.'

'But it's not working out like that?'

'It certainly isn't. From the moment I arrived – before, even, I've had Joy breathing down my neck, inviting me round, introducing me to people, volunteering me for things. This shop. It's not that I mind exactly. In fact this is the only thing I've enjoyed since I set foot in this town. But it should have been MY choice, don't you see?'

Madge nodded. 'I'm afraid you get a lot of that round here. People trying to organise your life. It's because they haven't got one of their own, I always think. But that's no consolation to you.'

'And to top it all, Joy's trying to fix me up with this ghastly man who can't stop eating and only speaks in monosyllables.'

Madge raised her eyebrows. 'Wouldn't be Adrian Mills by any chance?'

Ruth nodded. 'Do you know him?'

Madge was laughing. 'I do a bit. I've never heard him described like that before, but it certainly fits. If you think he's funny about food, you should meet his wife.'

'She actually exists, does she? I was beginning to think perhaps he'd made her up. People keep mentioning her but she never seems to appear.'

'Oh, she exists all right. But that's about all she does do.'

Ruth's curiosity was aroused. 'What exactly is wrong with her? I mean, why won't Joy let her in the house? She lets some pretty awful other people in.' She stopped in case this had caused offence but Madge merely cackled more heartily.

'Rowena's got bulimia. Nothing wrong with that, so long as you keep it to yourself, I say. Ro made the cardinal mistake of throwing up in Joy's house. I've only eaten there once myself, but basing it on that I'm surprised it doesn't happen all the time.'

'She's not all that good at cooking,' Ruth conceded.

Madge became serious. 'It's wrecking her life, poor cow. Not just because Adrian refuses to take her anywhere, but it feeds on itself – no pun intended. The more she does it, the more she worries about it, the more she does it. As I say, she's an intelligent woman. You never know how things are going to affect you.'

'What brought it on, do you know?'

'They were trying for a baby. At least she was trying. I don't know about the wunderkind. Too much of a baby himself, I should think. Wouldn't want the real thing stealing his thunder.'

'It's hard to think of Adrian making thunder of any kind,' mused Ruth.

Madge exploded with laughter. 'True, but apparently he made some film about a cellar when he was in his twenties and it won an award. He's been living off it ever since.

'Anyway, the sad thing was she had a phantom pregnancy. Swelled up like a balloon. Had the doctors fooled and everyone. Even after they told her there was no baby she still kept putting on weight, just as though she was expecting. This is before I knew her. She was very young when she married him, I gather. Second wife. Been his assistant or something. Anyway that bastard Adrian, once he'd got over his relief that he wasn't going to have to fork out for a pram and the rest, started having a go at her for being fat. Well, you've seen him. He's like a beanstalk. That's when it started. Small things at first. She didn't like this, she'd got an allergy to that . . . In the end she was throwing up left, right and centre.'

Madge took another biscuit and ate it ruminatively. Ruth picked up the coffee cups. 'She might get over it. Grow out of it, whatever.'

Madge shook her head. 'I doubt it as long as she's with that prat.'

'Perhaps she'll meet someone else.'

'I don't think she wants to. She's crazy about the bastard. God knows why. Still, who's to say what people see in each other? She was very matey with Bill at one time, but Adrian soon put a stop to that. Now he hardly lets her out of the house, except to go to work.'

'You make her sound like a prisoner.'

'She's made herself one. She feels guilty about it all, and that suits Adrian fine. She's completely under his thumb. Wouldn't blow her nose without asking him first. Not that you'd know it

• Sarah Grazebrook

to meet her. Very smart. Always the latest styles. That's half the trouble, as well, of course. The women of Westbridge don't like to be upstaged.'

Ruth nodded, thinking by 'women' Madge probably meant Joy and her circle.

Madge stood up and dusted the crumbs off her jumper. 'No, her best hope was the harem, but I don't think even Bill Bartholomew could have coped with her long-term.'

'What harem?' asked Ruth, fascinated.

'Oh whoever he takes a fancy to at the time. He's usually got a couple of them in tow and a few more on the back burner. Doesn't like commitment, does Bill. He had a bad first marriage. Shook his confidence. Now he prefers safety in numbers. Seems to get away with it, too. Don't ask me how. He's not what you'd call a looker, is he?'

'No,' said Ruth.

Madge laughed. 'He's quite a charmer, though, in his way. Wouldn't you say?'

'I don't know that I would,' said Ruth a trifle haughtily. To her mind 'Let go this minute, you dozy bugger' was not the ultimate chat-up line. Madge glanced at her but said no more.

They were invaded by a group of teenage girls looking for things for a Sixties' Night party.

'How did you get involved in this?' Ruth asked as they were closing up.

Madge shrugged. 'Don't know really. They needed someone. I'm fond of animals. The house is full of them.' She sighed. 'I needed a break from Leonard, I suppose, if I'm honest.'

'Leonard?' asked Ruth tentatively.

'My husband. He's dead now. Been dead five years. He had Parkinson's.'

'I'm sorry.'

'Yes, it's a rotten thing. It drags on and on, you see. Still, he's out of it now. Life goes on and all that.'

She shoved the remaining biscuits back in their sack, locked the till and waited while Ruth collected her things. They walked together to the car park. 'You coming in on Friday?' Madge asked suddenly.

'Yes, of course. That's if you need me?'

'I can't say I need anyone. I'm used to doing it on my own,' said Madge brusquely. Ruth felt slightly hurt. 'But it's nice to have someone to talk to. Someone with half a brain, that is.'

Ruth accepted this as the nearest she could hope for a compliment. She was getting into her car when Madge came loping back to her. 'If you want you can have a bit of lunch after,' she said ungraciously.

Ruth smiled. 'Thank you. That would be very nice – if you're sure it's no trouble.' Madge shrugged. 'All the same to me,' she said.

9

On Wednesday Ruth bought the local paper and scanned it earnestly in search of part-time work. It made depressing reading. The only jobs on offer seemed to be early morning cleaning, child-minding, or a weekend custodian of the local castle, which might have suited her, had the advertisement not stipulated that 'non-graduates need not apply'.

'It's come to something,' she told Lollo aggrievedly, 'if you've got to have a degree to make sure no one steals a wretched castle.' Lollo smirked complacently and hiccupped up another of her cod liver oil pills.

Ruth was gradually weaning her off them, along with the other noxious supplements that the Taylors obviously considered essential for a decent doggie life. Lollo had shown no objection and indeed seemed more than willing to transfer her affection from dope to the butcher's offcuts if mixed with sufficient dog biscuits and followed by a bowl of warm milk.

On Friday Ruth rose early and took her for a walk. The dog clearly sensed something afoot, for she refused to come back when called and managed to get a thorn in her paw while interfering with the Taylors' ornamental rose bush by the gate.

Ruth consequently arrived at the shop late, without the bunch of daffodils she had bought at great expense from a garage the night before. 'I'm afraid I forgot the flowers,' she apologised.

'What flowers?'

'I'd bought some flowers to give you, but I left them on the kitchen table. Lollo will probably have eaten them by the time I get back.'

• Sarah Grazebrook

'Oh well,' said Madge, reddening slightly with pleasure, 'vitamin C. She probably needs them more than I do.'

At a quarter to eleven Bill Bartholomew brought back the clothes he had bought for the wedding. Madge seemed quite unphased by this, despite the fact that she had accepted twenty pounds for them the week before.

'How did it go?' she asked as she hung them up.

'All right,' said Bartholomew. He seemed slightly out of sorts.

'Oh, come on, Bill,' said Madge. 'You knew she'd marry him in the end. You said yourself it was the best thing.'

'Did I?' asked the Scotsman gruffly. 'Well, happen I was wrong.'

'That'll be the day,' said Madge matter-of-factly. 'She was far too young for you. You said so yourself.'

'That doesn't mean I meant it,' said Bill peevishly. 'She was opening like a flower before my very eyes.'

'You mean her legs were,' said Madge ruthlessly. 'Stop feeling sorry for yourself. I've got a lovely pully for you here somewhere.' She went into the back.

Ruth and Bartholomew eyed each other suspiciously while she was gone. 'Madge tells me you're a writer,' said Ruth, when she could bear the silence no longer.

'Aye,' said the man with exaggerated Scottishness.

I am a divorced woman whose husband has gone off with an American dental technician, passed through Ruth's mind, but instead she said, 'The dog I'm looking after got a thorn in her paw this morning.'

Bartholomew stared at her for several seconds. 'Is that a typing exercise?' he asked.

'No,' said Ruth, annoyed. 'I just thought you might be interested, seeing that you've got a dog.'

'Not really,' said the man dejectedly. 'I'm nursing a broken heart.'

'Whose?' snapped Ruth callously.

To her surprise this made him laugh. Madge returned at this point with a very loud jersey. 'Look at this. Just what you need to cheer you up.'

Bartholomew surveyed it critically. 'I'd rather have a bottle of whisky.'

'Well the last one's gone. Shall I find a bag for you?'

'All right, if you must. You know I think there'd not be a creature alive if it weren't for what I fork out here.'

'I daresay you're right,' said Madge prosaically.

'How much do you want for it?'

She shrugged. 'Give me a pound.' Bartholomew gave her two.

'Aren't you going to try it on?' asked Ruth, unsettled by the transaction.

'No need,' said the man. 'Madge knows what suits me.' He winked and Madge snorted and gave him one of her biscuits.

'He likes you,' she said to Ruth when he had gone.

'Oh come on,' Ruth protested. 'I've only spoken to him twice and one of those he was cursing me.'

Madge shrugged. 'He likes you.' She did not elaborate and Ruth did not pursue the matter. She didn't care greatly whether the Scotsman liked her or not since she didn't particularly like him. Although she was still slightly intrigued by the prospect of his harem, given that most of the women she had met so far in Westbridge looked better suited to a hockey team than a Celtic seraglio.

She followed Madge home in her car. If Bell Cottage had seemed remote, Peppers was a great deal more so. The road to it was unadopted. More like 'exposed on a hillside', thought Ruth as she bounced along the cratered surface a good deal more slowly than Madge, whose Mini was leaping like a robot from a video game.

Rounding a corner they came to the house. It was long and low and looked as if it might have been converted from a stables. Madge stopped her car, rather more suddenly than Ruth had expected. She screeched to a halt behind her, then got out and followed Madge round the side of the building, passing three cats and a small chicken run in which glossy bantams pecked energetically at the gravel.

Madge unlocked the back door and two Irish setters flew past them and made for the paddock behind the house to the obvious irritation of a couple of goats already stationed there. 'They hate being in,' Madge remarked, leading the way through

• Sarah Grazebrook

the untidy lobby to an even untidier hall. She took Ruth's coat and showed her into the living room which was contrastingly neat and animal free.

'What will you have?' asked Madge, indicating an awesome array of alcohol ranged along a dresser. Ruth gazed. 'Have you got any sherry?'

'Nope,' said Madge. 'No communion wine, either. How about a gin?'

'Thank you,' said Ruth, chastened. Madge poured two navy rations and dampened them with tonic. 'Ice,' she said and stomped off.

'I don't do puds,' she informed Ruth, dropping ice cubes into the glasses. Ruth took a sip. Then another. She felt strangely relaxed.

'Drink all right?'

'Very nice.'

'Just cheese,' Madge went on. 'And I might have some apples left.'

'Very nice,' said Ruth again, giving her a silly smile. To her amazement Madge came over and removed her glass from her hand. 'That's too strong for you,' she said, tipping half of it over a geranium and topping it up with tonic. 'Got to work up to my level. I always forget that. Don't have all that many visitors and Bill can drink me under the table.'

Ruth sipped the now pallid aperitif. 'Just going to prod the sprouts,' said Madge. 'I'll give you a yell when it's ready.'

Ruth looked around the room. It was light and airy, with a huge television in one corner and several squashy armchairs plonked in front of it.

She could imagine Madge with her feet up, gin in hand, watching it through the dark winter evenings. It in no way struck her as a lonely prospect.

There were several photographs on the mantelpiece, mostly of dogs past and present, and a rather sweet one of a round-faced man holding a little girl on the back of a donkey. Leonard, presumably, and a daughter?

'Grub's up,' came Madge's voice. Ruth made her way to the kitchen where Madge was ladling food on to two plates. 'Don't mind eating out here, do you?' she asked, handing one to Ruth.

'Not at all,' Ruth assured her. Madge produced a French loaf and hacked it into chunks, then plonked a bottle of red wine between them. 'That should do it,' she said cheerfully.

'That was delicious,' said Ruth when they had finished.

'Not bad,' Madge agreed.

'I used to enjoy cooking,' Ruth went on, 'but I'm afraid I've rather got out of the habit. You tend not to bother when you're on your own, don't you?'

Madge shook her head furiously. 'Rubbish. You don't get out of the habit of eating. Why should you get out of the habit of eating well? It's a cop-out. All these single women living off Prozac and Mars Bars. Then saying they don't know how to fill their time. No wonder they get depressed. Their stomachs get depressed. Show me a happy stomach and I'll show you a happy person. Or animal for that matter. Look at my two. You'd think they were pups. One's eight, the other's ten. What's the secret? They like their grub.'

'I expect you're right,' Ruth agreed, thinking of Lollo's stack of uppers and downers.

'Of course I'm right. Want some cheese?'

Madge fetched the cheese and some lumpy apples which tasted superb despite their appearance.

'What are they?' asked Ruth.

Madge shrugged. 'God knows. I get them off that tree in the paddock. Look like nuclear fall-out, but they taste okay. Bill wanted to make scrumpy with them but there weren't enough.'

'How did you get to know Bill Bartholomew?' Ruth asked.

'He wanted to marry my daughter,' said Madge.

'What?'

Madge looked up and burst out laughing. 'No, that's just a joke between us. Sylvia was visiting at the time, and he definitely took a shine to her, but the truth is he came to interview me. He was doing an article on battery hens and he wanted to talk to someone with a few free-rangers. Someone put him on to me. We just sort of hit it off. He stayed to supper. Got legless. Proposed to Sylvie. Nearly beat Leonard at draughts. Like one of the family. He got Tyson from me. Mind you, he spoils that dog. I keep telling him so. Takes no notice. Have you got room for a brandy?'

'Oh, no,' Ruth insisted. 'I've got to drive home. I wouldn't mind some coffee if you've got some.'

Madge made coffee and lit a cigarette. 'Funny bloke, Bill,' she ruminated. 'I've known him ten – twelve years now. He moved down here when he split with his wife. They'd been here on holidays, I think. I suppose he thought it would be like one long holiday. He certainly behaves that way sometimes. The village gigolo. I can't think why he didn't go somewhere hot if that was what he was after. Men are odd things, aren't they?'

'I take it your daughter didn't accept his offer?' Ruth asked. To her surprise Madge's eyes suddenly filled with pain. 'No,' she said gruffly. 'Sylvie had better things to do.' She did not continue and Ruth felt instinctively the subject was better left.

There was a howling from outside as the setters demanded to be let in. 'Time for their walk.'

Ruth stood up. 'I'd better get back and see what mayhem Lollo's created. Thank you so much for lunch. Perhaps you could come to me next Friday, if you're not too busy?'

Madge grunted. 'I'll see how I'm fixed.'

Ruth could hear Lollo howling as she drove a little unsteadily up the lane towards Bell Cottage. It was an eerie sound. A slight twinge of panic flickered through her as she thumped the accelerator and rattled up the drive.

'It's all right. I'm back. Stop that stupid noise at once,' she ordered as she searched for her keys. There was a silence, followed by renewed wailing.

'Oh for goodness' sake,' Ruth grumbled. She pushed the door which sprang open, almost unbalancing her, and Lollo shot past and disappeared down the driveway, out into the lane. Ruth stared after her in confusion. 'Lollo,' she called half-heartedly. 'Come back here at once, you idiot. I'm going to take you out. Come BACK, do you hear me?'

If she did, Lollo certainly had no intention of obeying. She had been shut up far too long. There had been no free newspapers all morning and the Ruth woman had omitted to leave her anything cuddly to put in her nest. She was out for revenge.

Ruth did not know this as she stared hazily down the drive, trying to decide what to do. The animal would not go far. There was no traffic between here and the beach. The worst Lollo could do would be to roll in another pile of fish bones. The thought of this sent a quick spurt of adrenalin gushing through Ruth's veins. She groaned and went to fetch the lead.

After twenty minutes of whistling and calling she decided the dog must have doubled back. She was cold and cross as she tramped back up the drive.

There was no sign of Lollo quivering in the porch, however. She went round to the back, then down to the compost heap. Lollo had not been there. For the first time a feeling of genuine anxiety crept through her. Where could the wretched animal be?

It was beginning to get dark as she set forth again, this time with a thicker coat and gloves. She went as far as the boathouse, then turned and retraced her steps, still calling. She didn't know what to do. Ring the police? Did they still have time for women who had lost their dogs? Suppose they asked her for a description? A fat hairy sausage. She tried to think of any distinguishing features. None came to mind. An autopsy would doubtless reveal a stomach lined with newspapers. She shuddered and tried to organise her thoughts.

The main problem was that she had had too much to drink. And she had driven home. How to explain that to the local constabulary? She could see it all. 'A dog, you say, Madam? Fat and brown. Would you mind breathing into this, Madam?'

What would Joy say? And Duncan? He'd probably withdraw her maintenance altogether if she got sent to prison, on the grounds that she wouldn't have to pay for anything in Holloway. No, she couldn't possibly call the police. Poor little Lollo would have to meet her fate alone. A lump rose in her throat.

She was about to turn round again when a figure loomed out of the darkness by the back door. Ruth froze. The figure approached. As it came nearer it was possible to discern that he was carrying something. Ruth's heart began to swoop up and down, colliding sharply with her stomach on the way.

'Who's that?' she croaked, backing towards the gate.

• Sarah Grazebrook

'Who the bloody hell do you think it is?' came the exasperated reply, as Bill Bartholomew came up to her, a soaking wet Lollo wrapped in a blanket in his arms. 'Where've you been? I've been stood outside there for twenty minutes. You'll be lucky if the dog's not got pneumonia.'

'You've found her,' was all Ruth could manage.

'She found me, more like. She was prowling round the yard, looking for Tyson, I should think. Randy little tart. I opened the back door to see what the noise was and the next thing I knew she'd scuttered off and fallen in the fish pond. I had the devil's own job getting her out of there.'

Ruth started to laugh, partly from relief and partly because for once she wasn't responsible for the animal trying to drown herself.

'I'm sorry,' she spluttered, sensing that the Scotsman did not share her amusement. 'Will you come in? You must be frozen.'

'I am,' he grumbled, holding Lollo in front of him like a sacrificial lamb. The dog, who had had a very severe fright, whimpered miserably and tried to snuggle up to him. 'Get off me, you drippy floozy,' he chided.

Once inside Ruth went in search once more of the hairdryer.

'Do I not get a drink?' came the man's plaintive voice up the stairs. Ruth hurried back down.

'Yes, I'm sorry. What would you like? I've only got wine or some brandy.'

'No whisky?' asked Bartholomew disappointedly.

'I'm afraid not,' said Ruth, thinking she could hardly be expected to buy drinks she didn't like in case she had visitors she didn't want.

'It had better be brandy then,' said the man.

She found the bottle and poured a generous measure. Or so she had thought, for Bartholomew immediately reached for the bottle and topped up his glass. Ruth smiled politely.

'Are you not having one yourself?' he asked.

'I think I might have a small one. To celebrate Lollo's safe return.'

'If I had a dog like that I'd celebrate her safe disappearance.' Bartholomew tipped his glass and swallowed the entire contents.

Ruth remembered what Madge had said about his drinking capacity.

'Help yourself to another,' she said unwillingly. 'You must excuse me. I have to dry Lollo.' She hauled the protesting animal into the kitchen, lecturing her on what she thought of dachshunds who ran away, fell in fish ponds and, most heinous of all, brought home disagreeable Scotsmen to polish off her brandy.

'Talk to yourself a lot, do you?' Bartholomew was standing in the doorway watching the pair of them. Lollo licked her chops, in anticipation of either her supper or a flaring row between the humans. In the event she got neither.

Ruth took a breath. 'No more than most people who live alone, I don't suppose.'

Bill Bartholomew nodded. 'You're right about that. Still, at least no one argues with you when you're on your own.'

Ruth sat back on her haunches. Lollo took the opportunity to escape. 'It's funny you say that,' she replied, 'because almost all the conversations I have with myself are arguments between me and someone else.'

Bartholomew grinned. 'Who wins them?'

Ruth smiled very slightly. 'I suppose I do.'

'Oh, aye? And what happened in real life?'

'What do you mean?'

Bartholomew laughed. 'Oh come on. You know what I mean. All these perfectly rehearsed quarrels are just re-runs of the ones you lost when you had them. Right or wrong?'

'I really can't remember,' said Ruth coldly. 'Would you like me to drive you home? It's the least I can do after all your kindness.'

Bartholomew studied her with interest. 'Well, that's me told,' he said at last. 'Yes, you can drive me home. Why not? That's what neighbours are for, after all, are they not?'

Some neighbour, thought Ruth, as she struggled up the perpendicular track that led to Bill Bartholomew's cottage. Did no one in Westbridge live on a tarmacked road?

'Here we are,' said Bill, who was feeling quite jovial after the brandy. 'Will I ask you in for a snifter?'

• Sarah Grazebrook

'No thank you,' said Ruth. 'I'd better get back before Lollo decamps again.' Tyson barked in the distance. Bartholomew shrugged. 'They're worse than bairns, aren't they, the animals?'

Ruth sniffed. 'They are a bit.'

'Still,' he sighed sentimentally. 'They love us.'

Yours might, Ruth reflected, driving back to the ravenous Lollo. Mine is just using me.

10

The following day brought a letter. Ruth got to it just before Lollo and was surprised to see it had a local postmark and was clearly handwritten.

Dear Ruth, it said in blotchy biro, *Please excuse the nerve and all that, but I was wondering if you [and of course, lovely Lollo], would like to come to supper tomorrow night, [Saturday]. Nothing much, as I'm a lousy cook, and please don't even bother to acknowledge if you've got something super planned, [short notice and all that] but it would be such fun to see you. We could talk about Things! Yours, Gwen [Pritchard]*

Ruth had never seen a letter that depended so heavily on parentheses. It reminded her of those cards which say *Happy [birthday], [anniversary], [Christmas], etc.* and the purchaser merely has to ring the appropriate occasion and message, thus avoiding all personal contact with the recipient.

Supper with Gwen. To discuss Things. It was hardly the most tempting offer in the world. Yet again it was the weekend, and she had had no other. She dialled Joy's number.

'Hello?'

'Joy, it's Ruth.'

'Ruth, dear. How are you?'

'Fine, thank you. Could I leave a message for Gwen?'

'Gwen? What sort of a message?'

Tell her the cocaine's in the boot of the car, came to mind, but Ruth resisted. 'Could you say we'd love to come to supper tonight? We'll be round about eight, unless I hear differently.'

There was a pause. 'Gwen has invited you to supper?'

'Yes. Is it a problem?'

• Sarah Grazebrook

'No. NO. I just thought she was planning to finish my curtains tonight. Silly me. I expect I got it wrong.'

If Ruth had had doubts before about accepting Gwen's invitation, this effectively resolved them.

As they drove up to the house she could see that the Blakeneys also had company. There were a couple of cars parked in the driveway, one of which she recognised as Adrian's. I'm well out of that, she thought as she fumbled round to the back where steps led down to Gwen's basement.

Unsurprisingly the flat was full of ethnic wall-hangings and talismans, some so alarming that Ruth had to look close to make sure they were not shrunken heads. 'Do you like those?' asked Gwen excitedly as Ruth backed away from a particularly gruelling leather mask.

'I don't think I've seen anything quite like it before,' she responded tactfully.

'No, isn't it wonderful? A friend of mine – well, Henry's really,' Gwen paused delicately, 'gave it to us. He makes them. Carves them, whatever. He's got his own studio in Worthing. Under an old people's home. He's doing frightfully well.'

As well he might, Ruth reflected, thinking of the wealth of potential donors. She stifled an urge to giggle.

Lollo, on the other hand, did not find the mask at all funny. She approached it commando style, hairs on her neck Mohican with dread. A low rumble escaped her throat, erupting into a savage snarl as she came within sniffing distance.

'I think perhaps the leathery smell's unsettled her,' said Ruth, lifting the object prudently on to a higher shelf.

'Oh, poor Lolly,' Gwen sympathised. 'Is oo fwikened? Come with Gwenny and she'll find you a lovely choccy biccy.'

'She's had her supper,' Ruth protested – hopelessly, for the two of them had already disappeared down the passage into Gwen's kitchen.

Ruth remembered she had bought a bottle of wine and followed. 'Here,' she said, handing it to Gwen who was in the process of opening a fresh packet of biscuits. 'She really shouldn't have those, Gwen. She's on a bit of a diet.'

Gwen looked at her appealingly. 'Just one? After all it is a special occasion.'

Is it, thought Ruth nervously, watching as Lollo swallowed the biscuit whole. She hoped it was not Gwen's birthday or anything she ought to have known about. She struggled to remember the date. February the twenty-second did not seem unduly significant.

Gwen went over to her stove and took the lid off a large saucepan. 'Nearly there,' she said. 'Oh goodness me, is that for us?' as she spotted Ruth's bottle.

'It's nothing special,' said Ruth. 'Would you like me to open it?'

'Would you? That would be awfully nice. I've got some glasses somewhere.' She hunted around and produced two tumblers that looked as though they'd been hewn from milk bottles with a meat cleaver. Ruth poured some wine.

'Cheers,' said Gwen. 'Gosh, this is nice. I usually drink beer. Henry had a friend who brews his own and I sort of got the taste for it, but this is lovely,' she added hastily. Ruth smiled and made a mental note to make hers last.

'Come in the other room,' invited Gwen. 'I've got loads of things I want to ask you. Are you sure Lollo can't just have one more biccy?'

'Absolutely,' said Ruth. Gwen sighed but accepted the decree. Not so Lollo, who set up a piteous whining, till Ruth suggested she be allowed out in the garden for a few minutes.

'Now,' said Gwen as they sat down, 'first things first. You know what date it is?'

Again Ruth's heart sank. 'Ummm . . .' she said feebly.

'It's February the twenty-second,' Gwen went on excitedly.

'Oh . . . Yes. I'd almost forgotten,' mumbled Ruth.

Gwen continued, undismayed. 'The reason I asked you round, apart from being dying to see you, of course, is that I need your help.'

'I'm not awfully good at sewing,' Ruth intercepted, determined not to be roped into lining her sister-in-law's curtains. Gwen looked at her a little strangely but soldiered on. 'You're so good at sort of saying things. And besides, you've been through it.'

'Through what?' asked Ruth gingerly.

Gwen shrugged. 'Well, you know – IT. Breaking up and all that.'

- Sarah Grazebrook

Ruth took a deep gulp of her wine.

Gwen watched her anxiously. 'I haven't upset you, have I? I didn't mean to, really I didn't.'

Ruth shook her head. 'No, of course not. But I really don't think I can be of much help to you, Gwen. I've only recently got divorced, and I certainly don't consider myself an expert.'

'Not divorce. Oh no, nothing like that,' Gwen shook her head in mortification. 'No, I want your advice because I've decided what I'm going to do.'

Ruth smiled kindly. 'Forgive me, but isn't advice what you usually ask for before you've made up your mind, not after?'

Gwen gave a tinkling laugh. 'Well, yes I suppose it is. But, you see, although I've made up my mind what to do, I'm not absolutely one thousand per cent sure HOW to do it, if you see what I mean.'

Ruth took another swig of her wine and wished she had brought two bottles. 'Perhaps you'd better tell me what you have in mind.'

'I'll tell you over dinner,' Gwen promised and led her into a cubicle which just managed to contain two chairs and a foldaway table over which Gwen had flung a batik cloth and lit a candle in the shape of Rudolph Nureyev.

'This is nice and cosy,' said Ruth, hitting her knee on the table leg.

'Isn't it?' Gwen sighed. 'Joy and Christopher are so kind, letting me have this lovely flat, and they hardly charge me a thing. I feel so guilty.'

'You are helping Joy with her curtains,' Ruth reminded her. 'It would cost a fortune to have them done professionally.'

Gwen smiled deprecatingly. 'It's the absolute least least I could do.'

She served her casserole, tastier than Joy's, and some home made bread, which was not. She had made a fruit salad, mainly of dried figs as far as Ruth could tell, and doused it in yoghurt made by 'a very dear friend that Henry had introduced her to'.

'I take it you're not from round here?' asked Ruth, as Gwen went to fetch the home-brewed beer.

Gwen turned in surprise. 'Yes, I am. Why do you say that?'

'I don't know really,' Ruth floundered. 'I sort of assumed

because Henry had introduced you to all these friends of his that perhaps you were new to the district.'

Gwen looked depressed. 'No,' she said. 'I've lived here all my life. Henry comes from Birmingham. But he was always so much better at making friends than me.'

'But surely,' Ruth pointed out, 'you must have had some friends before he arrived, if you've lived here all your life?'

'Yes I did,' said Gwen forlornly. 'But Henry didn't seem to get on with them all that well. I think it was because he came from a city. He used to say they were a bit . . . I don't know . . . parochial. I expect he was right. He knew so much more than me, you see.'

'What is Henry's profession?' asked Ruth, loathing him by proxy.

'He's going to be an actuary,' said Gwen proudly. 'When he passes his exams.' She must have registered the shock on Ruth's face because she added shyly, 'He's a bit younger than me, you see.'

Ruth surmised that Gwen could be no more than twenty-eight. 'How much younger?' she asked, prepared to offer motherly advice.

Gwen hesitated. 'Twenty-sevenish.'

'And he hasn't taken his exams yet?'

'Oh yes. He's taken them three times, but he's terribly sensitive, you see. Every time he gets into the exam room he has a panic attack and has to leave almost immediately. It's a dreadful shame because everyone says he'll make a marvellous actuary when he does get there.' Her head drooped. 'I sometimes wonder if it was something to do with me that made him fail.'

Ruth clucked dismissively. 'I'm sure that wasn't the case. How old was he when you met him?'

Gwen flicked through her fingers. 'Twenty-six. Ish.'

Ruth stared. 'You mean you've only known him a year?'

'A bit more than that. It was just after his birthday, you see. And that's in July. Nearly two years, really.'

'And he's failed his exams three times since you met him?'

Gwen looked confused. 'No, he's only taken them once since he's known me. But that was the worst. He thought he was being chased by a mad cow.'

• Sarah Grazebrook

Silence seemed best at this point. Ruth drank some water.
'If you want my advice, Gwen . . .'
'I do. I do. You see, the reason I've asked you, apart from . . .'
'Yes, yes, I know.'
'Is that I want you to help me with my plan.'
'What plan?'
'My plan for the twenty-ninth.'
'Twenty-ninth what?'
'Of February. It's Leap Year, isn't it?'
'Is it?' asked Ruth who had lost count.
'Yes. That's the point. My plan is to go up to Henry on the twenty-ninth of February. And propose. Women are allowed to, you see, on Leap Year Day. It's traditional. And I thought if he saw how much I loved him, he'd – well, you know – he might agree to give it another go. I mean, I know it was all my fault. I shall tell him that. I was silly to go on the way I did. After all, it's only money, isn't it? When it comes down to it.'

'What is?' asked Ruth, her head reeling from Gwen's logic and the disgusting beer.

Gwen paused. 'Oh, yes of course, you don't know, do you? How Henry and I came to split up?'

Ruth shook her head. 'You don't have to tell me if you don't want to.'

If Gwen noted the unspoken plea she chose to ignore it. 'I would like to tell you,' she said, giving her head a brave little toss. 'I feel I can trust you. I know I've only known you a little while, but I'm very intuitive about people. I can tell almost straight away if I'm going to get on with them.'

Obviously, thought Ruth, if Henry's anything to go by.

'I met Henry at a hedgerow preservation meeting. Joy had organised it, so it was she who introduced us really. I owe her so much. Anyway, Henry was down here staying with a friend from college and this friend, it's the one who makes the beer, brought him along, and I was standing at the back of the hall because there weren't enough chairs and Joy said I should because I was the tallest, which made perfect sense, of course, and Henry and Gavin – that's the one who makes the beer, came in a bit late because I think they'd stopped for petrol on the way or something, and Henry, just by accident, stood on my foot, and was so apologetic. You'd think he'd broken it or something, but he was so nice and insisted I go and have a drink with them in the pub afterwards, and we just sort of hit it off.

'He was down here for a fortnight and we saw ever such a lot of each other. I showed him where all the good pubs were, and then I would drive him and Gavin home afterwards, and once when Henry was feeling a bit glum I took him out to dinner at the Crossbows. It cost a fortune. I couldn't really afford it, but it was worth it just to see how happy it made him. And he told me all about his studies and how he was going to be an actuary and things, and then he had to go back to Birmingham, and of course I was devastated. I was so frightened he'd forget all about me once he was back in the bright lights of the city.'

'And did he?' put in Ruth, who was getting pins and needles where Lollo had slumped on her foot.

Gwen shook her head. 'That was the marvellous thing. I didn't hear from him for ages, although I wrote and wrote. Well of course, he was so busy with his exams and things so it was perfectly understandable, and then a funny thing happened.' She paused dramatically.

'What was that?' Ruth prompted obediently.

'I had this great uncle. I didn't know him very well. He lived miles away – Cumberland or somewhere. We hardly ever communicated, just Christmas cards and things. Anyway he died, and it turned out he'd left me quite a lot of money. Oh, not a fortune or anything, but enough to put a deposit down on a little place of my own. My parents moved out to Spain, you see. They used to own the village shop in Harbury, but they sold up and took early retirement. It's a video shop now.'

Ruth felt that some response was required to this but could not think of one so merely nodded.

'Anyway, I was feeling a bit light-headed, I suppose, and I wrote to Henry and told him all about my bit of good luck, and I must have been feeling really brave because I said if he wanted to, he could come and share my flat – the one I was going to buy. And the next thing I knew, he rang me up and said he was coming to see me, and that's how it all happened.' She looked across at Ruth who was struggling to contain her disbelief.

'Oh I can see what you're thinking. 'Some people always fall

• Sarah Grazebrook

on their feet', and I suppose I have, at least up till now. But that's why I'm planning to go over to the flat on the twenty-ninth and take the bull by the horns. After all it worked before. Why shouldn't it work now?'

Ruth, who could think of a thousand reasons, was silent. 'How exactly did you and Henry come to break up, if you don't mind my asking?' she said at last.

Gwen sighed. 'Well, it was my fault, of course. Henry was being a bit funny about money. I was between jobs, you see, at the time.'

'Henry, I take it, wasn't working either?'

'Not money working, no. Well, he had so much studying to do. He didn't want to jeopardise his chances again. Anyway, things got a bit tight and we had this most awful row and he said I should either get another job or I'd have to move out.'

'Hang on,' said Ruth sharply, 'I thought you said it was your flat.'

Gwen looked at her wide-eyed. 'Oh, didn't I say? It was both of ours. Henry said we should have a joint mortgage, because once he'd passed his exams and was earning all that money it would make sense for him to get the tax relief and anyway, he'd be paying all the bills and that. He didn't want me to work once he was established, you see. So it was all perfectly fair.'

'And now he's thrown you out,' Ruth reminded her.

Gwen shrugged. 'He didn't really throw me out. It just seemed better for us to be apart for a bit. At least,' her eyes became alarmingly moist, 'that's what Henry said. But everyone's been so terribly kind. Particularly Garth Forland and, of course, Joy and Christopher . . .'

Ruth listened resignedly while Gwen ran through her lexicon of generous neighbours, '. . . and of course, now I've managed to get myself this little job in the bookshop. It's not very well-paid and it is terribly hard work, but I had to do something. I just had to.' She fixed Ruth with her spaniel gaze. 'I'm sorry to go on like this. You must be awfully bored of listening to my problems when you've got so many of your own.'

'Have I?' asked Ruth, jolted back to reality. 'Oh, I wouldn't say that.' In truth she had been trying to work out how she could persuade Gwen to relinquish her job at the bookshop in favour of herself. Despite what she had been saying, Ruth doubted very much that a few afternoons in a bookshop could amount to a contravention of the EEC rules on humane employment conditions.

'There's just the tiniest possibility,' Gwen continued afresh, 'although it's probably frightfully bad luck to mention it, but I overheard Adrian Mills talking to Joy the other evening, and he was saying he'd need a research assistant if he's going to be in charge of videoing the pageant, and I'm hoping against hope he might consider me for it but, of course, that's ages away.'

'Of course,' Ruth repeated automatically.

'So, what with all that, I really do think Henry will probably change his mind in the long run and ask me to come back.'

'Sometimes these things are for the best,' Ruth murmured unconvincingly. Gwen nodded vigorously and blinked her eyes. 'It's just I do so miss him.' Her shoulders began to tremble.

Ruth took a deep breath. 'I'm sure you do, Gwen, but if you want my honest advice, I really think you'd be better discarding this plan of yours for the twenty-ninth.'

Gwen stared at her in anguish. 'But why? I haven't told you my plan yet. Oh, you mustn't worry. I'm not going to go in while SHE's there.'

Ruth wondered what Gwen had put in the coffee. 'Who is SHE?' she asked steadily. Gwen gave a dismissive little snort. 'She's his wife, but they've been separated for years now. I don't know why she suddenly had to show up. If you ask me she's only come down to make trouble. Let's go next door. I've got some really nice slivovitz. It's made from parsnips. A friend of . . .'

'Henry's,' murmured Ruth without thinking.

'Actually it was Adrian's. Adrian Mills,' said Gwen with the tiniest hint of asperity.

Over the parsnip slivovitz Gwen confided her plan of campaign. She would arrive at her erstwhile flat at seven fifty in the evening, purporting to be a Takeaway Pizza courier. SHE, her intelligence informed her, was a devotee of the National Lottery and would not be prepared to leave the television at so crucial a moment in her destiny. Henry, therefore, would come to the door to be confronted by Gwen, sporting her polka dot vest and cycling shorts and a *quattro stagioni* pizza from Safeways.

• Sarah Grazebrook

She knew her man. He would not be able to resist. By the time SHE had accepted another week of pauperdom Henry would be hers for eternity.

Ruth, almost breathless with disbelief, refrained from enquiring what would happen if SHE won nine million pounds while Gwen was entwining Henry with broccoli and melted mozzarella.

'So,' said Gwen when she had finished. 'What do you think?'

Ruth swallowed. 'I think it's very original.'

'You like it?'

'Gwen, how can I tell? I don't know Henry. Or this – person, for that matter. I do agree you should get your flat back, but I honestly wonder if Henry is the right man for you. Or even if he is, whether this is the right way of going about things.'

Gwen treated her to a smile of sickening sanctimoniousness. 'You would say that, of course, after all you've been through. But trust me, Ruth, I know what I'm doing.'

As she and Lollo zigzagged away from the house, Ruth took with her the enduring memory of Adrian Mills' face on discovering the two of them retching quietly into the rhododendron bush by the gate. 'Not you as well?' was all she could remember from their conversation.

11

Ruth spent Sunday worrying.

It was not something that came to her naturally, but events of the previous few days had led her inexorably towards it.

She was in a strange place, with very strange people; she was in charge of a dog over which she had no control; she had insufficient money to survive on, and now she had been made party to a plan by an unbalanced female to seduce a man who was married to someone else, by means of a polka dot vest and *quattro stagioni* pizza. The weight of her years pressed upon her.

Lollo sat by her feet chewing ruminatively on a slipper she had found in one of the cupboards. She was oddly subdued. Ruth wondered vaguely if she were missing her owners, but she had showed no visible signs of pining. If anything, she was eating more than ever. Perhaps she was suffering from the same thing as Adrian. Perhaps she had worms? Ruth hoped with a passion she had not. Apart from her natural revulsion to the thought it would entail a visit to the vet, and that really would finish her off. She'd be reduced to locusts and wild honey till Duncan's next cheque arrived.

Martin rang in the evening. He was planning to come down the next weekend 'to stroll round the improvements'. Ruth couldn't help laughing as she noted a large damp patch over the front door. 'I don't think there are many improvements.'

'That bad, is it?' asked Martin.

Ruth sighed. 'No. I'm exaggerating. It'll be good to see you. I could do with some normal company.'

'I'm normal?'

- Sarah Grazebrook

'You are compared to some of the people here.'
Martin laughed. 'Mum . . .'
'Yes?'
'Would it be all right if I brought someone with me? A friend?'
'Yes, of course. I'm afraid you'll have to share a bedroom. Who is it? Jack?'
'No. Actually it's a girl. Her name's Kate.'
Ruth hesitated. 'Well, if she doesn't mind it being a bit spartan. You'll have to sleep in the sitting room, or you can have my room and Kate can have the spare and I'll sleep down here. Yes, that would be best.'
'Mum,' Martin cut across her meanderings, 'there's no need. Kate and I will sleep together.'
Ruth retired to bed even more worried.

On Monday she cleaned the spare room. By the end of the morning it smelled more like an operating theatre than a boudoir. Lollo sniffed around suspiciously.

In the afternoon Ruth walked her down to the town and looked in the window of the Job Centre. Pile drivers seemed to be at a premium in the area, but apart from that there was nothing other than the jobs she had seen in the newspaper.

Walking back past the newsagent's she saw an advertisement for Ann Summers' representatives, guaranteeing 'a lot of fun, a good income and free peekaboo panty set for each party hostess'. She toyed with the idea of enquiring further, but the thought of Joy, Grace and the redoubtable Violet Sampson bickering over spray-on penis stiffeners was more than she could bear.

Gwen Pritchard was sitting on the porch step when she got back. She leapt up and came running towards them as they entered the gate. Lollo bounced joyfully in anticipation of more chocolate biscuits but Gwen hardly noticed her in her excitement.

'I just had to bring you my news. It's so good I could hardly believe it. SHE's gone.'

Ruth dragged her mind back from penis extenders and tried to fix it on Gwen and her news. 'Is she . . . ?'

'Yes, that's right. I met Grace down town this morning. She was going to her osteopath and she happened to let drop, quite by accident, that she had seen Henry down at the station this morning, seeing her off. Isn't that wonderful?'

'Is it?' asked Ruth, struggling to untangle Lollo's paws from the lead. 'Look, Gwen, it's a bit chilly. Why don't we go inside? I'll make some tea and you can tell me all about it – if you want to.'

'Oh I do, I do.'

They went into the cottage and Ruth set about the laborious task of boiling the kettle and listening to Gwen's ecstatic description of what the unfortunate SHE had been wearing on her departure [a brownish coat] and carrying [a small suitcase and two canvas holdalls]. 'THAT sounds fairly permanent, wouldn't you say?' Gwen demanded, in between asking whether she should have her hair bobbed before Saturday, and if Ruth thought a pink lycra body stocking would be better than the vest?

Ruth, who couldn't see either garment exciting much lust in a man who hallucinated about mad cows, murmured noncommittally and busied herself with the tea things.

'So now we don't have HER to worry about, everything should be fine. You don't mind, do you? I know it's a frightful bind at that time of night and everything, and I wouldn't ask, but you've been so kind, and given me so much good advice and everything. And after all, you have been through it, too, so you know what I'm suffering – have been suffering, that is. You're a real chum.' Gwen's face saddened briefly. 'I only wish I could do the same for you. Still, who knows? One day . . .'

An icy chill began to descend on Ruth. 'I'm a little bit confused,' she interrupted tentatively. 'I . . . Is there something I said I would do the other evening, Gwen? I know I had quite a lot to drink.'

'No, of course you didn't, Ruth.' Gwen fairly shook with girlish mirth. 'It's just you were so supportive. So was lovely Lollo, too, of course.' She reached down and gave the dog a squeeze. Lollo burped. 'No, the only thing would be if you could possibly just drive me round there. I mean it would look a bit funny if I were to arrive on a bicycle, wouldn't it? I mean the pizza would be cold for a start. I don't think Henry would be too pleased about that.'

Ruth reflected that cold pizza was probably the least of his problems. 'I'll drive you there if you want me to, Gwen, but you know I do feel this scheme of yours is a little ill-advised. As I said before, you have all my sympathy regarding the flat and that, but I do think there may be better ways of going about things. Have you tried the Citizens Advice Bureau? They're awfully good at legal matters.'

Gwen flapped the idea away. 'It's not the flat I'm interested in. It's Henry. What would I want to go setting solicitors on him for? They do more harm than good ninety-nine times out of a hundred.'

Ruth could not deny the truth in this. 'What time would you like me to call for you?' she asked wearily.

Gwen hissed with dismay. 'Oh, I don't want you to call for me. Someone might see. I wouldn't want Joy or anyone to, you know, guess what I had in mind. No, it's a big big secret between you and me. I'll meet you on the corner by the library, if that's all right. About a quarter to eight. It's ever so close to the flat so we won't be late.'

'But if this – person's gone, is it absolutely necessary to arrive during the Lottery draw, still?'

Gwen's brow clouded and Ruth immediately regretted having introduced a variable.

'I see what you mean.' Gwen's face contorted with indecision. 'But yes, I do think that would be the best time, if it's all right with you.'

'Perfectly,' said Ruth, as one choosing between the noose and the bullet.

Gwen departed. Ruth fed Lollo and set about preparing her own supper. Halfway through she realised with a sickening thud that Saturday was when Martin and Kate would be with her. Not that it would take a whole evening to drive Gwen to Henry's flat, but she had been planning to cook them a nice dinner. Hang the expense. She still had her credit card and she was not having Martin's girlfriend pitying him for the sake of a few pounds.

She might even take them out to dinner. Or would that be ostentatious? Particularly as she didn't know anything about the local restaurants. No point in making a thing of it, she told herself, vividly aware that the longer she could keep the pair of them out of the connubial bed the happier she would be. That was absurd. Martin was a man now. Presumably he'd been sleeping with this girl for some time if he were prepared to install her under his mother's roof, albeit for one night only?

She went and had another look at the spare room. It still smelled like a clinic but now it was freezing as well. A morgue, thought Ruth, dejectedly. She shut the window and went back to her supper.

'I've had a thought,' Madge informed her when she got to the shop next morning. 'You know what you were saying about work and money and that?'

'Yes,' said Ruth half-heartedly. She had all but given up hope of supplementing her income and was on the verge of ringing Duncan again and reneguing on their latest agreement.

'Well, I was thinking and it occurred to me that you should get in touch with Rowena.'

'Rowena?'

'Mills. The one I was telling you about, that's married to that twerp, Adrian.'

'Oh?' said Ruth, wondering if Madge thought she needed to lose weight.

'She does market research. Organises it. She's always on the lookout for new interviewers. Apparently the turnover round here's pretty high. They run out of mates to try the products on. That's why you'd be good. You don't know anyone. Ro wanted me to do it but I told her no. I can't stand all those stupid questions. 'How often do you eat turkey?' 'How many times do you open your bowels each day?''

Ruth blinked nervously. 'That sounds a bit medical for me.'

Madge shrugged. 'Just an example. You get your petrol money. Would you like me to have a word with her or not? I can ring her from here.'

Ruth considered. She might as well investigate. Maybe she could stipulate 'no bowel surveys'. Money was money. 'Yes, please,' she said. 'I'd be very grateful.'

'She's going to call in. She's having her hair done and then she'll drop by on the way back.'

Ruth was sorting ski wear from football kits and fending off the woman with the headscarf who had returned with a view to helping the freezing of Thailand for a maximum of one pound fifty.

Madge, seeing that she was under siege, came stalking across the room and ripped a pair of salopettes out of the woman's hands. 'They're very small in Thailand,' she growled. 'Try the children's rail. As much as you can carry for thirty pounds.' The woman retreated.

Rowena Mills was not as thin as Ruth had expected. In fact she looked quite robust for someone who allegedly threw up four good meals a day. She was tanned, 'sunbed', Madge whispered, and immaculately dressed. Her nails were manicured, her shoes shiny and her hair sleek. The very picture of a woman in charge of her own life.

Only her eyes betrayed a hint of panic as she shook Ruth's hand, flicking between her and Madge as though anticipating a possible attack from either of them.

She was about the same age as Gwen Pritchard, prompting in Ruth the ignoble thought that more women cracked up in their twenties than during the legendary menopause, particularly if confined to east Kent.

Her voice was low and husky, which surprised Ruth. She had expected something more high-pitched. 'Madge has told me all about you,' Rowena said. Since it was Madge and not Joy who had done the telling, Ruth felt reasonably assured that she had kept it to the minimum.

'There's a training course,' Rowena continued. 'It's just a couple of days. To familiarise you with the various types of survey we do, and then on your first job someone goes out with you to iron out any difficulties. After that you're on your own. The pay's pro rata. I can give you an application form, if you're interested.'

'Thank you,' said Ruth. 'Could you just give me some idea of the sort of thing I'd be required to do.'

Rowena smiled. 'Nothing too dire, I promise you. I suppose Madge has been terrifying you with tales of blood and urine, has she?'

Ruth swallowed. 'She did say something about bowels. I don't think she mentioned blood and urine, did you, Madge?'

Madge snorted with laughter. 'I only use that on the people Ro won't want. It's easier than telling them they'd be no good.' She turned to Rowena. 'She'll be fine. Take my word for it.'

Rowena handed her the forms. 'Have a look through. See what you think. It would be really nice to have someone new on my list. We've got a huge soup job coming up and I honestly don't know how I'm going to fill it. They're looking for people who eat soup twice a day, on top of everything else. I mean, who does that nowadays?'

Only Adrian, thought Ruth, but refrained from saying so.

'How are you finding Westbridge?' Rowena asked. 'Madge said you were staying in the Taylors' house.'

'Yes, that's right. It's certainly a change from London,' Ruth replied.

'Yes, isn't it?' said Rowena vehemently then, blushing at her own temerity, continued more calmly, 'I do hope you'll decide to give this a go. It can be quite fun if you like meeting people. The secret is not to take it too seriously, wouldn't you agree, Madge?'

Madge, who had been folding jumpers in the corner, looked up. 'I certainly would. And you'd do well to remember that yourself, young lady.' Rowena laughed awkwardly and fiddled with an expensive bracelet on her wrist.

'I understand you've met my husband?' she said to Ruth.

Ruth nodded. 'Yes, at . . . at . . .'

'At Joy and Christopher's. Yes, I was so sorry not to be there. Pressure of work, I'm afraid. There's rather a lot of paperwork involved in market research. Only for me,' she added hastily. 'Don't let me put you off before you've even started.'

Ruth smiled. 'You won't. I need the money.'

Rowena nodded anxiously. 'Yes, isn't it a swine? I hate money. When I think of all Aid's projects that haven't got off the ground, just for lack of investment. It makes me want to scream. He's so talented. It seems so unfair when you see all the rubbish that does get made, and there's him, with all these marvellous ideas and no one with enough imagination to back him.' She shook herself. 'There's me on my hobby horse again. I'm sorry. But you've met him. You must see what a waste it is. I mean the man's a bloody genius. Anyone can see that. It's such a waste.' She stood up.

• Sarah Grazebrook

'I must go. Let me leave these forms with you. Anything you want to know, give me a ring. I'm home most evenings.'

I bet you are, thought Ruth, as she watched Rowena driving away.

She took the forms home and filled them in, stating that she had no criminal record or history of mental instability, then posted them while walking Lollo.

She was a little surprised to receive a phone call on the Thursday morning from the head office of the company, saying that a training class had been scheduled for the following week and they would be delighted if she could attend. It would take place in Canterbury but they would be prepared to provide lunch on both days and reimburse her travelling expenses. Ruth accepted with some alacrity.

She flipped through the information pack that Rowena had given her. The pay was not good, but the work did not sound particularly arduous. She had herself been approached in the past by respectable females enquiring which brand of tea she preferred and whether she had ever microwaved a cake. No one, so far as she could remember, had ever asked for her blood or her urine in the street. And it was money.

Feeling distinctly more optimistic she looked up the restaurant section of the Yellow Pages and booked a table for three at The Crossbows for eight o'clock on Saturday.

Alarmed by this extravagance she then dug out all her mince recipes with an eye to providing lunch for Madge on Friday and Martin and Kate over the weekend.

In the event she went to the supermarket, armed with her trusty credit card and once more spent enough to send Mervyn Parsons into hysteria.

Joy rang on Thursday evening, ostensibly for a chat, but actually to inform her that Adrian had mentioned his wife's intention of involving Ruth, when trained, on the 'soup biggie', and her own availability as a recipient of free food if Ruth were to find it 'all too much for her'.

Ruth thanked her politely and said she would certainly bear this in mind, at the same time making a mental note to flush any remaining soup down the lavatory before she let it pass the lips of her sister-in-law.

There was another 'Household Event' at the shop on Friday morning. The woman with the headscarf was there, but she seemed to be losing heart in the face of Madge and Ruth's united opposition, and actually paid seventy pence for a pair of men's pyjamas which could not have protected a corpse from a cobweb, let alone a nomad from the sirocco.

To Ruth's surprise and embarrassment Lollo snarled at Madge when they arrived back at Bell Cottage. Madge, however, was unalarmed. 'She can smell McGuigan and Conte,' she explained, giving Lollo a cursory tweak. Lollo ceased snarling and began an obsequious display of lovableness which Madge also ignored. This only intensified her efforts till Ruth, sick of the dachshund's ridiculous little twirls all over the kitchen, banished her to the back garden.

'By the way, I forgot to say, I'm going on a training course for Rowena's market research next week,' said Ruth as she fetched the coffee. Madge grunted. 'Some right nutters on that,' she said. Ruth wondered if this applied to herself, and if not, why Madge had recommended she enrol.

'Well, at least it'll be a bit of cash.'

'Exactly. Who's minding the dog?'

'No one. It's only two days.'

'They don't like being left, you know.'

'No. Still I don't see I've got any option.'

'Shouldn't have them if you don't want them.'

Ruth was on the verge of saying that she didn't want Lollo, and that the main purpose of her applying for the job was so that she need no longer have her, but something in Madge Jordan's eyes told her it would not be a good idea.

12

Ruth liked Kate. She was not particularly pretty, but she had a kind of earthiness that was decidedly attractive. Ruth surmised she was probably a year or two older than Martin.

Despite all she had told herself – that Martin was nineteen, that it would be more worrying if he hadn't slept with a girl, that these university affairs never lasted, she had still anticipated the arrival of Kate with the kind of despair she had thought confined to mothers whose sons have decided to enter a monastery.

The sound of Martin's car crunching over the gravel was very nearly equalled by the thudding of her own heart as she went out to greet them.

'I don't know why men always think they can read maps,' Kate announced before they had been introduced. 'If I'd listened to Martin we'd be nearly in Devon by now.'

'Excuse me. I am reading Anthropology,' objected Martin.

'Perhaps you should think about changing your course,' said Kate. 'You couldn't understand a word that man said to you at the petrol station.'

'He had a cleft palate,' Martin retorted.

'What'll you do if you come across a Zulu with the same problem?' demanded Kate.

'Run like hell,' said Martin.

They took Lollo for a long walk in the afternoon. Ruth prayed silently that they would not meet Bill Bartholomew and Tyson, and fortunately they did not.

When they got back Martin watched the football results while Kate folded slices of newspaper and sealed the cracks through which the north east wind was wailing. 'We'll go to B & Q tomorrow,' she promised Ruth. 'We passed it on the way. Martin can fit you some of that proper stuff.'

Martin accordingly groaned and said he had come away for a rest.

'You shouldn't have brought me then, should you?' Kate observed, which greatly endeared her to Ruth.

Lollo, plainly hoping for the same reaction from the newcomers that her slobbering inspired in Gwen Pritchard, slithered over and rubbed herself obsequiously against Kate's legs. 'Get off,' said Kate, holding her teacake firmly away from her. 'You're fat enough already.'

'You say that about everyone,' said Martin, running a wary hand over his stomach.

'Only when it's true,' said Kate cheerfully.

'Or me.'

'Or you, obviously. But that was because you said I walked like Fergie. Revenge was essential.' She turned to Ruth. 'Don't you agree, Martin's mother?'

Ruth laughed. 'I think he got off very lightly under the circumstances. Do you think you could call me Ruth? "Martin's mother" makes me feel like an Indian squaw.'

'The Indians have got it right,' Martin observed. 'Much better call people something that suits them than naming them after flowers or footballers or whatever.'

Kate nodded vociferously. 'You could be "Washes No Socks".'

'All right, Walks Like Fergie, how far do you want to take this?' Martin cupped his arm round Kate's neck and hauled her towards him.

'Let go of me, Lump with Sharp Elbows,' squawked Kate, struggling to get free. Lollo bounced ecstatically beside them, snapping with pleasure at the prospect of violence.

Ruth cleared the tea things away.

When she came back Kate and Martin had resolved their differences and were snuggled on the sofa counting their money.

'We're going to take you out for a meal,' Martin explained.

'Oh, no.' Ruth shook her head. 'I'm taking you two out. It's all arranged. I've booked.'

'Well, we'll pay,' insisted Kate.

'You certainly won't. You're my guests. Anyway you can't possibly afford to go buying people meals on a student grant.'

The two of them looked at each other. 'What shall we do?' Kate asked Martin. Martin shrugged. 'It was just going to be a Chinese or something, Mum. Is that what you had in mind?'

Ruth hesitated. Somehow she didn't think The Crossbows qualified. 'Look,' she said, 'let me pay for this and you can take me for a pub lunch tomorrow. I'd like that.'

Their faces brightened slightly. 'Are you absolutely sure?' asked Kate.

'Of course I am. Besides . . .'

'Besides what?' asked Martin.

'I've sort of promised to give a friend a lift somewhere on the way. That won't be too much of a problem, will it?'

'Why should it be?' asked Kate.

'Ummm . . .' said Ruth. 'Well, if you two are okay I'll just give Lollo her tea. We need to leave about seven-thirty. The water's hot if either of you wants a bath.'

'We can have one together,' said Kate.

'Oh. Right,' said Ruth and retreated to the kitchen feeling a thousand years old.

'Where exactly are we picking up your friend?' asked Martin, as they circled the library for the third time.

'Ummm . . .' said Ruth. 'Oh, there she is.'

Emerging from the shadows like some Gothic emissary came Gwen, a long navy raincoat over whatever she had finally settled on to stir the fires of Henry's passion.

Ruth slid to a halt and Gwen scurried forward, one hand clutching a flat cardboard box, the other grappling with the door handle. Kate reached across and opened it for her. Gwen leapt back. 'You've got passengers,' she wailed.

Ruth nodded. 'This is my son, Martin, and Kate. We're going to try The Crossbows. I thought we could drop you off on the way.'

'Oh.' Gwen seemed undecided whether to continue with the operation. 'Do they? . . . Have you? . . .'

'I told them we had to give you a lift, Gwen,' said Ruth as patiently as she could. They were already in danger of losing their table.

• Sarah Grazebrook

'Oh. Right. Thank you.' Gwen squeezed herself into the back beside Kate, clutching her cooling pizza like the secret of eternal life.

Kate held out a hand. 'Hullo. I'm Kate.'

'I'm Gwen,' Gwen responded jerkily. 'I'm a friend of Martin's mother.'

'Washes No Socks,' Kate murmured to herself.

'Kate's at university with Martin,' Ruth broke in quickly.

'How lovely,' said Gwen as though she had announced the ending of the world.

'Here we are.' They swung round the corner of the road and came to a stop outside a large house divided into flats. The place looked ominously dark. 'Are you sure you'll be all right, Gwen?' Ruth asked anxiously. 'Do you want us to wait a few minutes?'

'Oh, no. Thank you. Please don't wait. Everything will be fine. I'm just a little . . . You know how it is.'

If there was one thing Ruth didn't know, it was how it felt to descend on the man who had thrown you out, clad only in a mackintosh and cycling shorts and clasping a tepid pizza. She tried to sound suitably empathetic. 'Good luck.' Gwen gave a brave little hiccup and let herself out of the car. The wind caught in her raincoat and blew it upwards.

'I don't think your friend's got anything on under that,' said Martin, fixing his mother with an inquisitor's eye. 'Exactly what is going on, Mother?'

Ruth laughed awkwardly. 'It's a bit complicated. Not at all what you think.'

'What do I think?'

'Well, I don't know. That she, Gwen, that is, is . . . well, you know.'

'Completely mad?' suggested Kate from the back.

'Oh, she's definitely that,' said Ruth, 'but not . . . you know . . . well . . .'

'On the game,' said Martin.

'Well, she isn't. It's nothing like that.'

'You don't have to tell us if you don't want to,' said Kate kindly.

'Yes she does,' said Martin.

'It's not what you think,' Ruth repeated feebly.

'Tell us what it is and then we'll tell you if it's what we think or not,' Martin persisted remorselessly.

Ruth sighed. 'It's nothing to do with me. I met Gwen at your Auntie Joy's.'

'That figures,' Martin grunted.

'Don't interrupt. She's living in their basement at the moment, because she's split up with her boyfriend. He's apparently thrown her out of the flat – the one back there where we dropped her, and she thinks she can get him back by turning up on him unexpectedly, in her sexiest underwear and pretending to be a Takeaway Pizza courier.'

A noise like a motor horn came from the back seat where Kate had dissolved into hysterics.

'Like a Stripogram?' asked Martin. 'But what's she going to do with the pizza?'

'Don't ask,' whinnied Kate. 'And whatever it is, I'm NOT, so you can get that clear right away.'

'I think they were just going to eat it,' said Ruth weakly, 'but that's not the end of it. Today being the twenty-ninth of February she plans to propose to this wretched Henry. She seems to think shock tactics work best on him. Anyway, now it turns out he's got a wife, although Gwen thinks she may have gone back to Birmingham or something. The whole thing really does seem to me to be fraught with peril.'

'How did you get involved in all this, Mum?' demanded Martin. 'I thought you'd come down here to get away from it all.'

'So did I,' Ruth moaned. 'I'd've been better off in the Balkans. Gwen asked if I could drive her there tonight, that's all. She thought Henry might be suspicious if she turned up on foot.'

'I wish you'd said,' said Martin, 'I could have painted "PAGE'S PIZZA PALACE" all over the car.'

Kate mopped her eyes. 'It's better than being bored, though, isn't it?'

Ruth reserved her judgement.

'This is very posh,' Kate remarked as two youths rushed forward and offered to park Ruth's car for her. She declined and the youths retreated, looking relieved. Metros were not the sort of cars people usually came to The Crossbows in.

'What on earth made you choose this place, Mum?' asked Martin, handing his bomber jacket to a man in a dress suit.

'I didn't know it was like this,' Ruth replied, casting a look at the assembled diners. It was Joy's cocktail party, times four. The women wore puffy sleeved evening dresses and even puffier hair, the men wheezed uncomfortably in dinner jackets.

'It's a bit OTT for a country pub, isn't it?' said Martin.

'I think it's lovely,' said Kate, swirling her skirt.

'Do you have a booking, Madam?' asked a thin man with a moustache.

'Yes. Page. Mrs Page. For eight o'clock. Three of us.'

The man consulted his ledger and nodded very slightly. 'If you'd like to come this way.' He threaded his way between the tables to a far corner of the dining room where, once seated, they were surrounded by the wine waiter, a waitress and a very young girl who was presumably being trained, from the look of abject terror on her face.

'Grief, Mum. Have you seen the prices?' hissed Martin. Even Kate was looking a bit pale. Ruth smiled brightly and cursed Gwen Pritchard with all her soul.

'It's a treat,' she assured them. 'Don't worry about the cost. Please.'

Martin shrugged. 'Dad only took us to a pasta place, didn't he, Kate? Then he moaned about the price of the wine all evening.'

'He is an economist,' said Ruth crisply, annoyed that Martin had introduced Kate to Duncan before herself.

'We bumped into him after the Bjork concert,' Martin continued. 'I made him take us for a meal. He tried like mad to worm his way out of it, and then it was just a spaghetti. I think he only agreed so that Laureen could have four puds.'

He glanced at Ruth impishly and they all three burst out laughing.

'Well, have what you like tonight,' said Ruth. 'It's on your father.'

They had just ordered coffee when the young trainee, looking as though she had a gun to her head, came scurrying towards them. 'Mrs Page?' she asked in a terrified whisper.

'Yes?'

'There's a lady asking for you outside. She wanted to come over, but Mr Fletcher said best not.'

'A lady?'

'Yes, please.'

'Did she give you a name?'

'I don't think so, Madam. She's a bit all . . . wet.'

'Wet?' Ruth repeated, immediately thinking of Lollo. 'You did let the bath water out, didn't you, Martin?'

'What's that got to do with it?' asked her son, wondering if he should offer to drive them home.

'Only, if you could come, Madam,' pleaded the girl.

'Yes, of course,' said Ruth. 'You two stay here. I won't be a moment.'

She followed the girl.

Gwen sat in the foyer, guarded by the two parking attendants, raincoat draped indecorously over her thighs, hands drooping between her knees, the very picture of 'prostitute apprehended', as Ruth could not help thinking.

She hurried over to her. 'Gwen . . . Is everything all right?'

Even through three glasses of wine this struck Ruth as one of the silliest things she had ever said.

Gwen raised tear-soaked eyes to her. 'Oh, Ruth,' she sobbed, and buried her face in her hands. The attendants shifted uneasily and stared out of the front entrance. The young waitress stood transfixed, gaping unashamedly at the spectacle.

'Do you have somewhere quiet we could take this lady?' Ruth requested briskly. The girl gazed at her hopelessly. 'I don't know, Madam.'

'Could you ask?' Ruth commanded. 'Immediately.'

The girl pattered away, to return shortly with a fierce blonde woman in black. 'My friend's feeling a little unwell,' Ruth began.

'Certainly, Madam,' said the woman who clearly felt as unhappy about Gwen's presence as Ruth. She led them behind Reception and along a corridor where she unlocked the door to the Conference Room and ushered them in.

Ruth turned to her. 'My son and his girlfriend may be looking for me.'

• Sarah Grazebrook

'I'll tell them,' said the woman and left.

'Now, Gwen, what happened?' said Ruth, trying to sound sympathetic and practical at the same time.

Gwen swung dramatically round and covered her face once more.

'Take your time,' said Ruth, wishing she'd had her coffee. Gwen clearly took this as carte blanche to perform two more circuits of the table, sighing and shuddering, and periodically stopping to gaze out of the deep arched windows bordering the drive.

'Would you like a glass of water?' said Ruth to remind her that she was still waiting.

Gwen turned. 'What? Oh . . . Yes, please. I don't think I could drink it. It would make me choke.'

Ruth resisted the urge to force one on her. 'Sit down, Gwen. And tell me what happened. Unless you'd rather not . . . ?'

This had the usual effect of opening the flood gates of Gwen's confidences. 'Oh, Ruth, it was so terrible. So terrible.'

Ruth waited.

'I went up the stairs to the flat. My heart was in my mouth, as you can imagine, but I was absolutely resolved to go through with it. Is that your son's girlfriend, by the way, that was in the car?'

'Yes,' said Ruth, thrown. 'I suppose she is.'

'She looks far too old for him,' sniffed Gwen. That's rich, thought Ruth, coming from you. 'But anyway, I rang the bell. There were no lights on or anything, so I rang and rang. And then I heard footsteps.' She stopped to blow her nose.

'And?' Ruth prompted.

'It was the man from up above. He'd heard me ringing, you see, and came to see what was going on. When he saw me he said, "Oh, it's you, is it?" which I thought was so terribly kind, and so I said, "Yes. Just me." And then he went back into his flat.' She paused to allow Ruth to take in the significance of the exchange.

'And what happened then?' repeated Ruth, seeing none.

'Well, I rang a few more times, then I remembered I had a key, so I thought "perhaps he's just popped out for a few minutes", and I had this brilliant idea to let myself in, put the oven on very low.'

'Gwen, you didn't plan to . . .' Ruth exclaimed, thinking that even a low oven in Gwen's case could well have proved fatal.

'Yes, yes. Warm the pizza up. Because remember, I'd been waiting on the corner for ten minutes before you came to collect me.'

This struck Ruth as grossly unfair but it did not seem the moment to protest. 'So you let yourself into the flat, Gwen. What happened next?'

Gwen screwed her eyes tight shut and clenched her fists at the memory. Henry in flagrante with his wife seemed the most likely scenario. 'He wasn't there,' she mumbled.

'What?' said Ruth sharply.

'He wasn't there.'

'He'd popped out?'

Gwen shook her head and bit her lip savagely. 'All his things had gone. His clothes, his CDs, everything. His shaving mug. Oh it was so terrible, Ruth. You can't imagine. I wanted to die.'

Ruth waited a moment to let Gwen compose herself. 'So what did you do, Gwen?' she asked quietly.

Gwen took a breath. 'Well, I ate the pizza. Most of it. I didn't bother to heat it up. I just ate it cold.'

'And then?'

'Then I looked around, just to make sure he hadn't left anything. A note, or something, but there was nothing. Oh, Ruth, my poor flat. All my things gone, and now all Henry's gone as well. It looked so . . . well, lonely. Do you know what I mean?'

Ruth nodded obligingly, trying to imagine what a lonely flat looked like. All she could think of was how lucky Gwen was to have got rid of the cad so easily, although her feelings were spiced with some sympathy for any man who got himself involved with Gwen. She really was an exhausting woman.

'So then I thought the best thing I could do was come straight here.'

Why? sprang to mind. 'How did you get here, Gwen?'

'In a taxi.'

'Is it still waiting?'

'No, he wouldn't wait, although I begged and begged.'

'Would you like a lift home?'

• Sarah Grazebrook

'Could I? That would be so fearfully kind of you. If it's no trouble.'

'Not at all,' sighed Ruth, 'trouble' being relative.

There was a tap on the door and Kate popped her head round it. 'We wondered if you were all right,' she said.

'Yes, come in, Kate. Gwen's feeling much better now.' Gwen eyed Kate suspiciously but brightened noticeably when Martin appeared. 'You must think me the most frightful nuisance,' she murmured coquettishly, tossing her wild curls and hugging her raincoat to her.

'That's all right,' muttered Martin, staring fixedly at a point on the table.

'We're going to give Gwen a lift home,' said Ruth blandly. 'I'll just go and sort out the bill.'

'I feel so foolish,' said Gwen again as they drove up the lane to Harbinger House. 'I expect Martin thinks I'm a neurotic woman, don't you, Martin?'

'I wouldn't know,' said Martin sulkily. He was plainly unsettled by Gwen's unabated flirtatiousness. Kate, on the other hand, seemed unperturbed.

'I'll let you out here,' said Ruth. She had no wish to bump into Joy and have to undergo a further interrogation.

'Funny friends you have, Mum,' said Martin pointedly when Gwen had tiptoed off down the steps to her flat.

Ruth shook her head. 'I'm so sorry about that.'

'You didn't even get your coffee,' said Kate, who plainly thought that the worst part of it. 'I saved you your chocolate.'

'What happened to mine?' asked Martin suddenly.

'I ate it. I did it for your own good.'

'Well, if you're so worried about my own good, how come you made me sit in the back with that sex maniac?'

Both women turned to look at him. 'I don't think you can call Gwen that, darling,' Ruth reproved him. 'She doesn't always dress like that. And it was a rather special occasion.'

'What did she do? Offer you a peek at her pizza?' Kate enquired cheerfully.

'And the rest,' said Martin crossly. 'She kept rubbing her foot against my leg.' He sounded so offended that both the women burst out laughing. 'I don't see what's so funny,' he complained. 'If I'd done it to her I'd've been done for sexual harassment.'

'Well, I wouldn't try charging Gwen. She's got enough problems as it is,' Ruth coaxed. 'She was just a bit het up. I'm sure she didn't mean anything.'

'She'd better not have,' said Martin aggressively. 'I'm not into cycling shorts and dirty macs.'

'Aren't you?' asked Kate ingenuously. 'What on earth am I going to wear tomorrow?'

When they got home Ruth found the brandy and Martin's good humour returned. Gwen is the end, she thought as she took Lollo for a late night stroll. Poor Martin, he's led a very sheltered life. She really put the wind up him. Still Kate will sort him out. He's a lucky boy.

'Come on, Drives Everybody Mad,' she called to Lollo who, as if to prove the truth of this, took no notice at all.

13

The training course for Fawcett Research Services was less harrowing than Ruth had feared. No mention was made of syphoning blood and urine from the passers-by, rather the emphasis was on how to distinguish a badly-dressed lawyer from a well-dressed tramp and, having done so, how to persuade them to sample plain-wrapped products of varying degrees of nastiness.

There were two other trainees with Ruth, an enormous woman with home-bleached hair called Mel, and a silver-quiffed man of about fifty who introduced himself as 'Vince – No, not THAT one'.

Ruth, who had no idea to which 'THAT one' he referred, smiled politely and helped herself to coffee.

Rowena was late and arrived looking slightly less *soignée* than previously. She soon regained her calm, however, and spent a lively morning fending off fatuous questions from Vince and trying to explain to Mel why bookmakers, barrowboys and butchers were not necessarily examples of Group B in terms of social grading. Mel took this in good part, going on to cite Canadians for Group C and doberman pinchers for D.

Vince, apparently, had done all this before so interspersed Rowena's patient explanations with heavy sighs and much rolling of his eyes upwards.

Ruth found the instructions simple enough to follow, her only fear being that she would lack the nerve to speak to anyone in the first place, but the constant reminder that she could earn up to thirty pounds a day was more or less sufficient to quell her doubts.

• Sarah Grazebrook

Rowena said that after lunch they would go into the city centre and try a few dummies. Mel raised her hand and asked how they would know if the people were dummies or not, at which point Ruth was afflicted with a fit of coughing and Rowena suggested it might be time to order the sandwiches.

Vince hogged most of these, at the same time regaling them with tales of his previous successes as a naval commander, a wine taster, a buyer for Harrods and the chief mechanic for the Williams' Formula One racing team.

Ruth forbore from asking him what exactly had attracted him to market research but was, nonetheless, treated to a fulsome explanation.

'I'm a People Person, you see. Can't get enough of them. They seem to warm to me, if you get what I mean. Not sure why. Just something in the old chemical makeup I suppose. Not everyone's got it.' He cast a meaningful look at Mel who was eating an enormous Danish pastry she had fished from the bottom of her bag. Rowena sat to one side ogling it wistfully.

Ruth took her plate and sat down by her.

'How long have you been working for Fawcett?' she asked.

Rowena dragged her eyes away from the pastry. 'Oh, about three years now, I think. I started off as an interviewer, then when our area supervisor left they asked me if I'd like to take over.'

'You must have been awfully good,' Ruth remarked, 'for them to put you in charge so soon.'

Rowena laughed a trifle forlornly. 'I think it was more a case of "needs must". There weren't that many candidates for the job.'

'Why not?'

Rowena shrugged. 'Long hours. Not much money. There's an awful lot of paperwork involved. A lot of people can't spare the time. You know, people with families.' Her voice trailed away. Ruth sought to change the subject.

'Madge Jordan's nice, isn't she?' she said brightly. 'To be honest, I was a little bit nervous about meeting her at first. Grace Forland had made her sound like an ogre.'

Rowena laughed. 'Well she is rather, isn't she? But a nice one, you're right.' Her face became serious. 'She's been a good friend to me. She and Bill. I expect you know him?'

'A bit,' Ruth demurred.

Rowena sighed. 'Everyone knows everyone in Westbridge. And everything about them, which is worse.' She looked at her watch. 'I think perhaps we'd better make a start if everyone's finished?'

They set off, Mel eating a Mars Bar and Vince prancing ahead in a dayglo waistcoat. His chemical makeup did not seem to be working too well for him that afternoon, or perhaps it was his habit of calling the men 'squire' and the women 'my good woman' that accounted for the flurry of refusals he was getting.

They had been given a very simple questionnaire to try out. Even Mel seemed to have got the hang of it at last, although Rowena did have to have a discreet word with her about the difference between a confident approach and a physical assault.

Ruth did all right. Her initial nervousness wore off once the first interview was over. If anything it all seemed too painfully simple. Surely no one got paid for asking people whether they ever bought a Sunday newspaper? Her confidence was marginally shaken by a drunk who followed her into the cathedral precincts demanding to know what colour knickers she was wearing but, as she reflected, he would probably have done that anyway and she really shouldn't blame it on market research.

Arriving home she found a lemon yellow envelope sitting in solitary splendour at the bottom of the wire basket she had fitted over the letter box.

It was from Gwen thanking her for being a true friend and outlining her intention of buying Henry out of his share of the flat and selling it, because it was now a place 'so full of sorrowful memories' for her.

Setting aside the mush, Ruth was relieved that Gwen had adopted so pragmatic an approach and almost felt tempted to ring her and say as much. The call would have to be channeled through Joy, however, so she decided instead to drop Gwen a line endorsing her plan and wishing her the very best for the future.

This had an enticingly final air about it, though she doubted that Gwen would take the hint.

• Sarah Grazebrook

After supper she studied her market research notes. They made no sense at all to her. She wondered how she had ever thought she could cope but, alongside Gwen's note, had come a bill from her book club reminding her that there were fifteen pounds outstanding from her last order and respectfully requesting that a cheque be forwarded straightaway. I must cope, she told herself. I must make some money.

Lollo was in a bad mood and lay chewing menacingly on what remained of her slipper. Ruth reflected that it was just as well she didn't know she would be out all day the next day as well. It did seem a bit rotten to keep leaving the poor thing on her own. She sighed. I'm doing it for her, she told herself.

The phone rang. It was Joy. 'Ruth, dear, how are you?'

'Fine, thank you, Joy.'

'Only we hadn't heard from you for so long we thought perhaps you were dead.'

Ruth bristled slightly at the implied criticism. 'I've been quite busy, actually, Joy. You know how it is.'

'Do I ever? In fact that's why I rang. I've found something for you to do.'

Ruth wondered briefly if Joy ever took in what anyone ever said to her. She waited. 'I'm sending you to a class.'

'A what?' she stuttered, completely thrown.

'A class. A writing class. Oh, you needn't worry. You don't have to be any good. None of them are. That's why I'm sending you. But we need a script. God knows I've tried everything else. Even got Chrissie to pen a few lines but, bless him, he's so steeped in legal jargon. It was all full of "heretofores" and "whomsoevers" and the like. Marvellous stuff, but you'd never get the meaning across to the hoi polloi, would you? That's why I thought you'd be good. I mean, you went to university so obviously you can spell, but you've got what I'd call a simple mind, and that's what we need.'

'I'm afraid you've lost me, Joy,' said Ruth, her face hot with annoyance, 'only having a simple mind.'

Joy tinkled with laughter. 'Oh, I didn't mean it like that. You're so amusing, Ruth, when you want to be. By the way, have you seen anything of Adrian? He couldn't stop talking about you the other evening. He's obviously very smitten.'

'What rubbish,' said Ruth brusquely. 'He's hardly spoken two words to me, and they were all about his stomach.'

'The way to a man's heart . . .' said Joy, in a silly voice.

'I've met his wife,' Ruth broke in, to forestall any further discussion. 'She's very nice.'

'Rowena?' said Joy curtly. 'I'm surprised you think that. Mind you, we all thought she was okay to start with.'

'I'm hoping to do some work for her,' persisted Ruth. 'Market research. In fact I'm on a course at the moment.'

If this was meant to deter Joy from her plan it signally failed. 'Well, there you are. You must be bored witless if you've been reduced to that. No, this writing lark can be quite fun, Gwen tells me. She's on it so you'll have someone to talk to.'

Ruth contemplated hitting her head against the wall. 'Why don't you get Gwen to write your pageant for you, then? She could certainly do with some distraction at the moment.'

'Oh, you've heard?' said Joy indifferently. 'Well, it was bound to happen. He was heaps younger than her. And then when the mother turned up . . . At least we'll be able to get her out of the basement now. I've never heard of anything so ridiculous. What did she think would happen, for heaven's sake. You can't go cradle snatching and expect to get away with it.'

Ruth shook the phone to make sure she had heard correctly. 'I'm sorry, Joy. I thought . . . that is, Gwen told me this Henry was only a year younger than her.' Joy bubbled with laughter. 'And that it was his wife who turned up, and now he's gone back to join her. In Birmingham.'

'Well, that's a new version. These writing classes are obviously working for Gwen. You must definitely enrol. No, Gwen picked up Henry, who is nineteen or thereabouts, by the way, installed him in her flat, proceeded to drive him mad and then, when he threatened to leave, came rushing over to us with tales of a carving knife and the rest.'

'Henry threatened her with a carving knife?' asked Ruth, forgetting how justified she had thought it the other night. Joy laughed. 'I doubt it. Henry was the type who liked his food cut up for him. That's why Gwen was so useful, I suppose. Anyway, as soon as she'd up and run, he was obviously on the phone to Mummy because Grace Forland saw the two of them

• Sarah Grazebrook

at the station last week. All packed up and ready to go. Mummy carrying the luggage, of course.'

'But what about the joint mortgage?'

'What joint mortgage?'

'The one Gwen's got with Henry.'

This time Joy was silent. 'She really has been spinning you a yarn, hasn't she? Gwen inherited that flat from her grandmother. She owns it. That's why it was so annoying having her camped out with us. I knew it wouldn't last, otherwise I'd've turfed her out ages ago. Still at least I got my curtains done. Anyway, I'll sort out with her about the writing class. I think it's a Tuesday, down at the high school. You'll love it. It'll take you out of yourself.'

'Joy,' murmured Ruth, still reeling from what she had heard, 'I really don't think . . .'

'Just a basic outline. Julius Caesar through to the Channel Tunnel. Keep it simple, that's the secret. No rhyming couplets. We don't want it sounding like a limerick contest. About twelve scenes, a couple of minutes each. Shouldn't be too hard.'

'It sounds impossible, not hard,' Ruth argued hopelessly.

'Rubbish. It's a doddle. Just think yourself lucky I haven't put you on costumes.'

As Ruth took Lollo for her late night wander she wondered how she was going to retain her sanity.

The second day of Ruth's course consisted of more practice interviews, preceded by a discussion of the different types of survey carried out by the company.

Mel was still having trouble with her Social Grading, having been exceedingly sharp with a cleaner whom she had optimistically graded 'A' on the assumption that everyone who worked in a hospital must be a consultant.

'You said "forty-five to fifty-four",' Ruth heard her berating Rowena as she was led away from a party of Japanese tourists queuing to see the cathedral.

'Yes, that was the age group I wanted, Mel. Not the number of people in the party.'

'Daft if you ask me. Time for a bun?'

By the end of the morning Ruth was wondering why Rowena had ever worried about being overweight. The sheer strain of a morning with Vince and Mel would be enough to shift ten pounds from the average person.

Vince had got into a row with a traffic warden whom he had accused of being a government lackey when the man refused to be questioned about his drinking habits.

A small crowd had gathered and the situation had only been eased by the arrival of a foreign coach which the warden felt duty-bound to shout at. Rowena took the opportunity to summon them all back to the hotel for a résumé.

They had lost Mel, who turned up twenty minutes later with a bag of shopping and two pairs of new shoes, at which point Rowena resorted silently to the Ladies.

After lunch they went over what they had learnt – very little in Mel's case, and nothing at all in Vince's, if their comments were to be believed.

Rowena closed the session at a quarter past three, loading them with notes and reminders and promising to get in touch as soon as suitable work became available in their area.

If Lollo had been disgruntled by Ruth's absence the day before, she was downright livid by Thursday's. The telephone had been displaced. A letter from Ruth's solicitor enclosing a bill for downgrading her maintenance had been savagely gnawed through the mesh. Her raincoat had been dragged from its peg by the back door and scrunched into a heap under the table, and the bowl of dog biscuits had been distributed throughout the house like clues in a treasure hunt.

'You've made an awful mess,' Ruth complained as the dog rushed past her into the back garden, returning minutes later covered in mud which she shook all over the kitchen floor. 'That is very mean of you,' said Ruth, struggling to grab her before she could further desecrate the house. 'Gosh, you're getting fat, Lollo.' She couldn't think why it should be. The dog presumably got more exercise now than she had with the Taylors, even allowing for days like this. And she had cut out half the stupid vitamin supplements in favour of real food. Oh well, she had done her best. A couple of weeks of market research and she'd have enough to put her back where she belonged. Then her life would be her own at last.

• Sarah Grazebrook

As if to disprove her theory, Joy rang on the dot of six to say that she had arranged for Gwen to meet her at a quarter to seven on Tuesday evening at the entrance to the high school so that she could enrol for Creative Writing.

'I haven't said I will, Joy,' said Ruth, feeling rather more belligerent than usual in view of her newly acquired skills.

There was a pause. 'Ruth, dear, please don't let me down over this.' A plaintive note crept into Joy's voice. 'I sometimes think there's no one left I can depend on.'

That's because you depend on them for such unreasonable things, thought Ruth. She sighed. 'I tell you what, Joy. I'll go once and give it a try, but I am not promising anything beyond that.'

Triumph oozed from Joy's voice. 'No, of course not, Ruth, dear. No one would dream of asking you to. Just give it a try, that's all I'm asking. After all, it is for the community. Otherwise I wouldn't ask.'

Ruth put the phone down, aware that she was being succoured. Still, one night wasn't going to wreck her whole life.

Madge Jordan listened, blank-faced, while Ruth told her about the course. 'They've got some big soup job coming up. Five days, at least, Rowena said. That would be,' Ruth calculated, 'well, at least a hundred and thirty pounds after tax. That would keep Lollo in the kennels for . . .' Their eyes met. 'Four days,' said Ruth dejectedly. 'Oh, God, Madge. Isn't it ridiculous? Here's me, working five days in order to board someone else's dog for four. I'm beginning to think I should ask Duncan to come back to me.'

'Too late for that,' said Madge brusquely. 'Anyway that's the last thing you want, just when you're beginning to find your feet.'

'Some feet,' said Ruth gloomily. 'The only thing I seem to be able to do with them is thrust them down my throat.'

Madge snorted with laughter. 'You'll be all right. Stop feeling sorry for yourself and make us a cup of coffee. You sound like one of your sister-in-law's orphans.'

Ruth smiled forlornly. 'I'm not that bad, am I?'

Madge shrugged. 'Not yet. But you want to watch it. She's got a lot of scalps hanging from her belt. They all started out as normal human beings.'

Ruth laughed. 'I take it you were a candidate?'

Madge nodded grimly. 'I certainly was. So was young Bill, though for possibly different reasons.'

Ruth stared at her. 'You're surely not suggesting Joy had her eyes on Bill Bartholomew?'

Madge shrugged. 'Only from the purest intentions, I'm sure. I think she rather saw him as Lancelot to her husband's Arthur.'

'There's nothing all that pure about that,' Ruth reminded her.

'Well, you know what I mean. Joy Blakeney always strikes me as the sort of woman who prefers to do her courting in public.'

Ruth nodded. 'I think I understand. I'm sure she'd never cheat on Christopher. She's furious with Duncan for the way he's treated me. And he's her own brother.'

Madge reached into a rubbish sack and pulled out a packet of bourbon creams. 'Just wait till you cheat on him,' she said.

On Monday morning Rowena Mills telephoned to say that she had had the details of the soup survey and she would be very grateful if Ruth could be available to do some work on it.

'How much work?' asked Ruth hopefully. She had received her Visa bill that morning and was already regretting she had not let Kate and Martin take her for a Chinese meal as planned. Particularly since, if they had, they might all have avoided the spectacle of Gwen dripping across the foyer of The Crossbows in quite such public display.

'Five days initially,' said Rowena. 'It's a total of twenty interviews, plus recalls.'

'When does it start?'

'Friday. It might involve a bit of weekend and evening work. Sometimes that's the only time you can find people in. Would that be a problem?'

'I can't think why it should be.'

'Fine. It's just some people have such a hectic social life they can't fit it in.'

'Oh,' said Ruth dejectedly. 'Do they?'

'I'll pop this in the post to you, then, shall I? It's all local work. I'll come out with you on the first day to make sure you're okay.'

- Sarah Grazebrook

'Thank you,' said Ruth, thinking she should make the most of what was likely to be the highlight of her social calendar.

Gwen Pritchard telephoned later in the day to say that Joy had told her how keen Ruth was to join the Creative Writing class and how excited she herself felt to have been asked to take her under her wing.

Ruth held the phone away from her ear in an effort to quell the pitch of Gwen's enthusiasm. 'I'll see you at a quarter to seven, then,' Gwen finished, when she had explained that Ruth mustn't be even the teeniest bit nervous because everyone was terribly friendly and encouraging and their teacher was the most marvellous man who ever lived, and terribly talented, and really it was a wonder that he could find the time to pass on his knowledge to, let's face it, a bunch of amateurs, not that some of them weren't terribly talented too. All of them, really, in their way. [Except, of course, herself, who was quite quite useless, and really she didn't know how they put up with her, but there it was.]

'He's the one I was hoping might help with the pageant script,' she added confidentially, 'but sadly he's too busy. I thought he would be.'

'A quarter to seven,' Ruth sighed, wishing she had the courage to renegue on promises the way Duncan and Joy did.

14

Gwen was waiting just behind the concrete post that marked the entrance to Westbridge County High School. Ruth's heart gave a sickening jerk as she recognised the raincoat and more or less identical flanking movement that had heralded the start of the Leap Year escapade. She hoped to God Gwen had something more on underneath it tonight.

Her pulse slowed somewhat as she noted the familiar dirndl skirt poking out beneath it as they made their way towards the office for Registration.

'My friend here would like to enrol for Creative Writing,' Gwen told the secretary, as though Ruth spoke no English. The woman nodded and hunted for a form.

'It's only for one week,' Ruth interjected. 'I just want to see what it's like.'

The woman paused in her search. 'I'm afraid I can't enrol you for less than a term. It would be pro rata because you've missed three weeks, but you'll still have to pay for the remaining six.'

'How much would that be?' asked Ruth aghast.

The woman calculated. 'Twenty-six pounds thirty, unless you're unemployed.'

'How much would that be?'

'Seven pounds fifty.'

'I am unemployed.'

'Right. Could I just see your UB 40?'

'My what?' stammered Ruth.

'Your UB 40. Your card, for when you're signing on.'

'I'm not signing on,' said Ruth in confusion.

The woman sighed. 'You're not unemployed then, are you?'

• Sarah Grazebrook

'I am,' Ruth persevered. 'I haven't got a job, so I must be unemployed.'

'Not so far as the KCC is concerned. Do you want to enrol, or not?'

'Yes,' said Gwen quickly, before Ruth could refuse. 'She does. Oh, please, Ruth. It is for the town, remember. Joy said I absolutely wasn't to let you back out, whatever happened.'

'In that case she can pay for my classes,' snapped Ruth, aware that a queue was forming behind her. Gwen's eyes became huge and moist as she fumbled in her canvas bag. 'I'll pay for my friend,' she said to the secretary, who shrugged and began to fill in the form.

'Of course you won't, Gwen,' said Ruth through her teeth. 'I never intended anything of the kind. It was a joke.' Bitterly she extracted her cheque book. The last thing she wanted was to be financially indebted to Gwen Pritchard.

And the second last was to be sat in a room full of people intent on unburdening their literary angst for two hours every Tuesday till Easter, she thought morosely as Gwen led her in the direction of Room G.

'This is Ruth. She's new,' she told anyone who would listen. There were about a dozen people present. Several well into retirement, a few around her own age, and two – a man and a woman – who looked extremely young and frighteningly angry. They were seated next to each other, staring grimly at the blackboard on which was inscribed a map of Italy and some facts about its economic development since the war.

Ruth couldn't see why it should annoy them so greatly.

'This is Reg,' said Gwen, tapping a bald-headed man on the arm. 'He's writing the most brilliant science-fiction novel, aren't you, Reg?'

Reg shrugged modestly. 'Not too bad, though I say it myself,' he said. Ruth smiled politely.

'Is Jimmy coming this week?' asked Gwen.

Reg's mouth curled downwards peevishly. 'I hope not,' he said and returned to his notebook.

Gwen introduced Ruth to two elderly women hugging the radiators. 'Gay and Mona, I'd like you to meet Ruth.'

Gay and Mona smiled benignly and asked what sort of thing

she wrote. 'Letters, mostly, I suppose,' Ruth answered.

They chortled deliriously. 'Letters, mostly. That's very good. I expect you're going to be one of our comedians, dear, aren't you?' said Mona. 'We always like to have some funny people in the class. There's young Tanya, there,' she jerked her head in the direction of the scowling young female. 'She's hilarious. And so clever.'

'So clever,' echoed Gay.

'You finished that poem yet, Gwennie?' asked a skinny man with sticking up hair. He twitched so alarmingly when he spoke that Ruth was surprised he stayed on his chair.

'Not quite,' said Gwen, dipping her eyes. 'I'm having trouble with my ending.'

'Just keep taking the tablets,' said a man in a brown suit who had a laptop computer in front of him. Gwen giggled. 'You're awful, Tony.'

'But I like you,' said the man in a camp voice, which made Gwen giggle all the more.

'This is Ruth,' she told him.

'Quilp. Tony Quilp,' said the man. 'Can we come and sit next to you today, Tony?' asked Gwen. 'I don't expect Ruth wants to be at the front on her first evening, do you, Ruth?'

'No,' said Ruth. 'Not in the least.'

They settled themselves down, Tony continuing to make puns in a monotone voice till a woman behind him with long dark hair and an Alice band asked him to be quiet so that she could concentrate. 'Pardon me for breathing,' said Tony and put his finger on his lips.

'Late again,' said Reg, swinging his arm up to look at his watch.

'Stop complaining,' snarled Tanya. Reg polished his glasses peevishly.

Ruth had been trying to work out, by dint of surreptitious glances, whom amongst those present might be recruited to fill her soup quota when the door swung open to reveal their class tutor.

'Sorry I'm late, everyone. Some idiot's parked their car right across my short cut.'

Ruth put her head in her hands.

• Sarah Grazebrook

Bill Bartholomew flung down his jacket, unloaded a pile of papers on to the desk, rubbed the map of Italy off the board and settled down to teach the class.

'I'd like you all to write down the first thing that comes into your minds,' said Bill, searching vigorously among his belongings for a packet of sandwiches which he proceeded to eat while flinging carefully compiled folders at the heads of most of those present.

'Ow,' whimpered the twitcher as his body projected itself into the flight path of a particularly hefty missile.

'Sorry, Karl,' said Bartholomew. 'Can you give it to Heather? Too many adverbs again, Heather. Try writing without any at all.'

'It wouldn't be the same without adverbs,' wailed the woman with the Alice band.

'Precisely,' said her teacher. 'And Karl would still have his left ear. Reg—'

Reg perked up. 'Yes, Oh Mighty One?'

Bill threw Reg's offering with particular venom. 'What did I say last week?'

'Never say "the earth moved" in science fiction,' Reg murmured guiltily.

'Precisely.'

Ruth noticed that Bartholomew was softer on the women than the men. Perhaps this was his harem, she thought, casting a sceptical eye round the room. Tanya was too young, and far too cross – angry, she corrected herself. Surely Mona and Gay were a bit old, although they certainly looked extremely game in their identical mauve blouses and crimplene slacks? Heather looked as though she would run any man through who threatened her with so much as a cup of coffee, and Gwen – well, Gwen was obviously still pining for Henry.

'Okay,' said Bill, 'how are we doing? Karl, what was the first thing that came into your mind this evening?'

'My ear hurts,' said the twitcher sulkily.

'Brilliant.' Bartholomew turned to his blackboard and wrote 'ear hurts' in untidy letters right across it.

'Heather, what about you?'

Heather pursed her lips. 'Hedonism is dead,' she suggested.

'In a pig's ear,' smirked the Angry Young Man, doing horrible things to his fingernails.

Bartholomew turned to him. 'Okay, Neville. What have you got for us?'

'I haven't got anything yet. I'm not ready.'

'You mean you haven't had a single thought since you arrived?' asked Bill mildly.

'I've had a lot but none that this lot could cope with,' said Neville dismissively.

'Try them.'

'Vice is nice but incest's best,' said Neville.

Gay put her hand up. 'It's an anagram,' she said.

If Ruth had not got hiccups it is possible that she might have passed the whole class without the tutor noticing her. He certainly had a very cavalier attitude towards his register, which he completed without requiring anyone to acknowledge that they had actually turned up.

'What are you doing here?' he demanded, when the volume of her burps had assumed a level no one could ignore. 'Apart from making that noise?'

'I'm writing a pageant,' Ruth established, between eruptions.

'What about?'

'Westbridge.'

'A pageant about Westbridge?'

'Yes. And Julius Caesar. All that.'

Bill Bartholomew's eyes narrowed suspiciously. 'Do you know a woman called Joy Blakeney?'

'She's my sister-in-law.'

'You're prepared to admit to that, are you?'

Afflicted though she was, Ruth was not prepared to accept the public denigration of a relative by a man whose own credentials were so questionable.

'Why shouldn't I be?' she hicked haughtily. 'As I understand it, my sister-in-law has done a great deal for the community of Westbridge.'

'I agree,' said Bill. 'She's turned it into the plague centre of South East England. By the way, I hope you're planning to include a leper colony in your pageant. We wouldn't want you missing out the best bits.'

- Sarah Grazebrook

'I don't know what you're talking about,' Ruth retorted, relieved to find that her indignation had cured her hiccups.

'Ask little Gwennie,' said Bartholomew. 'Now, if you don't mind, I think we'd better get on with the lesson.'

'By all means,' said Ruth. 'I wasn't aware that it had started.'

There was a definite frisson in the air as Bill turned to ask Tanya what the first thing that had entered her mind that evening had been.

'I was wondering how it was possible for women in holy orders in Medieval Europe to "give" themselves to God, bearing in mind that "God" at that time was considered to be entirely masculine in essence, and whether in fact that very sacrifice of their womanhood was perhaps a subconscious desire to be subjugated by the male member, bearing in mind that "God" is often represented as holding a rod or staff.'

Bartholomew took a last bite of his sandwich and threw the crust in the bin. 'That's not a thought, that's a sermon,' he said.

Mona and Gay said they really couldn't think what their first thoughts had been, but Gay thought it was probably to wonder whether their bus home this week would be as late as it had been last week. Mona echoed this with uncanny precision, which clearly did not surprise their tutor in the least.

Tony said his first thought had been how lovely Gwen looked, accompanying his confession with what could best be described as a leer, and Gwen, whilst pretending to be utterly thrown by this announcement, managed to confess to a yearning reminiscence of her happiness as a young girl on the school trip to Tours when she had fallen in love with, and been tentatively kissed by the teenaged son of her host family.

Looking around the room Ruth could see no justification for this memory, but since it was rapidly topped by Reg who said his was whether the cosmos was female and if so, whether life as we knew it was not the result of a giant penetration by a universal prick. This sent Mona and Gay into spasms of giggling and managed to drag the corners of Heather's mouth even further towards her chin.

'That is certainly a thought,' said Bill Bartholomew with the sort of wonder usually reserved for the criminally insane. 'Mrs

Page, what have you written down as your first thought on joining my Creative Writing class?'

Ruth scanned her empty notepad, willing it to supply her with something suitable. Nothing came to mind.

'Oh come now,' said Bartholomew in the softest possible tones. 'I can't believe you came here with a completely empty mind.'

Their eyes met. 'I should like to think I came with an open mind,' said Ruth coolly.

'And nothing has entered it since?'

'Quite a few things have.'

'What was the first?'

Ruth cast a quick eye round the classroom. 'Hell is all around us,' she said authoritatively.

'Are you going to read us some more of your latest, Reg?' Gwen asked in the coffee break.

Reg shrugged. 'I doubt we'll get round to it if he continues at this rate,' he said sulkily.

The first half of the evening had been spent discussing last week's homework – a dialogue between an escaped convict and a schoolmistress whom he had taken hostage.

Ruth was amazed by the similarity between the various offerings, setting aside that Gay and Mona did theirs together and had managed to make both protagonists sound like two women at a Bring and Buy sale.

Neville's was riddled with swear words, which made sense for the convict, but not really for the schoolmistress who, he maintained, was the spinster head of a village primary.

Heather's had had a bit more drama to it. The convict had tied his victim to the end of the bed and then, having divested himself of his prison clothes, proceeded to quote large swathes of Milton to the unhappy woman, who could only manage a few miserable lines of Dante through the slit in her gag.

For someone so fond of epic poetry, Heather's voice was depressingly monotone. Bill finally called a halt just as the convict was about to compare himself to Lucifer for the fourth time.

'That's coming on fine, Heather. Now I want it back next week without the adverbs, okay. See what that does for it.' Heather

• Sarah Grazebrook

opened and shut her mouth several times, but they had moved on to Karl who had set his piece in the eighteenth century – a fact denoted by his use of 'thee' and 'thou'. Nobody seemed unsettled by his use of an air pistol to threaten his victim.

Tony appeared to have taken the exercise as an occasion to try out his latest batch of *Reader's Digest* jokes.

Tanya said she wasn't prepared to read hers out loud because nobody wanted to hear it. This piece of perspicacity raised her several notches in Ruth's estimation but the effect was immediately spoilt by several people crying in loud voices that they certainly did. Ruth noted that Heather kept her head well down during the protestations.

Tanya's creation was full of sex and violence, which doubtless accounted for Tony's desire to hear it and possibly Mona and Gay's, who giggled and squeaked excitedly at every new molestation.

Although Bill Bartholomew asked for comments at the end of every reading, very few were forthcoming. Ruth wondered if this was because they inspired no criticism or because the class operated a cartel, whereby no one would slaughter your own effort if you kept stumm about theirs.

Gwen, it was true, kept up a running stream of *brilliants* and *wonderfuls* under her breath, but these could hardly be construed as literary dissection.

Nor did it do her any good when it came to her own effort. She made the cardinal mistake of copying Tanya's approach, but because she was neither surly nor 'hilarious', and possibly because she had a less rigorous grasp of the four-letter word, no one opposed Gwen's plan to remain silent, and she was forced to fold up her homework and tuck it modestly back inside her bag without so much as an introduction.

Reg snapped that he had been too busy with 'the novel' to attempt the exercise. Bill said nothing but Ruth thought his eyes were surprisingly eloquent.

All this had brought them to the halfway point when they had adjourned into the school hall for coffee.

Mona and Gay came pattering over to join them. 'How are you finding it?' they questioned Ruth.

'It's . . . interesting,' said Ruth guardedly.

'Yes, isn't it?' they trilled. 'I expect you've got lots of ideas you want to write about, haven't you?'

'Not really,' said Ruth. 'Writing's not something I've given much thought to previously.'

Mona and Gay nudged each other. 'Isn't she funny?' they affirmed.

A bell sounded and the pupils drained their cups and hurried back to the classroom. Bill was screwing the top on a thermos flask as they came in. 'Oh, poor Mr Bartholomew,' said Mona. 'Drinking your coffee all by yourself.'

From the look on Bill's face it was the first piece of luck he'd had all evening. 'I'm going to give you next week's homework before we begin the second half,' he said. 'Mrs Page, I'd like you to attempt the exercise the others did last week, and the rest of you, I want a piece of dialogue between an immigration officer and a man who has broken his false teeth during the flight and can't find his passport. Okay? Any questions?' Heather raised her hand.

'Yes, Heather?'

'I have to say that I think the situation you have just described to us might possibly lead to unintentional humour.'

Bill scratched the skin between his eyebrows thoughtfully. 'You have a point there, Heather. Unintentional on your part, I'm sure it would be. I was rather hoping that one or two of the others might get some intentional humour into it.'

'But what would be the point of that?' asked Heather in some distress. 'We're not here to write jokes. We're here to become creative writers.'

'And humour has no part in creativity?' asked Bill.

'Well, it has a part, naturally. But not a very important one, surely? I mean look at *Paradise Lost*. You could hardly say that was full of humour, yet it's clearly one of the finest literary achievements in the English language.'

Bill nodded. 'And what about Bill Shakespeare? Where would you place him on a sliding scale?'

'Oh well, Shakespeare,' said Heather petulantly. 'You always cite him to prove your point.'

'Only because he does,' said Bill cheerfully. 'Anyone else got any objections to the homework?'

- Sarah Grazebrook

Ruth put up her hand. 'I won't be here next week.' Bill looked mildly surprised. 'Why not?'

'I've only come for one week.'

'What on earth for?'

Ruth felt slightly embarrassed. 'I promised my . . . Joy . . . Mrs Blakeney I would.'

Bill surveyed her critically. 'That sounds a fairly peculiar promise.'

'Oh you know what I mean,' flustered Ruth. 'She wanted me to come and learn to write a pageant, so I said I'd come for one evening. I didn't realise it was a course.'

Bill nodded slowly. 'So although some of my students here have been coming for seven years and still haven't perfected their first short story, you felt confident that after two hours, one hour forty, if you deduct the coffee break and registration, you are competent to sit down and recreate the entire vista of human history from the beginning of Time to the present day? I congratulate you. Perhaps you should be taking the class, not me?'

Ruth could feel herself blushing. 'That isn't what I meant and you know it,' she muttered crossly.

'My mistake,' said Bartholomew mildly. 'What did you mean?'

'Not that,' said Ruth.

'What then? Do you think that in the remaining,' he glanced at his watch, 'forty-five minutes your inspiration will be so absolute that you will achieve your aim without further tuition from me?'

'I meant,' snapped Ruth, goaded beyond belief, 'that I didn't want to come in the first place and I certainly don't want to come again.' There was an audible intake of breath around the class.

To her surprise and alarm, Bartholomew burst out laughing and clapped his hands together. 'Excellent. Well done, Mrs Page.' He turned to the others. 'That, as I'm sure you'll appreciate, was a superb example of how a simple dialogue between two total strangers can develop into a tension-packed encounter with a surprise ending. THAT is what I'm looking for in the exercises I'm giving you. NOT predictable little tête-à-têtes between a couple of cyphers. Life is not like that. Conversation is not like that. Different people have different brain patterns, different ideas, different reactions. Try and get some variety into your work. It doesn't matter how incongruous it may seem to you. Branch out. Experiment. Dare to be wrong. That's where creativity starts. In the unexpected. Right. On. We don't have much time if Mrs Page is to finish her pageant before the pubs shut.'

Despite herself Ruth found she was laughing. The others, presumably more used to their tutor's methods than she, seemed largely unaffected by the incident and continued to churn out examples of their imaginative powers with all the invention of the compilers of a laundry list.

15

The details of the soup survey arrived the next morning. Ruth's heart sank when she felt the weight of the package, and plummeted even more when she sat down to read the contents.

Rowena's idea of local obviously covered anything between Westbridge and the Wash. She had pinpointed certain areas as those most likely to yield avid soup eaters but none of them were within a twenty-mile radius of Bell Cottage.

At first sight the quota looked quite simple. She merely needed to find twenty people between the ages of twenty-one and seventy who would be prepared to try a new variety of soups and comment on them. It was only when she got down to the fine print that she began to appreciate Madge's cynicism.

Five of the people had to be vegetarian, five 'A/B' category, five living alone, and five with both children and an elderly relative in the household. Added to this the 'A/B's could not be vegetarian although they could be living with elderly relatives and children, but could not be entered in both categories. The single people could be vegetarian and/or 'A/B's and could be entered as both, provided they did not eat soup more than twice a week. The vegetarians could be living with elderly relatives and children but in that case they should be female and not older than forty-five.

By the time Ruth had read it three times she was no longer even sure what kind of food she would be offering her wretched victims.

There were four varieties of soup, two in packet form and two in tins. One of each kind was suitable for vegetarians and the alternative tin was specially recommended for old people.

• Sarah Grazebrook

It didn't say why. Probably to drop from a great height on the interviewer, Ruth thought morosely as she filled yet another sheet of paper with five bar gates.

By half past eleven she had all but despaired of the whole idea. She rang Rowena but only got the answerphone, in the form of a toneless message from Adrian suggesting she call back at a more convenient time.

She stuttered incoherently into the machine, requesting that Rowena get in touch with her as soon as possible on a matter of great urgency, at which point the front door bell rang and Lollo, whose patience with market research surveys was as limited as Ruth's, set up a ferocious barking and began systematically lobbing herself at the door in the hope of driving away whoever was the other side of it.

Ruth hoicked her out of the way and opened it. Gwen Pritchard was standing in the porch with an enormous bunch of rhubarb.

'I'm not disturbing you, am I?' she asked breathlessly. 'I just had to pop round to see what you thought.' She waved the rhubarb triumphantly in Ruth's face.

'Don't tell me you grew it yourself?' asked Ruth with artificial enthusiasm.

Gwen's brow clouded briefly then cleared. 'Oh, not the rhubarb. That's just a little gift. A "thank you".'

'"Thank you" for what?' asked Ruth, horribly afraid that Gwen had lined her up for another tortuous escapade. Gwen gave her curls a girlish tweak.

'Oh, just for being nice, I suppose. Being you. You know . . .' She gazed at Ruth with moist eyes. 'I don't suppose I could pop in for just a teeny teeny moment? If you're not too awfully busy?'

Ruth cursed herself for having once turned down the chance of an assertiveness course. 'No, that's fine, Gwen. I was just going to make some coffee. Would you like a cup?'

'Oh, that would be so lovely. If you're sure it's not too much trouble?' She pressed the rhubarb into Ruth's unwilling arms and followed her in.

'Go into the sitting room. It's warmer in there. I won't be a minute.'

As she boiled the kettle Ruth could hear Gwen telling Lollo

how beautiful she was. When she took the tray through she found that the dog had taken this praise as carte blanche to sit on all her study notes.

'Get off those this instant, you swine,' she exploded, attempting to push her with her foot. Gwen immediately came to the rescue, explaining how it was all her fault.

'Is this your homework?' she asked aghast, smoothing out the crumpled sheets of paper.

'What homework?'

'The exercise that Bill set last night. I always like to work on mine first thing, too. While it's still fresh in my mind. I'm so terrified of forgetting something he's said in the lesson. Because it's all so wonderful and useful, isn't it? It would seem almost criminal to forget something and get it all wrong.'

'Actually it's far more important than that,' said Ruth callously. 'They're my notes for the market research survey I'm going to work on.'

'Market research? I didn't know you did that. You really are so clever, Ruth. Did you do it in London before you came down here?'

'Not a lot,' said Ruth, reluctant to admit her rookie status to Gwen.

'I could never do anything like that,' Gwen observed ruminatively. 'I'm far too shy. I'd feel I was intruding, turning up on people's doorsteps without being asked and just expecting them to invite me in.'

Ruth struggled nobly with an urge to strangle Gwen. 'I dare say you'd be rather good at it,' she observed grimly.

'Do you think so? No! But, anyway, I couldn't spare the time, what with the bookshop and everything.'

'Are you working this afternoon?' asked Ruth hopefully.

'No, not today. I always take Wednesdays off so that I can concentrate on my writing. I should be doing it now but then I thought, poor Ruth's probably feeling absolutely lost. I know I did after my first class. I'll just pop round and make sure she's all right.'

'That was very kind of you, Gwen. But you mustn't let me keep you from your homework. I wouldn't want Mr Bartholomew's inspiration to wear off.'

• Sarah Grazebrook

'He is wonderful, isn't he? Can I let you into a tiny secret?'

'I'm not very good at keeping secrets,' said Ruth, momentarily inspired herself.

'Oh, don't worry. It won't be a secret for long. I just wanted you to be the first to know because you've been so . . . you know. It's about Bill and me.'

'BILL and you?' Ruth repeated, staring at Gwen incredulously.

'Yes. But don't tell a soul, will you?'

'Tell them what?'

'Anything. You know . . .'

There was another ring at the front door. Ruth, her head still reeling from whatever Gwen had not told her, went to answer it. This time it was Rowena Mills, almost hidden behind two cardboard boxes.

'I'm so sorry,' she apologised as she dropped them on the hall table.

'What for?' asked Ruth, who was beginning to sound like a quiz show hostess.

'Well I always try to get to the "newies" before the instructions get to them. I've lost so many good interviewers that way. They take one look at the office gobbledygook and that's them finished. PLEASE don't tell me you've sent in your resignation?'

Ruth laughed. 'I was tempted, I can tell you. Come in. I've just made some coffee.' She lowered her voice. 'I'm so glad you've arrived. I've got a visitor I can't get rid of.'

Rowena tossed her shiny head. 'Well, if it's anyone local the sight of me will probably do the trick.'

Ruth paled in mortification. 'I didn't mean . . . Oh, Rowena, I'm so sorry . . . I didn't mean . . .'

The two women gazed at each other in mutual dismay then, suddenly, without warning, both burst out laughing. They laughed till the tears ran down their faces. They clung to each other for support. Lollo spent so much time on her hind legs trying to attract their attention that she finally fell over backwards and lay squawking feebly on the hall floor, ignored by the gurgling females till Gwen, intrigued by the noise and irritated by the lack of attention, came tiptoeing out to see what was amiss.

'Oh,' she said when she saw Rowena. 'It's you.' And without another word, bent down and righted the flailing dachshund. 'Poor, poor Lollo,' she cooed exaggeratedly. 'Is oo all upside down?'

This had the effect of setting Rowena and Ruth off again, but eventually calm, or relative calm, was restored. Ruth made more coffee and they all four repaired to the sitting room, where Lollo installed herself on Gwen's lap and Rowena set about resolving Ruth's confusion with soup quota.

After a while the two of them became conscious of heavy sighs issuing from Gwen's direction. Ruth turned to her. 'I'm so sorry, Gwen, but I really do have to get this sorted out.'

Gwen smiled sweetly. 'Oh, don't mind me. I'm just sitting here trying to think about my writing. I'm used to doing it in a quiet place, but don't worry about that. I'm sure Bill will forgive me if it's not up to my usual standard.'

'I'm sure he will, Gwen,' Rowena remarked, addressing her for the first time. 'He's forgiven you a lot worse.'

Gwen glanced at Rowena and her fulsome lips looked suddenly thin. 'Bill says the class is much better since you went,' she blurted out. Rowena reddened slightly but otherwise her face remained impassive.

'Oh well, that's all right, then,' she said quietly. Ruth sensed that the situation might be getting out of control. She stood up. 'I'm so sorry, but I'm going to have to take Lollo for her walk, survey or no survey.'

Rowena stood up too. 'Of course. I'm so sorry, Ruth. I've taken up far too much of your time. I think we've sorted out most of the gremlins now. If you think of anything else, give me a ring. I'll see you on Friday about two and we'll break the back of it. Bye, Gwen.' She crossed to the door. 'Give my love to Bill when you see him.' Gwen flushed angrily but said nothing.

Ruth saw Rowena out. She felt she ought to say something, but what? The two women obviously disliked one another but it wasn't her fault if they chose to descend on her at the same time. Really the network of relationships in Westbridge was more complicated than the Book of Kings if you came into it unprepared.

Her heart sank as she returned to the sitting room. Everything in Gwen's body language reeked of an oncoming confidence.

• Sarah Grazebrook

'You must be wondering what all that was about,' Gwen began as soon as she had sat down.

'All what?' asked Ruth casually, piling the coffee cups on to a tray. 'Look, I'm awfully sorry, Gwen, but I really do have to take Lollo for a walk.'

Gwen's face fell. 'Oh dear. I was so hoping we might be able to have one of our chats.'

Ruth gestured helplessly to the maze of papers around her. 'I'm sorry.'

'Perhaps another time?'

'Perhaps.'

'Unless . . . ?' Gwen glowed with inspiration.

'Unless what?'

'How would it be if I were to take lovely Lollo for an ickle toddle, so that you could get on with your work, and then, when we come back, we can have our talk just the same? There's so much I want to tell you. I need you to advise me, you see.'

'Oh Gwen, I don't think my advice would be of any use to you. It certainly wasn't last time.'

Gwen frowned slightly but then rallied. 'Yes, it was. It's just it wasn't the right advice for the situation. That doesn't mean it wasn't good advice.' She smiled forgivingly and Ruth found that she had tied the tea towel into a reef knot.

Blank with despair she watched the two of them trotting off down the path. Briefly she considered leaping into her car and driving to the other side of England before they got back, but she was down to her last gallon of petrol and the car tax was due at the end of the month. She was trapped, doomed to a life of soup surveys, dogs, poverty and neurotic neighbours. I could live for another fifty years, she thought.

She was not feeling much better by the time Gwen and Lollo returned. Gwen, however, was positively ecstatic.

'The most exciting news,' she squealed, letting go of Lollo's lead so that it caught on the rickety telephone table and upset it yet again. 'He's coming over.'

'Who is?' asked Ruth, setting the table right and shaking the receiver to make sure it was not completely broken.

'Bill. I met him just now. Down by the boathouse. He was

exercising that lovely dog of his and he and Lollo had a lovely play together and Bill and I had a little chat.'

She paused delicately and Ruth was tempted to ask if one little chat a day might prove sufficient for her conversational needs, but Gwen continued, 'I do hope you're not too terribly terribly cross with me, but he recognised your dog – well, who wouldn't when you're as pretty as Lollo? and he said what was she doing with me, so I explained and he said he wanted to have a quick word with you about something and did I think it would be all right if he popped over, seeing as I was coming back anyway, if you see what I mean. So I said, "no, I was sure it would be", so I hope you don't think it wasn't?'

'By all means,' murmured Ruth, hoping that this would cover whatever form of reply Gwen expected from her.

Bill Bartholomew, when he did finally appear, looked decidedly less elated than his forerunner. 'Morning,' he grunted when Ruth opened the door.

'Gwen said you wanted to speak to me about something,' said Ruth briskly. She had no intention of wasting more of the morning on the blossoming of the couple's passion, which she assumed was what Gwen intended to reveal to her, no doubt while entwined coyly round the object of her desire.

'Oh aye?' Bill looked surprised. 'She just told me YOU wanted to see ME. I had some vision of you weeping over your writing desk, unable to continue till I came and rescued you from your creative torment.'

'That must have seemed highly probable,' said Ruth caustically. Bill scratched his head.

'Well, to tell the truth I wasn't entirely convinced, but I thought it was worth a detour on the off-chance.'

'I'm sorry I can't oblige,' said Ruth. 'I'm sorry you've had a wasted journey.'

'It's not wasted. I like you dry as well as wet.'

'Yes, well you can save your flowery talk for Gwen. She's obviously more susceptible to it than I am.'

'Young Gwennie's susceptible to everything. I prefer a bit of a challenge.'

'Really?' said Ruth crossly. 'In that case I challenge you to get

• Sarah Grazebrook

her out of the house so that I can get on with the things I'm meant to be doing.'

She led the way into the sitting room where Gwen put on a very decent pretence of being amazed to see Bill. He nodded to her, then turned to Ruth. 'You're sure there's nothing you want me to clear up while I'm here?'

'Nothing, thank you. Unless you can explain these soup instructions to me? The more I read them the less I understand.'

Bill picked up a packet and studied the label. '"Cut along the dotted line. Mix well with half a pint of cold water. Bring to the boil and simmer for five minutes".' He replaced it on the table. 'Did that help at all?'

'Ha ha,' snapped Ruth.

There was a little cough from Gwen. 'If nobody minds me interrupting . . ' she paused, plainly expecting to be silenced by one or both of them, then continued a little jerkily, 'now that we're all together, would it be a good idea to have a little talk, just the three of us, about our writing?' She looked imploringly at Ruth. 'After all, it is awfully lucky that Bill happened to call round when we were both together like this. It's almost like Fate, wouldn't you say?'

'I'm not sure that I would,' Ruth muttered to herself through gritted teeth as she savagely grated cheese for their welsh rarebits.

It was now nearly one o'clock and Gwen was still sitting cross-legged on the carpet, gazing raptly at Bill Bartholomew as he carefully explained the difference between a sonnet and a lyric poem. From the examples Gwen had produced so far Ruth would have thought she was more in line for a jingle competition than a rival to Shelley or Byron.

She herself had done everything in her power to shift the pair – tidying up her papers, stacking the soup neatly in alphabetical order and then again in size order when the pile collapsed, all to no avail. And what was all this about 'our writing'? From the moment Gwen had sat down she had done nothing but talk about her own creative masterpieces which, just by chance, it appeared she always carried in the pocket of her coat. No wonder they were so sharp with her at the evening class.

Ruth scraped the toast grumpily. It wasn't even as if she wanted to talk about her own writing. Particularly as she hadn't done any and had no intention of doing any. It was just the principle.

'Do you need a hand?' Bill Bartholomew, looking as though he had taken part in one of Violet Sampson's triathlons, hurried into the kitchen and closed the door, pressing his back firmly against it.

'No thank you,' said Ruth coldly. 'I'm afraid it's a bit thin. I've had to add more milk. I wasn't expecting visitors, you see.'

Bill looked patently embarrassed. 'I wasn't expecting to visit, I can tell you. I was on my way to the pub when young Gwennie pounced on me. She practically begged me to come.'

'Really?' Ruth raised an eyebrow. 'That's not what she told me.'

'She did. She said you were in a shocking state about your homework but you were too shy to phone me and ask for help. She seemed to think this would be the ideal solution.'

'She what?' Ruth confronted him, hands on hips. 'I cannot believe what I'm hearing. If you must know I hadn't given your blasted homework a second thought. I've got enough on my plate with all this soup.'

'Try a bowl,' said Bill.

'What?'

'A bowl. For the soup. It runs off a plate. Did you know that welsh rarebit's burning?'

'What? Oh no,' Ruth spun round just in time to watch the last piece of cheese turn black. 'Oh now look what's happened. That's the last of the bread. Honestly I could scream. I really could.'

'What about some of that lovely soup you've got piled up out there?'

'I can't use that,' said Ruth, horrified. 'That's work.'

Bill opened the bin and emptied the welsh rarebit into it. Lollo leapt up and went to investigate. 'Come on. I'll take you to the pub for lunch. I was on my way there anyway, when I was kidnapped.'

'Where is Gwen now?' asked Ruth suddenly, imagining her sobbing into her sonnets.

'Gone.'

'Gone? How can she be gone? She hasn't said goodbye. Gwen would never go without saying goodbye.'

Bill shook his head. 'She wanted to, but I said she should just creep away and I would explain.'

'Explain what?'

'That she realised you felt a little overwhelmed by the quality of her poetry, and that it would be better if I were just to have a quiet word with you on your own so that you wouldn't worry about holding her back. Especially now I've given her three more exercises to complete by next Tuesday. She really felt perhaps she should get on with it straightaway while the muse was still upon her.'

'Why don't Gwen and Rowena like each other?' Ruth asked as they sat by the fire in the pub. She was feeling a lot more cheerful, having drunk half a bottle of wine and lunched off home-made steak and kidney pie, rather than dried-out welsh rarebit with Gwen extolling her versatility as a cook.

Bill did not answer immediately and when he did his reply was evasive. 'Who knows? People rub each other up the wrong way sometimes, don't they? Happens more in a small community like this than most places, I daresay. Look at Madge and her daughter.'

'Don't they get on either?' asked Ruth.

Bill made a whistling sound through his teeth. 'Chalk and cheese,' he said. 'Sylvie's a cold fish.'

'Is that because she didn't want to marry you?'

Bill looked up, surprised, then burst out laughing. 'Madge told you about that, did she?'

Ruth nodded.

Bill shook his head. 'I think it goes back further than that. Sylvie's an ambitious woman. Nothing wrong with that, but I got the idea she was a bit ashamed of Len and Madge. Too outspoken for her kind of friends. And then when Len got ill and started dropping things and forgetting where he was and that, she really didn't want to know. I don't think Madge has ever forgiven her for that. They're hardly in touch these days, but it hurts Madge like hell, I know that.'

'I see,' said Ruth. Bill gave a half laugh and hunted around for his wallet. 'Do you?' he said.

'You must let me give you some money,' said Ruth as he reached for the bill.

'What for?'

'Well, there's no reason for you to pay for my lunch, is there?'

Bill shrugged. 'None in the world, except I've just had a whopping great cheque from the *Mirror*.'

'That must be nice,' said Ruth enviously. 'Even so . . .'

'Even so, it's my treat. And if you argue I shall make you listen to five more of Gwennie's poems before you leave your seat.'

Ruth laughed. 'I think you win. Thank you. That was lovely. The best meal I've had for ages.'

'We must do it more often.'

Ruth smiled awkwardly. 'Actually, I'm going to be rather busy for the next few weeks, what with all this soup to get rid of.'

'Well, if you get stuck I'm fond of a drop myself.'

'I'll bear it in mind if I get desperate.'

'Story of my life,' said Bill without rancour.

He walked back with her as far as the cottage, Lollo greeting him like a long lost father. He reached down and gave her ear a tweak. 'That dog of yours is getting fat,' he remarked. 'But you'll come to the class next Tuesday?'

Ruth grimaced. 'I don't honestly think there's much point.'

'What about your pageant?'

'They'll have to manage without me.'

'I'll tell cousin Joy.'

'I wish you would,' Ruth replied with genuine feeling.

Bill laughed. 'Not too many adverbs,' he said and gave her a peck on the cheek. She watched him go then went inside. How silly, she thought, to be pleased about something like that.

16

'"Break the back of it",' Ruth muttered bitterly as she breathed on her frozen hands and tried to unnumb her brain sufficiently to decide what sort of category she still needed to find.

The trouble with market research, she was discovering, was that, like pyramid selling, it was a lot easier to start than to complete.

Rowena had accompanied her while she placed six tins and five packets, by which time she had used up her quota of vegetarians, women under forty-five and two of her singles. She had then departed to type some letters for Adrian, leaving Ruth with a surfeit of compliments and encouragement, but no direct advice on how to get rid of the rest.

Now she was standing outside the offices of Hayman and Ratchett [Solicitors], in the hope of waylaying one of them on his way home.

A passing vicar took pity on her, offering the promise of children, elderly relatives and status in one fell swoop. It transpired that his parish was the other side of Canterbury, but by then Ruth was well past caring and the two of them parted with a mutual exchange of blessings, Ruth's being by far the more fervent.

'Good evening, Mrs Page. How's the pageant going?' Ruth jumped. Bill Bartholomew, smelling distinctly of alcohol, was standing at her elbow.

'Oh, it's you. You gave me a fright. Very well, thank you. I think I've got the hang of it now.'

Bartholomew raised an eyebrow. 'Then you'll have time to do your homework. Remember what I told you.'

'No adverbs,' Ruth cut in rather sharply. 'Look, you'll have to

• Sarah Grazebrook

excuse me. I'm rather busy.' The last thing she wanted was to be making soup placements with a drunken Scot in tow.

Bill took a step back and surveyed the alleyway cautiously. 'I hesitate to ask what you're doing, being busy in a dark alley by yourself on a winter's evening.'

'I'm waiting for a man, if you must know,' snapped Ruth. Bartholomew burst out laughing. 'Won't I do? I've just had a cheque, remember.'

Ruth glanced away in embarrassment. 'I didn't mean like that.' The glass door opened and a bright young man shot past and away towards the car park. 'Excuse me,' Ruth called lamely, but he was gone. 'Blast,' she said. 'Now I've missed him.'

'Was that my fault?' asked Bill.

Ruth glared. 'Yes, I think it was, to be quite honest. If you hadn't disturbed me it might all have been over by now.'

'You're a mighty quick worker,' said Bill.

Ruth searched around for a handkerchief. 'And can I just say I find that kind of innuendo extremely wearing.' She blew her nose savagely.

Bill sighed. 'Sorry. Too much exposure to Tony Quilp.'

Ruth picked up her bag. A tin of soup fell out and rolled into the gutter. Bill retrieved it for her. 'Gumbo Beans and Radish,' he intoned solemnly. 'That sounds pretty exotic.'

Ruth snatched it back. 'Now it's bent Gumbo Beans and Radish,' she said fretfully. 'Who's going to want to eat it now?'

'Aha,' said Bill. 'Now I understand. You're on the Rowena mission. No wonder you're in such a foul mood.'

'I'm not in a foul mood at all,' said Ruth wearily. 'I'm just cold and tired and fed up.'

'Will I buy you a drink?'

'I ought to be getting home. I've left the dog all day again. Heaven knows what she'll have got up to.'

'Another half hour won't hurt her.'

'Even so . . .'

'Even so you don't want to have a drink with me?'

'I didn't say that.'

'You didn't have to.'

'Look, it strikes me you've had a few already.'

'I have.' He sniffed forlornly. 'It's my birthday.'

Why me, thought Ruth. She smiled politely. 'Happy birthday.'

'I'm forty-five,' Bill continued gloomily.

Ruth fiddled with her car keys. 'Prime of life.'

'What's prime about it?' asked Bill aggressively. 'I've had three cards and two of them were from the same person.'

'Well, there you are. Someone must love you. Look, I really must be going.'

'Just one?'

'Oh, all right then. Just one. But you must let me buy it.'

'Why?'

'Because it's your birthday.'

'I'm having dinner with Madge,' said Bill as she set the whisky before him. 'She remembers my birthday.'

'That'll be nice.'

Bill sighed. 'Yes. I'm very fond of Madge.'

'I am too. She's one of the few . . .' she stopped.

'Few what?'

Ruth shrugged. 'I don't know. I was going to say "genuine" people round here, but that's not really fair.'

'True, though. How's your soup going?'

'It's a lot harder than Rowena said it would be.'

Bill laughed. 'Ah, Rowena.'

'What does "Ah, Rowena" mean?'

'Just that. Will I take a tin to help you out?'

'You can't.'

'Why not?'

'Because I know you.'

Bill burst out laughing. 'You are new to the game, aren't you? Anyway, you don't know me. What do you know about me?'

'I know you're forty-five.'

'You don't know what I've been doing for the other forty-four years though, do you? You know nothing about me. What I like, what I don't like . . .' He picked a tin out of Ruth's bag and scrutinised the label. 'Crispy Pork and Rowanberries for a start. How can it be crispy if it's in soup? I'm going to

• Sarah Grazebrook

contact the Trade Descriptions mob and have it taken off the market.'

'Oh please don't,' Ruth pleaded, laughing. 'Not till I've got someone to taste it.'

Bill put it back. 'I shall make an exception, seeing it's my birthday. Come on, which one do you want me to have?'

'I suppose I could use you for one of my singles,' said Ruth dubiously. 'You're not a vegetarian, are you?'

Bartholomew curled his lip menacingly. 'Do I look like a vegetarian?'

Ruth rummaged in her bag. 'How about this?' She handed him a packet.

'Haddock and Mango Chunks? What pervert came up with that? Can't I try something else?'

'No, because that's the one no one else wants either. Please. You'd be doing me a huge favour.'

The Scotsman's eyes narrowed craftily. 'In that case you can do me one.'

'What?' asked Ruth.

'You can come to my class next Tuesday.'

'Is that all?' said Ruth, surprised.

'Certainly not. You can have done your bloody homework.'

'Bill, you know I can't write.'

'I know nothing of the kind. Anyway it's nice to see a fresh face.'

'In that case can't I just sit there, looking fresh?'

Bill shrugged. 'Not unless you want me just to sit there, looking at your soup.'

'I'll come if you let me do my recall afterwards.'

'What's that?'

'You have to tell me what you think of the soup.'

'I could tell you that now.'

'After you've eaten it.'

'Sadist.'

Driving home, Ruth thought about Bill and his three cards and dinner with Madge on his birthday. A sense of loneliness engulfed her. It was only three months till her own. Still, a lot could happen in three months.

* * *

Joy rang on Sunday morning to say they were having a few friends round for drinks that evening and she was most welcome to pop in.

'How are you getting on?' she asked.

'Fine,' Ruth replied, 'thank you. I've got a bit of a cold from . . .'

'With the first draft?' Joy interrupted.

A sickening feeling swept over her.

'How long do you think it will take?' Joy persisted. 'Only I've got Kevin Mulcahy coming from the district council and he says if we're to get this EEC grant he'd better have something to show them pretty soon.'

'What EEC grant?'

'Oh, didn't I tell you? We've applied for a Tout Ensemble grant for the pageant. Part of it will go towards the staging costs, but there's quite a hefty slice available for the script and any original music. Since dear old Harold's based most of it on *Rule Britannia*, that leaves a fair old chunk for whoever comes up with the words.'

Ruth put her hand to her head. 'When you say "a fair old chunk" . . . ?'

'A thousand, or thereabouts. Chrissie and I thought you could probably do with a bit of cash in hand. He met that creepy little bank manager of yours at a do the other evening and from what he could gather, Duncan's being a bit of a pain.'

'He certainly is.'

'So we thought why not get poor Ruthy to write it for us? We need the script, she needs the dosh. Hey presto!'

Ruth tried to take it all in. 'Joy, I'm not sure that's entirely ethical. I mean, there must be dozens of people who could come up with a better script than I can.'

Joy hissed dismissively. 'Rubbish. They had their chance. But you'd better get a move on. See you tonight. Adrian might pop in, by the way.'

Ruth replaced the phone, her head swirling. A thousand pounds. For that she could dispose of Lollo, tax the car, perhaps buy herself some new clothes and who knew, take a short holiday?

A thousand pounds. And all she had to do for it was produce

twelve short scenes depicting the history of England from the Roman Invasion to the opening of the Channel Tunnel. By six o'clock that evening.

Her heart sank to irretrievable depths. How would she possibly manage that? Her history was abysmal. She couldn't write. She wasn't even sure she had any paper in the house. And it was Sunday.

Lollo waddled in and sat on her foot. Ruth gazed down at her. Not much inspiration there. 'Come on, Podge,' she said. 'Let's go for a walk. You need exercise and I need to think.'

They stopped off at the newsagents where Ruth bought a pad of scented notepaper, the nearest approximation to manuscript they could come up with.

They had covered the whole of the beach from the church to the boathouse and still she had got no further than 'Scene One. Enter Julius Caesar. J.C.: "Veni, vidi, vici."' She didn't even know what happened next. Presumably there was some kind of a battle. What then? She could hardly fill the script with 'there followed two thousand years of peace'.

Back at home she made herself some coffee and settled to her task. The notepaper smelled of lavatory cleaner which did not greatly assist her efforts.

'Scene One,' she wrote. 'Enter Julius Caesar. J.C.: "Veni, vidi, vici."' She went back and inserted 'and soldiers' after Caesar, then 'a rousing cheer' after 'vici'. Things were beginning to flow. 'MUSIC', she wrote with a flourish and whipped the sheet off the notepad. 'Scene Two', she wrote at the top of the next page.

By twelve o'clock she had completed six scenes. The action had moved from the invasion through Ethelred the Unready, who was always good for a cheap laugh, to the Norman Conquest. This brought her approximately half-way to the twentieth century. Her fingers were white with cold, her head aching with concentrated effort and the smell of the notepaper, but she was getting there. 'That's five hundred pounds under my belt,' she told Lollo who snorted as though such considerations were beneath her.

Heady with achievement she went to ring Martin. 'Hullo,' came his befuddled voice.

'Martin, it's Mum.'

'Mum?' Martin sounded shocked. 'Why? What's happened?'

'Nothing,' said Ruth, a little unsettled. 'I just thought I'd give you a ring. Did I get you out of bed?'

'No,' said Martin quickly. 'Well, yes. Is everything all right?'

'Of course it is. I just wondered how you were. How you both were. Do thank Kate for that lovely note she sent, won't you? I hope you'll be able to come down again soon. The weather's getting a bit better now.'

'Oh,' said Martin. 'Right. Look, I've got to go, Mum. See you. Okay? I'll ring you in the week. Bye now.' He put the phone down.

'Bye,' said Ruth into the dead receiver. 'I'm just earning a thousand pounds.'

She went back to her script, but inspiration was definitely on the wane. She rummaged around in her memory. What had they done at school? The Tudors, the Stuarts, the Wars of the Roses? What about the Crusades? Lots of colour in that.

'Scene Seven,' she scribbled. 'Everyone goes to Jerusalem.' Somehow she didn't think the EEC would cough up too much for that. She put a line through it. 'A time of hardship and Magna Carta. Much jousting among the nobles. MUSIC.'

'Scene Eight. Harvest time. Dancing and jollity. MUSIC.'

It occurred to her that so far seven out of the eight scenes had ended in music. Setting aside Old Harold's penchant for *Rule Britannia*, there was a very real fear that he might have to create some original stuff if she carried on like this, thereby eating into her own share of the grant. She went back and crossed it out in all but the first and last scenes, inserting 'THUNDER' for two of them and 'DAWN CHORUS' for the rest.

She was nearly there. All that remained was for her to make the quantum leap between Morris dancers in the sixteenth century to hard-hatted navvies tunnelling under the sea.

With a burst of imagination that Spielberg might have envied, she managed to amalgamate the two world wars, several royal weddings, and the opening of the Eurotunnel into four noisy scenes, climaxing in the return of Julius Caesar to witness the cavalcade, complete with traitors' daggers in his back. This Ruth considered her *pièce de résistance*, since it offered the poignant reminder that nothing is as it seems. 'NOTHING IS AS IT

• Sarah Grazebrook

SEEMS!' she wrote in capital letters and underlined it three times. 'MUSIC. THE END'.

Exhausted she went to scramble herself an egg.

When she came back Lollo had chewed up three of her opening scenes and transported the rest to her nest.

'I'm having a bit of trouble reading some of this,' said Kevin Mulcahy, gazing distractedly at the crumpled blur in front of him. Though Ruth had managed to sponge most of Lollo's slobber off it, there was no denying a lot of the ink had got blotched.

She had intended to copy the whole thing out, but the wretched notepad only contained fifteen sheets, so by the time she had re-written scenes one to three there was nothing left.

'It's only rough,' she apologised again. 'If you like I could get a clean copy to you during the week.'

'I really need something to show the Belgian Arts Minister,' Mulcahy fretted. 'There's a meeting on Wednesday. I absolutely must have it by then.'

'Oh you would. You will,' insisted Ruth, trying to prise the shrivelled pages away from him. Mulcahy sniffed suspiciously.

'What did you say happened?'

'It was on the way here,' she lied. 'I stopped to get some petrol and the wind sort of swept it out of the car, right into a puddle.

'A very putrid puddle, judging by the smell. Lucky you didn't lose it,' said the councillor. 'I must say I think it's a bit careless to leave it lying on the seat like that, if you don't mind me saying. I thought you writer people were a bit more protective of your creations.'

'Yes,' said Ruth humbly. 'I am. We are. Usually.'

'You're sure you can get it to me by Wednesday?'

'Oh, absolutely.'

'Only I've had another offer from a couple of the chaps in the printing room. They belong to this Sealed Knot caper.'

'Ah,' said Ruth, feeling sick.

'Can't say they've got your journalistic experience but they're pretty darned hot on historical accuracy. Still,' he reached round and took a lemonade off the table. Joy, who had been monitoring this exchange, closed in.

Mulcahy nodded at her politely. 'Just saying to your sister-in-law, I wonder whether we shouldn't let the lads in the print room have a stab at this pageant script, too? After all . . .' He got no further.

Joy set down her glass and fixed him with a look that would have quelled Ghengis Khan. 'I hope I'm not hearing you right, Kevin. Are you seriously suggesting that you turn down a script from one of the leading academics in the field of Kentish history in favour of the lads from the print room?'

Mulcahy swallowed. 'It's just that you know what these EEC chaps are like, Joy. They like to think they've got a choice.'

'They have,' said Joy imperiously. 'They can choose between a professional script from a renowned expert or the resignation of the entire organising committee.'

'Ah,' said Mulcahy, looking as though he was tempted by the latter.

'Bearing in mind,' Joy continued rapidly, 'that the cost of the advertising is being sponsored by my husband's firm.'

Mulcahy accepted defeat. 'I should like three copies, please,' he told Ruth a trifle brusquely. 'On my desk first thing on Wednesday morning.' Ruth retreated, feeling as though she'd been given a hundred lines.

Adrian detached himself from a small group of females to whom he was explaining his plan to video the pageant in the making. 'You mean a fly-on-the-wall sort of thing?' quavered one of them excitedly.

'Something like. Only more intimate. I like to put my mark on my achievements. People can always tell an Adrian Mills production.'

I bet they can, thought Ruth, endeavouring too late to get away from him. 'There you are,' he told her. 'Rowena says you're helping out with this soup fiasco?'

'Yes,' said Ruth. 'Is it a fiasco? I hadn't realised.' Adrian tutted. 'Everything Ro gets involved in is a fiasco. Goes without saying.' For a brief moment Ruth wondered if Duncan had ever been this disloyal to her. She pushed the thought from her mind.

'I don't think it can be at all easy,' she said, 'trying to organise a market research survey.'

• Sarah Grazebrook

'Nothing to it,' said Adrian. 'Are you telling me you can't find twenty people to eat a tin of soup?'

Although she couldn't, Ruth had no intention of admitting it to Adrian. 'It's not only that, though, is it? She has to organise all the people to do it, and train them in the first place.'

'Yes, well I grant you, that can't be too easy, judging by some of the morons she manages to recruit.'

'Thank you,' said Ruth. 'Would you excuse me? I want to talk to Christopher about something.'

'Have you two had a tiff?' Joy enquired later, having noted Ruth's rather pointed avoidance of Adrian during the evening.

'Christopher and I?' asked Ruth guilelessly.

'No,' Joy clicked impatiently. 'You and Adrian? I couldn't help noticing . . .'

'That man is a pompous self-opinionated bore,' said Ruth savagely. 'I'm sorry, Joy. I know he's your friend and I'm a guest in your house, but really I do find his behaviour insufferable.'

'Goodness,' said Joy in amazement. 'Whatever has he done? I know he's married and all that, but you knew that, too, didn't you? It's not as though he made any secret of it.'

'No, and it's not as though he made any secret of his contempt for his wife,' said Ruth sharply.

'Oh, well, Rowena . . .'

'Yes, Rowena,' snapped Ruth. 'I happen to think she's a very nice woman, and a great deal better than he deserves. And if there's one thing I hate, it's a man who puts down his wife in front of total strangers. Particularly when she's not there to defend herself.'

'Quite right,' said Christopher admiringly. 'And it's about time you started inviting her again, Joysie. Enough's enough.'

Joy gazed at them as though they had both gone mad. 'That's what I get for trying to help people, is it?' she said resentfully and swept their glasses away to the kitchen.

'Oh dear,' said Ruth. 'I'm sorry about that. It was my fault.'

'Rubbish,' her brother-in-law soothed. 'Do her good to hear the truth occasionally. I love my wife dearly, but her habit of playing God I could do without.'

'Still,' said Ruth. 'She did mean well. And look at this money she's trying to get for me. She lied through her teeth to that council man. She told him I was the greatest living authority on the history of Kent, or some such. I just stood there and let her. And what's going to happen on Wednesday when he sees what I've written. Joy'll probably end up in prison for perjury.'

'Nonsense.' Christopher laughed. 'He was doing the same thing. These two lads of his are probably his wife's cousins. That's how things get done in the country. Believe me, it's dog eat dog.'

Ruth jumped at the recollection. 'It was dog eat script, in my case.'

'That bloody animal,' said Christopher. 'I'm so sorry you got landed with that. I told Joy it wasn't on, but you know what she's like.'

Ruth smiled. 'Never mind. That's why I'm doing this soup thing, and the script. What would I have done if I hadn't needed to earn some money? Sat around feeling sorry for myself, more than likely. No, Lollo has her uses, you know.'

She went and apologised to Joy who seemed to have forgotten the entire incident and was busy trying to persuade a very elderly man, who turned out to be the famous Harry Clifford, that *Rule Britannia* was not positively the only piece of music required to make the pageant go. 'You tell him,' she incited Ruth, but Ruth was learning fast in the matter of business self-interest. '*Rule Britannia*'s very suitable,' she reassured him. 'And there's nothing like a clap of thunder to add a touch of drama.'

17

In the cold light of day it came to Ruth that her script was not worth a thousand pounds in any language. The obsequious Kevin Mulcahy had tried one last shot in favour of his print room protégés. 'I wonder if you could let me have a copy in French for the Belgian minister?' he had suggested as he was putting on his coat. Seeing Ruth's mouth drop, he had added, 'Lee in the print room is bilingual. I wonder if I should ask him . . . ?'

Once more Joy came to her aid. 'I can't see the point of it being in French. Unless, of course, we're expecting the entire population of Brussels to come over for the evening?' Mulcahy was silenced.

Riffling through the script, now smelling like a cabbage field in spring-time, a sense of despair enveloped her. She had bought some proper cartridge paper and even rooted out her portable typewriter from the box where it had lain since her arrival.

The more professional the presentation, however, the more paltry seemed the content. For a start, what had taken up two sides in her scrawly handwriting was now eclipsed to a paragraph and a half. She tried double spacing but it still looked horribly bare. She wondered if she should copy out the notes of *Rule Britannia* but even Kevin Mulcahy would be bound to spot they were the same if she did it seven times.

It was raining again, underlining her gloom.

The phone rang. It was Bill Bartholomew.

'Oh,' said Ruth, deeply surprised to hear his voice.

'Have you done your homework yet?'

'Oh God, no not yet. I haven't had time.'

- Sarah Grazebrook

There was a pause. 'I've eaten my soup.'
'What was it like?' asked Ruth.
'Bloody awful. How could you do that to me?'
'You did offer,' Ruth defended herself. 'Was it really that bad?'
'It took four glass of malt to get the taste out of my mouth.'
'Perhaps you should have had the whisky first?' Ruth suggested. 'It might have altered your perception of it.'
'Altered perceptions should be confined to hard drugs, not secreted in packets of soup.'
Ruth laughed. 'I'm sorry it was so beastly. Really I am.'
'And you haven't done your homework for me.'
She groaned. 'No, I'm afraid not. I'm sorry, but I'm in the most awful trouble.'
'What sort of trouble?'
'It's my own fault, but I really don't know what to do.'
'Someone's died from eating your soups?'
'No. This is far more serious.'
'More serious than death? You don't know what to wear tomorrow night?'
'Oh, stop it,' said Ruth, laughing hopelessly. 'It's to do with this wretched pageant script, if you must know.'
'I thought it was going so well.'
Ruth blushed. 'Well, no, it isn't really. I just said that.'
'I thought maybe you had.'
'And now I'm in awful trouble.'
'Why?'
'Because there's money involved. A grant from the EEC. And some minister's coming over from Brussels on Wednesday and he wants to see the script, THREE COPIES, to decide whether they're going to back the project or not.'
'And you haven't started it?'
'I have,' said Ruth indignantly. 'I worked all yesterday on it.'
'And?'
'And then Lollo went and ate half of it and slobbered over the rest. It really is so unfair.' A self-pitying note had entered her voice. She tried to pull it back. 'I don't know why I'm telling you all this. It's entirely my own fault. I've only myself to blame. It's just that . . .'

'You could do with the money?'

'Yes. I know that makes me sound terribly mercenary, but it's for Lollo, mainly. So that I can put her back in the kennels. She'd be far happier there. And so would I be – with her, there, if you see what I mean.'

'Hmmm,' said Bill ponderously. 'You're in a bit of a hole. Can't you re-write what you did by Wednesday and take a couple of photocopies?'

Ruth fiddled with the phone wire. 'It's dreadful,' she said finally.

'What is?'

'My script. My version, whatever you call it. It's truly awful.'

'Come on, it can't be that bad.'

'It is. It is. I haven't even got the history right. Lollo was probably right to chew it all up. I shall have to ring the council and say I just haven't got time to do it. It's just that the money would have been so handy. Never mind. It's my own fault.'

'I think that's where I come in,' interrupted Bartholomew. 'Look I've got a job on today but if you'd like to hang around after the class tomorrow night I'll see if I can give you a hand. Any good?'

'It'll be too late by then,' wailed Ruth. 'It's got to be on his desk by nine o'clock on Wednesday morning.'

Bill snorted with derision. 'Masses of time. Have you never heard of deadlines? I used to be a journalist, remember.'

'Are you sure it wouldn't be too much trouble?' asked Ruth, hardly daring to trust her luck.

'I wouldn't offer if I didn't mean it,' said the Scotsman brusquely.

'Thank you very much,' twittered Ruth, feeling as though the world was falling from her shoulders. 'I really am terribly grateful.'

'So you should be,' said Bill. 'And in return I want two pages of dialogue between a prisoner and a schoolmistress.'

'Oh yes. Yes. Anything.' She put the phone down and practically danced into the kitchen.

She returned home tired and dispirited from her soup recalls.
One housewife accused her of having switched the packet for

• Sarah Grazebrook

washing powder, and the vicar who had seemed so friendly on Friday now pronounced himself unavailable for interview before the thirtieth of March.

The only light on the horizon came from Bill Bartholomew's promise to help with the pageant script. She supposed she had better do something about the dratted homework he had set her. She couldn't think why he was so persistent. It must be perfectly plain to him that if she couldn't string together twenty-four lines on the history of Britain, it was highly unlikely she'd be able to come up with something that required real imagination.

Still, a promise was a promise. And if she didn't have anything to show him he might withdraw his own offer. She shuddered and went to fetch her biro.

Gwen rang on Tuesday afternoon to 'beg, beg, beg her' to go to the class again.

'I am going,' Ruth had said when Gwen paused for breath.

'Oh, please do. I know it's a bit unnerving the first time, but everyone will be so disappointed if you don't. We do so love to have new people. It's like fresh blood being piped into our literary veins.'

'I am going,' Ruth repeated, wondering how many times Gwen had rehearsed this appeal and if it had ever worked.

'What did you say?'

'I said I am going. I'll see you there, shall I?'

'Oh, Ruth, this is marvellous news. I'm so glad. Really pleased. You mustn't mind Bill's manner. He really is the most marvellous teacher in the world and so encouraging. I was terrified of him at first, but now we're – well, you know – much closer. You just need to get to know him.'

'Yes,' said Ruth.

'See you tonight then.'

'Yes.'

Bill was punctual that evening. He seemed in a good mood as he collected the various offerings from his students, although his eyes narrowed slightly when Reg professed yet again to have had no time to do the work he had been set. He said nothing, however, and they were soon involved in a rousing discussion about whether characterisation was more important than plot, or vice versa.

The second half of the evening was comprised of video extracts from films old and recent, which Bill used to demonstrate the use of dramatic irony. This led to another lively debate in which the loudest voice was that of Reg demanding that he be allowed to read them the latest chapter of his novel. No one took any notice.

'Tony's asked me to go to the pub. Everyone's going, apparently,' Gwen informed her as the bell rang. 'Would you like to join us? It would be so lovely.'

'Erm, no I'm afraid I can't,' said Ruth, guiltily. For some reason she didn't want anyone to know about Bill helping her with the pageant. Not because it was cheating, but because she was beginning to resent the way everyone minded everyone else's business in Westbridge. Essentially a private person, she longed for a little space away from the caring eyes of the entire population of the town.

'You can give me a lift,' Bill told her as she hung around at the exit.

'What about your car?'

'I walked.'

'Right,' said Ruth.

'And we'll stop at the Indian on the way back. I can't create on an empty stomach.'

'Right.'

'I read your homework in the coffee break,' said Bill blandly as he climbed back into the car with a carrier full of food.

'Oh,' said Ruth. 'What did you think?'

'There wasn't a lot TO think on the strength of a page and a half, was there?'

'I found it rather hard,' Ruth mumbled defensively.

'Not as hard as I did to read, I should think?'

Ruth shifted in her seat. 'You obviously thought it was rubbish.'

'Oh yes, there's no doubt about that.'

'I told you I couldn't write.'

'I'll never doubt your word again.'

Ruth pulled into his drive. 'Well, if you feel like that there's clearly no point in my coming in. It would just be a waste of your precious time.' She jerked the car to a halt in front of his front door.

'Hold up,' said Bill, 'you can't give up that easily.'

'Why not? I've had a beastly day asking all these people about this blasted soup and now you're saying I should't be let loose with a pen in my hand.'

'Did I say that?'

'As good as.'

'No I didn't. Nothing of the kind. Come on. You've still got to ask me about my soup, remember. And I'm certainly not going to eat all this by myself.'

'I'm not hungry,' grumbled Ruth. 'You can just tell me about the soup and then I'll go.'

'Shan't,' said Bill, stamping his foot on the gravel.

'Don't be so silly,' said Ruth.

'Oh, I'm silly, am I? It's perfectly all right for you to act like a nine-year-old, just because I offer you a bit of constructive criticism.'

'What's constructive about saying I shouldn't be let loose with a pen in my hand?'

'Those are your words, not mine. Did you expect me to say it was the greatest thing since Shakespeare? "The wit of Pope, combined with the sagacity of Jane Austen and the narrative skills of Homer". Is that what you wanted me to say?'

'No, of course not.'

'Christ, woman, you may have a problem with dialogue but that doesn't mean you can kill off one of the characters before she's opened her mouth.'

'It was dramatic irony,' said Ruth sulkily.

'If you ask me, it was taking the piss. All I wanted was a few lines of conversation between a man and a woman from widely differing backgrounds.'

'I don't know anyone like that.'

'Don't you just,' said Bill, fumbling angrily for his door keys. He let them in, was leapt upon by Tyson whom he managed to restrain, and led the way through to his kitchen where he dumped the carrier and hunted silently for a bottle opener. Ruth hovered.

'I'm sorry,' she said finally. 'I can see how it must look to you.'

'How?'

'As though I didn't take your class seriously.'

'It had occurred to me.'

'I suppose the truth is, I don't. I mean there are so many odd bods there. None of them strike me as the kind of people who are going to make careers as writers.'

Bill turned on her. 'You're right. They're not. Same as the people who go swimming at the sports centre are never going to make the Olympics. And the women who make jam for the animal welfare are never going to open restaurants. That doesn't mean they're nothing, their efforts are nothing, their dreams are worth nothing.

'Do you think I thought I'd end up teaching evening classes in a seaside town in the back of nowhere? I was going to be the greatest living novelist of my generation. Does that mean I'm rubbish? I don't suppose you thought you'd end up the way you have when you were twenty, did you? There must have been the odd dream tucked away somewhere inside that creative torrent you call your mind.'

Ruth was silenced. Bill opened the fridge and pulled out a bottle of wine which he attacked savagely with the corkscrew. 'I got you some of this,' he said bitterly. 'I had an idea you liked it.'

'Thank you,' said Ruth and searched for her handkerchief.

'Oh God,' said Bill awkwardly. 'Don't start all that. I didn't mean to upset you.'

'Yes you did,' snuffled Ruth.

'Yes I did. But you upset me.'

'Why? You know I can't write. That's why you offered to help me, I thought. I don't know why you have to be so horrid. I was only doing my best.'

'Your best?' Bill snorted with laughter. 'Your best? "Page One. Enter Burglar. Schoolmistress: 'Who's there? Don't shoot.'

GUNSHOT. Schoolmistress: 'Aaaagh.' Burglar: 'You shouldn't have done that.' Schoolmistress: 'You've shot me. Aaagh.' Burglar: 'I didn't mean to. It was an accident.' Schoolmistress: 'Aaargh.'" etcetera, etcetera. If that's your best, you'd better stick to shopping lists from now on. Here,' he poured her a tumbler full of wine and one of whisky for himself. 'Cheer up. You're not completely beyond hope.'

'You make me sound as though I am.'

'No, no. It would look wonderful in Braille. Let's eat this before it's stone cold and then I'll show you what I've done.'

What Bill had done was to map out a dozen scenes, each with a narrator and half a dozen lines of dialogue between the protagonists. It was dramatic, informative and concise, covering the essentials and colouring in the background. Ruth read it with amazement.

'What do you think?' he asked when she'd finished.

Ruth gazed at him. 'How long did that take you?'

'About two hours. Why?'

'It's brilliant.'

'Hardly.'

'It is compared with mine.'

'That's just possible. You'll want to make changes, obviously.'

'Will I?' Ruth asked anxiously.

'Well, of course. That's just a rough outline. You may want to prune the narrative a bit and add to the dialogue.'

'May I?' said Ruth drily.

Bartholomew laughed. 'A couple of "aaarghs" in the right place might make all the difference.'

Ruth smiled. 'If you don't mind I think I'll leave it as it is – for the time being. Once I've got tomorrow over I can work on it at my leisure.'

'If they accept it.'

Ruth looked up surprised. 'Oh, I'm sure they will. It's much too good for Westbridge.'

Bill looked at her with interest. 'That came straight from the heart.'

Ruth shook her head sadly. 'I'm sorry. I'm just a bit off the place at the moment, I'm afraid.'

Bill nodded. 'I know how you feel,' he said. 'Do you want another drink?'

'No.' Ruth stood up. 'I must be going. I'll have to get up early to get some copies of this.' Bill reached into his briefcase and silently handed her two more photocopies.

Ruth smiled as she took them. 'You knew I wouldn't want to alter it.'

Bill grinned. 'Let's say I knew you wouldn't have time to.'

At the door Ruth turned. 'I forgot to ask you about the soup,' she said. Bill waved her away.

'Tomorrow. Come round tomorrow night and I'll cook you a meal. You can tell me how the pageant went down and I can tell you how the soup did.'

Ruth smiled. 'It ought to be me cooking you a meal after all you've done.'

Bill shook his head. 'You're a working woman. When your survey's over you can, if you still want to.'

Ruth nodded then said hesitantly, 'Of course, if the script's accepted I must give you some of the money.' She paused. 'All of it, I suppose.'

Bill burst out laughing. 'Oh don't worry. I shall exact my price in due time. I'm a Scotsman, remember.'

As Ruth drove away she wondered how much the remark had been meant as a joke.

18

'He thinks it's marvellous. Quite the most brilliant thing ever.'

Ruth listened to Joy gabbling about the success of Bill's script with the Tout Ensemble committee. Her relief that it had been accepted was tinged with guilt that her only contribution had been to deliver it in a brown envelope at five to nine that morning. Still, the worst was over. As Bill had said, she would probably have to work on it – put in the commas and quotation marks, which she had noticed he was very lax about. Yes, there would certainly be plenty for her to do. 'It's only a rough draft,' she told her sister-in-law. 'It was very rushed. I still have quite a bit of polishing to do.'

'Oh yes, yes, we could tell that,' agreed Joy, who couldn't see a single thing wrong with it, 'but even so, it's a very worthy first attempt.'

What happened to 'brilliant'? thought Ruth.

'To be honest, we were none of us sure you'd be able to pull it off. Not in such a short space of time,' Joy added hastily. 'You never told me you could write, Ruth. I'd never have sent you to that pea-brained writing course, if you'd said. I feel such a fool.'

'The class was extremely useful,' said Ruth quickly.

'Yes, but they're just a bunch of amateurs, aren't they? You don't have to tell me. I've seen some of the stuff Gwen comes up with. It's dreadful. None of her poems rhyme. And as for that Bartholomew chap who runs it . . .'

'He was excellent,' put in Ruth before she could start. 'If it hadn't been for Bill I don't think I'd've got it done at all.'

Joy sniffed slightly. 'You're too modest, Ruth. That's always

- Sarah Grazebrook

been your problem. Mind you, now I think about it, Duncan was always very good at English. He won a book token in the fourth year for his essay about building a Channel tunnel.'

'Was he for it, or against?' asked Ruth without interest.

'Oh against. Definitely. And, of course, he's been proved entirely right. Those shares of his are practically worthless. All he can do is scoot backwards and forwards in it for a pound a go.'

'That must be very satisfying for him.'

'Yes, well naturally you'd be pleased, and I don't blame you. Apparently the woman won't go with him. It makes her ears go funny, according to Duncan. Not that I've spoken to him for months. It was just I asked him to get me some gin, so he popped in with it on his way home the other week. I didn't give him dinner,' she added hastily, not wanting to offend her author's sensibilities.

'Joy, I must go. I've still got a couple of recalls to do. Thanks for ringing. I'm glad they liked it.'

'Oh they did, they did. Kevin said he wouldn't have thought you capable of it. That's high praise from him. Oh and I knew there was something I meant to tell you. I bumped into Adrian down the town and, of course, I had to tell him your good news. He's planning to invite you out for a drink sometime, when he can fit it in, so you see you were wrong to think he wasn't interested. Why don't you get your hair done or something? There's quite a good woman in the high street. She does Violet Sampson's for her. I could get you the number if you like?'

'Thank you, Joy, but I'm sure I've got it somewhere.'

'Righto. I'll let you get on. I had a postcard from the Taylors, by the way. They're having a marvellous time. Missing the dog like crazy, though. Perhaps you could drop them a line, just to let them know everything's okay? I'll give you the address next time I see you.'

'Yes, of course,' sighed Ruth, wondering if she should mention to them that they now had no cushion covers.

She had only just got back to the pile of ironing which had been accumulating all week when the phone rang again. It was Rowena Mills, sounding quite frantic. 'Ruth, is that you?'

'Yes. Is anything the matter, Rowena?'

'Yes, I'm afraid there is.' She hesitated. Ruth waited to be told that Adrian had revealed his plan to take her for a drink and that she was about to be named as the Other Woman.

Rowena, however, had other worries on her mind. 'I've hit a bit of a problem with the soup job.' She paused again. Ruth rehearsed how many of her contacts would have had time to put in a major complaint so far.

'It's Vince,' she heard Rowena saying.

'Vince?'

'Yes. I'm going to have to reallocate his quota.'

'Why?' asked Ruth, thinking he couldn't have done worse than she had.

'He's under arrest.'

'He's what?' Ruth shook the phone to make sure she was hearing aright.

'Under arrest. Apparently – of course it hasn't come to court yet, so we don't know if it's true – but there have been several complaints from people whose homes he visited that items were missing afterwards. Anyway the police got in touch with Head Office and it turns out his references were completely false and that he has a record for fraud. It's all a bit of a disaster.'

A bit, thought Ruth. 'So how does that affect the survey?'

'Quite badly, as you can imagine. I'm going to have to abandon everything he's sent in and start the whole thing again. That means I need twenty fresh interviews.'

Ruth's heart began its customary descent.

'I was wondering if you could possibly fit in a few extras?' It was less of a request than a prayer. Ruth braced herself. 'I don't think so, Rowena. I've had enough trouble getting people for my own quota. I honestly don't think I could find the people in Westbridge to fill the bill.'

'No, I realise that,' Rowena broke in quickly. 'I said so to Head Office. They have agreed that, because of the short notice and everything, it would be perfectly acceptable for you to travel outside your own area. They would pay all your mileage, naturally, and any overnight expenses you might incur.'

Ruth groaned inwardly. 'When you say "outside my area"?'

'Tonbridge is a very fertile town for "A/B"s.'

'And how much is the overnight allowance?'

'Fifty pounds.'

• Sarah Grazebrook

Ruth did a quick calculation. Fifty pounds a night. It was not to be sneered at. But then what would she do with Lollo? The wretched animal was kicking up enough of a fuss when left alone for a morning. There was no way she could leave her in the house for the best part of a week. Images of her postcard to the Taylors flashed across her mind. 'Everything fine. Dog dead.' She shook herself.

'I'm sorry, Rowena. It's just not practical. I'm supposed to be looking after the owners' dog while they're away. I couldn't possibly leave her all night on her own, even if I could get someone to pop in during the day.'

There was a pause. 'I see,' said Rowena.

Ruth pictured her, head bent low over the lavatory. 'What about Mel?' she asked gently.

'Mel's not quite got the hang of it yet,' said Rowena in a voice eloquent with despair.

Ruth sighed. 'Could you possibly leave it with me till tomorrow?' she asked. 'I'll see if I can work something out.'

'Oh, would you? Yes, yes, of course. I knew I could rely on you, Ruth. When Aid first mentioned he'd met you I thought, "this woman sounds like my kind of person." He said you reminded him of me, you see. He's very very perceptive when it comes to people. That's what's so great about him.'

'I'll see what I can do,' Ruth said gently, and put the phone down. Lollo, who had been sitting on her foot, gazed at her resentfully and went out into the garden to sulk.

'Brilliant, eh?' said Bill Bartholomew, turning the chops on the grill pan and cursing as the fat shot up and spattered him. He had on an enormous apron complete with inflated breasts and nylon G string which Ruth would have considered tasteless in a joke shop, but made her laugh inordinately on him.

'Marvellous, brilliant – everything. The best thing since William Shakespeare,' she added to please him.

'The woman's a complete idiot,' said Bill, looking pleased.

'I can't thank you enough. Actually, you would have laughed. First of all she said she never thought I had it in me, which, of course, was perfectly true, then somehow she managed to trace it back to Duncan winning a prize for an essay on the Channel tunnel thirty odd years ago. I might have known she'd drag the credit back to her side of the family.'

'When in fact it belongs to yours?' said Bill drily.

Ruth blushed. 'Well, no, of course it doesn't. It belongs to you, but I couldn't tell her that, could I?'

'Certainly not. She'd've flushed the whole thing down the lavvy.'

Ruth was sitting at the kitchen table, a large glass of wine in front of her. She had offered to help but Bill had shooed her away. 'You're my guest. You do nothing. If I come to your place, I do nothing.' She wondered idly if he was fishing for an invitation but decided to ignore it. After all, there was a purpose behind this visit. She had to fulfil her quota. Her old quota, that was. The thought of finding another twenty people to taste her soups was too depressing to contemplate. Think of the money, she told herself. The fee, plus two hundred and fifty pounds for subsistence. Only a fool would resist.

She had bitten the bullet and booked Lollo back into Pets' Paradise for the following Monday. By Friday the animal would be settled and she would have no need to fetch her back. She wondered how long she would have to wait for the thousand pounds Joy had promised her. She also wondered how much of it she would have to pass on to her host.

'So what happens next?' asked Bill when they had finished dinner.

'I ask you what you thought about the soup, I suppose,' said Ruth, reaching for her bag.

'Not that. The pageant. What's the next step?'

'Do you know, I haven't a clue. I don't even know when it's taking place. Hopefully I'll be gone by then.'

Bill looked up. 'I thought you were staying till the owners got back.'

Ruth nodded. 'Yes I am. But I thought that I might go away somewhere for a few days, with the . . .' She hesitated.

'Money?' Bill finished.

'Well, some of it. What's left after, well, you know.' She put her glass down. 'How much do you want? I do wish you'd tell me, then I'd know how much I've got over. I mean, do you want it all? You'd be perfectly entitled.'

Bill shook his head angrily. 'I don't want any of it, woman. What do you take me for? Isn't it enough one of my pupils has got something into print?'

'Yes, but I didn't write it,' wailed Ruth. 'You must take some of it. I feel guilty enough as it is.'

Bill frowned at her. 'Bloody middle-class consciences,' he grumbled. 'Tell you what, you can crawl to Tonbridge on your knees and we'll call it quits. How about that?'

'Don't mention Tonbridge,' Ruth moaned.

'Why not?'

'Because one of Rowena's interviewers has been arrested for robbery and she wants me to do another twenty interviews. In Tonbridge. I wish I'd never agreed.'

'Why did you?'

'For the money. Why else?'

'You're obsessed with money.'

'I'm not. Really I'm not. It's just I've never had to manage on my own before. I never realised how much everything costs.' She looked up. 'You despise me, don't you? Middle class, never had to pay for anything. I don't blame you. Especially as I'm making such a complete mess of it all.'

Bill got up and poured them both a brandy. 'I don't despise you. Why should I? I don't think you'd get my vote as Financier of The Year, but not many people would. You're doing the best you can. What's wrong with that? By the way, I've decided what to give you for homework next week.'

Ruth shook her head. 'I'm not coming to your class any more, Bill. I thought you understood. I was only doing it till the pageant thing was sorted.'

Bartholomew sat back. 'I see. I've served my purpose and now that's it?'

'It's nothing like that,' Ruth protested. 'But you've seen for yourself how hopeless I am. I'd only hold things up. You can't really want me there?'

Bill shrugged. 'Not if you don't want to come.'

Ruth looked at him helplessly. 'It's not that I don't want to come. It's just that I'm no good at writing. I've proved that beyond all conceivable doubt.'

'No you haven't. You've proved that you haven't found your

voice. Give it a chance. You've got a brain, imagination. Let it free for once. It's trapped inside your stupid middle-class head, that's all.'

'Thank you very much,' said Ruth.

'And don't pretend you're offended. You know what I'm saying as well as I do. I'm saying here is a chance for you to offload some of the frustration that's making you so miserable.'

'I'm not miserable.'

'You're not happy, though, are you?'

'And writing will change all that?'

'Who knows? Maybe. Maybe not.'

'I still don't see what schoolmistresses and mass murderers have to do with it.'

Bill slapped the table. 'There you are. Last week it was a petty burglar, now it's a mass murderer. There's hope for you yet.'

Ruth laughed. 'You're ridiculous.'

'I want you to write a letter,' Bill went on.

'What about?'

'It doesn't matter.'

'I can't just write a letter if I don't know what it's about.'

'Hold on a minute. I haven't told you who it's to yet. It's to the man who shot you when he broke into your home last week.'

'What?'

'You are a middle-aged schoolmistress lying in your hospital bed. The man who shot you is now safe behind bars. I want you to write him a letter.'

'What about, for heaven's sake?'

'Anything. Your feelings, your fears, the pain you're in, the resentment you bear him, the pity you feel for him. Whatever. Use your imagination.'

'Why do I have to be middle-aged?' grumbled Ruth.

Bill burst out laughing. 'Sorry. Perhaps it was asking too much for you to imagine that as well.'

Ruth crumpled up her napkin and threw it at him. 'Soup,' she said.

'Soup,' said Bill.

19

Ruth took Lollo back to Pets' Paradise on Monday morning.

She had bought a chicken for their Sunday dinner and the two of them had eaten it together, Lollo pushing her bowl around under the table while Ruth chewed miserably on her roast potatoes and told herself that it was all for the best and that both of them would be happier without each other.

This did not stop her feeling like Judas Escariot as she loaded Lollo, complete with leather holdall, into the back of her car and set off for the kennels.

The owner, Stella Francis, was bright and brassy and not at all the sort of person Ruth thought should be in charge of other people's pets.

'Let's sort out the finances first of all, shall we?' she had said with a hard bright smile. Ruth made out a cheque for the week. The woman peered at it as though Ruth were a well-known forger. 'We usually ask for a month in advance,' she explained, baring her hard bright teeth.

'I'm sorry,' Ruth stammered. 'I wasn't aware . . . I'm afraid . . .'

'That's all right,' said the woman. 'Seeing that we know the owners. Weekly will be fine. In advance, of course.' She turned to where Lollo, unnaturally subdued, was sitting pressed against Ruth's leg. 'Come on, Lollo. My goodness, you've put on a bit of weight, haven't you? We'll have to see about that. I think it's going to be half rations for you for a while.'

'She's had plenty of exercise,' Ruth intervened. 'I think perhaps she wasn't very happy with her previous diet.'

The woman gave her a scathing look. 'I think perhaps these things are best left to professionals, Mrs . . .' She picked up Lollo's

• Sarah Grazebrook

lead and led her away down a passage, Lollo peering anxiously over her shoulder at Ruth, who stood helplessly beside the holdall, like a parent depositing her child at prep school.

The youth who had first landed her with Lollo came in whistling. He glanced at her incuriously. 'Can I help you?' he asked, dumping a bag of cat litter in the doorway.

'No, no thank you.' Ruth took a deep breath, turned her back on the bag, and hurried away to her car. Opening the door she saw that Lollo had left the rubber bone she had bought her for a goodbye present. She picked it up, but changed her mind and tossed it back on the seat. She then drove very fast to Tonbridge, crying all the way.

Rowena Mills had been right about Tonbridge and particularly Tunbridge Wells which was just over the bridge. Ruth had considerably less trouble in finding suitable guinea pigs than in Westbridge.

Rowena had called round on Saturday with fresh supplies and renewed thanks.

'I'd've done the wretched things myself,' she assured Ruth earnestly, 'but Aid's getting a bit het-up about a couple of projects he's got in the offing, and I don't really want to go away and leave him just when he needs me. Otherwise I'd never have dumped you in it like this.'

Ruth smiled with what sympathy she could muster. 'Where does he get his funding from – for the projects that are commissioned, I mean?'

Rowena's alabaster brow furrowed anxiously. 'That's always the worst part. Of course, Aid's awfully good at getting people to cough up – he can be very persuasive when he wants to. I expect you've noticed?' She smiled shyly to show she knew other women must envy her. Ruth grunted non-committally and helped Rowena carry the soup into the house.

She had brought Ruth a home-made cake, dripping with cream and chocolate, which had slightly unnerved her. She wondered if she should offer her a slice but decided against it through squeamishness. She and Lollo had made inroads into it throughout the weekend, which was probably the reason the poor creature was now to be starved back to fitness.

She found a small Bed and Breakfast not too far from the

centre and booked herself in till Friday. Although it already seemed clear that the work would not take as long as she had expected, she salved her conscience by reminding herself that the money was not for her. She bought a local paper and planned what she would do with her evenings.

She had intended to go to the cinema that night but it had started to pour. Instead she had a meal, bought some wine in an off-licence and returned to her room to catch up on her paperwork.

By half past nine she had finished, so she had a bath and went to bed early. Sleep, however, evaded her. She couldn't rid herself of Lollo's dopey brown eyes gazing back at her as she was led away to be starved. It was worse than anything in *Lady and the Tramp* or *Greyfriars Bobby*. Soon she was sobbing all over the duvet cover.

This is ridiculous, she told herself. I didn't cry like this when Martin went, certainly not when Duncan did. I must pull myself together. I can't go out interviewing people tomorrow with eyes like footballs. Think of something else. Do something else. But what? The paper was full of sad stories, her book was about a marriage break-up. Outside the rain was clattering against the window. Was there nothing to take her mind off her misery?

What was it Bill had said about her being miserable? He was right, whatever it was. She'd forgotten to tell him she would be away all week. Now he'd think she really had been using him. She must ring him in the morning. She could get his number from Madge at the shop. He'd still think she was trying to duck out, though.

An idea came to her. She would do his silly homework for him. She might as well. There was nothing else to do here and he seemed to think creative writing was the panacea for all ills. Now was her chance to find out. She got out of bed and tore a couple of response sheets from her spare questionnaires, then settled herself back among the pillows.

A letter from the wounded schoolmistress. She concentrated as hard as she could. It was almost like being in hospital, here in the stark little room with a glass of water by her side and her clothes stacked away in the corner. She closed her eyes, hoping for inspiration, then opened them again when none was forthcoming. The blank page stared up at her. She must begin somewhere. A letter to a criminal.

'Dear Vince,' she wrote.

Ruth had less luck the next day than on the Monday, partly because it was still raining and partly due to a dearth of vegetarians in the shopping centre. She went and hung around by the health shop.

While she was there she remembered that she must phone Madge. A man's voice answered the shop phone. 'Is that Westbridge three six six seven three five?' she asked confusedly.

'That's right. How's it going?'

She realised that it was Bill Bartholomew. 'What are you doing in the shop?' she asked.

'I'm filling in for you. What do you think I'm doing?'

'In the shop?'

'Why not? I spend more time in here than most people.'

'Yes, but . . .'

'Madge has gone to the bank. Do you want to leave a message?'

'Yes. No. The message was for you, for Madge to give you, that is.'

'So you want to give me a message to give to Madge to give to me?'

'No, of course I don't.'

'What's the message?'

Ruth felt suddenly awkward. 'I'm afraid I can't come to the class tonight.'

'Why not?'

'Because I'm here. In Tonbridge. I'm here all week.'

'What have you done with the dog?'

Ruth drew a breath. 'I've taken her back to the kennels. It was the best thing. It wasn't fair on her, me being out all day and all that. Madge agreed. She said it was the best thing.' She paused.

'Right,' said Bill. 'Thanks for letting me know. See you some time.'

'Bill,' Ruth almost squealed down the phone. 'I'm coming next week. I promise. It's just this blasted survey. I was going to come this week. Honestly I was.'

The Scotsman cleared his throat. 'Fine,' he said coolly. 'I didn't mean you to think you were under pressure.'

'I've done my homework,' Ruth blurted out.

'What homework?'

'You know. The letter from the schoolmistress to the prisoner.'

'Good. Fine.'

'You don't believe me, do you?' she said resentfully.

'Of course I believe you.'

'I'm going to post it. You'll get it tomorrow. Then you'll see.'

'Then I'll see,' Bill agreed.

Ruth put the phone down feeling like an outcast. Madge was cross with her for leaving Lollo, Bill was cross with her for missing his class, and she was heartily sick of herself for managing things so badly. Added to which she couldn't even find a beastly vegetarian outside a health shop. She bought herself a Danish pastry and ate it sitting on a seat for the disabled outside the public conveniences.

By the end of the day she had placed all but three of the soups. She rang Rowena who was so pitifully grateful that she had done as much as she had, that Ruth began to wonder whether she was working too hard for her own good.

By the end of the week she was beginning to feel as though there were no other food than soup, and no genuine way of describing it apart from 'foul'. She drove home tired but grimly satisfied with her achievements.

In an odd way she was looking forward to getting back to Bell Cottage. Although the guest house had been clean and the water hot, it had lacked the homeliness which she now ascribed to the Taylors' lurid wall colourings and the demonic cooker.

She had had a nice week, going to a concert and two films, choosing clothes she would buy when she had money, looking in estate agents' windows and balking at the price of local property.

She wondered what would happen if and when the house in London was sold. She had always assumed she would buy a small flat somewhere in the same neighbourhood, but if prices in the suburbs were this high, how on earth was she going to find a place in London? She took a yogic breath and dismissed the thought. That was for another day. Now was now.

'Now' came furnished with its own supply of problems for no sooner had she unlocked the door and carried her case into the hall than the phone rang. It was Joy.

'Ruth, where on earth have you been? We thought you were dead. I was going to get Chrissie to break in but he's had to go to Norwich on a case. If you hadn't answered today I was going to call the police.'

'Tonbridge,' said Ruth.

'What?'

'Tonbridge. I've been to Tonbridge. Doing some market research for Rowena. I'm surprised Adrian didn't mention it to you.'

Joy sniffed. 'I haven't seen Adrian for ages,' she said dismissively. 'He seems to be spending all his time with Gwen Pritchard these days. Something about her assisting him with a video. She'll be about as much help as a chocolate teapot, if you ask me, but at least it keeps her out of the shop for a bit. Poor Jenny Redwood's at her wits' end.'

'Well, she would be if she works Gwen as hard as she says she does and she's not there anymore.'

'Gwen? Work hard? You must be joking. Gwen's the laziest person I've ever met, and that's saying something. That's what comes of having unearned income, mind you. It breeds sloth. I don't need to tell you that.'

Ruth was unsure how she should take this remark since, to her certain knowledge, Joy had never had a job in her life.

'If Gwen doesn't need the money, why does she work in the bookshop then?' she enquired. 'She certainly doesn't seem to enjoy it.'

'Because she owns sixty per cent of it, that's why. And she doesn't like them to forget the fact. Her grandmother left her the best part of a hundred thou, as well as the flat. She took a fancy to Paul when they first moved down here, and agreed to invest in Penny Dreadful. If you call floating in and out and trying to get the customers' trousers off "working". I suppose some people might.'

Ruth rubbed her aching head. It was all too much for her. 'Was there a reason you rang, Joy?' she prompted.

'Yes of course there is. Apart from finding out if you were still alive. I must say, I do think you might tell us next time, if you're planning to flee the country, Ruth. We've been terribly worried, what with that breakout from Barlan and everything.'

'What breakout?'

'Oh, haven't you heard? No, I suppose you wouldn't have if you've been living it up in Tonbridge all week. Three men have escaped from Barlan. Wednesday, I think it was. They were on Day Release, helping some old biddy cut her privet hedge when they just up and legged it. She'd gone inside to make them a cuppa and when she came back they'd gone. Where the warder was, God only knows. Probably in the pub. Anyway, they're in the area, everyone's fairly sure, so I wouldn't go leaving your windows open tonight. Oh, and I should check your outbuildings – garage, whatever. That's just the sort of place they love to hide. You can see now why we were so worried. Still, all's well that ends well. I bet you're glad now you've got that dog around.

'By the way, the real reason I rang was to say, could we have a copy of the pageant script ASAP, please? We've got our first casting session on the fifteenth and we need it for people to read from.'

Ruth swallowed and dragged her thoughts back from images of Magwitch and Jack the Ripper. 'Oh, yes, yes, of course. As soon as I can. Actually I think Kevin Mulcahy has them all.'

'No he hasn't. He's sent them back to you. You should have got them by now.'

Ruth cast a quick eye over the pile of envelopes in the basket, chiefest of which was a package marked Westbridge District Council. 'I think I can see them. I've only just got back. I'll get a copy off to you as soon as I can.'

'If you would. I'd come and get it myself, but what with those murderers roving around . . .'

'Murderers?' squawked Ruth, her stomach giving an uncontrollable lurch.

'Well, probably not, but definitely psychos. Chrissie told me not to leave the house on my own after dark whatever happened.'

'How sensible,' said Ruth, preparing to book herself into a hotel.

'You're so lucky,' came Joy's voice, 'having a dog to protect you.'

Ruth locked the doors, front and back, put an armchair in front of the french windows, poured herself a stiff brandy and settled down to await her fate.

It came in the form of the third envelope she opened.

The first had indeed been the three copies of her pageant script, together with a compliments slip from the Leisure and Recreation Department and an injunction from the Public Utilities Department not to waste water unnecessarily.

The second was another bill from her solicitor, reminding her that she had not yet paid the first, and the third, dated Tuesday, was from Pets' Paradise, demanding that she ring them immediately on a matter of grave importance.

Ruth's heart stopped in her mouth. Tuesday. It was now Friday. Lollo was definitely dead. The Life Support System had been turned off at noon that day, failing any response from the person in charge of her.

Sickly she scanned the letter heading. 'Office Hours: 9–7' it read. It was ten to seven. She went into the hall, sat down and dialled the number.

There was a click and the answerphone message came on. 'It's not seven o'clock,' bellowed Ruth, half in frustration, half in relief. Now, whatever it was, she wouldn't know till the morning. There was another click. 'Pets' Paradise. How may I help you?' said a very young voice. Ruth recovered herself somewhat. She took a breath. 'It's Mrs Page here. I have a letter from you, dated Tuesday the twenty-fourth. It says that I should get in touch urgently.'

'In connection with which client?' asked the girl with less animation than the answerphone. Client, thought Ruth. How ridiculous. 'Lollo. The dachshund,' she said evenly, her heart thumping. There was a pause.

'I think I'd better get Mrs Francis. Please hold.'

On came the dratted music, but Ruth hardly heard it. She sat and waited for what seemed an eternity before she heard the distant taps of heels approaching.

'Mrs Page?'

'Yes.'

'It's Stella Francis here. We thought you'd be in touch before now.'

'I've been away,' said Ruth weakly. 'I gather there's some sort of problem with Lollo?'

'There certainly is,' came the woman's sharp voice. 'In fact, Mrs Page, we would be quite within our rights in refusing to keep her under the circumstances. Quite within our rights. The terms and conditions do state that any relevant information concerning a pet's state of health must be declared at the time of admission.'

'Why. What's the matter with her?' asked Ruth frantically. Obviously she was still alive, but by how much?

Stella Francis sighed. 'You're not telling me you were unaware that the animal is in pup?'

'In what?' screeched Ruth.

'In pup. Pregnant. In fact quite far advanced, which is going to make it a lot more difficult for Mr Groves. That's why we were so surprised that you didn't respond to our letter. I have rung the number you gave us several times.'

'I've been away,' Ruth repeated limply. Lollo, pregnant. No wonder she'd seemed so podgy and lethargic lately. Pregnant. But when? How? Oh, my God, she thought, as images of Lollo spreadeagled under Tyson rose before her eyes.

'I've spoken to Mr Groves,' Mrs Francis was saying, 'and he's prepared to go ahead, although, as I've said, there is some risk involved. I would have to ask you to sign a disclaimer in the event of the animal's death. I can arrange for it to be done early next week. The sooner the better, according to Mr Groves. He'll bill you directly. I think you'll be looking at something in the range of four hundred pounds and of course, I don't need to remind you that boarding fees are payable, even during a client's temporary absence.'

The words washed over Ruth as she tried to clear her thoughts. 'Pregnant', 'death', 'four hundred pounds' were the ones that stuck.

'Who is Mr Groves?' she heard herself saying.

'He's the vet. The one we use. He's not local but he specialises in pedigree animals so we thought it best to call him in.'

• Sarah Grazebrook

Ruth pulled herself together. 'What exactly is the matter with Lollo, apart from being pregnant?' she asked.

Mrs Francis sounded surprised. 'Nothing. The animal is remarkably healthy. Healthier, I may say, than when we took delivery from the Taylors.'

'So why does she need an operation?'

If the woman had been surprised before, this question totally flummoxed her. There was a pause while she reflected on the disadvantages of having to deal with idiots, albeit for large sums of money.

'The operation is to terminate her pregnancy,' she explained kindly. 'I assume that the Taylors had no intention for her to be put to stud while they were away? There's certainly nothing on my notes about it.'

Ruth felt suddenly cold. 'You say there might be some risk to Lollo's life from this abortion?'

'Termination. Yes, naturally, there is always some risk, particularly at this late stage.'

'How close is she to giving birth?'

'Mr Groves thought three to five weeks. She's more than half-way, certainly.'

'How great is the risk?'

'That you would have to ask Mr Groves.'

'I don't want her to have it.'

'But, Mrs Page, I'm not sure if you understand. These are not pedigree pups. Or if they are, they are certainly not Kennel Club registered. I would not be fulfilling my responsibilities to Mr and Mrs Taylor who are, after all, the animal's owners, if I were to let the whelping go ahead.'

Ruth closed her eyes and pictured Lollo, struggling to deliver Tyson's puppies.

'I'll speak to you in the morning,' she said.

20

Ruth sat with her five bar gates before her.

Two weeks of market research had inured her to placing every combination of circumstances into a category. A vegetarian could not work shifts, a judge could not live with his mother. Thus her mind had begun to work. Ten days on the job and two in the classroom were finally beginning to bear fruit.

She looked at her chart. 'Lollo: Pups', a plus sign. 'Lollo: mongrel pups', a minus, and so on.

So far she had more pluses than minuses for allowing the abortion to go ahead. The Taylors; the Taylors' wrath; the impracticability of a] keeping, b] disposing of the puppies; Joy's wrath; the kennels' wrath; the expense. It seemed to go on and on. Against were the simple facts: the risk to Lollo; the expense to Ruth; the sadness of it all.

Whichever way she turned the figures, the operation came out on top.

At a quarter to ten, on her fourth gin, she finally admitted defeat and put away the sheet of paper. The operation would have to go ahead.

At a quarter past ten, as Ruth sat sightlessly watching *News at Ten*, there was a knock on the door. Her blood froze.

In one fell swoop Yugoslavia, the balance of payments, the Middle East, even Lollo, were swept from her consciousness, to be replaced by mass murderers, privet-hacking psychopaths and the ghost of Julius Caesar, seeking vengeance for his lines.

'Oh no,' she moaned, clutching desperately at the sides of her armchair. 'Go away. Oh no.'

• Sarah Grazebrook

The knock came again. 'Help,' she whimpered, sinking down below the back of her chair. How many prisoners did Joy say had escaped? Six at least, and all of them rapists and serial killers. How could Duncan do this to her? For it was he who had sent her to this wilderness of savages. Why had she not resisted his attempts to force her into this alien territory, peopled with sadists and throat slitters? If it was the last thing she did she would cancel her life insurance.

'Mrs Page . . . Ruth . . . Poet Laureate . . .'

Ruth sat up.

'Would you mind opening this door? I've come to talk to you about your homework.'

'Don't ever do that again.'

'What?'

Bill Bartholomew was sat with a glass of brandy, Ruth's homework spread across his knees and a plate of ginger biscuits at his elbow.

'Frighten me like that.'

'What's frightening about knocking on someone's door?'

'Nothing. In the daylight. Do you know there are ten mass murderers on the loose from Barlan?'

Bill looked mildly surprised. 'I didn't. No.'

'I expect that comes as a bit of a shock?' Ruth remarked a trifle smugly.

Bill nodded. 'I have to say it does. Particularly as they're all first offenders.'

Ruth frowned. 'How do you know that?'

'I teach them.'

'What? Mass murdering?' She was now on her fifth gin.

'Something like. I like to call it "Creative Writing", but I have to say a lot of it ends up in gore.'

Ruth swirled her glass. 'Well that's only to be expected, isn't it?'

'Why?'

'Because that's the sort of people they are.'

Bill set his glass down and looked at her. 'That's the sort of people they'd like to be, Ruth. The people they actually are are petty thieves and confidence tricksters.'

Ruth felt confused. She wished she had had a bit less to drink. 'That's even worse.'

'Why?'

'Because those are horrid, mean little crimes. Nothing grand about that.'

'Precisely. That's why they all pretend they're in for GBH.'

'So you don't think these men who've escaped are dangerous?'

Bill shrugged. 'Who knows? Who knows what a wounded animal will do when it's cornered?'

'That's a bit dramatic,' said Ruth uncomfortably.

Bill laughed. 'Probably. To be honest, from the ones I've taught, I should think they're likely more frightened than anyone, poor sods.'

'They are criminals,' Ruth reminded him.

Bill nodded. 'So they are. Half of them are in for non-payment of fines and the rest for fiddling their gas meters. A real underclass they've got at Barlan and no mistake.'

Ruth looked at him accusingly. 'Were you always so liberal?'

Bill accepted the criticism. 'No. You're right. They're a pain in the butt, most of them, but I don't think you need to worry about being dead in your bed by the morning, that's all I was trying to say. Which brings me to your homework.'

Ruth sat up attentively. 'Did you like it?' she asked. Bill's expression belied a struggle between tact and artistic integrity. 'It was better than the last one,' he said finally. Ruth's face fell.

'A lot better.'

She brightened slightly. 'I really felt I'd got inside the schoolteacher's head this time,' she told him. 'I wrote it sitting up in bed in the B&B and it was just like being in hospital except I hadn't been shot in the stomach. Did you sense that at all?'

'That you'd been shot in the stomach?'

'That I hadn't,' Ruth explained patiently.

Again Bill's face contorted. 'I sort of got the sense that you were in hospital,' he said.

'That would be from my description, I expect?'

'Yes, I think so. Can I ask you something?'

'Of course.'

'When you write to people – you know, ordinary letters to

• Sarah Grazebrook

friends and that, do you normally describe the room you're in?'

Ruth thought. 'Well, no I don't suppose I do. It's not usually relevant, is it?'

Bill nodded. 'You see, here,' he rummaged through the pages and found the place he was looking for, 'you write, "the walls are a crisp magnolia colour. In one corner is a wooden wardrobe, probably of the nineteen fifties genre, with metal hangers, brackets, not enough, inside it. The curtains are unevenly hemmed, allowing the early morning sunshine to trickle through, making straggly patterns on the bare cord carpet."'

Ruth glowed. 'I was rather proud of that bit.'

Bill's look of anxiety deepened. 'Were you?'

'Yes. Particularly as it was pouring with rain when I wrote it. I really let my imagination fly. It's not all as good, I know,' she added modestly. 'Why are you smiling? Would you like another brandy?'

Bill put down the letter. 'I think a cup of coffee would be very nice,' he said. 'I'll make it if you tell me where.'

Ruth stood up, disappointed that she was not in for a night of literary discussion and alcohol. 'No, I'll do it.'

Bill followed her out. 'It must seem funny without the wee sausage dog about.'

A lump rose in Ruth's throat. 'Yes,' she said briskly. 'I'm getting used to it, though. Shall we talk about my homework? I'm sure you've got heaps of criticisms to make.'

'Not heaps,' said Bill cautiously. 'Are you sure you want to hear them?'

'Certainly. I'm never going to improve if I can't take a bit of constructive criticism.'

Bill shrugged. 'Here goes. To start with I think, if I'd been shot in the stomach by a burglar, I probably wouldn't start my letter to him with "I hope you are well".'

Ruth glanced at him curiously. 'How else can you start a letter? I always start my letters like that.'

Bill nodded. 'Okay. It's hard to find a suitable beginning, I grant you. Perhaps it would be better to leave that and come back to it later, when you've written the rest. The other thing

I was a bit unhappy about, apart from the description of the room . . .'

'Excuse me,' Ruth interrupted. 'Are you saying now you didn't like the description of the room?'

'I'm not sure it was appropriate under the circumstances.'

'It was utterly appropriate. In fact I'd go further than that. I'd say it was absolutely essential.'

'Why?'

'Because I wanted him to be able to picture what it was like for her lying in a hospital bed with a bullet in her guts. That's why.'

'In that case, why did you write it like an estate agent's patter?'

'I didn't.'

'You did.'

'You said it was so good just now,' said Ruth sulkily, spilling the water as she poured it into the cups.

Bill looked remorseful. 'I didn't, Ruth,' he said gently. 'YOU did.'

'I suppose the rest is no good either?' said Ruth, sploshing milk angrily into the coffee.

'I don't take milk.'

'Too bad,' she snapped.

'Have you got any sugar?'

'No.'

'Can I have another brandy instead?'

'I've made this now.'

'Christ, woman, it's only a bit of criticism. I thought you said you could take it. You'd better stick to peddling soup, if you can't.'

'I said "constructive" criticism.'

'That's what I'm giving you.'

'No you're not. You're just picking holes in everything I've done. Just for the pleasure of it. That's why you want me to come to your class, isn't it? So that you can humiliate me in front of everyone. Well, that's it. I've had it. You can take your rotten homework, and your rotten pageant for that matter.' She stalked into the hall and returned with the three copies. 'And you can send me a bill for writing it and then I can send you a bill for the cost of Lollo's abortion and then perhaps we can call it quits.'

She sat down on a chair and burst into tears.

The Scotsman stood over her, not knowing what to do. 'What's this about an abortion?' he asked at last.

'As if you didn't know,' Ruth wept, searching fruitlessly for a handkerchief.

Bill reached across for the kitchen roll and tore her a long strip then sat down opposite. 'I don't. Honestly. Ruth, Mrs Page . . . Is it something I should know about?'

'It's only your bloody dog's fault,' sobbed Ruth, blowing her nose savagely.

'Tyson?'

'Yes, Tyson. That afternoon when we first came here and we met you on the beach and he . . . you know, and she . . . well, Lollo was in season, it turns out. And now she's pregnant, in pup, whatever they call it, and the woman at the kennels says she'll have to have an abortion because they're not pedigree and the Taylors would be furious, and it'll probably kill her because she's so far advanced, on top of which it's going to cost four hundred pounds which, even with what I earn from "peddling soup", I haven't got. So I hope you're satisfied.' She sat back exhausted and wiped the kitchen paper across her face. 'I hate this place,' she said tonelessly. 'I wish I'd never come here.'

Bill sat silently, staring at his hands. 'I'm sorry,' he said at last. 'I've really screwed things up for you.'

'You have rather.'

'It wasn't what I intended.'

Ruth gave a deep sigh and yawned. 'No, I suppose not.' She looked at him. 'Oh, it's not your fault. If it hadn't been Tyson it would have been some other dog. I didn't know, you see. And I should have. If it's anyone's fault it's my dratted sister-in-law's for landing me in it, like that. That's typical of Joy. She goes round acting Lady Bountiful and she never gives even the slightest thought to the consequences of her actions. Duncan's just the same. If it's anyone's fault it's his for getting me into all this in the first place. And if it's not his it's that fat witch he's living with. Joy was probably right. I bet Laureen put him up to it in the first place. I didn't think so at the time, but now I'm sure of it. What are you laughing at?'

Bill shook his head. 'I was just wondering how long it would take you to get back to God and his archangels.'

Ruth smiled forlornly. 'I suppose I was getting a bit carried away. It's just,' she waved her hands helplessly, 'it's not been a very good day, one way and another.'

Bill stood up. 'I'd better go. Will I pour you a brandy before I do?'

Ruth shook her head. 'I've had too much already. I'm sorry.'

'Nothing to be sorry for.'

'Yes, there is. What you say about my writing is true. It's about as lively as a train timetable.'

Bill grinned. 'But a lot more realistic. You'll get there. The trouble with you is you keep all your emotions locked up. Even in that letter. There's no anger, no resentment, no feelings of any kind. Think about it. If you can get this worked up about a bitch you don't like getting pregnant, just imagine what you could be going through if someone shot you. It's like rape. You've been invaded. Use your anger.'

Ruth nodded. 'It's just I can't really picture this burglar of yours. At least I can, but he always ends up as that pathetic little show-off on my market research course. It's very hard to get emotional over him.'

'What about Duncan?'

'What about him?'

'Can't you get emotional about him, after all he's done to you?'

'Oh, I couldn't possibly put down my feelings for him on paper.'

'Why not?'

'Well, because . . .' Ruth sought for an answer and found none. 'Well, anyway I couldn't. Not possibly. Never.'

'You don't have to use his name. Just his effect on you.'

Ruth shivered. 'I'd never do that. It's far too personal. I thought this was creative writing you were talking about. There's not much creative about describing real things.'

Bill smiled. 'Oh, well,' he said. 'I expect you know best.'

* * *

• Sarah Grazebrook

At two o'clock Ruth crawled into bed. Her eight-page letter lay on the kitchen table surrounded by coffee cups and discarded biros. I'd love to see his face, she thought, when he reads that.

She was woken by the sound of the telephone ringing. It was nearly half past nine. She lay for a few minutes listening to it then grudgingly hauled herself out of bed and made her way downstairs. She had still not got used to not seeing Lollo bouncing around at the foot of the stairs each morning. Her head ached miserably from the gin.

She picked up the phone.

'Ruth, it's Joy. Where on earth have you been? I've been ringing for hours. I thought you were—'

'Dead,' Ruth finished laconically. 'No, sorry, Joy. I'm not.'

'Don't be sorry,' said her sister-in-law a trifle nervously. 'Are you all right, Ruth? You sound a little . . .'

'I've got a bit of a headache. Nothing serious. What was it you rang about, Joy?'

'Nothing. Well, nothing urgent. Are you quite sure you're all right? Your voice sounds a bit . . .'

'I expect I've got a cold coming,' muttered Ruth. 'I might go back to bed for a bit once you've told me why you rang.'

Joy took the hint. 'Oh yes, I should. Good idea. I mustn't keep you. In fact this will probably please you. I've arranged for Grace Forland to pop in about ten and pick up those copies of the pageant and drop them round to me. Would that be all right?'

Ruth groaned inwardly. 'I don't see why not.'

'Ah but if you're going back to bed that probably wouldn't be such a good idea. I could ask her to come back this afternoon.'

'No, don't do that. I'll stay up,' said Ruth, determined not to prolong the agony.

'No, no, you mustn't do that. You're clearly not at all well. Look, why don't you just put them on that little shelf in the porch and she can pick them up without disturbing you at all? I'll give her a ring and tell her that's what you're going to do. You get back to bed. We don't want you falling ill with the pageant coming up and all that that entails.'

'I thought I'd done my bit,' said Ruth in some alarm. Joy laughed melodiously.

'Oh no, no. That's just the start of it. This is a community effort, remember. Now you've got the script out of the way we can start on the real nitty gritty. I'll give you a ring next week to tell you which committees you're on. Now you get back to bed and don't worry about a thing.'

Ruth was about to make herself a cup of coffee, prior to returning to bed when the phone rang again. Damn, she thought, anticipating Joy with a complete change of arrangements.

It was Martin. He sounded more hungover, if anything, than his mother. 'Mum, it's Martin.'

'Hullo, darling. How are things? When are you coming down again? The weather's getting a lot warmer. It's really quite spring-like. You could take Kate on a daytrip to France. They've got all sorts of offers in the local press at the moment.'

She sensed she was prattling on rather, but the fact that he had rung cheered her up. 'Actually,' said Martin glumly, 'that's why I rang. I thought I might come down at the end of the term, if that's okay.'

'Of course it's okay. Why shouldn't it be? Will Kate be coming?'

'Erm, no. It'd be just me.'

Ruth sensed that something was wrong. 'Oh, right,' she said brightly. 'Perhaps another time?'

Martin sighed. 'I don't think so, Mum. Truth is, we've broken up.' So that's why you've rung, thought Ruth, her maternal urges springing into action.

'I'm sorry,' she said gently. 'These things do happen, Martin. I know it's no consolation at the time.'

'It was my own bloody fault,' Martin blurted out angrily. 'I'm such a stupid bugger. Honestly, Mum, you'd think after what Dad did to you I'd know better.'

Ruth froze slightly. 'Why? What happened?'

'Oh I went to some stupid party. Got drunk. Kate had gone home to see her father for the weekend. I ended up in bed – Look, you don't want to hear all this. Anyway, she came back early, found us. That was it.' His voice cracked slightly. 'I really love her, Mum. I think I'll go crazy if I don't get her back.'

Ruth stared at the phone, willing it to supply her with some helpful advice. 'You won't go crazy, Martin. It may feel like it at

• Sarah Grazebrook

the moment. It always does. But these things pass. You're only nineteen. Believe me, you won't always feel this bad.'

It was useless and she knew as she spoke it was useless. Martin plainly thought so too. 'Thanks for the sermon,' he said angrily and put the phone down. 'What was I supposed to say?' Ruth shouted at the top of her voice. As if in answer she turned to see Grace Forland's tormented face pressed against the glass panel of the front door. She stood for a moment wondering whether to flee or open the door and ram the telephone down the nosey woman's throat.

Grace raised a hand and tapped lightly on the glass. Reluctantly Ruth opened it. 'Hello, Ruth,' murmured Grace, her brow criss-crossed with anxiety. 'Everything all right?'

'Yes, thank you, Grace.'

'Only Joy said the copies would be on the porch shelf and they don't seem to be there?'

'No, I haven't had time. The phone rang just as I was fetching them. Do come in a minute.'

'No, no I won't, thank you.' Grace backed away. 'A hundred and one things to do. Garth's waiting for me in the car. How's the little dog, by the way?' She glanced around nervously. 'I rather expected to see her.'

'She's gone,' said Ruth ominously. Grace swallowed.

'Well, if I could just take the copies.'

'I'll get them for you.'

Grace collected herself. 'No, no, you mustn't. You get back to bed. Just tell me where they are and I'll be on my way.'

'They're on the kitchen table,' said Ruth, having no wish to prolong the visit. 'If you really don't mind, I think I will get back to bed.' She shivered dramatically. 'I think I may be running a temperature.'

'Yes, yes,' Grace insisted. 'I'll find my own way out. You just get better as soon as you can.'

Ruth snuggled down under her duvets and tried unsuccessfully to go back to sleep. She heard the front door close and the sound of the Forlands' car driving away. When she felt confident that they were gone, she got up again, ran herself a bath, took two aspirins and braced herself to meet another day.

21

Joy Blakeney stood at the open french windows signalling violently to her husband who was busy making a bonfire down the garden. 'Chrissie,' she squawked. 'Chrissie ... Chrissie ... CHRISTOPHER.'

A posse of rooks shot into the air and sped away to more peaceful surroundings. Christopher Blakeney, who had heard her the first time, reluctantly pulled off his gardening gloves, gave the fire a rebellious poke and went to see what Joy wanted.

'Quickly,' she incited as he plodded across the lawn. 'Can't you move any faster?'

'No,' said her husband.

'Where are you going now?' as he headed off towards the kitchen.

'To take my boots off.'

'Never mind that now. This is serious. Come in this way. Ruth's gone MAD. There. You can put your feet on that.' She laid a newspaper on the carpet.

'For God's sake, Joy, can't I just leave them in the kitchen?' Blakeney grumbled as his feet were guided to the sports section of the *Telegraph*. 'I haven't read that bit yet.'

'Never mind. Never mind. You won't have time for reading when I tell you what's happened. Just sit there and listen.'

'Any chance of a cup of coffee?'

'No, there isn't. Honestly, Chrissie, this is an emergency. We've got to decide what we're going to do. Grace has gone to fetch Adrian, and Garth seems to think we ought to call the doctor, but I'm not at all sure that would be such a good thing. I said we must ask you before we did anything.'

• Sarah Grazebrook

'Apart from inviting the entire neighbourhood in,' said Christopher.

'It's not the entire neighbourhood. It's a few trusted friends. By the way, Violet Sampson might drop in for that sponsorship money. If she does you must send her away immediately. She's a frightful gossip.'

Christopher Blakeney sighed deeply and waited to be enlightened. Joy went into the hall and returned carrying a pile of papers. Solemnly she handed them to her husband. 'What do you think of that?'

Christopher glanced at them unemotionally. 'What am I supposed to think? It's three copies of that blasted pageant you've been on about for months now. I've seen it already. It's fine. Very good. Brilliant. What else am I supposed to say?'

'Not that,' snapped Joy, snatching them away from him. 'THAT.' Her fingers stabbed at a batch of handwritten pages lurking at the bottom. 'Grace picked it up when she was collecting the scripts. She didn't realise at the time. They were all together.'

Christopher squinted at the first page. 'This looks like a personal letter,' he said, laying it down.

'It is. It is,' said Joy excitedly. 'Read it. Go on. Read it.'

Christopher frowned. 'I'm not going to read a private letter to someone else. I wouldn't dream of it. And nor should you.'

Joy Blakeney hopped up and down with frustration. 'I wouldn't normally. Of course I wouldn't. I wasn't going to read that one, but it was with all the rest of the stuff, and I just happened to cast my eye over it before I realised what it was, and really, Chrissie, you have to read it. For Ruth's sake. So that you can tell us what we should do. Oh, there's Adrian. Oh no. He's brought that wretched Gwen Pritchard with him. Is there a man alive she hasn't had her hooks in? Really, you would think people would think, wouldn't you, at a time like this?'

'Why did you ask him anyway?' said Christopher crossly. 'I thought this was meant to be a private family matter, not a cocktail party.'

'It is. It isn't,' said Joy obtusely. 'I asked him because he's got a mad wife. I thought he might be able to throw some light on matters.'

When she had gone to let them in Blakeney tried to overcome his natural reticence. It didn't look exactly like a letter. There was no address or date at the top, and his conscience was eased marginally by the fact that it didn't seem to be to anyone in particular or, more oddly, to several people at once, as he noted the names 'Vince', 'Bill' and 'Duncan' all scribbled through. The most recent addition seemed to be a Messrs Millet and Bailey, although there were also signs of a 'Mervyn' and possibly a 'Francis'.

'Dear' whoever it was, he read. 'I expect this letter comes as surprise to you.'

It certainly did to Christopher, containing as it did some rather graphic details of what Ruth would like to do to the recipient and what she appeared to think he had done to her. Theft was mentioned, as were houses, serial killers and abortionists, though whether the last two were connected seemed a little confused, even in the mind of the writer.

He was prevented from reading further by the invasion of Adrian, Gwen, Grace and Garth Forland and the elderly Trent couple who ran the pottery class and had a nephew who practised psychotherapy. 'I met Enid in the chemists',' Grace apologised. 'I thought she might be able to shed some light.'

Joy looked unconvinced by this, but dispensed Gwen to the kitchen to make coffee for eight. 'Make the real kind,' she called after her. Christopher frowned, as instant was quite good enough for this lot.

'It'll take her forever,' Joy whispered sotto voce. 'Now,' she raised her hands like a prophet. 'Everyone sit down please. There's no time to lose. I have gathered you here,' Christopher Blakeney closed his eyes, 'to discuss what can be done to help my poor sister-in-law.

'Not all of you will be familiar with the contents of the letter which has fallen into my hands. Providentially, may I say.'

Mr Trent raised his hand.

'Yes, Arnold?'

'Would it be in order for Enid and myself to see this missive?'

Joy shook her head emphatically. 'That won't be necessary. I really think the fewer people who have access to it, the better.' Noting the couple's annoyance, she added, 'Some of the passages are truly disturbing. I wouldn't want to inflict them on my best friend.'

Gwen came tiptoeing in to ask which cups she should use.

'The ones at the back of the cupboard, but be sure to put everything else back,' said Joy, winking elaborately at her husband. Christopher noted a slight stiffening of Gwen's back as she retreated. 'My husband,' Joy continued, indicating Christopher as though he were an item for auction, 'has seen the contents and he is going to suggest the best way to progress in this delicate matter.'

There was an expectant pause.

'Aren't you, darling?' Joy prompted. Christopher roused himself.

'I haven't had time to read the whole letter,' he said.

'But most of it,' Joy intervened. 'Just cast a quick eye over it again, darling. To refresh your memory.'

Christopher sighed and flipped through the pages. It was certainly racy stuff and not at all in keeping with the mild, ironic woman he knew as Ruth.

Having dispensed with the recipient's physical details which ranged from his blackening teeth through to his unfortunate habit of eating spaghetti as though he were sucking it through a straw, the letter went on to describe what it was like to have a bullet fired at close range into one's navel.

Christopher had a nasty suspicion this was some kind of metaphor for pre-menstrual tension or, worse still, intercourse, which brought the likely culprit back to Duncan, although who knew what Ruth had been doing in her spare time since her husband had left her? Whatever it was it obviously hadn't been giving her much pleasure.

The final sheets dealt with some ghastly plan she had to force her attacker to live in a freezing cold damp cottage with no access to toothpaste for six months, but the writing was becoming more blurred and Blakeney set it aside, feeling he had captured quite enough of its essence to agree that his sister-in-law was in a very bad way.

'I think perhaps,' he began cautiously, and was mightily relieved to hear Gwen rattling along the hall with her burden of coffee.

'Oh Gwen, not now,' said Joy savagely, glaring at Adrian who was behaving for all the world as though he had never seen the woman before in his life, let alone been carrying on a heated affair with her, if what Grace Forland said was to be believed.

'Isn't there any cake, or anything?' Mills asked casually.

'No,' said Joy, then, 'Oh yes, there might be. Could you go and look for us, Gwen dear. There's a pet.'

Gwen trudged away, somewhat mollified by the softening in Joy's tone. She rather wished Adrian had said something to allow her to stay. After all she was his Personal Assistant now, having agreed to put quite a lot of money into his short about Neville Chamberlain's sex life. And she'd promised him lunch at the Indian restaurant. And she was a friend of Ruth's. Her best one, probably. It seemed a bit mean to exclude her from the discussions, particularly since the letter sounded like a Creative Writing exercise that the lovely Bill Bartholomew might have set Ruth for homework. She sighed at the thought of him, then rallied a little, thinking how sweet was her revenge on Rowena. She'd always been Adrian's PA up till now.

'Now, where were we?' asked Joy. 'Chrissie, darling, I think the best thing might be for you to tell us what the alternatives are and then we can decide which would be best.'

'Well, if you ask me the woman's mad as a hatter,' put in Garth Forland suddenly. 'Look at the way she treats that dog. Always trying to drown it, from what Grace tells me.'

'I didn't exactly say that,' murmured Grace.

'Yes you did,' snapped her husband. 'Where is it now, by the way? Shouldn't be left with her if she's finally flipped.'

'Actually,' said his wife, going rather pale, 'I asked about Lollo this morning and Ruth said she'd gone. I didn't think much about it at the time, but now . . .'

'Told you so,' Forland thumped the table. 'Woman should be certified and that's all there is to it.'

'Oh I'm sure Ruth would never do anything to hurt the Taylors' dachshund,' said Joy nervously. 'She knows it's a pedigree.'

'My nephew says mad people always kill their loved ones first,' said Enid Trent.

• Sarah Grazebrook

'You're not supposed to call them mad,' prompted her husband. 'They're . . .' but his memory failed him.

'I really think perhaps one of us should go over there,' said Joy, looking directly at Christopher.

'Well don't look at me,' he responded grumpily. 'If anyone goes it should be you.'

'Me?' exclaimed Joy as though it were the silliest suggestion in the world. 'Why me?'

'Because she knows you. You're her closest relative down here.'

'That's no reason. Besides, Enid's just said mad people go for their loved ones first. I should be the very last person to go.'

'I said you were her closest relative, not her closest friend,' Christopher pointed out. 'On Enid's reckoning, you should be the safest of us all.'

'What on earth do you mean by that?' demanded Joy, insulted but not sure why.

'Look at the way you've treated her. From the day she arrived, and before that even.'

'Exactly. I've done everything in my power to make things easier for her. I found her somewhere to stay . . .'

'Complete with damp walls and a bloody dog she didn't want.'

'It was company for her. It's not my fault if the Taylors don't heat their home properly.'

'No, but it's your fault if you stuck Ruth there. There must be masses of holiday cottages round here that are empty in the winter. You just wanted to get in with Rodney Taylor so that you could captain the ladies' golf team next season.'

'I did not,' said Joy, going quite pink. 'Anyway I can't go up there.'

'Why not?'

'Because I have to stay here to co-ordinate matters.'

There was a nervous cough from the doorway. Everyone turned. Gwen was standing there with some stale malt loaf which she had buttered and a packet of economy digestives that Joy kept for the workmen. 'This was all I could find,' she said shamefully. To her surprise and delight Joy hurried over and took the tray from her. 'Gwen, my pet, how clever of you. Just what we could all do with. Now I'm just going to ask you one tiny favour more and then I shall leave you in peace, I promise.'

'What's that, Joy?' Gwen asked, anticipating tree felling at the very least.

'I'd like you to be an absolute angel and pop over and see how Ruth is. She wasn't feeling all that well this morning and we're all a bit worried about her. You've been such a good friend to her, I'm sure she'd rather see you than boring old us.'

Gwen glowed with gratification. 'Of course, Joy. I'd love to do that. Oh, poor Ruth. I do hope she's not feeling too icky. Do you think I should take her some soup, or something? She probably hasn't managed to do any shopping.'

Joy frowned with concern. 'I think possibly it might be better to go straight over and see how she is first. You know what it's like when you're ill. Sometimes you want one thing and sometimes you want something completely different.'

'Oh yes, of course. Silly me. I should have thought.'

She turned a coy smile on Adrian who had consumed three pieces of malt loaf and was now stuck into the biscuits. 'Would you be an absolute angel, Aid, and drive me over?'

'Can't you take a cab?' asked Adrian, surprised at her temerity, but for once Gwen was sure of her position. 'It would be quicker if you drove me,' she said meekly.

'Yes, go on, Adrian,' said Joy briskly. 'And for heaven's sake, stop eating those biscuits. I've got the plumber coming on Monday. I'll have nothing to give him.'

They departed, Adrian moaning about his Indian lunch. Garth Forland and Christopher took the opportunity of Gwen's departure to sneak away to the pub.

Joy and Grace were left to fend off the Trents' ever more personal enquiries, which they both felt far exceeded their entitlement as aunt and uncle of a shrink.

As they left Violet Sampson came cycling round the corner and nearly ended all of their lives. Joy dispatched her with one pound fifty in five pence coins that she had been keeping to use for parking, and she and Grace settled down with large gins to discuss what should be done.

'Let's have a look at that letter again,' said Joy. Grace handed it to her. 'You see,' she said when she had scrutinised it again, 'she seems very unclear about what this man has done to her, apart from shooting her, which is clearly Freudian. And who's it to? I mean, is it Dunc for deceiving her, or this Vince person for stealing her jewellery? Ruth hasn't got any jewellery, by the way. Only that ring her mother left her and that's only rubies.' Joy flipped the pages. 'And here she says something about being forced to walk the streets because she's got no money left. Now that's plainly linked to sexual frustration. I know Dunc's been a bit of a pain about things, but he certainly wouldn't want his ex-wife to go on the game. Suppose it got in the papers? No, the bit that really worries me, though,' she glanced surreptitiously over her shoulder as though fearing the room might be bugged, 'is this bit about Millet and Bailey.'

'Who are they?' whispered Grace, infected with the urge for secrecy.

'That's it. They're our family solicitors. In the City. Dad didn't think anyone south of the Thames knew anything about money. They're frightfully dear, but they've always done good by us. I'd hate to think of Ruth setting fire to their offices or whatever it was she was thinking of doing.'

'I don't think it was their offices she was going to set fire to,' murmured Grace.

'Yes, yes, but that was clearly Freudian,' Joy dismissed her. 'Plainly what she was referring to, albeit indirectly, were their offices. Now the last thing we want is to offend them. They were awfully good about the fence when that ghastly man wanted to build his garage overlooking our bathroom. And to be honest, I'm not sure if Chrissie ever paid them the last part of the bill. Imagine the trouble it would cause if Ruth did anything silly and it came out she was related to us.'

Grace looked grave. 'Of course,' she said, wondering if Joy would ever offer her another gin, 'people often fantasise about doing awful things. It doesn't mean they actually plan to carry them out.' Joy looked somewhat relieved.

'No, that's true. Perhaps we're all getting worked up over nothing.'

'Mind you,' said Grace, who never liked to let an opportunity to spread gloom get away from her, 'there is the question of the missing dog.'

Joy clapped her hand to her mouth. 'Oh Lord, I'd forgotten all about that. Wasn't there something about hanging, drawing and quartering?' She ferreted wildly through the pages. 'There. "Hanging, drawing and quartering would be too good for you. You should be pounded down and made into dog meat." Oh my God, how horrible. Oh dear. I really think perhaps a GP might be the best answer to all this after all. I know it's Saturday but there's bound to be a locum on call somewhere. Actually, it would be better anyway if Dr Frederick wasn't involved. He might ask us to move. Oh dear, I don't know what to do now. Do you think Gwen's there yet? She must be. They've been gone simply ages. Do you think I should ring? Where IS Christopher? That's men all over. They're never there when you need them.'

'Might I have one of those?' asked Grace, as Joy poured another hefty gin into her glass.

'What? Oh yes, yes of course. Help yourself. I'm just topping mine up a little. I never drink at midday, normally. I shouldn't now. I need to keep a clear head.'

When Christopher and Garth Forland finally returned from the Forresters they found their respective wives giggling convulsively. The men stood uneasily by till Christopher Blakeney, particularly incensed by Joy's reference to what she called 'his secret sorrow', brought them all back to earth by asking if anyone knew why an ambulance had been seen racing up the road in the direction of Bell Cottage?

22

While the collected wisdom of Westbridge was debating her fate Ruth, newly bathed, breakfasted and aspirined, set out for Pets' Paradise.

She had thought long and hard about the alternatives. Her letter – homework, whatever it was, had helped to clear her mind. She had shifted a lot of angst, pent-up anger and bitterness on to those scribbled sheets of paper.

Duncan had come off worst, closely followed by the bank manager, both sets of solicitors, the odious Stella Francis and, finally, Bill Bartholomew. Not because it was his dog that had set this latest disaster in train, but because he had caused her to doubt herself, something she was very good at doing.

She had thought when she came to Westbridge that this would be a new beginning; that people would accept her for what she was – not the wife of Duncan Page, DTI economist; not the divorcee set aside for a dental technician, but Ruth Page, woman. And they had not.

From the very first evening she had been singled out as a person to be helped, pitied, patronised. Only Madge and Bill had taken her for what she was, and of those two, Bill had chosen to unsettle her.

She had not felt sexual interest in a man for twenty years, setting aside the evenings spent ogling Harrison Ford on late night movies. She wasn't sure that that was what Bill aroused in her now. She only knew that she had tried, for whatever reason, to impress him and had signally failed.

She no longer cared what he thought of her latest effort, wherever it was. She had looked for it that morning, thinking she had left it on the kitchen table, but it was not there. Maybe she had thrown it away. She really couldn't remember. The important thing was that she had written it and with it had offloaded a welter of resentment and frustration.

Now she could think more clearly, plan her future, take positive steps. And the first of these would be to bring Lollo home.

Mrs Francis was not around when she presented herself at Reception. 'Could you find her for me then, please,' said Ruth briskly. The girl scurried away, returning to say that the proprietoress would be with her shortly as she was attending to some urgent business. Ruth's courage began to waver.

After ten minutes of hanging about she was all for turning tail. The more she thought about it, the sillier her scheme became. She would sell the puppies, restore Lollo to her normal size and deliver her to the Taylors for all the world as if nothing untoward had happened in their absence.

Her spirits were not much revived by the sound of raised voices, one of them Stella Francis'. 'There is absolutely no way I could agree to such an arrangement. It is NOT merely a question of finance, I can assure you. I have the welfare of the animal to consider. Mr Groves has assured me that this is the most sensible course of action and anyway, I would certainly never agree to release a client to someone not authorised to take charge of it. You could be anyone. You could be a puppy farmer for all I know.'

'Better a farmer than a murderer,' came the unmistakable tones of Bill Bartholomew as the two of them rounded the corner, still arguing. Stella Francis caught sight of Ruth. She looked almost pleased to see her.

'Ah, Mrs Page. I'm so glad you've come. Do you know this gentleman at all?'

Ruth swallowed. 'I . . . Yes. What are you doing here?' she asked.

'What are you doing here?' came the response.

'I've come to pick up Lollo. I decided I couldn't let her go through with it. I'll think of something. Sell the puppies. I don't know. Something.'

'Snap,' said Bill.

'What?'

'I came to do the same thing but this lady,' he threw Mrs Francis a very caustic look, 'says she won't let me take her without written permission from the owners.'

'I suppose that makes sense,' Ruth acknowledged.

'Don't you start.' He turned to the woman who had not yet decided whether to be relieved or annoyed. 'Right, well now the lady who does own the animal is here, perhaps we could get on with it?'

Annoyance won the day as Stella Francis folded her lips into a very thin smile. 'I'm afraid it isn't as simple as that.'

'Why not?' demanded Bill.

'Because this lady is not the official owner. She is merely looking after the animal while the owners are away.'

'Yes, but surely . . .' Ruth interrupted. 'You were perfectly happy to accept my authority when it came to agreeing the abortion.'

'Termination.'

'Why don't you call it what it is?' roared Bill angrily. 'It's a bloody abortion and she's not having it. Okay?'

Mrs Francis ignored him but her right eye began to twitch slightly. She sighed. 'It is, of course, up to you, Mrs Page. If you are prepared to take the responsibility for the dog's health and future wellbeing . . .'

'I am.'

'I have to remind you that it is very unlikely the Taylors will be able to mate the bitch with a pedigree dog if she has already produced mongrel stock.'

Ruth took a breath. 'That's not really my concern,' she said quietly. 'My concern is for Lollo now and I can see no justification for putting her through an unnecessary operation at this time. That is my final word.'

Stella Francis raised her eyebrows. 'If you're quite sure.'

'I am,' said Ruth, her head throbbing.

'I must ask you to sign a disclaimer to say that you chose to ignore the advice of the professional staff here and that any future mishaps with regard to the dog's health are none of our responsibility.'

'Right.'

• Sarah Grazebrook

'There is of course the matter of next week's boarding fee, in lieu of notice of withdrawal.'

'I understand that.'

'And Mr Groves' consultation fee which is fifty-nine pounds.'

'What?' Ruth's jaw dropped. 'You can hardly expect me to pay for a consultation I didn't request in the first place.' Mrs Francis looked supremely smug.

'It is in the agreement,' she said, turning to the fine print at the back of the contract. Ruth paid.

Any resentment she felt about the cost of ransoming Lollo was amply repaid by the joy she exhibited at being freed. She bounced around them, albeit a little heavily, squeaking and rushing between their legs till they were all but hobbled together. 'Stop it, you daft animal,' ordered Bill to no effect. He lifted Lollo's belongings into Ruth's car then turned towards his own. Ruth ran after him. 'Bill . . . I mean, well, thank you. Thank you very much for what you were going to do.'

Bill shrugged. 'That's okay.'

'No it isn't. I mean it isn't okay for you just to say "okay" and go like that. I mean, could you, would you like . . . ? Have you got time for a coffee?'

Bill grinned. 'I should think so. Will I follow you home?'

Ruth nodded. 'Yes all right. You can look at my latest writing attempt.' Bill shuddered dramatically.

She laughed. 'Actually, you needn't worry because I've lost it. I think I must have thrown it away. I was a bit drunk last night. I don't know if you noticed.'

'Not at all,' said Bill.

They stopped in the lane outside Bell Cottage, mainly because the ambulanceman was trying to make room for his colleague to reverse. Ruth leapt out, followed by Lollo, who took this invasion of her property very seriously and immediately rushed round the back of the house barking and snarling like the Hound of the Baskervilles.

'What on earth's going on?' Ruth asked the ambulanceman. The man frowned. 'Do you know the occupant, madam?' he asked.

Ruth stared at him. 'What do you mean "know" her? I am her,' she spluttered. The man gazed at her in utter confusion. 'Come again?' he said.

'I live here. I'm staying here while the owners are in Australia. What on earth's happening?'

The man took a step backwards. 'One moment, Madam,' he said, fumbling for his walkie talkie. Bill joined her. 'What is it?' Ruth shook her head. 'I don't understand. It seems as though they're here for me, but God knows why. I've never been hospitalised for a hangover before.'

The man came back to her. 'Are you a Mrs Ruth Page, Madam?' he asked in a level voice.

'I am, yes.'

'Would you have any identity with you?'

Ruth produced her library ticket and a letter from the bank. The man shook his head. 'Excuse me one moment,' he said, punching the numbers on his mobile phone. 'Hullo, Mick. Look, mate, cancel the fire engine, will you? . . . I'll tell you later . . . No, better than that . . . Okay, mate. Ta.' He slid the phone back into its case. 'I'll be back in a moment,' he said breaking into a run and galloping towards the house. Ruth and Bill followed.

The sight round the back of the cottage was interesting.

Gwen, balanced precariously on a ladder held none too steady by Adrian Mills, was tapping frantically on the lower pane of Ruth's bedroom window. 'I think I can see movement,' they heard her cry. At which moment Lollo, excited by so many friends at her homecoming, took a joyful nip at Adrian's ankle. Adrian gave a screech like a banshee, let go of the ladder and sank to the ground, clasping his leg.

Gwen, suitably alarmed, turned to see what had happened, lost her balance and fell with alarming force on top of him. The ladder followed.

At this point the fire engine, which the ambulanceman had not succeeded in cancelling, arrived with siren blasting, followed by a passing police car whose crew were down on their crime clear-up quota.

While the ambulanceman explained to the fire captain that his services would not be required to force an entry, the policemen unleashed an alsatian which ran with leopard-like speed round the back of the house to the further excitement of Lollo who began a canine equivalent of the Dance of the Seven Veils.

The alsatian, being a professional, ignored her and ran straight

• Sarah Grazebrook

to where the scrum was thickest. Here he effectively saw off both ambulancemen who were struggling to untangle the bodies and, having allowed them to remove a weeping Gwen, placed one paw either side of Adrian Mills' head and stood over him, growling menacingly if he so much as blinked. It was thought that at this point Adrian passed out.

Gwen, however, who had sustained very little injury, barring a bruise on her bosom where she had hit Adrian's chin, convinced herself that he was dead and had to be forcibly detained by a policeman from throwing herself across his lifeless torso before they had had time to remove the alsatian. Having seen the effect she could have on a grown man, they were not prepared to risk their star contender for the local Police Dog Trials, which might yet restore them in the eyes of their sergeant.

It was at about this time that a cub reporter from the local paper turned up, having been alerted by the sound of sirens. He took a few pictures and returned to his desk to compose a suitably hysterical article.

Meanwhile, back at Harbinger House, Joy Blakeney was marshalling her husband and the Forlands into her car as they set forth to investigate the reported ambulance heading for Bell Cottage.

Ruth listened disbelievingly as the ambulanceman explained that they had had a call from the lady now sobbing helplessly in the arms of Mick and a spare policeman, to say that she had tried to gain entry to the house of a very dear friend, whom she had every reason to believe was lying seriously ill in bed, and unable to come to the door.

The ambulance had duly arrived, only to find that they too could not get any answer from the occupant. Gwen had then thought of the ladder, but the men's union forbade them to risk life and limb in the pursuit of patients, so they had duly sent for the fire brigade who were trained for that sort of thing. No one knew why the policemen were there, and they themselves certainly had no intention of revealing their motive.

Everyone duly departed, Adrian on a stretcher, now fully conscious and demanding the instant execution of Lollo and, though more tentatively, a similar fate for the police dog.

Gwen had been taken to hospital too, for a check-up, although she had been more than willing to have her bosom examined by anyone ready to comply. 'She was awfully lucky,' Ruth remarked to Bill as they inspected the mangled remains of the ladder. 'She could have broken her neck.'

'Or his,' said Bill ruminatively. 'Still, you can't win 'em all.'

'That's a terrible thing to say,' said Ruth disapprovingly.

'I know. Particularly since I meant it,' said Bill and gave her a wicked grin. Ruth started to laugh till the tears were pouring down her face.

'Look at her. She's quite hysterical,' gasped Joy from the back of the car, craning her neck to see what Ruth would get up to next. 'There's no sign of Gwen. Do you think . . . ? Oh no, that's too terrible . . . That ambulance . . . Christopher, can you see any sign of Gwen? Oh, look. Thank God, that's Adrian's car. Well, if his car's still here nothing too awful can have happened.' She sat back relieved. Christopher Blakeney allowed himself a moment's reflection on the holes in his wife's logic. 'Isn't that that bloke you don't like?' he asked casually, indicating Bill with his head.

Joy had made no secret of the fact that she had considered Bill Bartholomew little better than the devil incarnate for some years now. It stemmed from a sad little episode, in which, befuddled with summer punch, she had made a rather explicit suggestion to him and been rejected. Kindly, courteously, but rejected none the less.

That she had been too drunk to perform so athletic an exertion, that Bill had known full well that she would regret it to her dying day if she had, and that he had some regard for her husband with whom he had shared the odd pint in the first few months of his stay in Westbridge, had never been allowed to enter Joy's reading of the equation.

It had occurred about the same time that his name had first been linked with Rowena Mills' and, although Joy would never have admitted it, Bartholomew's obvious preference for the youthful blonde from London had done a lot to harden her own reaction to Rowena's later difficulties. The only good to come out of the liaison was that Gwen Pritchard who, for some years, had been working her way unchallenged through the male population of Westbridge, had had her nose very severely disjointed by the episode and although, as far as everyone knew, Bill and Rowena's affair was long over, she had never got over the disappointment of having to stand in line for a lover.

In Joy's own mind the saga had served as an example of the Scotsman's unbridled lechery, rumours of which had grown with every year that passed, largely fuelled by her own and Grace Forland's zeal in keeping them alive.

'Oh no,' groaned Ruth, her laughter dying away as she caught sight of the new arrivals. 'I don't believe it.'

The Blakeneys' car came to a halt and out piled all four occupants. Lollo, who had been having a lie down after all the excitement, leapt to her feet again, preparatory to starting the second show of the day.

'Get down, get down,' squawked Joy, flapping her hands and staggering a little. She wished now she'd had time for lunch.

'Well, the dog seems to be all right,' remarked her husband. Garth Forland scowled. 'It's put on a lot of weight. They don't like it, the small breeds. It plays dickie with their hearts.'

Grace shushed him, and the four of them approached stealthily. Bill and Ruth watched.

'Say something,' Joy hissed to Christopher, endeavouring to smile at the same time.

'Hullo, Ruth,' called Christopher. 'Feeling better?'

'Not that,' hissed Joy again.

'Well, what?' demanded Christopher sulkily.

'Something . . . I don't know . . . Different.'

'Looks like we're in for rain,' he shouted, indicating the clear blue sky above.

'Do you think so?' asked Ruth, wondering why he was shouting. 'Hullo, Joy, Grace.' She nodded to Garth Forland. 'You all know Bill, I expect?'

There was general grunting. 'Do you want to come in for a moment?' Ruth asked, wondering how she was going to get rid of them.

'Oh yes,' said Grace.

'No,' said Joy in the same breath.

'We might as well, now we've come all this way,' snapped Forland ungraciously.

Christopher Blakeney merely shrugged and raised his eyes to heaven.

Ruth unlocked the door and they all filed in, Grace making little whooping noises to show that she admired Ruth's improvements, Joy hugging her cardigan to her and still trying to fend off Lollo who associated her with bowls of batter. Garth Forland's eyes roved minutely over the living room for a place where Ruth might store alcohol.

Christopher sat down and gave Lollo a pat. She leapt thunderously on to his knee and endeavoured to lick his face. 'Good God, Ruth, what have you been feeding this animal?' he wheezed. 'She weighs a ton. Anyone would think she was . . .' He stopped as he caught Ruth's desperate expression. 'Heavy bones, dachshunds,' he mumbled, as though he knew what he was talking about.

'I think I'll be off,' Bill murmured to Ruth as she went to make them all coffee. Ruth grabbed his arm.

'Oh please don't go. I'll never get rid of them on my own.'

Bill hesitated. 'Yes, but your sister-in-law and I don't get on all that well. I think it might be better if I skedaddled.'

Ruth, who had had as much as she could take for one morning, rounded on him. 'If you go now and leave me with this lot, I shall never speak to you again.'

Bill raised his eyebrows quizzically. 'That's a threat, is it?'

'Please, Bill,' she begged. 'Just stay for half an hour. Just till they've gone.'

Bill sighed. 'Why have they come, anyway? Have you established that yet?'

Ruth shook her head. 'No, but I wouldn't be surprised if Garth Forland had a strait-jacket tucked away somewhere. He's giving me the most peculiar looks.'

Bill laughed. 'That's just his squint. All right. I'll stay. I shall make you pay for it, mind.'

'Anything.'

'Anything?'

Ruth caught his eye and blushed. 'Almost anything.'

They knew as soon as they entered the room, Bill carrying the

• Sarah Grazebrook

tray and Ruth following with a plate of biscuits, that they had been talking about them. The soft hiss of sibilants immediately ceased to be replaced by loud bright chat about the weather, the date of Violet Sampson's half marathon and what had happened to the man who used to deliver the milk.

Bill took the tray round and everyone accepted a mug, muttering their thanks like communicants making the responses. Ruth followed with the biscuits which all but Christopher declined. 'Malted milk,' he declared cheerfully. 'They remind me of Christmas.'

'Honestly, Chrissie,' Joy whispered as though they were in a dentist's waiting room, 'I do wish you'd concentrate.'

'What on?' asked Christopher, spraying crumbs all over Lollo. Ruth cleared her throat. 'It's lovely to see you all,' she said and could think of no way to proceed.

There was a silence then Grace Forland leaned forward like a primary teacher prompting the school play. 'It's lovely to see you, Ruth. Looking so WELL.'

This was obviously the cue for her husband to say his piece for Garth Forland, harumphing mightily and wondering why no one had offered him any sugar, put down his mug and strode across to the mantelpiece. Resting his elbow on it he surveyed Ruth critically then demanded, 'Settling in all right?'

'Yes. Thank you,' she replied in some surprise.

'Good,' said Garth, casting a meaningful look at his wife. 'No problems?'

Ruth shrugged. 'Just the usual ones. Nothing particular.'

'Ah,' said Forland, not quite sure how to continue. 'Nothing particular, eh?' Grace Forland coughed quietly to show that he was straying from the point. Forland glared at her and resumed his interrogation. 'Ever had ECT at all?'

Ruth stared at him. 'ECT?' she repeated.

Forland nodded. 'Electro . . . electro . . .' He clicked his fingers irritably.

'Convulsive therapy,' his wife breathed, staring at the toe of her shoe.

'Good for depression, that sort of thing. Does wonders, so I'm told.'

'Really?' said Ruth, wondering if he was quite mad.

Forland took a breath. 'So there it is,' he said in a tone of relief and went back to his sugarless coffee. There was another silence. Joy seemed to be experiencing some kind of fit.

Ruth decided it was time to take the bull by the horns. 'Exactly why have you come?' she asked, aiming her question at her sister-in-law as the most likely instigator. Joy tried to pull herself together. She had a splitting headache and was no longer entirely sure herself why they were there. Probably it was something to do with their solicitors and Ruth being ill. Before she could speak, Christopher Blakeney lifted Lollo carefully off his lap, stretched his legs which were riddled with pins and needles and said, 'To be honest, Ruth, it's all to do with some letter you wrote – which none of us had any right to look at,' he added, throwing a vicious look at his wife. 'Joy got it into her head that you had some problem with a man, of some sort. Not that it's any of our business, but then we heard there was an ambulance on its way here, and I'm afraid it all got a bit out of hand, as things tend to do in small communities. And that's the sum tale of our presence here. Anyway, I'm glad to see you're okay. I'm sure we've taken up quite enough of your precious time for one day, so we'll be on our way and leave you in peace.' He jerked his head commandingly at Joy, who could do no more than open and close her mouth several times before allowing herself to be escorted back to the car, trailed by the Forlands.

Ruth followed them to the door. Bill, who had said nothing throughout, came with her, just in time to hear Joy's newly regained voice demanding to know 'What have they done with Adrian?' before Christopher all but threw her into the car and sped away.

He put his hand on Ruth's shoulder. 'Some relations you've got,' he said musingly. For some reason Ruth did not resent the remark. She glanced at him and smiled. 'You should meet Duncan,' she said, 'if you think Joy's a pest.'

23

Ruth emptied baked beans over the toast. 'I'm sorry it's not more exciting. I haven't had much time to do any shopping lately.'

Bill laughed. 'I can't think why. This is fine, honestly. Wonderful. A feast.'

'Don't overdo it,' Ruth warned him. 'I'm not susceptible to flattery.'

'Everyone's susceptible to flattery. You've just got to know which bits to flatter.'

Ruth glanced at him ironically. 'I should think that's something you're rather good at.'

Bill surveyed her. 'What's that supposed to mean?'

'Well, you have half the women of Westbridge falling at your feet, if the rumours are true.'

'Oh, they're true all right,' said Bill airily. 'Would I be right in supposing you belong to the other half?'

Ruth laughed. 'I think I probably do. I've got enough problems without dying of unrequited love.'

'How do you know it's unrequited?'

Ruth looked up and saw that he was still watching her. She smiled awkwardly. 'Let's call it intuition,' she said brightly. 'Do you want some more beans? I can open another tin.'

'No thanks,' said Bill. 'That was fine. So, what will you do with young Lollo now you've got her home? And the pups, for that matter?'

Ruth looked worried. 'I wish I knew. It seemed such a good idea at three o'clock this morning. Now I can't help thinking I've made an awful mistake. I mean, what do I know about puppies, for God's sake? I can't even look after my own son.'

Bill looked surprised. 'I didn't realise you had children.'

'Only one. Martin. He's nineteen. He's just broken up with his girlfriend. He rang me this morning in an awful state and I was just no use to him at all.'

'In what way?'

'Oh I just said all the wrong things. Stupid useless things about Time being a great healer and all that rubbish.'

'It's true rubbish.'

'Yes, but it's not what you want to hear, is it, when you're feeling like that?'

Bill sighed. 'I suppose not. It's not a problem I've had to deal with. Children.' He was silent for a minute, then roused himself. 'Anyway, back to the pups. Have you been in touch with Madge?'

'Madge?'

'She knows all there is to know about dogs and a bit beyond. Why don't you have a word with her?'

Ruth hesitated. 'To tell the truth, I think Madge is a bit annoyed with me. She had a go at me about leaving Lollo alone so much. She was the one who said I should put her back in the kennels if I couldn't look after her properly. I don't think I dare tell her what I've done now.'

Bill laughed. 'You don't want to worry about Madge's temper. No one escapes that for long. Give her a ring. I'll bet you ten quid she never even mentions you've had a row.'

'It wasn't exactly a row. More like a dressing down.'

'There you go then. Eat humble pie. Say you were wrong. She's not one to gloat. And she really is our best bet.'

'Ours?' said Ruth in some surprise.

Bill shrugged. 'I am the father of the groom.'

Ruth smiled. 'Well, in that case, perhaps you could make the call?'

Lollo sat like the Queen of Sheba on a bean bag in the middle of Madge's lounge. She had been prodded, albeit gently, squeezed and had her tongue inspected. Now the large woman with the deep voice was pronouncing on her.

'Three weeks max, I'd say. Four pups minimum. She's in pretty good shape, considering.' Ruth lowered her head. 'What have you done about a whelping box?'

'A what?' asked Ruth.

'Whelping box.' Madge did imaginary measurements with her outstretched arms. 'Three by four, I should say, to be on the safe side. You'll need an infra-red. Don't want the poor mites freezing to death, do we? I can lend you one, if you like.'

'Thank you,' said Ruth, quite overwhelmed by the prospect of what lay ahead.

'You'll need to keep the vet informed. Just in case. I use Jenkins. He's a bit past it, but he'll come out for me. And he's cheap, compared to those nancies they use at the kennels. Start saving your newspapers. They get through a mass of those. Here,' she scribbled mightily on the back of an envelope. 'You'll need to lay in these.'

'What are they?' asked Ruth, staring hopelessly at the physician's scrawl.

'Supplements, and a few bits and bobs for cleaning up etcetera. Main thing is to keep her happy. That's always the recipe for a healthy litter.'

'How am I supposed to do that?'

'Lots of love and affection. Heavens, woman, you're a mother. I shouldn't have to tell you about that.'

'I'm sure I didn't have to have half of this for Martin,' Ruth grumbled as they drove away.

'You mean you didn't feel the urge to tear up newspapers?'

'Can't say I did.'

'Call yourself a mother? D'you hear that, Lollo? Your mother here thinks you're a pest.'

'Don't you start,' said Ruth.

'Start what?'

'Talking to her as though she's human.'

'She's more convincing than you are. Sometimes,' he added quickly.

Ruth grunted. 'Do you want me to drop you at home?'

Bill looked pained. 'I thought we were going to make a day of it. Go into town. Choose the trousseau, post the bans. Where do you suppose you post a dog's banns?'

• Sarah Grazebrook

'On a lamp-post, I should think. I hope you're going to make this whelping box for me, by the way. I'm hopeless at building things.'

'Call yourself a New Woman? Leave it to me. I have a way with wood. What are we going to have for supper?'

They bought some food, then took the dogs for a walk.

Ruth cooked steaks and they watched television, then tore up the lottery tickets Bill had insisted they buy down the town. 'I didn't want to win anyway,' he said, tossing the pieces into a bin.

'Why buy a ticket then?'

'So that I could say that and impress you with my strength of character.'

'You'd've impressed me a lot more if you'd won.'

'I wouldn't have said it then.'

Ruth laughed. 'I thought not.' She chucked her pieces into the bin as well. 'I do wish I'd won. I wish it like mad.'

'Why? What on earth would you do with ten million quid?'

Ruth closed her eyes. 'So much.'

'What?'

'Well, for a start I'd get the heating fixed in this cottage. Joy's right. It's the coldest place I've ever stayed in.'

'What else?'

'Oh I don't know. The usual things. A new car. A holiday. A decent whelping box.'

Bill had spent an hour and a half trying to construct a square from four planks of wood.

'It is a decent whelping box – will be when I've finished anyway.'

Ruth started to giggle. 'You're the only person I've ever known who could make four pieces of wood into a triangle.'

'It's not a triangle,' Bill protested. 'It's just a bit crooked.'

'That's because you've nailed one of the bits to the top.'

'That was an experiment. I may not leave it like that.'

'I sincerely hope you don't. The puppies will all fall out of the bottom.'

'Trust me. It'll be all right on the night. I have a way with wood.'

'So you said. You didn't say it was the way of a death-watch beetle.' She suddenly became aware that he was watching her again. She stopped laughing. 'Why are you staring at me like that?'

Bill roused himself. 'Was I staring? Sorry. I was just thinking how pretty you look when you're laughing. Quite different.'

'Oh thank you,' said Ruth, the blood rushing to her face. 'I think that's what's called a double-edged compliment.'

'It's not a compliment at all,' said Bill matter-of-factly. 'It's a statement of fact. And a warning.'

'Thanks for the warning,' said Ruth.

Bill continued to look at her. 'Now I've offended you.'

'Of course you haven't.'

'Of course I have. I have a wonderful habit of saying the wrong thing to people.'

'The "wrong thing" being the truth, I dare say?' Ruth observed dejectedly.

Bill shrugged. 'My version of the truth. I'm not always right, you know.'

Ruth threw up her hands in amazement. 'Whatever gives you that idea?'

Bill chuckled. 'I asked for that, didn't I? Are you coming to my class on Tuesday?'

'If you really want me to.'

'I do. I missed you last week.'

Ruth smiled. 'I'm sure you did amongst the adoring literati of Westbridge.'

'A little adoring never did anyone any harm. You should try it some time.'

'No thanks. Anyway, I should think you've got more than enough from Gwen Pritchard. She's pretty smitten with you, you know.'

Bill laughed. 'Ah Gwen,' he said.

'Yes,' said Ruth, 'and what about "Ah Rowena" while we're at it?' As soon as she had spoken she regretted it. Bill's face changed from amusement to something close to anger.

'I think we can leave Rowena out of this,' he said coldly.

'I'm sorry,' Ruth stammered in bewilderment. 'I didn't mean to upset you. It was supposed to be a joke.'

Bill's face softened slightly. 'I know. It's just that Rowena's a joke to a few too many people round here. She's a nice woman. She's had a lot to put up with.'

'You don't have to tell me that,' said Ruth energetically. 'That husband of hers for a start.'

'That prat,' Bill spat the words out. 'I could kill that man when I think of what he's put her through. I take it you've heard the history?'

'Madge told me,' said Ruth warily. She had never seen Bill so angry before. He sat for a moment, his hands clenched on the table in front of him, then looked up and caught her eye.

'It's not too much to ask, is it?' he said quietly. 'A baby?'

'No,' said Ruth. 'But it's not always possible. It's not anyone's fault. It's just the way things turn out.'

Bill nodded. 'Maybe. Would you have wanted more?'

Ruth thought. 'Yes, I suppose I would. I don't know. It's all so long ago. I stopped thinking about it years ago, once it became clear Duncan and I weren't going to be happy together. I concentrated on other things. You have to.'

Bill roused himself. 'That's right. That's what you have to do. Or find someone else.'

Ruth looked across at him, cursing herself for what she was about to say. 'Did you find Rowena, or did she find you?'

Bill gave a short laugh. 'Neither, really. It was a sort of mutual arrangement. Oh I've slept with her a few times, but it's more for comfort, if you see what I mean.'

'Not really,' said Ruth, depression settling on her like a shroud.

'She's crazy about the bastard. I was just a shoulder to cry on. She did a fair bit of that. I suppose it made me feel good at the time. Useful. I thought I was in love with her, but then when I thought about it again, I decided it was only lust.' He sighed. 'I suppose that's all it ever is unless you're very lucky.'

'I wouldn't know,' said Ruth.

'Yes you would,' said Bill and, leaning over, took her face in his hands and kissed her forcefully on the mouth. Ruth wrenched herself away from him.

'Why did you do that?' asked Bill curiously.

Ruth stared at him furiously. 'Because I'm not one of your "harem", as Madge calls them. I may be divorced and lonely and presumably fair game as far as you're concerned, but,' she fumbled for words to express her resentment. 'I'd ... I'd just like you to know that I am not available for evenings when Gwen Pritchard's laid up with someone else, and Rowena Mills has her own husband around to be sick over.'

Bill looked palpably shocked. 'I seem to have got this a bit wrong,' he said slowly and without another word, picked up his coat and left the house.

Ruth heard the sound of his car churning away down the drive. She sat for a while then got up and wandered into the kitchen. Lollo followed her. Silently the two of them surveyed Bill's efforts at a whelping box. 'Men,' said Ruth miserably. Lollo licked her hand in commiseration.

The following day Joy phoned to say that Adrian Mills had broken a bone in his foot and had severe bruising to three ribs. He was to be kept in till the doctor had seen him again on Monday. Gwen had been discharged on Saturday evening, having waited five hours in Casualty, before a doctor pronounced her a very lucky woman and sent her off into the night with a prescription for witch hazel and a long hot bath.

Joy, now recovered from the effects of her gin, had decided in the cold light of day that of the two of them, Gwen was indisputably the madder, and as such had downgraded her position on the pageant committee from 'producer's assistant' to 'matron', which basically meant she had to look after all the children whose parents could not be persuaded to remain with them while the event was in progress. Gwen had whimpered a great deal when informed of this change, but to no effect.

All this Joy imparted to Ruth whom she had now concluded needed occupation above all things, particularly as she seemed to have fallen under the spell of the egregious Bill Bartholomew who would obviously do all in his power to thwart the success of the spectacle, possibly by undermining Ruth's confidence in her excellent script.

Having re-read Ruth's letter between paracetamols the night before, Joy was firmly convinced that, if indeed it had been written by Ruth, this was merely a temporary aberration, and as such would be best forgotten, at least until the pageant were out of the way. In this her husband totally concurred.

- Sarah Grazebrook

Ruth had spent a troubled night, worrying about how she would cope with Lollo's pups, what, if anything, she should tell the Taylors, and most of all, how to come to terms with her own feelings for Bill Bartholomew.

She told herself that she was being stupid. He plainly saw her as just one more potential conquest and not a very vital one at that, since he had seen fit to boast about his previous amours in a manner that was scarcely short of confessional. Perhaps he saw her as 'a shoulder to cry on', although from the way he had kissed her that was not her prevailing impression. And why had she kicked up such a fuss? Where was the harm? She was free, unattached. Opportunities like that were hardly likely to come her way on a daily basis from now on. She should have taken the chance while she had it. Common sense told her Bill would not be likely to try his luck again.

And yet she was glad she had not succumbed. Not only because of his past, his reputation, his cavalier approach to the whole affair. She was glad because, however little she meant to him, he had come to mean rather a lot to her and when she left Westbridge she would like her memory of him to be a happy one, one that she could work upon in her dreams, rather than a sordid little reminder of how low her self-esteem had sunk.

24

Part of Joy's plan to occupy her sister-in-law lay less with a desire to see her happy than a firm intention of prising Gwen Pritchard away from Adrian Mills.

Although in her heart she found him singularly tedious, Mills had always come in useful as a 'spare' man, even before she had banished Rowena from the house.

Joy saw her gatherings at Harbinger House as an entrée for many to the 'beau monde' of Westbridge, her own position being accordingly elevated. It behoved her therefore to have on hand an adequate supply of spare men to sit with aged aunts, plain daughters and, more recently, rejected sisters-in-law.

She had never intended that anything should come of her energetic matchmaking between Ruth and Adrian. Awfully though Duncan had behaved, she was too much his flesh and blood to allow an ex-wife to betray him on her doorstep. With Adrian she had known herself to be safe, since even he must recognise the difficulties of training another woman to quite the degree of subservience he seemed to have achieved with Rowena. Besides, Ruth had no money, an even deeper disincentive to any involvement as far as Adrian would be concerned.

The dratted Gwen, however, was another matter entirely. She was well off, constantly available, and quite drippy enough to throw herself under an oncoming train if Adrian suggested it might make a good picture. Well, if Gwen thought that would give her automatic entry to the Blakeneys' sceptred circle, she had another think coming.

With this in mind Joy rang Ruth and suggested that she might

• Sarah Grazebrook

like to visit Adrian in hospital. To her surprise Ruth was rather brutal in her refusal.

'You could take him some chocolate,' she persisted. 'Apparently they've put him on a liquid diet. He's taking it rather badly.' She refrained from adding that the reason for such stringent treatment was Adrian's avowed intention of staying in hospital till the result of his rabies scan was available. Since this would take a minimum of six weeks, the doctor had seen no other way of ensuring his rapid eviction.

'No,' Ruth repeated. 'I'm sorry, Joy, but I honestly can't see the point of going and sitting by someone's bed when I have nothing at all to say to them and they have even less to say to me.'

'That's because he's shy,' suggested Joy half-heartedly. Even she could sense she was on to a loser. 'Well, if you're absolutely sure . . . ?'

'I am.'

'In that case can I get you to give Grace a hand with the togas? She's doing awfully well but she does seem to think forty-two may be more than she can handle. She could drop the material round to you. I've got it all here. It's terribly simple. You just have to hem along the edge and then bind them with blue and gold.'

'I'm not very good at sewing.'

'No I know, but needs must. By the way, I've got you down to help Gwen Pritchard with the charioteers.'

'In what way?' asked Ruth rather sickly.

'Clearing up. We need two people to walk behind the horses just in case there are any little accidents. I'd send Violet but she goes faster than the horses. Some of the mothers have complained because the children are barefooted. Lot of fuss over nothing if you ask me. Are you coming to the auditions, by the way?'

'What auditions?'

'For the parts, of course. I thought you might like to sit in on them, seeing that you wrote the damn thing. Oh, I didn't mean that, Ruth. It's absolutely brilliant. Things are just beginning to get a bit on top of me, that's all. There's so little time and so much to do.'

'Even so, I think it might be better if you did the auditioning without me, Joy. I really know very little about that sort of thing.'

'Oh, you wouldn't have to do anything. It would just be nice to have you along. Moral support and that.'

'When is it?'

'Wednesday night. You could pick up the togas at the same time.'

Ruth arrived to collect Joy and the togas with a decided sense of misgiving.

The other members of the panel were already in situ, seated in a row at the far end of the village hall, shuffling lists and looking for all the world like magistrates about to sentence a gang of grave robbers.

They consisted of the local vicar who, in keeping with Christopher Blakeney's predictions, had been inveigled into accepting the role of director on the promise of a service to 'bless the pageant' and a portion of the ensuing profits.

A faded man with a permanently embarrassed expression, he sat on the end, together with Garth and Grace Forland, Kevin Mulcahy from the council and finally Joy, who made them all change seats before installing herself in the middle and demanding to know if any of them had reconsidered offering themselves for the role of Julius Caesar. There were grunted negatives from all present, at which point she turned to Ruth who had found herself a seat at the side of the stage and was endeavouring to hide behind the curtain.

'What about you, Ruth? After all, you wrote it. You shouldn't have any trouble learning the lines.'

Ruth peered out from her refuge with ill-concealed alarm. 'But I'm a woman.'

Her defence was treated with the contempt it deserved. 'Oh we take no account of sex here,' Joy informed her cheerfully. She turned to the others. 'Do we?'

'No,' they all affirmed, though Ruth noticed Garth Forland had gone a rather curious colour.

'Who would follow the chariots?' she reminded them. This had a far more telling effect and it was generally agreed that

• Sarah Grazebrook

they would have to try and find someone from the assembled hopefuls now lining the corridor.

The auditions began. They were for speaking roles only, since anyone who merely fancied being a centurion or a morris dancer could lay claim to their part by filling in a list Joy had stuck to the notice board in the lobby.

There was a slight hiatus when Garth Forland, practically comatose with boredom after the fifth rendition of 'Once more unto the breach, dear friends,' by those aspiring to the part of Ethelred the Unready, asked that the Saxon maidens, composed almost entirely from the sixth form of Westbridge High, should be allowed to parade before the panel.

'Why?' Joy demanded, glaring at him from behind the dark glasses she had adopted for her role as impresario.

'Because . . .' Garth's heavy hands flapped despondently around.

'Perhaps we should see some of the ladies next?' murmured the vicar whose voice was as faded as his appearance.

'Good idea,' snapped Mulcahy. 'We've been here nearly an hour and all we've had are these Ethelred people. Give it to that first bloke. He was all right.'

Joy studied her list. 'Lee Cartwright?' she said.

'That's the one,' said Mulcahy.

'That wouldn't be the Lee Cartwright who works in your office, would it, Kevin? The one who's so good at writing?' Joy gave him a withering smile. Mulcahy went pink and said he didn't care who got the part so long as they got a move on. Grace suggested a coffee break which everyone agreed to, and afterwards matters proceeded rather more quickly since half the auditioners had lost patience and wandered off to the pub.

By nine o'clock they had their Julius Caesar, a red-faced man with a stammer and a splendid Roman nose. The nose had won out over the stammer, which Joy had insisted was nerves. No one saw fit to point out that if he was nervous in front of five people in a village hall, how on earth would he feel before the assembled masses of East Kent? Truth was, no one much cared by then.

The part of Thomas à Becket had been allocated, in absentia, to Adrian Mills, on the grounds that Grace had made the archbishop's vestments too short and that now Mills was confined to a wheelchair (at his own insistence), he would be amply covered by the material. It would also serve to conceal his video camera, thus allowing him to film the spectacle from a magnificent vantage point. Joy drew the line at his wheelchair-cum-throne being mounted on a rotating pedestal to facilitate better coverage of the event. 'He'll just have to twist about a bit,' she decreed.

Ruth was interested to note that, despite Joy's own protestation that sex was no barrier, all of the women who came to audition went away with the parts of 'handmaid to Britannia', 'second serving wench to King Ethelred', 'nun', however passionate their delivery of the pieces they had chosen to perform.

At a quarter to ten the janitor appeared and began to make noisy passes with his broom. 'Not much longer, Mr Jay,' whimpered the vicar. 'He likes to be closed up by ten,' he confided to the panel, smiling nervously.

Garth Forland, who had been asleep, jumped violently as the janitor dropped a chair behind him. 'What? Oh my God. Yes,' he said, blowing his nose heartily. 'Are we off?'

'Not quite,' murmured his wife. 'Are there many more on your list, Joy? Only . . .'

Joy shook her head. 'I think we've about cracked it,' she said, folding up her lists and preparing to put them in her bag.

'You finished now, Vicar?' asked the janitor meaningfully.

'Yes, yes, I think so, Mr Jay. Thank you very much.'

'What about the others, then?' demanded the man. 'Only I like to be shut by ten.'

'What others?' dithered the vicar.

'The women. There's two of them out there. Been there all evening. Only I like to be . . .'

'Yes, all right. We know that,' cut in Joy. 'I don't know what they can be here for. All the women's parts have been cast. Ask them to add their names to the list for nuns. We need lots of those. Would you?'

The man looked perplexed. 'I don't think they want to be nuns. They say they're here for Britannia.'

'Britannia?' It was Joy's turn to go a funny colour. 'What on earth can they mean? The role is cast. Perhaps you'd be kind enough to say so.'

The janitor hunched his shoulders. 'Nothing to do with me,'

• Sarah Grazebrook

he said. 'You tell 'em. They've been there all evening. I doubt they'll take it kindly.'

Joy sighed. 'I sometimes think I have to do everything in this life. All right. Ask them to come in, please.' The man shuffled off.

Garth Forland was frowning mightily. 'I think I might have dropped off for a minute,' he observed.

'Forty, more like,' snapped Joy.

'But who is playing Britannia?' Garth persisted.

'Yes,' Mulcahy added. 'Who is?' The vicar, too, looked a little bemused. Joy stared at them as if they were mentally deficient. 'I am, of course,' she said finally. 'I should have thought that was obvious.'

'Is it?' asked Garth belligerently.

'Well, who else is there?' asked Joy kindly. 'Grace?'

Grace's face lit up for one brief moment till she realised the suggestion had been made sarcastically.

'Don't see why not?' said her husband loyally, although having seen her hips and the proposed costume he thought it was probably a long shot.

'Oh really,' said Joy, trying to maintain her good humour. 'Anyway she'd hate it, wouldn't you, Grace?'

Before she could answer Kevin Mulcahy stepped in. 'If these women have been waiting all evening, we owe it to them to see them,' he said firmly. 'After all, it's rate-payers' money we're using. What do you think, Vicar?'

The vicar made a mewing sound at which point the janitor returned to say that one of the women was going but the other wouldn't budge. 'Tell them we'll be delighted to see them both,' said Mulcahy authoritatively and sat down. The others followed suit. Mr Jay retraced his steps.

Gwen was the first to appear. She came tiptoeing round the door with the stealth of a cat burglar and the timidity of a mouse.

'Ah,' said Garth Forland, looking more animated than he had all evening. 'It's young Gwen.'

'I don't believe it,' muttered Joy, taking off her sunglasses and passing a hand across her forehead. She leaned forward. 'Gwen, dear, what on earth has got into you?'

Gwen stopped and seemed about to retreat, but Forland was having none of it. 'She'd make a champion little Britannia if you ask me,' he informed his confrères. 'Just the right . . . just the right . . .' He stopped, having caught his wife's eye. 'Anyway,' he said sulkily. 'Give some of the young'uns a chance, eh, Vicar?'

The vicar jumped, having been called upon to make a decision. 'Er,' he said, 'possibly so. Why not, after all?' He got no further as Joy quelled him with a look.

'Gwen has absolutely no experience of acting, have you, dear?' she stated.

'Well,' said Gwen, dimpling very slightly.

'It's a pageant, for God's sake,' bellowed Forland. The vicar blanched. 'She doesn't have to act. She just has to sit there looking . . .' Again Grace caught his eye.

'Exactly,' said Joy. 'Anyway, who's going to look after all those adorable children? Not to mention the charioteers? Thank you so much for coming in, Gwen. Perhaps next time?'

Even Gwen could not fight this. She tiptoed out again, the droop of her shoulders as expressive as anything from the commedia dell'arte.

Violet Sampson was not so easily disposed of. She came striding down the centre of the hall with a look that said, had she had a trident handy, two at least of the panel would now be impaled on it.

'I've been out there for hours,' she accused before anyone could speak.

'I really am terribly sorry,' twittered the vicar who was hoping to ask her to run for the church roof. 'We . . . there was a bit of confusion. We thought . . .' He looked at Joy for support.

'Violet, have you gone stark staring mad?' was the best she could offer.

Violet's nostrils retracted, making her look more like a horse than ever. 'I don't know what you mean,' she countered. 'You advertised auditions. I assumed that meant they were open to anyone?'

'Yes, indeed,' said Kevin Mulcahy anxiously. He didn't want any letters to the press. 'We're very grateful that you've spared the time to come along. Was there any particular role you had in mind?'

- Sarah Grazebrook

'Britannia,' said Violet uncompromisingly, and launched into a high-pitched rendition of 'Daffodils'.

'Ah,' said Mulcahy and looked to his colleagues for assistance.

'Britannia's cast,' said Joy. 'You can be a nun if you like. There are plenty of those.'

'No, thank you,' said Violet, looking her straight in the eye. She had not forgiven her for all those five pence pieces, half of which had turned out to be centimes. 'Who exactly is playing the part?'

'That will be announced later,' said Joy sharply.

Violet continued to glare. 'Well, it isn't Gwen Pritchard, that's for sure.'

'How do you know?' asked Grace quickly.

'Because she's in the lav crying her eyes out,' said Violet indifferently.

'Oh, I say.' Garth Forland half rose, then sank back as his wife glanced at him.

'And since she and I were the only people interested in the part, it seems a bit odd that you say it's already cast.'

There was a clearing of throats. 'I think I shall let Mrs Blakeney explain,' said Mulcahy, sitting back in his chair and folding his arms, Pilate fashion.

Joy shrugged. 'Violet, it's sweet of you to have turned out like this, particularly when we all know how busy you are. And PARTICULARLY knowing how much you hate appearing in public, even when it's for a good cause like the Westbridge pageant. It is appreciated, do take my word for it. Unfortunately, or fortunately even,' she allowed herself a deprecating giggle, 'the author has insisted that I play the part of Britannia on this occasion. It is, after all, a new work, and the roles have been created in some instances with certain people in mind. I have been chosen for Britannia. Goodness knows, I would rather have taken a back seat, considering all the other things I have to be responsible for but,' Joy spread her palms with gallic sangfroid, 'there it is.'

Violet's thin face thinned to a pencil point. 'That is a pity,' she said fiercely, 'because Roddy Brown up at Malvern Farm was going to let me use his shires for the chariot.'

Kevin Mulcahy sat forward. 'What's he charging?' he demanded. Violet affected to look unconcerned. 'Oh, he was going to lend them for free. But only if I was in charge of them, obviously. They can be a bit tricky to handle.'

The panel exchanged glances. 'That would save us a fortune,' Forland said cautiously. 'Those buggers at the brewery wanted two hundred. Plus insurance.'

'Are they insured?' asked Mulcahy.

'Naturally. But only for an accredited handler.'

'And you are accredited?'

'I am,' said Violet ponderously.

Silence fell.

'There was also the question of him lending a couple of wagons for the floats,' said Violet presently. 'Still, if you've made your minds up . . .'

'We have,' said Joy savagely. Mulcahy held up his hand for peace.

'Nothing is settled yet,' he said firmly. 'May I take your phone number, Mrs . . . Miss . . . ?'

'Mizz,' said Violet and wrote it for him on an envelope.

Duncan Page rang just as Ruth was going to bed.

Lollo could no longer get up the stairs and she had taken some time to settle her. Although she had never let her sleep anywhere but the kitchen, the size and obvious discomfort of the animal was beginning to worry her. She had left her copious bowls of water, warm milk with glucose, as prescribed by Madge, and supplies of *Radio Times* to shred, but Lollo was twitchy and fractious and, more to the point, had ignored a chocolate biscuit which Ruth had given her as a concession to pregnant cravings.

The dog had finally collapsed unwillingly into her basket, ears damp with sweat and dark eyes luminous with uncertainty.

When the phone rang Ruth grabbed it, hoping beyond hope that it was Madge Jordan, allerted by a sixth sense to her anxiety and offering to drive over immediately with cold compresses and an unerring knowledge of what would be right to do.

'Ruth? Is that you?'

Her heart sank. 'Duncan?'

'Who else did you think it would be?'

'I am in constant touch with Downing Street,' said Ruth with the sort of forlorn wit that she knew would be wasted on her ex-husband.

There was a pause. 'Are you all right, Ruth?'

'Yes, I'm perfectly all right, Duncan. Why have you rung?'

'We've sold the house.'

'What?' A blanket of ice descended on her.

'We've sold the house. I've had an offer. It's not very good, but it's definite. Some army officer, back from Hong Kong. They were buying a place in Turnham Green and it's fallen through. Survey no go. Want to move in as soon as possible. Obviously we can't do a thing till the Websters debunk but it's looking good. I just wanted to check it was okay to proceed?'

Ruth tried to say something but found that her voice had disappeared.

'Ruth, are you still there?'

'Yes,' she croaked.

'Well, don't play silly buggers with me. The offer's for a hundred and eighty. I know it's a drop, but to be frank I think we'd be fools to hang on for more. I know they keep saying the market's picking up but there's no sign of it round here, I can assure you. A hundred and eighty minus the mortgage, that's a hundred, minus the estate agent's fees and the solicitor and all that, should be around eighty-five clear.'

Ruth, though dazed, was not sufficiently comatose to put up with this. 'Duncan, that's rubbish. How can an estate agent and solicitor possibly come to fifteen thousand?'

There was a pause. 'Well, it may be a bit more than that. I was just rounding it down to be on the safe side.'

You weren't, thought Ruth, you were trying to pull the bloody wool over my eyes. That's why you rang last thing at night. Like the police, raiding people's houses at dawn. You don't get me like that.

'I can't possibly give you an answer straight away, Duncan. Call me in a few days.'

'A few days? What on earth for? I've told you the facts. The man's desperate. I can't keep him hanging about. He'll offer for somewhere else.'

'Let him.'

'"Let him". Ruth, have you taken leave of your senses? This is a house we're talking about, not who wants the last cake at one of your blasted charity boot fairs.'

Ruth steeled herself. 'I know it is, Duncan, and that's why I want time to think about it.'

'But . . .'

'And there's no need to start "iffing and butting". I've made up my mind. I want time to think about it. As you said yourself, it's a very meagre offer and I have my future to consider.'

'I understand that, Ruth, but so have I. And so has Martin. I really don't see how I can continue to support him at university without some capital. I've done my best, but to be honest, funds are running very low. I've looked at it from all angles, and this is definitely our best bet. You know me. I'm only thinking of him.'

Ruth looked at the phone. I hate you, she thought. You horrible self-interested creep. And I hate your fat voracious concubine. 'I'll speak to my solicitors in the morning,' she said coolly, 'but I wouldn't like to raise any false hopes.'

25

Ruth's solicitors, needless to say, advised a quick sale. For a start they could see very little likelihood of their bill being settled till their client got hold of some real money. Secondly they had been given a very hard time by the firm of Millet and Bailey, the senior partner having turned out to be Master of the same lodge as Ruth's representative. They recommended immediate acceptance – the market was unstable, the purchaser sound, no chain was involved, delay would be costly.

Ruth acceded.

From what she could gather the sale would be completed by the end of June. Suddenly the sojourn that had seemed like half a lifetime when she arrived in Westbridge in February, had become a matter of weeks.

Between now and completion she must quit the cottage, find somewhere else to live, dispose of a litter of mongrels and decide what she was going to do with the rest of her life. It all seemed a bit much for a woman who had spent the last twenty years getting from Monday to Friday with no more taxing decision than when to pick up the cleaning.

She lay in bed listening to Lollo shuffling about below. It's all right for you, she thought. You've got me, and Madge. Who have I got? She permitted herself a few self-pitying sniffles, then turned over and tried to look at the positive side. She would have some money. The uncertainty would be at an end. Now she could put her marriage behind her and get on with whatever lay ahead.

At first glance it did not seem awfully promising. A very small flat in a cheaper area of London, far away from everything with which she was familiar. She would have to work, obviously, but doing what? She wasn't precisely qualified and it didn't take genius to remind her she was the wrong age for practically everything except osteoporosis and delivering Meals on Wheels.

She lay on her back and stared at the ceiling. Am I always going to be such a pessimist, she wondered. Look at me. I'm here. I'm managing. I'm a trained market researcher. They must be crying out for people like me in London. I'm free. I need never speak to Duncan again, unless Martin gets married and then I'll be drunk. I shall be happy in a little flat. I won't have to spend half my life cleaning it. I shall go to the theatre and concerts and have my ears pierced. I shall buy long flowing skirts with elasticated waists and never be uncomfortable again. I shall do an OU course and go to summer schools and meet interesting men who look like Michael Caine and Harrison Ford.

She fell asleep dreaming of balmy June nights spent discussing literature with Alan Rickman whose velvet tones acquired an unaccountably Scottish burr as the night progressed.

She woke some hours later convinced that she was doomed to pass the rest of her days working as dog trainer for Adrian Mills who had inherited a circus from his uncle, Julius Caesar. After that she fell into a more peaceful sleep and was woken by the sound of Lollo barking at the postman. She opened her eyes and stared at the ceiling again. It seemed much gaudier than she remembered. I shall have no yellow in my new flat, she decided, and went downstairs to see what was left of her mail.

Amongst the circulars was a travel brochure advertising the pleasures of French gites. Ruth was about to throw it away when her eye was caught by a particularly pretty stone cottage with a mountain rising high behind it and a dark blue lake in the distance. Wouldn't it be lovely, she thought, just to get away for a bit? Really away. Somewhere where no one knows me. Or almost no one.

She went into the hall and dialled Martin's number.

He sounded as depressed as ever when he came to the phone.

'Martin, it's Mum. I just wondered how you were.'

'Oh. Right. Okay.'

'Martin, I've had an idea. You can say no.' She waited for

him to do so, but Martin avoided the cue for a joke. 'What is it?'

Ruth soldiered on. 'I've got a brochure that came through the post this morning. It's for French gites. One of them, in the Auvergne, looks really lovely. I wondered if you fancied coming away for a week once your exams finish? You could go climbing, and I could just laze around and read or whatever. I wouldn't get in your way,' she added awkwardly. 'I just thought you might enjoy a bit of a break?'

There was a pause. 'Can you afford it, Mum? Because I haven't got all that much money at the moment.'

Ruth felt relief flooding over her. 'Of course I can, goon. I'm about to become a best-selling author.'

'What?' said Martin, utterly mystified.

Ruth laughed. 'Oh, of course, you don't know about that, do you? Auntie Joy's got me a grant from the EEC for writing her pageant for her. The least I can do is squander it in an EEC country.'

'You've lost me, Mum.'

'Never mind. I'll tell you about it when I see you. Shall I go ahead and book it then? First week of the hols? When do you finish?'

Martin sighed. 'The first of June, I'll be free.'

Ruth hesitated. 'It's only if you want to, Martin. I'm not trying to force you into anything.'

There was a pause then Martin said, 'I know you aren't, Mum. It's a lovely thought. I'd like to go climbing.' He sighed again. 'I'd like to go anywhere that isn't England.'

You and me, both, thought Ruth. She booked the gite that morning.

Preparations for the pageant were now in full swing. Parts had been allotted, with the exception of Britannia, the battle for which looked set to turn into a full-scale war as Joy and Violet Sampson marshalled their supporters.

On paper Violet's credentials looked insuperable but Ruth had a pretty shrewd idea that, come the day, it would be her sister-in-law bearing the trident aloft, possibly with Ms Sampson's entrails dangling from its prongs.

• Sarah Grazebrook

She had been kept busy with Joy's continuing demands, some of which she managed to avoid, but most of which she had endeavoured to fulfil, mainly from a sense of family duty, since the streets of Westbridge were by now strewn with the names of people Joy had offended, discarded or just worked to a standstill.

Rowena had telephoned her several times to do a day's work here and there and she had complied, mainly with a view to getting enough experience to sell herself to the more sophisticated London organisations on her return to the metropolis.

She had seen nothing of Bill Bartholomew. Madge had said something about his being away, but Ruth thought it more likely that he was just avoiding her and told herself she was grateful for it.

She was beginning to receive details from several London estate agents. She had applied to those in her own area first but soon found that she had been right in her assumption. There was nothing she could begin to afford without a mortgage, and without a regular income that was completely off the cards. She wondered about renting, but visions of a desperate old age when the money had run out frightened her off the idea.

She had been up to London and sorted out a storage firm. She had said nothing to either Duncan or Joy, who would doubtless have insisted on accompanying her or, worse still, forced Christopher to take another day off for the purpose.

It had been a depressing business. Though she had not had to enter the house, she had driven past it twice and it was impossible not to feel a lump in her throat at the sight of the familiar blue front door and her rose bush which looked a great deal healthier than when she had had the care of it.

She had arrived back at Bell Cottage tired and disheartened, having taken a detour round some of the areas she had been considering a move to. They were without exception, dry characterless places, suburbia at its worst. I'd be better off where I am, she thought bitterly. The spring had finally arrived and there was something reviving about the cool salty breeze and the fresh greenness of everything. She dismissed the thought as absurd. There is no way that I am going to live within fifty miles of

Joy and Christopher, she affirmed, not unless there's an electric fence all round.

Lollo didn't even get up to greet her. Ruth looked at her huge belly and decided it was time to phone Madge.

They moved Lollo in the next day. She was listless and irritable but showed few signs of objecting as the two women lifted first her basket then her into Ruth's car and drove in stately convoy to Madge's house.

'Where's that whelping box?' Madge demanded as Ruth unloaded Lollo's luggage.

'It's nearly ready,' Ruth demurred, having forgotten all about it since she'd dumped it in the garage after her row with Bill.

'Better bring it round this afternoon,' Madge ordained. 'She could be early by the look of her.'

Ruth hauled it out when she got home. It really was quite hopeless. Whatever Bill had had in mind, it was certainly not clear from the heap of tangled boards now sitting on her table. She tapped it lightly in an effort to straighten one of the sides. The bottom fell out. 'Oh my God, why does he have to be so useless?' she exclaimed in frustration. 'I might just as well have bought one in Harrods. It'd be cheaper in the long run.'

It was while she was trying to fit it in her car boot that Bill Bartholomew arrived. He was on foot and had a distinctly gypsyish air as he came round the corner, swinging a canvas holdall from which protruded various bits of wood and metal. He stopped when he saw her. Ruth stopped too, then continued her struggle. Bill watched her for some moments then approached and stood a few feet from the car, still watching. Ruth jabbed her arm on a corner of the box and yelped with pain, letting go of it as she did so. It clattered to the ground and another piece fell off. Bill stooped and picked it up.

'You've broken it now,' he said aggrievedly.

'It was broken in the first place,' retorted Ruth. 'You made it broken if you remember.'

'That's why I'm here,' said Bill solemnly. 'Madge phoned. Thought you might need some help. I've come to finish it.'

'Finish it off, more likely,' said Ruth, dabbing at her bleeding arm. 'And me with it.'

'I'm glad to see Time has mellowed you,' said Bill, taking

hold of her arm and examining it. 'You'll live. It's only a scratch.'

'Well, it hurts,' grumbled Ruth.

'Will I put a plaster on it for you?'

'Have you got a plaster?'

'Of course I haven't got a plaster. I thought you might have one. In the house.'

'I can't go back to the house,' snapped Ruth. 'I haven't got time. Madge says Lollo may be early with the puppies. She may need this any time. For all I know she's in the middle of giving birth at this very moment.'

'It'll be a bit late for it then, won't it?' said Bill with ruthless practicality.

'Exactly,' said Ruth confusedly. 'Anyway, I can't stand here talking to you. I must get over there.'

'Will I come with you?'

'Whatever for?'

'To finish the box. Just in case we're not too late.'

Ruth hesitated. 'There's really no need. I'm sure Madge will think of something.'

'Happen she will. I'd still like to come. If that's all right?'

Ruth sensed that this was less a request than a statement. She shrugged indifferently. 'All right. Could you put this thing in the car for me, please? I don't want to lose any more blood over it.'

'Oh I wouldn't worry about that,' said Bill, chucking it recklessly into the boot. 'I'm sure your sister-in-law will have the paramedics standing by. I passed her on my way here. She'll have alerted the rescue services by now.'

'Just as well,' said Ruth haughtily. 'Can you not put that bag on the seat, please. It's dusty.'

'So's the bag,' said Bill, dumping it on the seat.

'Thank you,' said Ruth icily.

They drove in silence to Madge's cottage.

If Madge was surprised to see them together she said nothing, directing them immediately to the outhouse where Lollo was now installed with several weeks worth of newspapers, a large bowl of milk and the remains of Gwen Pritchard's once precious scarf.

They stood awkwardly in the doorway like hospital visitors, ignored by the patient and too polite to leave.

'She looks a bit uncomfortable,' Bill observed eventually.

'Yes,' said Ruth and bent down to adjust Lollo's blanket. To her surprise and alarm Lollo growled at her. She retreated rapidly. 'I think that's a bit better.'

'Yes,' said Bill.

They stood for several more minutes, melting under the infra-red lamp Madge had positioned on a shelf. 'It's very warm in here,' said Bill.

'It is, yes. I expect she needs it.'

'Aye. How's your arm?'

Ruth glanced at it. 'Oh, fine.'

They fell silent.

'Look,' said Bill and Ruth in unison.

'You first,' said Bill.

'No, you.'

'I was just going to say,' said Bill, 'perhaps I'd better be going.'

'Yes. Right. What about the box?'

'What box?'

'The whelping box.'

Bill looked genuinely shocked. 'Oh yes. I'd forgotten about that. Momentarily. I'd better ...' he flapped his hands in carpenterly fashion.

'Yes,' said Ruth. 'I'll help you get it out of the car.'

'Oh right. Thanks.'

They returned to the car still exchanging polite small talk. This is ridiculous, Ruth thought. It's just like when Duncan and I used to go to a Parents' Evening after we'd had a row. The moment we were off the premises the whole thing started again. And it'll be just the same with Bill and me. I can tell.

She opened the boot and started to yank Bill's creation out. 'Careful,' said Bill fussily. 'You don't want to break it any more.'

'Don't I just?' snarled Ruth as a splinter entered her thumb. 'You get it out, then.' She stood back, examining her thumb as Bill endeavoured to get the construction out in one piece.

'There,' he said smugly, carrying it in front of him like the Victor Ludorum.

• Sarah Grazebrook

'Would you like me to phone the Tate?' called Ruth, still smarting from the pain of her splinter.

Bill turned to make a withering retort, stumbled over a piece of stone, and tripped. The box crashed to the ground, splitting into three.

'In a word,' said Bill, taking a very deep breath. 'Fuck.'

Ruth hurried over. 'Oh dear,' she said, her cheeks starting to wobble. 'Is it all right?'

'Is it all right?' Bill now let fly with a catalogue of invective that caused even Madge to come and see what the matter was.

'There's no point in all that,' she told him when he paused for breath. 'You'll just have to start again. Better get a move on. She's off her food. That's a sure sign.'

'I'd be off my food it someone wanted me to sleep in that,' said Ruth, who had given up trying to control her laughter.

'I don't know what you're finding so funny,' said Bill furiously. 'There's a lot of hard work gone into that.'

'Yes, still it'll make a lovely bonfire,' Ruth remarked cheerfully. She hadn't enjoyed herself so much for months.

'I've got an old chest of drawers in the spare room,' Madge interrupted. 'You'd better use some of that.'

They followed her into the house. Bill fetched his bag of tools and the two of them stood round the kitchen table handing nails to Madge while she constructed a perfectly sound whelping box. 'There,' she said when it was finished.

'Not bad,' Bill conceded, peering along the edges with a professional eye. 'Just wish I had my plane here to level up those corners.'

'It'll do,' said Madge, before Ruth could respond. 'Call for a drink?'

'Oh, I think so,' said Bill, wiping his forehead. 'It's heavy work, this carpentry. Anywhere I can wash my hands, Madge?'

While he was away Madge produced a bottle of whisky and poured them all a stiff measure. Ruth, who had formerly eschewed spirits, found she was taking to them more and more.

They lined the box with newspapers and transported it to the outhouse where Lollo was eventually persuaded to swap her basket for the new accommodation. Madge pressed and prodded her knowledgeably, Lollo making no objection. Ruth felt this was a touch disloyal.

Bill stretched. 'Better be getting back,' he murmured, his humour restored by the whisky.

'Do you want a lift?' asked Ruth, also feeling mellow.

Bill shook his head. 'No thanks, I could do with the walk.'

'One for the road, then?' said Madge.

Bill shrugged. 'Why not?'

Ruth drove away, feeling strangely unwanted. Added to this was the sense that Lollo had recognised Ruth's uselessness in her present predicament, and had accordingly transferred her affections to Madge, trusting in her to see her through the ordeal to come.

She made herself some supper and had another go at the laurel wreath Joy had asked her to make from the Taylors' treasured bay tree by the porch. She dreaded to think what they would say when they came back. She had had three tries already and the bush was beginning to look like the victim of a deforestation policy.

Shortly before ten the phone rang. It was Martin. He sounded positively jubilant. Ruth did a quick calculation to see whether he could have had his results yet, but his exams didn't start for another week.

'Mum, guess what?'

'What?'

'Great news. Kate and I are back together again.'

A great sweep of joy came over her. 'Oh, Martin, that's wonderful news. I'm so pleased for you. Both of you. That really is excellent. Do give her my love.'

'Yes . . . Mum . . .'

'Yes?' A moment's doubt came over her. She's pregnant, she thought. Oh no.

'You know our holiday?'

'Yes. Do you want to bring Kate? That would be fine. There are two bedrooms. It would be no problem.'

'Mum, I don't know how to say this . . .'

Ruth waited.

'It's just a few of us, we've had the chance of a trip to India. Backpacking. One of the guys has got a Landrover. I wasn't going

• Sarah Grazebrook

to go. Didn't want to go on my own, but now that Kate and I . . . you know. She'd really love to go. I think it would be good for us to get away together. Get to know each other again. I think that's important.'

You sound just like your father, thought Ruth, then cursed her jealousy. She tried to smile. 'Of course, darling. It sounds wonderful. You can't possibly pass up an opportunity like that. Kate will love India, I'm sure of it.'

Martin's relief was tangible. 'Oh, Mum. You're sure you don't mind? I feel dreadful letting you down like this. Kate said we shouldn't dream of going, but I said I'd speak to you about it. If you'd really minded I wouldn't have gone. We'd've come with you to France.'

'Would you?' asked Ruth, struggling to keep the tears out of her voice. 'That is sweet of you both. When are you off?'

'As soon as the exams end. We'll come down and see you before we go, if that's all right?'

'Yes, please do. I'd like that. We've had an offer for the house, by the way. I don't know if your father told you?'

'He did say something about it.' Martin sounded slightly embarrassed. 'I didn't know it was definite.'

'Fairly definite, I think, so I don't know where I'll be when you get back. I'll leave my new address with Auntie Joy. You can get it from her.'

'Yes, okay, Mum. I'll do that. But we'll be down before we go, I promise. You're sure you don't mind?'

'Don't be so silly, darling. Of course I don't mind. It was just something to cheer you up after your exams. India sounds far better.'

'I'll bring you something fab. What would you like? Your own personal buddha? A little green-eyed idol?'

Ruth laughed. 'That would be nice. Make sure it is little, though. I don't think my next home will have room for full-scale statues.'

'I'll get you the flat-pack version.' He paused. 'Mum?'
'Yes?'
'Did Dad say anything else to you?'
'What about?'
Martin hesitated. He was obviously debating the wisdom of

continuing, but he'd gone too far to retreat. 'Oh nothing, really. It's just he said he and Laureen might be getting married, when the sale was through and that. I wasn't really listening. I could have got it wrong.' His voice trailed away.

Ruth was silent.

'Mum, are you still there?'

She roused herself. 'Yes, I'm here. No, he hadn't mentioned it to me, but why should he?' She gave a silly false laugh. 'It's none of my business now. We're both grown up. We've got our own lives to lead. Like you and Kate. Look, darling, I must go. I've got a hundred things to do for this dreadful pageant Auntie Joy's roped me in on. I'll talk to you soon. Give my love to Kate.'

She put the phone down because she couldn't bear to hear any more. That's it, she thought. There's nothing left. No husband, no son, no home, no job, no holiday, not even the bloody dog. Some epitaph, that would make. 'Here lies Ruth Page, whom nobody needed.'

She put the chain on the door and turned the lights out. As she went upstairs the phone rang again. It was Bill. 'Sorry to bother you so late,' came his gruff voice. 'The doggie's gone into labour. I'm afraid it's not looking too good.'

'What do you mean?' asked Ruth, her heart thudding too loudly to hear what he was saying.

'Madge has sent for the vet. The puppies are too big for her. We'll have to wait and see. I just thought I should warn you.'

'I'm coming over,' said Ruth.

'There's no need for that. There's nothing you can do. I just thought you'd want to know.' He paused. 'I am so sorry, Ruth. So sorry.'

'It's not your fault.'

'I think it is. I should have kept Tyson on the lead. None of this would have happened.'

Ruth put her head in her hand. 'No. Still, what's done's done. There's no going back, is there?'

She put the phone down before he could reply.

26

They were still waiting for the vet when Ruth arrived. Hearing her car, both Madge and Bill appeared anxiously at the door of the outhouse. She parked and ran across to them.

'How is she?'

Madge shrugged but her face was grave. Ruth followed them in. Lollo was lying on her side, her silken coat bathed in sweat, her eyes dull and filmy. Periodically she would give a heave and her swollen body would contract in the effort to push the first puppy out. A fine line of foam speckled her jaw. Madge crouched down and wiped it away with a cloth. Lollo gave another heave and started to pant.

The sound of a second vehicle took them flying back to the door. This time it was the vet. He hurried in and quickly examined Lollo.

'She's worn out,' he said. 'I may have to do a caesarian. We'll try this first.' He reached in his bag for a syringe. The three of them stood round in nervous silence as he inserted it in Lollo's neck. She stiffened slightly as the needle went in but seemed otherwise unaffected. Gradually her panting began to subside.

Michael Jenkins, the vet examined the bedding. 'Waters have gone.' He turned to Madge. 'When did she start?'

Madge looked worried. 'We can't be sure exactly. We were in the house. Just came out to check on her and she was plainly in trouble. Must have been between seven and nine. I'm sorry I can't be more exact.'

The vet took Lollo's temperature. 'Not as bad as I thought. She's calming down. First litter?' Madge nodded. Jenkins put his hands round Lollo's stomach and squeezed slightly. He looked puzzled. 'They're very big for dachshunds,' he said curiously. Bill and Ruth exchanged glances.

'They aren't dachshunds,' Ruth said softly.

The vet looked at her. 'What the hell are they then? They feel like baby elephants.'

'They're half labrador,' put in Bill rapidly. 'My dog, Tyson, is the er . . . whatsit.'

Jenkins' face cleared. 'Well, why didn't you say so?' he asked. 'Jesus, man, no wonder she's having trouble. I thought it was one of these Kennel Club nancies and you were expecting a thousand quid for them.' He rolled up his sleeves. 'You may lose one or two but if they're mongrels you won't be that bothered, will you?'

'Yes,' Ruth broke in vehemently. 'Of course we'll be bothered.' Everyone looked at her, making her feel once more that she was out of kilter with the whole world. But this time she didn't care. 'Lollo comes first,' she said firmly, 'but just because they're mongrels doesn't mean the puppies don't matter.'

Michael Jenkins cleared his throat. 'I'm glad you said that,' he said. 'I was just testing the water. I'll do my best.'

He crouched down and very gently reached inside Lollo, massaging her pelvis as he did so and talking very gently to her in a low soothing voice. At first there was no response but very slowly Lollo began to heave again, more rhythmically this time.

'Got it,' said Jenkins and, as they watched he started to ease an opaque sac from the animal's body.

'Oh my God,' said Ruth, watching in fascination as the vet handed the puppy to Madge who immediately tore open the sac, wiping the puppy's mouth and nostrils as Jenkins pinched and cut the cord. 'Oh my God,' she said again, 'it's all right.' The puppy wriggled and squirmed in Madge's arms, its eyes tight shut. She turned to Bill. 'It's all right,' she told him, like a teacher reassuring a child. Bill nodded and smiled in relief.

'It's all right,' she told Madge.

'She certainly is,' said Madge with a proprietorial air.

'She's all right,' Ruth explained to the vet, but he was waiting for the next one.

Lollo had four puppies. Two bitches and two dogs, none of the other three a patch for size on the first one, now named Lola. The last one was decidedly underweight.

Michael Jenkins left at two in the morning, resolutely refusing their combined offers of brandy, gin and champagne, all of which Madge had produced once it became apparent that no fatalities were expected.

Lollo, in character, showed no interest in suckling her brood but, with the exception of Twiggy (the last arrival), the puppies had no trouble in finding nipples to attach themselves to and were soon clamped to her like so many sausages, sucking blindly till the entire family fell asleep.

Madge was of the opinion that Twiggy would want watching, but since her possessiveness towards the pup was bordering on the manic, Ruth and Bill finally acknowledged that they were surplus to requirements and wandered, daft with exhaustion, out into the courtyard.

'I know,' said Bill formally, 'that I said I didn't want a lift earlier . . .'

'But you'd like one now?'

'Yes, please.'

'Of course.'

They said goodnight to Madge who, like a first time grandmother, couldn't wait to get rid of them, and tottered back to Ruth's car.

She turned on the ignition. 'I thought I didn't like dogs,' she said absently as they drove away.

'But Lollo's an exception?' Bill enquired.

'Oh yes. I really hated her.'

Bill looked across at her. 'I don't think you could hate anyone. You're not the type.'

Ruth gave a dry laugh. 'I used to think that.'

'And now?'

'I wouldn't like to put it to the test.'

She turned into Bill's drive and bumped to a stop outside the house. The distant rumble of Tyson's bark greeted them. 'Shut up, you dozy bugger,' called Bill without malice. 'You're a father now. You'll have to start behaving.' He turned to Ruth. 'Will you come in for a cup of something?'

Ruth shook her head. 'I'd better get back.'

• Sarah Grazebrook

'Why?'

'Lollo . . .' She stopped and smiled. 'Yes, all right. I'd love some coffee.'

'I never thought she was going to make it,' Bill admitted, setting the cups down on a table. 'I swear to God I thought that was it. That's why I rang you.'

'I'm glad you did,' said Ruth.

'You didn't sound it.'

'Well, it wasn't exactly good news, was it? And besides . . .'

'Besides what?'

'I'd had some other bad news.'

Bill sat down. 'Do you want to talk about it?'

Ruth sighed. 'Not really. It's not "bad news" in the normal sense. In fact it's excellent news from everybody else's point of view.'

'But not yours?'

'Oh I'm just feeling sorry for myself. I'll be fine once I've got used to the idea. Anyway, it's none of my business any more. People have their own lives to lead. There's no reason why they should take my feelings into consideration.'

Bill put up a hand. 'Yes, we've had the "blessed are the meek" bit. Now why don't you tell me what these bastards have done to make you so miserable? Is it the lovely Joy, by any chance? I hear she's threatening to skewer half of Westbridge with a trident if she doesn't get her part in the pageant.'

Ruth laughed. 'No, it's not her. It's Martin, my son.'

Bill looked surprised. 'I thought you said he was okay.'

'He is. He's marvellous. That's why I should be pleased. You know I told you he'd had a row with his girlfriend and she'd walked out on him?'

'Yes?'

'Well, they're back together again. And they're going to go to India backpacking for the summer.'

'And you're worried?'

'No. Yes, of course. As much as you always are. But he's quite sensible and Kate's very . . . No it's not that. It's . . .'

'What?'

Ruth shook her head. 'This sounds very selfish of me. And

that's all it is – pure selfishness, but when they broke up Martin was so unhappy and I suggested, only to take his mind off Kate really, that we go away for a week. To France. Martin's very fond of hill-walking and I like just lazing around reading and things. I booked a gite in the Auvergne. Nothing fancy. I just thought it would be nice for us both to have a week away. Just to chat and eat and see each other, be together, I suppose. He's nearly twenty. Soon he's going to be out of my life completely. I just wanted, I don't know – one last swipe at being a mother. Ridiculous, of course. "Empty nest syndrome", as Duncan would call it.' She smiled. 'And the stupidest thing of all – for me to be upset about, I mean – is that Martin let drop that Duncan's planning to marry his dentist once the house is sold, which it will be very shortly, by the sound of it. I should be delighted. Instead I feel as though the ground is being systematically ripped from under my feet.'

Bill was silent, gazing into his coffee. 'Will you get free dental care?' he asked at last.

Ruth stared at him. 'What?'

'If he marries his dentist? It sounds a bit drastic to me. I can't even see mine in the street without breaking out into a sweat.'

Ruth burst out laughing. '"His dentist" is what I call the woman he lives with. Actually, I think she's more to do with selling equipment than anything as useful as filling a tooth.'

Bill sat back. 'Do you still love your husband?'

Ruth felt suddenly shocked. 'Me? Love Duncan? I don't think I've loved him since we came back from our honeymoon. I'm not even sure I loved him before I married him, come to think of it.'

'Why did you, then?'

'Oh I don't know. It was so long ago. I was in awe of him, partly, I think. He seemed to know so much more about life than I did. And of course, I was so amazed that he would even consider marrying me.'

'Why?'

Ruth shrugged. 'Because that's the sort of person I am, I suppose. There's no other excuse, is there?'

For answer Bill leant across and kissed her very softly on the mouth. 'That's the sort of person you were,' he said. 'People

• Sarah Grazebrook

change. You've changed. Even since I met you. You've come alive.' Ruth turned her head away wretchedly. 'No I haven't. What's alive about living in a freezing cottage, force-feeding people soup and making nylon togas in my spare time? It's about as alive as being under anaesthetic. Even my own son can't bear the thought of spending a week in my company.'

'Oh for God's sake,' said Bill sharply. 'Look at it the way it is, why don't you, woman? He's twenty years old. What kind of a lad would he be if he preferred playing snap with his mother to bonking his way round India with a girl he's crazy about?'

Ruth sat up angrily. 'Thank you for the counselling session. I wonder you're such an expert, considering you've got no children of your own and a broken marriage behind you, not to mention a reputation for "bonking your way" round Westbridge, as you so tastefully put it. I wonder you don't go and work for Relate. They must be crying out for people like you.'

'I think they probably are,' said Bill grimly. 'It's a lot easier to understand someone else's problem if you've had it yourself. I apologise for the lack of children. It wasn't for want of trying. I caught mumps when I was twenty-three and it had rather a radical effect. I hope that's "tasteful" enough for you to understand. It just means I'm fucking sterile. The reputation, as you call it, goes with the territory. As you pointed out yourself, there's not much else to do round here, apart from spreading unfounded rumours. Ask your sister-in-law.'

Ruth didn't know what to say. She studied her hands. Bill got up and left the room. She waited to see if he would come back. After ten minutes she picked up her coat and went to the front door. It was open.

Bill was sitting on a wall not far from the car. Although it was cold he had no jacket on. He seemed lost in thought.

Ruth walked quickly to her car and got in. As she switched on the lights Bill turned his head towards her. His eyes were red from crying.

Ruth sat for a moment then turned off the ignition and got out. She went over to where he was sitting. 'I am an awful woman,' she said contritely. Bill wiped his face with his sleeve and smiled slightly. 'I'll drink to that,' he said. He stood up. 'Take no notice of me. I get like this sometimes. Talk about you feeling sorry for yourself. You're a novice compared with me.'

Ruth stared at her feet. 'I didn't know,' she said, 'or I would never have . . .'

Bill put up his hand. 'I know,' he said gently. 'Do you think I don't know that? It's nothing. Christ, woman, mumps! It's a joke. Who knows? I'd probably never have had any anyway. It doesn't matter. I hardly ever think of it. I'll tell you something that'll make you laugh.'

'What?'

'It was seeing Lollo with all those puppies. What's it they say about women getting broody? I'm the worst case I ever came across.'

Ruth smiled. She suddenly felt very protective towards him. Tentatively she reached out her hand and touched his face. Bill looked down at her. 'Is this because you feel sorry for me?' he asked.

Ruth shook her head. 'I don't know what it's because of.' Bill took hold of her hand and kissed the palm.

'Will you stay with me tonight?' he asked.

Ruth felt an intoxicating flash of panic zipping through her. 'I don't know,' she began. Bill took her face in his hands and kissed her with an almost savage intensity.

'Yes, I will. All right I will,' gasped Ruth, feeling as though she had stepped on to another planet. 'But don't tell anyone. Promise not to tell anyone.'

27

The remaining weeks of Ruth's stay in Westbridge flew by. Not only did she have the puppies to consider, she was also inundated with last-minute panics from Joy who was becoming increasingly batty with every hour that passed.

The sale of her London home was going ahead. She still had no idea where she was going to live, but somehow the happiness she was experiencing with Bill made everything else seem insignificant. Something would turn up. Things would sort themselves out. She was riding high.

They told no one about their affair. It was their secret – shared, private – safe from the ever critical eyes of Westbridge. If Joy Blakeney thought she saw them walking the cliffs together she dismissed it as coincidence. She had enough to worry about without Ruth falling victim to a middle-aged Lothario. Anyway Ruth was far too sensible – and far too busy. She was also way behind with her togas.

They continued to visit Lollo, sometimes together, sometimes apart, and if Madge Jordan noticed any change in their behaviour she said nothing, preferring to concentrate on the puppies, a more reliable source of affection.

She had found homes for the two males and announced her intention of keeping Lola herself. Ruth was slightly alarmed at the prospect of one of the foundlings living so close to Bell Cottage, but she had sufficient faith in Madge to know that she could handle any problems that might arise with the Taylors.

She continued to attend Bill's class, more to escape Joy's committee meetings than from any great desire to improve her

- Sarah Grazebrook

writing skills which, despite Bill's insistence, she still considered non-existent.

She found, however, that she liked to listen to him as he alternately criticised and encouraged the others, all of whom clearly believed they would one day win the Nobel prize for literature.

She began to see what he meant about allowing people to dream. What did it matter if Reg's saga would never be finished, or Tanya's racy prose passed fit for publication? They enjoyed what they did. It was a strange lesson to learn for someone who had been taught to believe all her adult life that 'no result' meant 'failure'.

Gwen, fresh from her rupture with Adrian Mills (apparently he held her totally to blame for the breaking of his foot), had turned her attention once more to Bill.

It amused Ruth to see her cornering him at every coffee break, beseeching him not to think her too too stupid, begging him to spare her just five more minutes of his very valuable time. Bill took it in his stride, patiently reminding her that her best hope lay in reading the works of others, and occasionally lending her his own precious copies which, if he were to be believed, she only ever returned late at night.

Sometimes he would raise his eyes to Ruth over the bowed heads of his pupils and smile conspiratorially. It made Ruth want to shout out loud for happiness.

A series of anonymous letters began to appear in the local paper, demanding that Joy be chosen to play the role of Britannia, these being countermanded by a correspondent describing himself only as 'a patriot', and suggesting that Joy was not even British, but the illegitimate descendant of a Danish prince whose mistress had drowned herself when the prince refused to marry her.

This threw Joy into even greater turmoil, since it required either that she deny her royal heritage or forgo the leading role in the pageant.

'Poor Joy,' Ruth remarked, after a particularly frenzied phone call in which her sister-in-law suggested that she go immediately to St Catherine's House and spend a day retracing the Page family tree in the hope of resolving the mystery.

Bill was in the kitchen trying to change the fuse in Ruth's hairdryer. 'Why "poor"?' he asked.

'This correspondence in the paper about her being a Danish princess is really getting to her.'

Bill looked up. 'I must say I didn't think it would go on this long. I'm running out of things to say.'

Ruth gawped at him. 'You mean it's you who's been writing these letters?'

Bill shrugged. 'I thought it needed a bit of counterbalance. All those glowing reports about how she was born for the role etcetera.'

Ruth frowned. 'Yes, but she can't help that. If people want her to play it they're entitled to write in.'

Bill gazed at her incredulously. 'You really are an innocent, aren't you? Who do you think's writing all those?'

'Well, I don't know. People. Friends . . .'

'She writes them herself.'

'Oh, come on, Bill. That's not fair. How can you possibly tell?'

'Because she can't spell Britannia. She always puts two "t"s and one "n". It was the same on that cast list you brought home. She'd written that by hand.'

Ruth started to laugh. 'She only wants me to spend a day in London tracing the family tree.' Bill put his arms round her waist and drew her to him. 'I'm not sure I shall be able to spare you,' he said proprietorially.

'I'll tell her that, shall I?'

Bill grinned. 'I think that might be the final nail in the coffin,' he said.

Ruth's face became serious. 'I shall have to go up to London anyway.'

'Why?'

'To try and sort things out.'

'What things?'

Ruth was silent for a moment. 'Somewhere to live. I can go back to the house for a couple of weeks, but that's really all I've got. After that I shall have to . . .' Her voice petered out. Bill's hands slid away from her. He suddenly seemed very interested in her hairdryer again.

• Sarah Grazebrook

When he had gone Ruth lay on her bed and looked at the ceiling. She didn't know what she had wanted him to say. She just knew that he hadn't said it. 'A chapter draws to a close,' floated across her mind. It didn't seem all that funny.

Lollo was gradually getting back to shape, mainly through the pumping action of the puppies. Twiggy still had trouble feeding and Ruth had come across Bill more than once with the spindly creature cradled on his lap, a baby's bottle tucked between its jaws. 'I'm applying to adopt her,' he explained one day, when she remarked on the pair's likeness to Rafaello's Madonna and Child.

'What about Tyson? You'd be asking for trouble.'

Bill looked glum. 'I suppose you're right. I could have her spayed. Or him.'

'That's a bit drastic.'

Bill shrugged dismissively. 'No worse than mumps.'

Ruth stroked his hair. 'Why don't I have her?'

He looked up, surprised. 'You don't like dogs.'

'I didn't. People can change. You said so yourself. She'd be company for me.'

Bill was silent for a minute. 'I'm not, I suppose?'

Ruth turned away. She had been dreading this moment. Ever since the night he had chosen not to understand what she was asking. Ever since she had come to her decision.

'You are,' she said slowly. 'You know you are. But I've got to leave soon, Bill. The Taylors are coming back. My house is being sold. I've got to start putting my life back together again. I've got to start making decisions. This time down here – well, it's been like a sort of dream. Limbo. A breathing space. I can't prolong it forever, can I?'

Bill removed the empty bottle from Twiggy's mouth and wiped her jowls fastidiously. 'No, of course not. Well, I hope it's been of some use to you.' He laid the sleeping puppy in its box and walked past Ruth into the open air. She followed him.

'Bill, I didn't mean it to sound like that.'

'Like what?'

'So cold and . . . calculating, almost. I'm just trying to be practical.'

Bill was staring hard into the distance. 'Oh, aye. Very sensible.' He turned to her and smiled. 'You're right. Practical. I like that in a woman. Heaven defend me from clinging females. Speaking of which, I've had Gwen Pritchard on the phone again asking if she can come and talk to me about her poems.'

'What did you say?' asked Ruth.

'Nothing. It was the answerphone. Might as well have her round, though. Can't do any harm. Poor girl could do with a bit of encouragement.'

Their eyes met.

Ruth went home and started to do her packing.

It was now only a week till the pageant. Martin and Kate were coming for the night, before setting off on their Indian trip. Ruth had been unable to cancel her French gite but, encouraged by Madge who had promised to hang on to Lollo till the Taylors returned, she had decided to go on her own. Mervyn Parsons had been a lot more amenable about her overdraft facility since being informed of the imminent sale of the house.

Joy, who was looking and sounding more like Lady Macbeth every day, had told her she would be quite mad to go, and had produced several cuttings citing demented French foresters who apparently spent their free time gunning down tourists from their hidey-holes in the mountains. Remembering Joy's interpretation of the Barlan escape, Ruth bought herself a first aid kit and a copy of *Bravo Two Zero*, which she imagined would furnish her with all she needed to survive.

Compromise had finally been reached regarding the role of Britannia. Joy would take the part officially, on the understanding that Violet Sampson would stand beside her on the chariot, dressed identically and holding the reins of the four steeds. Joy would speak and Violet would steer.

The fact that neither of them was prepared to exchange so much as a syllable with the other had already led to several near fatalities during rehearsals as the horses twitched under Violet's wavering navigation, unnerved by Joy's rendition of 'Oh, to be in England,' as they never had been by simulated gunshot and bazookas.

Kate and Martin arrived about lunchtime and were somewhat

dismayed to find the cottage in a state of semi-desolation. Ruth had packed all but her most basic essentials into cardboard boxes and holdalls and these lay around the place, giving it the semblance of a transit camp, rather than a home.

The weather had turned hot and she had laid lunch in the garden which took their minds off the austerity within.

In the afternoon she took them over and introduced them to Madge and the puppies. She left them there cooing over Twiggy while she went home to get ready for her own part in the evening's proceedings.

Despite heavy canvassing on Garth Forland's part, Gwen had not succeeded in upgrading her role and seven o'clock found her and Ruth, dressed in leftover togas from the daily depleting ranks of Roman soldiers, positioned behind the hot and foaming stallions which Violet had falsely persuaded the organisers were shires.

The squads of children were proving predictably anarchic – those from the state school being heavily engaged in a battle with the private pupils which looked likely to prove more decisive than anything Julius Caesar had come up with.

Their mothers, either from indifference or fear, were making a great play of 'leaving it to the authorities' although, Ruth considered, had they known that 'the authorities' meant Gwen with her pleas for 'everyone to be kind to each other', they would probably have taken a keener interest in the outcome.

The floats had been gathering since five o'clock. Just when they were ready to set off there had been a cry from a young woad-stained Druid that she needed to go to the lavatory. This had precipitated a chain reaction as all eighty-five of the schoolchildren affirmed their similar requirement and the procession was put back for half an hour while the operation took place.

A representative party from the Tout Ensemble (Brussels) contingent had arrived that afternoon by catamaran. All but one of them had been seasick and had sought to counter the effect with English beer. This had proved somewhat stronger than their usual tipple and the VIPs were now to be seen swaying gently on their podium, interspersed with Kevin Mulcahy who was a teetotaller, the mayor who was a reformed alcoholic, and Joy Blakeney, who had calculated that she need not be in situ as Britannia till seven forty-five, the estimated time for the departure of the last tableau.

Despite their highly significant role in the proceedings, neither Gwen nor Ruth had so far received any instruction on what they were to do in the event of a 'little accident'. Ruth had promised herself that, no matter what the danger to the battling infants, there was no way she was going to pick up horse dung in the skirt of her toga. She mentioned this to Grace Forland who was swanning around in a voluminous chiffon ballgown. Grace paled several shades and hurried away to return twenty minutes later with a pair of Pooper Scoopers she had borrowed from the pet shop.

Gwen and Ruth duly tucked them into the folds of their costumes and, at a suitably safe distance, installed themselves behind the frothing stallions.

At half past seven the procession began to wend its way through the narrow streets. A party atmosphere prevailed among the onlookers who cheered and threw small change at the passing tableaux. Adrian Mills spent a wretched evening trying to avoid the flying coins, his mitre proving a particular attraction to the local darts team.

Violet's horses wasted no time in relieving themselves in steaming heaps on the roadway but, while Gwen ran hither and thither attempting to remove these, Ruth merely stood to one side and told the children to watch their feet, an injunction which all but the most wanton adhered to.

The danger over, as far as Ruth and Gwen were concerned, the procession settled into a calmer mode, the sturdy tread of the participants giving way to a plod as they trudged through streets they had not known existed till that night.

Doubts had already been expressed by the committee regarding the length of the route, but Joy had insisted that it was the right of the rate-payers to have full access to the spectacle, and not even Mulcahy could argue with this.

Loudspeakers had been attached to the principal floats to allow the protagonists' lines to be heard. These were to be repeated at regular intervals to enable the spectators to absorb this encapsulated history of their town. Unfortunately not all the microphones were working which meant that Ethelred's valiant sortie into the Welsh borders was missed by all but those closest to him, and they were, by and large, his understudies, who already knew his lines a great deal better than he did.

The evening wore on. Ruth had more or less forgotten that she was part of it till, rounding the corner by the library she heard Kate's voice pointing her out. Kate waved frenziedly while Martin edged backwards in a desperate attempt to disassociate himself from it all.

'Oh look,' trilled Gwen, waving back and blowing kisses. 'It's your lovely son. Is that the same girl who came down with him before?'

'Yes,' said Ruth firmly. 'They're practically engaged.' Gwen sniffed and continued to blow kisses. 'Oooh,' she squeaked in sudden excitement. 'There's Bill with them. I knew he would come. He's been so supportive lately. I don't know how I could have gone on without him.'

Ruth looked up sharply and was surprised to note that Bill did indeed seem to be of the party. Madge was there, too, looking severe. The two of them were taking periodic sips from a hip flask and seemed to be deep in conversation. Gwen sighed. 'Do you think he saw us? I waved like crazy.'

Ruth shrugged. 'I've no idea. Hopefully not.'

'He's been so encouraging about my poems,' Gwen continued airily. 'After Adrian started being so unkind to me I felt I had to get it out of my system, so I wrote a few verses, just to say how I was feeling and everything, and Bill let me bring them over to his cottage and read them to him. I thought that was so kind, don't you? Because he really is such a busy man and so brilliant. It seems such a shame he's all on his own, don't you think?'

'He's got a dog,' said Ruth tight-lipped.

'Oh he has, of course. And such a lovely one. Even if it is a bit rough sometimes,' Gwen added pensively. 'But then a dog's not the same, is it? Not really?'

'As what?' asked Ruth, who was beginning to hope one of the horses would kick Gwen in the stomach.

'Oh, you know,' said Gwen coyly. 'A companion. Someone who understands you.'

'I think,' said Ruth savagely, 'that there is very little to Bill Bartholomew that couldn't be understood by an earthworm.'

At this moment a wasp flew inside Violet Sampson's breastplate. Violet flapped her arms frantically in an effort to expel it. Unfortunately she had forgotten she was holding a whip and the tip of this caught the ear of the nearest horse, Charger.

The animal proved himself more than worthy of his name by first rearing then buffeting the hind quarters of the leaders until they broke into a trot, then a canter, and finally a gallop, at which pace they hurtled round the roundabout and took off along the pier at a right angle to the rest of the procession before being halted by the local butcher who could see his curbside barbecue being knocked into kingdom-come.

The Belgian officials, who had been nodding off despite the attempts of Kevin Mulcahy to keep them up-to-date with the proceedings, rallied visibly at this latest episode and began to make cheerful noises about twinning themselves with Westbridge.

'Voilà,' intoned Mulcahy, hoping to God that no one had been killed, and if they had that it might be Joy Blakeney, 'les chevaux qui portent Britannia.'

Down the street they came, foam bubbling once more from their mouths, eyes rolling dementedly. The butcher kept a firm grip on the lead rein, Violet Sampson showing no pressing desire to wrest it from him as she sat wheezing on the lower step of Joy's throne, alternately wiping her forehead and fanning herself with a loose piece of bunting.

Joy, who had also received rather a severe fright, had regained her position remarkably quickly, thereby demonstrating to herself and, she fervently hoped, to those who had doubted her, her inalienable right to symbolise all that was fine and true about the British.

Adrian, further down the line, had been entreated by all around him to film the charge, but his nerve had failed yet again and he had spent the entire episode cocooned in his cope while the video camera recorded several hundred feet of Grace Forland's tacking stitches to the accompanying sound of Adrian's frantic heartbeat.

By half past nine the procession had completed its journey. Floats were being dismantled, children reclaimed and the crowds

• Sarah Grazebrook

were dispersing to the pubs. The official party had withdrawn to a private buffet in the Mayor's parlour and all that was left of the Grand Pageant of Westbridge was the clearing up.

Ruth helped herself to some of the free lemonade on offer and went in search of Kate and Martin. She found them in a pub on the seafront. There was no sign of Bill Bartholomew or Madge.

'She had to get back to feed the puppies,' Kate explained. 'Bill went with her.' Ruth nodded. Martin went to fetch more drinks.

'He's nice, isn't he?' said Kate.

'Martin?' asked Ruth, amused.

'Martin? Oh he's scrummy. No, I meant Bill whatisname. Madge's friend.'

Ruth fiddled with her toga. 'If you two don't mind, I think I'll go on back to the house. I feel rather ridiculous in this. There's no need to hurry. I can give you a key.'

'Stay and have one drink with us,' said Martin, setting down a tray. 'We'll have to be off quite early tomorrow. Kate's promised to call in on her dad before we go.'

Ruth smiled. 'What did you make of it tonight?'

Martin rolled his eyes upwards. 'I think, Mum, the sooner you're out of Auntie Joy's clutches the better. You must be dying to get back to sanity.'

Ruth drained her glass and gave Kate the spare key. She leant over and kissed Martin lightly on the top of his head. 'Yes,' she said, 'of course I am.'

28

The night before Ruth left for France, Joy held another little *soirée* for her. It was conducted on much the same lines as the first, except that the chili had been exchanged for a vegetarian lasagne, equally solid, and Gwen Pritchard had been replaced at Adrian's side by his wife.

Though it was nothing to do with her, Ruth felt a genuine gush of pleasure at the sight. Rowena looked positively radiant as she guided Adrian to the most comfortable chair and laid his walking stick lovingly beside him. She waved cheerfully when she saw Ruth and beckoned her over. 'Ruth, come and tell Aid it's not his fault you're deserting us.'

Ruth smiled and joined them. 'How's your foot?' she asked Adrian.

'Bloody awful,' scowled Mills. 'I'm in constant pain.'

'He didn't want to come tonight,' put in Rowena, 'but I insisted. "It's Ruth's last night," I said. "And she's been such a good friend to us. You've got to come." So, of course, he relented.' She touched his cheek with such genuine affection that for a moment Ruth believed the man must be lovable.

'Anyway, he'd've been wretched if he'd missed you,' Rowena continued. She turned her head aside so that Adrian couldn't hear. 'To tell the truth, I think he's got a bit of a thing about you. Though of course he'd never say so. He's much too shy.' She grinned conspiratorially, and Ruth felt a sudden urge to hug Rowena and stab Adrian in the neck at the same time.

Violet Sampson came over to demand her sponsorship money for the Tibetan monastery and Garth Forland made a special effort and said he thought Lollo was looking fitter than when

• Sarah Grazebrook

the Taylors went away. Grace agreed fervently, though Ruth caught her looking nervously in the back of her car when she thought no one was about.

After the Trents had approached her and said how disappointed they were she had not found the time to join their pottery class, the party began to break up. Once more Ruth found herself seated opposite her brother-in-law while Joy made coffee for the three of them.

'So, how's it been, in the end?' he asked nonchalantly. Ruth could tell he was afraid she was about to sever all connections with the family.

'It's been fine, Christopher,' she said quickly. 'Just what I needed. A complete break.'

'And now? After France, I mean?'

Ruth shrugged. 'Who knows? I'll keep you posted. Thanks for looking after my stuff, by the way. I really am most grateful.'

Joy appeared with the coffee tray. 'Oh you mustn't be grateful,' she decreed magnanimously. 'It's been a pleasure looking after you, Ruth. And besides, it was the very least we could do.'

The imitation of Gwen was so obvious that they all three burst out laughing.

Ruth rose. 'Thank you, anyway, Joy. You've been to a lot of trouble on my behalf and I am grateful, believe me.'

Joy went very red and looked in danger of crying, whereupon Christopher said something about checking the back door lock and left the two women together.

Since this was the last time she would see her for some time Ruth felt an overwhelming fondness for Joy sweeping through her. After all, she had done her best to make her stay enjoyable and if it hadn't been, whose fault was that? Her own alone.

'Well,' she said emotionally.

'Bon voyage,' quavered Joy, sniffing into her sleeve.

Ruth blinked rapidly, gave Joy a quick squeeze and hurried into the hall to find her coat. Joy followed her.

'Ruth?'

'Yes?'

Joy hesitated. 'Nothing. It's just . . . I hope you don't think . . .' She faltered.

Ruth pulled her coat on. 'Think what?'

'Nothing. I don't know. It's just sometimes I wonder . . . I hope you don't think I've tried to interfere in any way – with . . . you know . . . anything, while you've been down here?'

Ruth looked at her sister-in-law. Joy's hyacinth eyes were wide with uncertainty, something Ruth had never seen before. She stopped looking for her car keys and seizing her by the shoulders kissed her affectionately on both cheeks.

'What rubbish you do talk sometimes, Joy,' she said. 'I'd've been nowhere without you. Nowhere at all.'

As she was driving away Joy came pounding down the drive behind her. Ruth stopped the car and wound down the window. Breathless, Joy thrust an envelope through it. 'Nearly forgot,' she wheezed. 'All the best, Ruth. From the bottom of my heart.'

When she got home Ruth opened the envelope. It contained a cheque, together with an invoice from Kent County Council for her services as Writer in Residence for the Westbridge Community Pageant. There was also a note of the current exchange rate for Belgian francs. One thousand came to twenty-two pounds twenty-three p.

Madge came round to see Ruth off. 'Place looks a bit bare,' she remarked, which was an understatement. Ruth smiled and nodded. For some reason she had an enormous lump in her throat.

Madge grunted and picked up two of her suitcases.

'Madge, don't you carry them. You'll do your back in,' Ruth pleaded.

'Rubbish. I've carried worse than these. You'll let me know, will you, about the puppy?'

'What do you mean?' asked Ruth. Madge glanced back at her.

'Twiggy. Whether you want her or not?'

Ruth was completely thrown. 'Madge, how can I possibly have a puppy? I don't even know where I'm going to be living in a month's time.'

Madge's face registered no surprise. 'Sorry. Must have got the wrong end of the stick. Something Bill said. He seemed to think you might be interested.'

• Sarah Grazebrook

Ruth blushed. 'Well, yes, I probably did say something about it, but that was before I'd thought it through. I mean it just wouldn't be fair, would it, to take Twiggy to some poky little flat and leave her alone all day?'

Madge said nothing, but continued to cart Ruth's luggage out to the car. Ruth had arranged for Christopher to pick up the stuff she didn't need immediately. He would store it until she found a permanent base. When everything was in, she checked once more for her passport, made sure the windows were closed, and locked up Bell Cottage for the last time.

Madge stood silently by the car, her face a study of indifference. 'Perhaps I'll see you some time,' she said gruffly as Ruth came over. Ruth grasped her hand, then gave her a bear-like hug. 'You're going to be my first visitor,' she promised. 'I can't thank you enough for . . .' Tears took over.

'Better get a move on,' said Madge brusquely. 'Don't want to miss your ferry.'

'Give my love to Lollo,' Ruth choked, then got quickly into the car and drove away.

The gite in the Auvergne was everything she'd hoped. Quiet, cosy, remote. She walked and read, drank too much wine and made plans. The plans themselves were a little hazy as they generally came after the wine, but they were positive bold ambitious plans, centring on her own success as a business woman, author and breeder of pedigree dachshunds.

It was only on the last night of her stay, with the prospect of suburbia looming, that she had a little trouble believing them. She sat out on the wooden verandah as she had every evening and looked down towards the lake, as blue and mysterious as it had been in the brochure. Behind her the coral light of the sun stretched across the mountain, sending long shadows on to the winding road that led down to the nearest town.

She was writing to Martin, though whether it would reach him she did not know. Far away she could see a car puffing its way up the incline. It never seemed to get any nearer until suddenly it disappeared from view behind the sharp crags of the overhang and then reappeared a good half a mile further on. She watched incuriously as it approached. It was red and battered and had a sticker of some sort in its front window. Ruth squinted to see what it might be.

It was in the same breath that she managed to distinguish 'GB' on the white plastic oval that she realised who was driving the car. 'Oh my God,' she said out loud. 'I don't believe it. I don't believe it.' She stood up and watched half-mesmerised as Bill Bartholomew crunched the vehicle to a halt, got out, stretched, scratched, and bellowed up the drive. 'Any chance of a drink for a desperate man?'

Ruth ran stumbling down the path. 'What are you doing here?' she asked incredulously.

'Just passing,' said Bill innocently. 'Thought you might be able to spare me a glass of wine. If it's too much trouble, don't worry. I've a stop in Morocco on Tuesday.'

Ruth shook her head hopelessly. 'How did you know I was here?'

'I didn't,' said Bill cheerfully. 'Madge showed me the brochure so I knew it must be around here somewhere. I asked in the village if there were any mad Englishwomen in the district.'

'And they sent you straight to me?'

'Certainly not. You were fifth on my list. Am I going to get this drink or not?' Without waiting for an answer he took hold of her arm and led her back to the house.

'Why have you come?' asked Ruth again as they sat outside in the gathering dusk. For once Bill had no ready answer. His face was in shadow and it was impossible to guess what he was thinking.

'Unfinished business,' he said at last.

'What's that supposed to mean?'

'You didn't say goodbye.'

'I thought we'd already said that.'

'When?'

Ruth reached across and snuffed out the candle which was about to set fire to her airletter. 'When I said I had to leave and you didn't ask me to stay.' Bill lowered his head. Ruth sought around for something to soften the accusation. 'I wasn't expecting you to, Bill. I'm not even sure if I wanted you to. After

- Sarah Grazebrook

all, I'd just spent twenty-odd years with one man. I certainly didn't want to throw myself into another . . . another . . .'

'Long-term relationship?' Bill finished.

'I suppose so.'

Bill laughed. 'I'd spent about the same amount of time avoiding one. I'm afraid you rather panicked me.'

Ruth smiled. 'I didn't mean to. I'm not always very good at expressing myself.'

Bill took her hand. 'Oh I don't know. You've got a lovely way with a shot schoolmistress.'

'And not quite such a good one with real people.' She looked at him. 'All I wanted to say was – is, you've been such a good friend to me.'

'Only friend?'

'Let me finish. A friend is what I needed. A lover – well, that was a bonus, I suppose.'

'I've been called a lot of things in my time. "Bonus" was not one of them.'

'Please try to understand what I'm saying. You know as well as I do that the physical bit is just, well . . .'

'Just what?'

Ruth struggled to find the words. 'Just . . . It doesn't mean anything, does it?'

Bill stared at her. 'How can you say it doesn't mean anything? How can you say that? It's . . . Christ, woman, we're not bloody animals, are we? We're not bloody dogs on heat.'

'You tell me,' said Ruth with more vehemence than she had known herself capable of. 'You tell me, with your bloody Westbridge harem. You tell me.'

Bill looked at her with utter hopelessness. 'You don't still believe that rubbish, do you?'

'Of course I do,' said Ruth, endeavouring to maintain her calm. 'The very first time I met you you were off to the wedding of some girlfriend of yours.'

'Second time,' Bill corrected.

'And what about Rowena? You told me about her yourself.'

'Two women in seven years. That makes me Casanova, does it?'

Ruth was silent.

'Well. Does it?'

'Not exactly.'

Bill set down his glass and looked at her intently. 'There's more to this, isn't there?'

'No, of course not.'

'There is. Why don't you tell me what you're thinking?'

Ruth shook her head. 'No, it's nothing. Really. It's none of my business anyway.'

To her shock and alarm Bill suddenly picked up his glass and flung it across the garden. It smashed on the low stone wall. Somewhere a cat yowled and ran away. 'Do you ever say what you're really feeling?' he bellowed. 'Have you ever done it in your life? Do you ever wonder if that's why your husband left you? Because you're so damned well brought up?'

Ruth put her hands up to her face then brought them down again. 'All right. What about Gwen Pritchard? Don't tell me you haven't been sleeping with her because I won't believe you. And I hate you for it. All right?'

Bill stood up and walked over to the wall. Carefully he picked up what he could find of the broken glass and piled it on the stones. 'I won't tell you then,' he said bitterly. 'You'll just have to find out for yourself.'

'I have,' said Ruth listlessly. 'She gave me chapter and verse during the pageant.'

'What did she say?'

Ruth shrugged. 'The usual. How wonderful you'd been, how understanding. How awful it was for you to be on your own. The script doesn't seem to vary much, does it?'

Bill gave a dry laugh. 'Poor Gwennie. I'm afraid her ideas for the perfect romance are a bit fixed. That's probably why she hasn't found it yet.'

'God loves a trier,' said Ruth.

Bill sat down at the far end of the table. 'I don't suppose you're interested in my version?'

'Not really. As I say, it's none of my business.'

He turned to her in exasperation. 'It is your business. For God's sake, woman, why do you think I came all this way? It's taken me nearly twenty-four hours. I had a puncture outside Orleans. I left my wallet in a lavvy on the autoroute.'

• Sarah Grazebrook

'There are no lavatories on the autoroute,' Ruth intervened brusquely. Bill looked momentarily confused. 'Well, I thought it was. There was a little fountain and a stone thing.'

'That would be a shrine.'

'Ah. Well, I expect you're right because my wallet was still there when I went back.'

Ruth felt a horrible desire to giggle. 'All right. You had a beastly journey,' she said severely. 'You still haven't told me why you came. Or was it just to say goodbye?'

Bill sighed. When he spoke he sounded suddenly tired. 'I guess that depends on you, Mrs Page.'

Ruth waited.

'I went round to see Madge,' Bill continued. 'After you'd gone. I wanted to speak to you before. Christ, I even went to that ghastly pageant, tried to ingratiate myself with your son . . .'

'How did you get on?' Ruth interrupted.

'Lousy. You'd think I'd been applying to adopt you. His girlfriend's nice, though. She took pity on me. Said the lad was suffering from an Oedipus complex.'

'She never did!' Ruth slammed her glass down on the table.

Bill looked nervous. 'Of course she didn't. That was a joke.'

'Worthy of Tony Quilp,' said Ruth sulkily.

This time Bill laughed.

'Why are you laughing?'

Bill shook his head. 'Because it's so ridiculous.'

'What is?'

'It. Us. Here we are, two middle-aged loonies, arguing as though we'd been married for thirty years.'

'Heaven forbid.'

'Exactly. Have you got no whisky in the house?'

'Of course I haven't,' Ruth said irritably. 'Do you honestly think I'd come all the way to France to buy whisky? I've got some brandy. Will that do?'

'I suppose it'll have to.'

'Don't force yourself on my account.'

'I won't.'

Silence ensued. Somewhere a bird, foreign and brash, let out its defiant song into the black night air.

'I love you,' said Bill very quietly.

Ruth sat for a moment. 'What did you say?' she said.
'I'm not saying it again.'
'Ever?'
'I shall say it again in twenty forty-two, if you're still alive.'
'I shall look forward to that.'
'But I won't marry you.'
'In that case I won't marry you, either.'
'At least we're agreed on something.'

Ruth, who had been close to tears for some while, wiped ineffectually at her eyes.

'Don't start that,' said Bill resignedly. He got up and came over to where Ruth was sitting. Gently he took her in his arms and cradled her to him. 'You're about to live happily ever after.'

Ruth wiped her damp face on his shirt. 'Ugh!' said Bill.
'Are you sure?'
'What about?'
'Living happily ever after?'
'Of course I'm not, you daft bugger. BUT,' he added, seeing that more tears were on the way, 'I have an alternative ending.'

'What?' Ruth turned her anxious eyes to him and Bill, for once, was ashamed of his callousness. '"To be continued",' he whispered. 'It's never been known to fail.'